SEASON OF THE HEART

As Max passed her, Elizabeth reached up, her finger-tips grazing his. It was barely a touch, but more than enough to make Max pause. She reached once again. This time their fingertips met and the touch lingered. She inched her hand upward, slipping it into Max's. His hand closed over hers, hesitated, then held tight. While he held her, one hand connecting two hearts, Elizabeth stood.

It was Elizabeth who touched first. Her fingers trailed to the top of his jeans, lingering on the worn leather of his belt. Max drew her closer. This had been so long in coming.

"Elizabeth," Max whispered, pulling away from her just long enough to touch her face.

Elizabeth gazed at him, her eyes bright with need, and want, and love.

Books by Rebecca Forster

RAINBOW'S END
GOLDEN THREADS
VANITIES
VOWS
DREAMS
SEASONS

Published by Zebra Books

Dolores,

Thank you! for having me!

REBECCA FORSTER

Rebecca

SEASONS

ZEBRA BOOKS
KENSINGTON PUBLISHING CORP.

ZEBRA BOOKS are published by

Kensington Publishing Corp.
850 Third Avenue
New York, NY 10022

First Printing: May, 1996
10 9 8 7 6 5 4 3 2 1

Printed in the United States of America

For Marigail Mathis
An exceptional designer
An exquisite friend

Prologue

1986

"Oh, Brad, don't you love the name? Emerald Isle. It sounds so exotic. Look, there's the park. It looks like a big green island, just like the brochure said."

Elizabeth MacMillan sat forward, seat belt straining across her huge belly. The fingers of one hand were spread on the window as if she could touch the lush green grass through the glass, the other lay directly over her baby. He kicked and she grinned happily.

"I think Christopher likes the name, too," she said, her Southern drawl softening when she talked about the new life inside her. "Feel."

Impetuously, Elizabeth took her husband's right hand and put it on her stomach. He pulled back.

"Honey, come on. I'm driving. I don't want to have an accident." The reprimand was so gentle Elizabeth didn't notice the edge to it.

"Don't be a grump. We're only going ten miles an hour," Elizabeth laughed. "I swear, sometimes I think you're going to be the worst father in the world. If you're always this careful, how's this boy ever going to learn to ride a bike? You've got to learn to live a little."

Elizabeth leaned across the seat and put her head briefly on his shoulder, talking low. She was so proud of Brad. "Probably wouldn't be seemly for a brilliant young college professor to do that now, would it?"

she teased. She poked him in the side, then sat up straight, tiring of the fun before Brad could decide if he were having any. Her green eyes widened and she pointed. "There! There it is. 1347. Our new house. Our home, Brad."

Brad eased the car toward the curb in the nick of time. If he'd been any slower, Elizabeth would have climbed through the window to get a better look. But he was out of the car before she managed to do anything more than push open the door. Laboriously, her eyes never leaving the house, she pulled herself upright.

Brad hung on the open door, pushed his sunglasses up his nose, and looked at the place that would tie him to a thirty-year mortgage at a whopping eight and a half percent. Then he looked at his wife waddling up the brick walk without him. He didn't have to see her face to know her grin was firmly centered as she chattered on about landscaping, curtains, things that would somehow magically appear once they moved in. Elizabeth had her rose-colored glasses firmly in place. Rosier than the rosiest ones in the world. His little cheerleader. Elizabeth.

Smiling ruefully, thinking fleetingly of what might have been if Elizabeth hadn't shined her light on him, Brad MacMillan closed the car door and followed. This peevish mood would pass. What did they call it? Buyer's regret. Should be called life regret, he thought sadly. Tenure hadn't been awarded yet, and the payments on this place were high. Sometimes the nine-year difference between him and Elizabeth seemed overwhelming. Where she felt challenged, he suddenly felt tired. Where she saw possibilities, he clearly understood why the dreams couldn't come true. But that was normal when things weren't going quite as you planned.

"Hurry, Brad," Elizabeth called and he did, brightening his smile because her golden beauty couldn't be ignored, her happiness couldn't be deflected. You had to embrace her energy when it came at you like a fireball, or you'd get scorched as it whizzed by. Eighteen months of marriage and Brad MacMillan was just beginning to realize that Elizabeth was actually infectious and he had a bad dose of the disease.

"It's a great house, sweetheart. Hope you like it as much in thirty years as you do now," he said, smiling wryly.

"Don't worry about that," she whispered, slipping her arms around his waist and pulling him as close as she could. The baby jumped beneath her dress, frolicking between them. In that instant Brad MacMillan's heart swelled and he loved Elizabeth, the baby, and this big house more than he loved anything in the world. Gently, he lowered his lips and let them linger atop her head, breathing in the scent of her freshly washed hair. She melted into him. What a lucky man he was! She gave so much and expected so little.

Holding Elizabeth aside, he inserted the key and held the door open. Elizabeth's big eyes were trained on him expectantly. Perplexed, he waved his hand impatiently, inviting her in.

"Aren't you going to carry me over the threshold?" she asked.

Before he could react, Elizabeth laughed and walked past, hands clasped against her breast as she looked around, leaving Brad on the doorstep.

Stepping inside, the August heat more oppressive in

this closed up house, he turned to close the door but was caught by the sight of the huge park they called the Emerald Isle. Instead of the lush green oasis of Elizabeth's heart, all he saw were heat waves shimmering off the black-top that surrounded it. Brad sighed. Nine o'clock in the morning. The sun was already burning hot and mean in the sky. He hated heat. Air conditioning would be expensive, but necessary.

Closing the door softly, Brad listened to Elizabeth's excited exclamations echoing through the house as he thought about air conditioning. He thought about his growing family. He thought about his impending tenure and tried to imagine himself a father.

But most of all, he thought about a change of season. That would be nice. Yes, a change of season would be very nice.

Part One

Summer

One

Words were funny things. So many had been spoken and Elizabeth remembered hearing so few. Perhaps, she'd been talking all these years and forgotten to listen . . . to what she said . . . what Brad said. She'd missed the clues.

It was summer again, and she was one summer removed from catastrophe. Well, that was the understatement of the century: *This* summer was going to be downright cataclysmic.

Either way, both summers—and the seasons between—were lost to worry, hurt, and fright. Elizabeth MacMillan, the mom who could pick up a snake or climb to the top of the jungle gym, was scared.

Twelve months ago, Brad had talked about needing time and space. She hadn't heard him. Nine months ago, he had left, calling every week to check in, coming occasionally to see Christopher and, she hoped, her. She'd said all the right words then, too: *Take whatever time you need. I'm here for you. I love you. I'll wait until you're ready to talk.* Now, there was no one to talk to. Four weeks since she'd last heard from him. Complete and utter silence. From her husband, for God sake! Husbands didn't just stop being husbands. Humiliated, Elizabeth was at wit's end. What had gotten into Brad? How could he treat her so callously?

And now this.

Being home with her misery and doubt was bad enough, but having to come here was like airing your dirty laundry in public. Hating to beg, she put on her best face, her most upbeat voice. Cheerleader to the last in a losing game, she walked up to the receptionist and tried not to let her voice shake.

"Hi, there," she began softly. "My name is Elizabeth MacMillan." She cleared her throat delicately. "My husband Brad is a contracts administrator in the air division."

The girl behind the high desk lowered her thick lashes, pointed to a list beside her console with an extremely long nail, then looked back at Elizabeth with polite disinterest.

"I'm sorry, he must not be in. I don't see him checked off."

"I know that," Elizabeth said, her voice a tad too loud, her Southern accent thick—sure signs she was nervous.

Elizabeth pushed back her long hair, then held her hand to the throat of her Laura Ashley dress. The dress had cost a fortune, yet here it was out of place. She lowered her voice, trying to be more businesslike. "I know he isn't here. I've been trying to reach him for weeks. First I was told that he wasn't at his desk. Then I was told he was out sick. Then he was on vacation. I'd just like to know which it is."

"You don't know where your husband is?" The girl's face was an open book, and Elizabeth's chapter was entitled *failure*. Summoning up her pride, Elizabeth pulled herself to her full, impressive height.

"I'm not here to *find* my husband. I want to talk to his supervisor." Elizabeth held up a piece of paper. It was wrinkled, moist with perspiration, but legible. "I'd like to see John Sawyer, if it's not too much trouble."

"Do you have an appointment?"

"No," Elizabeth answered icily. Her green eyes tried to hold the receptionist's gaze, but wavered. Verbal bravado was one thing; facing up to blatant curiosity was quite another.

She felt a sudden burst of heat followed by a chilling cold. Panic again. She should be home baking cookies, cleaning the house, working in the garden. What on earth was she doing downtown trying to intimidate an eighteen-year-old receptionist? An apology sprang to her lips, but she held it back and locked eyes again.

"This is important," she said firmly. "I need to speak with Mr. Sawyer. Now."

The girl hesitated, then reached for the receiver. Elizabeth, her manners inbred, leaned toward the young girl. "Thank you," she said. "I didn't mean to be rude."

The young woman nodded, and Elizabeth thought she saw a refreshing flicker of sympathy. Heaven knew, her so-called friends were sorely lacking in sensitivity. Elizabeth smiled shakily. She took a deep breath, flipped her long light hair over her shoulder, and shivered. The air conditioning was giving her a chill. She'd always preferred hot to cold. So unlike Brad who . . .

Elizabeth hugged herself, too antsy to sit, afraid to even think his name. She tightened the muscles in her calves, an old cheerleader trick she'd used to calm her nerves before a big game. Those were the days. Tighten a muscle, give a holler, shake a pompom, and the home team won. Well, the home team was looking pretty sad. In fact, the home team was breaking up.

Colder now, Elizabeth moved away from the air conditioning vent and wandered across the lobby, half aware of the people congregating there. A small group spoke in low tones. Others came off the elevator. Somewhere, someone laughed.

Elizabeth shook her head, but it wouldn't clear. She turned to look out the huge windows, across the ill-defined skyline of Los Angeles. How in awe she had been of all this. Brad's sudden abandonment of his teaching career had been amazing, but to become the wife of an executive in a company whose profits were counted in the multimillions—well, that had been astounding. How respectful and proud she'd been. Respect. Now there was a word that needed some down-home refining.

"Mrs. MacMillan?" Elizabeth started, her arms falling to her sides as she turned.

"Yes?" Elizabeth couldn't hide her disappointment. A woman of indeterminate age in an impeccable gray suit held out her hand. Elizabeth wasn't even worth Mr. Sawyer's time.

"I'm Carol, Mr. Sawyer's secretary. I'm sorry we didn't know you were coming." She smiled sweetly. Elizabeth took her hand, knowing she offered the same smile fifty times a day. "Mr. Sawyer is in a meeting and won't be available for some time."

"I don't mind waiting," Elizabeth assured her quickly. "I've called and haven't been able to get through to him all week, so I'd hate to miss him now that I've come all the way downtown."

"I understand that, Mrs. MacMillan." They broke the woman-to-woman connection, and Carol was all-business. "But you have to understand how busy we've been. . . . It's the end of our fiscal year. If you'd be kind enough to call again in a week or two, I'm sure Mr. Sawyer could see you then. Or, perhaps, I could help you."

"No, I don't think so. You see, I don't have a few weeks." Elizabeth's voice cracked. Damn it. She wouldn't shame herself by crying. The deep breath she took quavered, but she held back the tears. "My son . . ."

"Is he ill?"

"No," Elizabeth shook her head, thrown off by such immediate and genuine concern. "He was sick, but it was the insurance problem that made me think of Mr. Sawyer."

"Thank goodness." Carol's well-mannered hands clasped together at waist level, indicating everything was fine now. But it wasn't. Before Elizabeth could set her straight, Carol was making plans. "Well, we can take care of insurance things without bothering Mr. Sawyer. You'll want to talk to the benefits administrator. Won't that be better than waiting until Mr. Sawyer's available? I'll get you her name and number."

The secretary slipped back through the glass doors, leaving Elizabeth to marvel at her diplomacy. The conversation hadn't ended. It had been clipped off.

Elizabeth eyed her surroundings. The man who'd come off the elevator was gone. The knot of people who had been so intent on their report was breaking up. The receptionist was on the phone. Everyone had a job to do—Elizabeth, too.

Her renewed determination empowering her, Elizabeth walked toward the heavy glass doors. Driven by worries about the doctor, the bill, the bank, and Brad she pulled them open, walked through, and turned right into her husband's other life.

No bells. No whistles. Certain someone would stop her any minute, Elizabeth strode briskly down the long hall. On her right, office windows looked out to the world. On her left, carpet-padded walls carved out a honeycomb of cubicles in which young people labored over papers or talked secretively into phones. In the private offices, men and women not much older than Elizabeth did the same.

Emboldened, Elizabeth held her head higher, stopping suddenly in the doorway of an empty office. For a fleeting moment she imagined Brad there, his soft features pulled together in an expression of concern over a problem of business, not poetry. Had he enjoyed that? Elizabeth didn't know. She'd never asked.

She blinked. Brad's image disappeared, and she stood in the doorway to an empty room, nothing more. Most people spent half their lives in offices like these, unaware how hazardous it could be.

" 'Scuse me."

A young man hurried past. Dutifully, Elizabeth hugged the wall. A woman came toward her as she stepped into the hall again. Elizabeth let her pass without speaking. Knowing she couldn't wander around the place much longer without drawing attention to herself, she poked her head into one of the cubicles and muttered another " 'scuse me."

"Yes?" The sandy-haired man looked up.

"Mr. Sawyer?"

"Fourth door down. On the right. But I think he's in a meeting in the conference room."

Elizabeth would have grinned if she hadn't been so miserable. These people weren't so smart after all. She hurried on. One. Two. Three. God, she felt faint. *Brad. Brad MacMillan, I want to be at home. I want you to be there, too.* Four. *I want this all to stop now.*

Here.

Sawyer's office. She read his name on the door.

John Sawyer.

Her savior.

Elizabeth ducked in, fully expecting to be able to catch her breath while she waited for Brad's boss to finish his conference. Instead, she pulled up short. In the large, airy office, three men studied her curiously.

Strangely unembarrassed, she found herself completely aware of her surroundings. She saw the picture of the little girl and woman on the desk, the plant by the window that needed water, the curl of paper that had missed the wastebasket and lay on the gray carpeting. What she couldn't get was an impression of the men. She couldn't focus without seeing Brad in her mind's eye.

"May I help you?" The man behind the desk came toward her.

"Yes," Elizabeth breathed and stuck out her hand. *Bold. Be bold,* she reminded herself. "Mr. Sawyer? I need you to help me."

The man hesitated, obviously trying to decide if he should admit his identity. Executive that he was, he graciously ignored her outstretched hand and held out his own toward her back, cupping the air and somehow turning her backward so she faced the door.

"We're busy here. Why don't you call me in about an hour? What department are you in?" he asked.

"No, I'm not in any department, but I've been trying to see you for weeks." Elizabeth had taken a few steps toward the hall then stopped. She wouldn't go backward again. This was the right place and the right person, and she wasn't going to lose her advantage. "You *are* John Sawyer, aren't you?"

"Yes, I am, and I'm afraid I am in a meeting at the moment." He sounded peevish. The polite hand was now stuffed in his pocket.

Elizabeth looked at the other two men in the room. Her green eyes trailed back to John Sawyer. He moved self-consciously toward the desk as if he could read her mind. She was back in the game and came right at him.

"I realize that you, and these gentlemen, are in the middle of something very important, Mr. Sawyer, but I've been trying to get through to you for a week now. You're never available. I'm Elizabeth MacMillan, and all I want to do is talk to my husband."

Elizabeth chanced a glance at the men. They were still listening, so she went on.

"I need to see my husband, Mr. Sawyer." Elizabeth clutched her purse and straightened her shoulders. She lowered her eyes, then raised them again. "I'm not unreasonable, Mr. Sawyer. I know our problems aren't your problems, but I've got a situation with the insurance company and . . ."

"Mrs. MacMillan," John Sawyer began. Her name sounded awful the way he said it . . . slow and sad.

Elizabeth swallowed around a huge hole in her middle, as if someone had shot her with a cannonball. She felt faint and must have looked it, because John Sawyer watched her a split second longer than was necessary before addressing his companions. "I think we can pick this up later."

The two nodded and were out the door like a shot, murmuring their goodbyes. Making a beeline for Brad, she guessed and sat down, straight-backed in the soft chair still warm from its previous occupant. She squared her shoulders, absolutely determined not to let the words "I'm sorry" pass her lips.

"I'm so sorry, Mr. Sawyer."

Damn! Elizabeth glanced over her shoulder as if she could catch those words back before they filled up the room. Then she saw it. One of the men had closed the door on his way out. Either he didn't want them to be disturbed or he didn't want to hear what was going to happen in this office. Her head swiveled back. "Mr. Sawyer, I hope you know I wouldn't have come to see you if there were any other way."

"I understand, Mrs. MacMillan . . ."

"Elizabeth. My name is Elizabeth."

"Elizabeth, then," he said kindly. "I don't know how I can help you." John Sawyer raised a hand to punctuate his powerlessness. It was a feeling she'd come to know well over the last year.

"Just seeing me helps an awful lot," Elizabeth said. "I know that Brad thinks the world of you." She lied and hoped he didn't know that Brad had never said so much as a word to her about his boss. "So I understand he probably told you that we've been separated for almost a year now. I know this is no concern of yours, and I appreciate any advice you've been able to give him. Heaven knows, you don't need to hear from me, too, but I'm afraid I haven't been able to talk to Brad."

She wanted to die. She had to tell this stranger how she had failed her husband; she had to beg for this man's assistance in matters that should be between husband and wife. Elizabeth's shoulders sagged; it was such an effort to keep them squared and looking strong. Her voice was a monotone—and mournful. Suddenly, she was very tired.

"He was very specific about needing some privacy, and I tried to respect that. He's called often enough, even come home to see our son regularly." Elizabeth's fingers wound in the strap of her purse. "Look, I've got to talk to my husband, Mr. Sawyer, and pretty damn soon, sir. The insurance plan is disallowing a claim I made for our son, and your company hasn't put through the automatic deposit into our checking account. I know Brad listens to you, and I hope you'll ask him to—" Elizabeth swallowed the last of her pride. "—talk to me."

Her voice broke with such a snap that John Sawyer looked wounded by it. Tears that had been held deep inside suddenly surged forward, pushing through her eyes and over her lashes, but Elizabeth never lowered her head.

"Mrs. MacMillan." John Sawyer was on his feet, digging in the drawers of his desk for a tissue, his voice softly despairing. He handed her his handkerchief in lieu of the tissue, then stood away as though this would afford her some privacy in an awkwardly intimate situation. Elizabeth hated his pitying silence and filled it herself.

"Mr. Sawyer, I'm so sorry. Truly I am." Her voice trembled. She dabbed at her eyes. She studied the handkerchief, but she never stopped talking. "I've never done anything like this in my life. I'm a mother and a housewife. It's all I've ever been, and I want a chance to make things right. If I can't do that, then I need to have some information so I can keep my son well and safe."

Afraid no longer, she waited and found she had power. John Sawyer couldn't look at her any longer.

"I'm sorry," he said. Elizabeth's heart went stone cold. She knew he was sincere and his sorrow was for something deeper than being unable to provide her with insurance data. He couldn't look her in the eye, so he walked to the wall of windows and leaned against it.

"Please, I . . ." she whispered. "I'm not here to cause you any trouble."

"I know you're not, Mrs. MacMillan, but I can't do anything." There was a heartbeat before John Sawyer stepped on Elizabeth MacMillan's rose-colored glasses and crushed them. "I don't know where Brad is." He swung around, finally meeting her gaze. "Brad quit a week and a half ago. He picked up his check on the fifteenth, canceling the automatic deposit. I'm very sorry. I don't know where your husband is. If you don't, I doubt anyone does."

With that, John Sawyer left the room.

Elizabeth sobbed. Such an ugly sound. No wonder actresses didn't sob in the movies. Elizabeth swiped at her eyes with the back of one hand. Actresses didn't look like she did either when they cried. Swollen cheeked and red-eyed, nose running. She flexed her fingers around the steering wheel. She sobbed again and sniffled.

"Damn," she hiccupped through her tears. "Damn."

She'd never cried like this in her life. Not even when Christina Dewar ripped the ribbons off her ballet shoes before her solo at their third-grade recital. She'd never hurt like this in her life. Not even when Brad first told her he wanted to live apart.

She'd done everything she was supposed to do. Brad had said he wanted time. Time! She'd given him a year. Space. She'd given him that, but he wanted more.

"Damn. Damn. Damn."

Horrified, Elizabeth felt her foot press hard on the gas pedal, keeping time with her curses. She tried to ease up, but she'd lost control. The car sped dangerously over the road as her hands clenched on the wheel. Her entire body felt strange. On fire and cold as ice. A body that couldn't possibly be hers. She had shrunk to a dried-up old carcass of a woman, exhausted and afraid, with nowhere to turn. The man who had promised to take care of her was gone; he had walked out as if she and Christopher were nothing more to him than casual acquaintances. Twelve years of their life meant nothing.

Another sob, a horrid wrenching sound that came from her gut this time. Elizabeth swore, but a wail broke the word in half and she moaned. Tears streamed down her cheeks, pouring from under her sunglasses. She tried to wipe them away, half blinding herself as she knocked her glasses askew.

"Good Christ, Brad," she cried. "Where . . . are . . . you?"

Panic rising, she pressed ever harder on the accelerator, not caring if the car flew off the face of the earth. Even Christopher didn't matter. This moment was hers. This pain was personal, private.

She sped past the front entrance to Emerald Isle, vaguely conscious of propriety. Someone from the neighborhood might see her careening around streets rife with children-at-play warnings. Someone might notice her swollen red eyes, her lips quivering uncontrollably with terror. Elizabeth paralleled the wall surrounding Emerald Isle. That symbol of exclusivity all those years ago was now just the final barrier of a jail she had called home.

Angrily, Elizabeth flipped the wheel and turned toward the back lot. The gray car swerved sharply, the wheels spinning for an instant as they dipped into a shallow ditch. Suddenly Elizabeth was suspended, entombed in a machine that now had a life of its own. Maybe this was the way it would end. A crash, blessed darkness. For a heart-stopping moment, she imagined herself dead, and Brad's grief when he was finally found and told. But the car gained momentum, catapulting onto the gravel road once again. She was still alive. Scared, sobs silenced for now, tears still streaming, Elizabeth drove on. She wanted to be home.

She didn't notice the men working on the side of the road. She paid no attention to the trucks pulled onto the shoulder. The bare-chested man pushing the wheelbarrow was of no consequence to her, so Elizabeth was oblivious to his fearful face as her car bore down on him and he pushed the barrow over the lip of the road and leapt after it. She had no idea that the huge piece of metal narrowly missed cutting a man in two at the bottom of the incline.

All Elizabeth MacMillan knew was that she needed to be in her own house before the next wave of hysteria hit her broadside. In the trail of dust she left as she fled toward home, Elizabeth didn't notice the man who ran behind her, stopping only long enough to throw himself into a cherry-red truck to continue his chase.

On she drove, careening onto Greenwood Boulevard before flipping the wheel a hard right onto Sundance Lane.

And at last, Elizabeth MacMillan was home. Alone.

"Hey!"
Bang.
"Hey!"
Bang, bang.
"I know you're in there. Hey! Lady! I want to talk to you now!"

Elizabeth didn't move. Someone was pounding on her door, screaming and cursing, and she couldn't care less. She didn't care if Ann sat with an ear to her kitchen window or if Janie in the house behind hers lounged by the pool, her X-rated imagination in high gear. And Elizabeth didn't care who was at her front door or what he screamed.

"Lady? Lady!" Another whack. The toe of his boot met the brass kick-plate on her lovingly painted china-blue door. "Christ."

Elizabeth stayed still. If she sat there long enough, he would go away. And maybe, if she sat very still, Brad would come back and make him go away. The world would always be right if she sat very still. Her mother had told her that when she was a child. But she hadn't listened.

With her head cradled on one upturned palm, Elizabeth now did as her mother instructed. She didn't twitch or blink, only watched her tears fall to the beautifully polished table. She was so weary of weeping.

"Hey! Lady!"

Startled, Elizabeth let her hand fall away; her head snapped up. She wasn't alone anymore. A tall, dark man walked in from the patio right through the French doors Elizabeth seldom closed. A handsome man. Broad-shouldered. Slim-hipped. Dirty. His clothes were caked with mud, his face streaked with sweat. He didn't belong there, yet he walked right across her hardwood floor and up to the table as if it were his right. Elizabeth MacMillan stared blankly, oddly unafraid in the face of his fury. He leaned down, spread his hands on the table.

"I don't know what your problem is, lady, but you almost killed one of my men. Now, I don't usually try to break down doors. I don't usually walk into someone's house without so much as an invitation. But this is serious. My men are going to be out there for a good, long time building houses like this so women like you can have a nice place to live, and I don't want them looking over their shoulder every minute for a broad who can't keep her eyes on the road. Life's too short for that kind of worry, lady. Too . . . damn . . . short. Got it?"

Elizabeth held his dark gaze, and he faltered, backing off, hand to his forehead. He pushed back the hard hat—angry, frustrated, perhaps even surprised to find himself standing before her. A line of black dirt dissected his brow where the hat sat low on his head above skin the color of fawn. Elizabeth winced. His boots made hard, scraping sounds as he moved, and she worried about scratches on the floor.

Elizabeth put her fingers to her eyes. They felt enormous and they hurt. She wished the swelling would go away; she wished he would go away. Gently, she pressed; and when she looked up, the man was still there. He was talking again, his finger pointing through the open doors, past the oblong pool to a point on the horizon. His voice was lower now, as if he were fighting for control. Brad never raised his voice. Brad never . . .

"That road was plainly marked with neon cones. That road is wide enough for a dump truck. You had to have seen my men a mile back, and you still drove like a maniac. You could have killed someone. Christ! Think before you get in your car."

He whipped off his hat, showing Elizabeth a classic profile. She turned away, unable to look at this man with purpose, so filled with emotion. His mere presence reminded her of what she didn't have; his bearing was an example of what she'd never had. He was crazy, of course, filling her house with anger, and she had to get him out before Christopher came home.

But instead, she started to cry again. She had no more reserves to draw on: No strength, no indignation, no play-acting or putting on a front. She couldn't even lift her hand to wipe away the tears. The man in the jeans, a tool belt slung low on his hips, froze, closed his eyes, and fell into the chair beside her.

He reached out, touching her lightly on the back of her hand, letting his fingers linger thoughtfully. Only the tips of his fingers lay against her skin, but it was enough to make Elizabeth pull herself to the surface of her despair and float there, listening to his quiet speech. If he sang, a quiet part of her mind observed, he would be a tenor.

"My man's got a family and kids, a home. Maybe not as nice as this, but it's his, you know. It's not for you to take away."

Elizabeth pulled her hand away. She didn't want to hear about things being taken away, lost, or thrown off. She was an expert on the subject. He misunderstood her reaction.

"Okay. You're right. Who am I to lecture?" Breathing deep he put his hard hat back on. "We're going to be out in that back area a good long while. I'd appreciate being able to send everyone home when the job's done. Sorry to have barged in. I apologize. I just . . ." Those long-fingered hands were on his slender hips again; a muscle in his neck twitched as he looked into the distance, searching for the right words. Finding nothing to suit him, he said simply, "Life's short, lady. Don't make it shorter."

He was halfway across the patio when Elizabeth found her voice. "I'm sorry," she whispered to his retreating figure. "I'm so sorry."

Elizabeth MacMillan lay her head on the beautiful dining room table and looked out onto the perfectly appointed living room. She thought about Christopher. She thought about Brad, and the tears came again.

Max Marino yanked open the door of his truck, threw his hard hat in, then crossed his arms atop the cab, resting as he took three deep breaths. God, he couldn't believe he'd done that. His crew was probably having a good laugh at his expense right about now. Running off like an idiot, screaming and hollering. Jesus.

Raising one hand, he ran it through his thick, damp hair. He wouldn't have blamed that woman if she had had him arrested for breaking and entering. And the way he'd talked to her. Lord! He'd never treated a woman like that. Except that once. Just that once— when it was Anna.

Slipping into the truck, Max pulled the door closed but didn't turn the key. He sat staring at the gray station wagon and the house, thinking of the woman inside. Different as night and day, that woman and Anna. Still, there was something similar about them. It was the way she'd looked at him as he railed at her, that blind and confused expression of pain. Yelling hadn't made him feel better then, when it had been directed at Anna; it didn't make him feel better now. Max shook his head. Dumb. But it was over—almost.

Flinging open the door, Max swung his long legs out of the truck and headed back to the house, through the gate and past the toys in the yard and a long unused cat's dish. He made it all the way to the patio and was about to step up onto the bricks when he caught sight of the blond woman.

She half lay across her dining room table, her head turned away from the bank of French doors. Her golden hair spilled over the mahogany. One long, slender arm was slung out, and her head rested upon it. Her fingers were curled as if in sleep. He found it hard to look at that hand. She didn't move and he could hear the sounds of weeping through the still-open door.

As he watched, he thought of Anna, though the physical resemblance was unfathomable: One dark, the other light; one so small, the other tall; one content in her little house, the other living large. Yet he thought of Anna and the nameless woman as if they were inexplicably bound together. In this late afternoon moment, they were one and the same. Both alone, beyond help—his or anyone else's.

Turning from her, Max left the way he'd come. He drove slowly away from the big house in Emerald Isle, leaving the woman to her heartache.

Better he tend to his own misery than try to mend hers.

Two

"Burgers!"

Elizabeth brandished the long-handled spatula and a plate of uncooked meat. She grinned, but Christopher's nose stayed buried in a magazine. A green reptilian creature with four heads graced the cover. Ten years old, confused, hurt, and bleeding from wounds so horribly like hers, but with the added burden of a child's mind to rationalize it all.

"Feet off the table, buddy." Lightheartedly, she rapped the bottom of his huge tennis shoes. "Come on. Put that silly magazine down, and help me watch 'em cook. School's going to start soon. We're almost out of picnic time."

Christopher squirmed and recrossed his feet. Unanswered, Elizabeth turned away. Her smile disintegrated the minute her back was to him. She busied herself at the barbecue, turning knobs, trying to master the hulking grill that Brad had sworn by. Even when it was near freezing he had piled burgers on a plate, fired up the grill, and stood patiently watching the food cook. Now and again, the smoke had billowed, a bit of grease hitting hot coals, and his face had been obscured. She used to laugh and say he had his head in the clouds. Maybe it hadn't been such a joke after all.

"Damn," she muttered, her hand slipping on the igniter, bruising three fingers.

Elizabeth snapped it to ease the pain, checked the wound—nothing but a scratch that hurt like hell—and put it to her lips. Little things, tiny problems, were the worst. They made her feel like sitting down and giving up. The glass that broke in the dishwasher, the missing button on her nightgown, Christopher's decision to take down the posters of that animated purple dinosaur and replace it with a picture of Johnny Cage, Kung Fu killer. Brad's cleaning. They had actually called her to pick up Brad's suits. Elizabeth had left them.

"You've gotta turn these first."

Startled, Elizabeth stepped back. Christopher moved in, laying his surprisingly masculine hands on the barbecue. Elizabeth looked at them, grateful to see small indentations above the knuckles as if childhood lingered there, if nowhere else. She heard a pop, a whoosh, and the gas was on, the grill was heating. Elizabeth laughed.

"Honey, that's great!" False bravado, but better than tears. "I didn't know you could do that." Elizabeth reached for her son, who stood shoulder-tall to her, but he slipped out of her embrace as easily as if he were a waif. Tipping her chin, saving some degree of face, Elizabeth shrugged. "Well, guess you are getting kind of old for big hugs. Still, I could use a little one now and again. You let me know when you could, too."

Elizabeth turned to her task, knowing her observation had come out sounding more like an accusation. She'd have to watch that. Carefully, she lay the burgers on the grill, taking comfort in the sound and smell, the rote of the chore. Daring to look up, she treated herself to a deep breath. She hated looking up lately, for fear she'd find people looking back. But today, locked away in the backyard with Christopher, she felt free.

The trees swayed in a slight summer breeze; the impatiens were blooming. The pool sparkled. It all looked so lovely—so normal—as long as she was looking up. Eye level wasn't so pleasant.

Christopher was back on the patio, lounging on one chair, his feet on another. He tossed a ball into the air and made noises that excluded Elizabeth by decibel level alone.

A high cloud passed above them, and now the garden didn't look as beautiful. The tomato plants she'd tended so happily three months earlier were heavy with fruit spoiling on the vine. She couldn't find the energy to harvest them, or the desire to eat them.

She saw the house as it really was. Big, in need of repair. She saw herself for what she was. A wife whose child had come before her husband. A mom whose everyday life had been priority. Now, her son needed clothes and food and things. How sad they hadn't given Brad enough back to make him want to stay.

Pushing at a strand of damp hair and flipping the burgers one last time for good measure, Elizabeth called to Christopher when she turned off the grill and decided it was time to really talk to her son.

"Here you go, sweetie. Ketchup?" She slipped into her chair and raised the family-size plastic bottle.

"I don't like ketchup, Mom." Christopher reached for the mustard. "Dad does."

There it was. The signal. Elizabeth reached out gently and held Christopher's hand. Slowly, she took the mustard and set it aside. Both hands covered Chris'.

His eyes were down. He made no move to take his hand away; nor did he move closer to his mother.

"Guess it's time we talked, huh?" Elizabeth squeezed. His skin was so wonderfully smooth. There was great comfort in this connection—at least for her. She squeezed again, urging a response, tipping her head to try to look into his eyes.

"Guess so," he muttered.

Elizabeth smiled sadly. How dear this child was to her. Almost all the baby gone from him, chubbiness melting away into a body that was poised on the point of young adulthood. There was a great deal of Brad in Chris, but Elizabeth saw herself, too: her fair coloring, her straight hair, her way of lowering her eyes when she didn't want to face something hurtful—like the truth.

"Want to eat while we talk?" Elizabeth let her hands slip away, though she would have preferred to have pulled him toward her. She offered the bowl of potato salad. Christopher gave it his full attention, giving himself a wall of food to hide behind as he listened.

"I'll have some, too," Elizabeth said softly, energy flowing out of her the more he claimed silence for his own. She dished the salad onto her own plate, swatted at an imaginary fly, then began.

"Okay, sweetie, here's the thing. Daddy's gone."

"Mom," Christopher said, "I know that. Do we have to talk about it?"

"Yes, we do." Elizabeth felt anger pop inside her head. Anger at Christopher because he wasn't making this easy. But he was a kid. She was the adult. It wouldn't do any good to yell at him. Softly, she said, "Chris, look at me. Now."

Reluctantly, he swung his head her way. His lips were full and moist, tinged pink. Those lips were set in a horrid expression that would surely follow him into adulthood if she didn't find some way to get him past all this.

"Thank you. Now," Elizabeth began in her best mom's-on-top-of-things voice, "what I have to tell you is that Daddy is *really* gone. I don't know where he is. That's a whole lot different from his wanting to live somewhere else for a while." Elizabeth folded her hands on the edge of the table and concentrated on her entwined fingers. "Daddy isn't going to be here to help us anymore, and I don't have any way of finding him."

Christopher's eyes snapped her way. She could feel his gaze on her. From the corner of her eyes she saw that his face looked surprisingly hard in the afternoon light as he considered her intently.

"Are you scared?" There, in his question, were strains of an adult's voice and an adult's challenge. His tone startled her into truthfulness.

"Yes, honey. I am." She leaned forward as if this would underscore her sincerity. "I was going to lie, but I don't think it would make anything better, do you?"

Christopher shrugged, his gorgeous gray-green eyes skittering away again. Damn, it was hard to know what to say.

"Nope."

The conversation was over. The burger was in his mouth. That anger flashed again, way deep inside her like lightning in a next-county storm. Their future loomed large and dark, and Christopher was pouting. Maybe the mommy approach was wrong. He was a big boy. Elizabeth would start treating him like one.

"Okay, Chris. You may not want to talk, but we've got to. I don't know how long it's going to be just you and me; but even if it's for a day, we've got to make some decisions. Things are going to be very different. We'll have to watch what we spend. There won't be any money coming in for a bit . . ."

Christopher's face paled; his eyes deepened a shade as his lips pulled shut and he swallowed his food. She should have tipped over the table getting to him, wrapping her arms around him. Instead, hurt, Elizabeth played his game, ashamed but unable to help herself.

"Well, Chris, it's nice to know that something interests you," she drawled.

"Will we stay in our house? Will we have to live in the car like those people on the news?" This time the questions lost all the edges of attitude. Pretense gone, Elizabeth found herself horrified that she could be so cold. She had assumed he was worried about the things he wouldn't have, but it was the horrible world outside Emerald Isle he was afraid of. Pained at her own lack of sympathy, Elizabeth closed her eyes. Christopher needed for her to say the right things, and he needed to hear them now.

"We're not going anywhere," Elizabeth answered gently, her eyes open, the promise delivered without hesitation although she wondered if this were the truth. "This house has been our home since before you were born. But, Chris, it's not going to be easy to keep it. I'll have to work. There's no way around it."

"How long?" Christopher asked.

"Until Daddy comes home. Always, if he doesn't." She shrugged and hoped he understood it wasn't a sign of defeat, only of uncertainty.

"None of the other moms do," Christopher mumbled and Elizabeth refrained from sighing. A child's view of the world was so beautifully limited. Of course some of the other moms worked, but just not the ones they knew.

"I'll start a trend." She chuckled softly. Chris formulated his thoughts by chewing on his nails. The thoughts must have been very deep indeed. He looked at her, fingers poised lip-level.

"Can I still play baseball?"

"I'll put it in the budget," she answered solemnly, then warned. "But don't lose your mitt."

The fingers were almost in his mouth again, but he hesitated, watching her carefully. "Do you think Daddy will?"

"Will what?" she asked.

"Come back." She had known he'd meant that.

She sat very, very quietly, hearing Brad in Christopher's clipped question, seeing him in the way Christopher's brow furrowed. Her son, so much his father. How could she even venture a guess and answer that question when she hadn't even known how much Brad had wanted to leave? She shrugged again, defeated, and shook her head.

"I don't know what Daddy's thinking or doing. I'm mad at him for not telling me, but I'm not mad at him for having to do it. Sometimes people need very different things. Sometimes I wonder if I did something to make him go away."

"No." Christopher shook his own head adamantly. "You're a good mom. I remember Dad talking about stuff that made him mad, and you weren't one of those things. You don't have to worry about that."

A tremor of relief coursed through Elizabeth. Christopher believed in her. She *was* a good person. A good mom. But a good wife?

"I try," she said quietly, afraid to ask what Brad had told a child instead of his wife.

"You're the best, Mom," Christopher insisted. To her surprise, he touched her shoulder. Tentative . . . heavy . . . but the best touch Elizabeth ever remembered getting. How awkward he was. Afraid of her as a woman, needy of her as a mother.

She took his hand and pulled him into her lap. He didn't exactly fit, but neither of them minded. Elizabeth moved just enough to kiss his cheek. "I'll make sure we're okay, kiddo. I'll take care of you and me; and when Daddy comes home, I'll take care of him even better."

Without a word, Christopher put his arms around her and lay his head in the crook of her neck. She felt him breathing and held him close, but somehow couldn't find that place in her heart where just holding him made her feel strong and whole.

"Hi, Elizabeth. What brings you here so early in the morning? Come in, have a cup of coffee."

Elizabeth offered Betsy Colby a smile and shook her hair back, trying to look as normal as possible. Her hands stuffed in the pockets of her candystriper pinafore, Elizabeth MacMillan, hospital volunteer, had a favor to ask.

"Thanks, I can't. I'm due at the hospital in a few minutes. I'm really sorry to bother you so early, but would it be okay if Christopher came here after summer camp for the next few days? I know it's an imposition, and I wouldn't ask unless it were absolutely necessary . . ." Elizabeth's voice trailed off.

"Hope there isn't a problem, Elizabeth," Betsy said, opening her door, an invitation for girl talk.

"No, of course not." Elizabeth struck a more confident air and remained outside. Confessing to Betsy wouldn't help, especially since anything she said would soon be whispered up and down the block. Everyone knew Brad had moved out, but no one was aware that he had deserted his wife and son. So Elizabeth kept a stiff upper lip. "I have to work late, and I don't want Christopher in an empty house. It would only be for a week until I can make other arrangements."

"Sure, no problem. I'll bet Katy would love to have him over," Betsy cooed.

Liar. Twelve-year-old Katy would rather have her phone taken away than play with the "kid" next door. Elizabeth's expression remained gracious. Her choices were limited.

"That's so nice of you, but Katy doesn't have to change her schedule for Christopher. If he could just pop in around 4:30, I'll be home by 7:00 at the latest."

"Seven! My goodness that hospital is getting pushy, isn't it? Expecting volunteers to work hours like that." Dish towel still in hand, Betsy leaned against the door jamb. She had all the time in the world.

"Well, yes," Elizabeth muttered, plucking at the full skirt of her uniform. God, she hated this: begging, lying by omission, living in a fish bowl. "You're sure it's okay?" she asked, edging away. "For Chris to come over, I mean."

Betsy's face shadowed with disappointment: Elizabeth had provided little grounds for gossip. She flipped the towel in dismissal. "Of course, it's all right. Just have him call if he's going to be late."

"Thanks." Elizabeth heard Betsy's door close before she'd made it down the walk.

"One day at a time," she admonished herself, noticing that her hand shook when she put the key in the ignition.

"I really appreciate your seeing me on such short notice, Frank."

"It's okay, Elizabeth, but we're going to have to make this quick."

Elizabeth backed up quickly, almost run over by the man who was as wide as he was tall. He huffed and puffed as he made the short walk from the reception desk to his small office. Elizabeth scurried after him, well aware that she should be pushing the magazine cart through Geriatrics instead of chasing after the hospital administrator.

"I really appreciate the time you're giving me." Elizabeth closed the door of his office behind her but opened it again at his request.

"So damn hot. You know."

"Sure." Elizabeth took a seat, knowing it was poor Frank's weight that raised his body temperature.

"So, what's up? Still having problems with that nurse on five?" He was abrupt. He pulled a calculator toward him, but Elizabeth knew he didn't miss a beat. She smiled. Nurse Crachet, the platinum-haired volunteer-hater. Frank had been living with her nonsense for years.

"No, actually, we've been lucky. She's working the night shift," Elizabeth said, managing a real smile. Frank was a nice man.

"So, then . . ." He spread his small, soft hands on his desk as much to steady himself in his chair as to indicate it was time to get to the point.

"So," Elizabeth repeated, trying to ignore the butterflies in her stomach. The last time she'd worked was at Dixie Chicken when she was sixteen. "I've never done this before, Frank, so you've got to help me a little bit, if you don't mind. I need a job. A real one. With a paycheck."

"Sorry to hear it," Frank said, and Elizabeth believed him.

"Me, too," she agreed softly.

"You've got a kid, right?" He speared her with a sharp eye. Elizabeth's embarrassment grew.

"Yes. Christopher's ten." This was a far cry from what she had expected. He should have questions about her competency, her experience, anything . . . but not about her child.

"Thought so," Frank said and pulled his hand across his brow. "We raised two boys. Good boys, too. Lot of it was 'cause their mom stayed home. Any chance you could get by without a job?"

Elizabeth shook her head. Nice man that he was, Frank pretended not to notice that she was swallowing hard.

"Gotcha."

The heavy man sighed. He opened his desk drawer and pulled out a bunch of papers. He slid them across the desk to her.

"Fill these out, Elizabeth, and we'll get the ball rolling. Got a college education, do you?"

"Yes. Oh, yes," Elizabeth said quickly. "University of Georgia."

"Shoulda guessed, huh?" He laughed, and Elizabeth's relief was overwhelming.

"Just wanted to know. Makes a difference." He breathed hard, wheezed a bit, and coughed; but his attention was all hers. "Only thing we have open right now is in Admissions. Think you could do that?"

"I can do anything. I'm good with people. Paperwork doesn't scare me." Nothing scared her. Not anymore.

"You don't know what paperwork is till you've been in Admissions for a few weeks. When can you start?"

"Tomorrow?"

"How about Wednesday? Gotta do some shuffling around with schedules. I may make this look like a piece of cake, but it isn't. It's tough."

"Wednesday, sure. Frank, I can't thank you enough. I thought it would be so hard. I thought . . ." Elizabeth was half out of her chair, hand out.

"Thought I'd grill ya, huh?" Frank's eyes twinkled as he teased her, but he was serious an instant later. "Look, Elizabeth, we don't really have an opening, but you've been around here a long time. Done good work. You're a straight shooter, and darn nice to boot. I know you wouldn't ask if it weren't important. Just do a good job. Don't make me have to stand up in front of some damn committee to explain why I hired you without experience or references."

"I promise. I promise."

"Just so we understand each other." He offered a

curt nod. "Take all that paper, fill it out, and bring it back here. Show up on Wednesday, eight forty-five. Now, I gotta get you out of here, okay?"

"Sure. I'll have these back this afternoon. Thank you so much. You'll never know what this means. . . . You'll never regret it."

"Elizabeth," Frank's eyes were on her, and she saw something more than the gentle giant he appeared to be. "I don't want to know why you need work, but I'm sorry that you do. I like families the way they used to be: mom at home, kid at school, dad at work. If it can't be that way, then I figure I should help out. It's the ladies that don't take care of their own because they don't feel like it that get my hackles up."

"You can get sued for saying things like that, Frank."

"It's the way I feel, and I'm too old to change. Now, get outta here. I'm really swamped."

"Yes, sir!" Elizabeth exclaimed. For the first time in a long time she started to feel hope.

Maybe things wouldn't be so bad after all.

Every bit of her body ached: Her head from thinking, her eyes from reading, her foot from tapping, and her hand from filling in blanks that asked about her life in detail. What a pitiful exercise. All too often she had written "not applicable" where others would have jotted down sterling examples of a competent professional life. Wearily she turned the page and started in again. Her pen hovered; the question stumped her. Whom would anyone contact in an emergency? Mom dead. Dad dead. Brad gone. Christopher? A ten-year-old boy? Any one of a hundred acquaintances who weren't close enough to call friends in an emergency?

Automatically Elizabeth reached for her coffee. Her fingers closed around the Styrofoam. She raised it to drink, her eyes wandering from the application to the budget figures doodled on a napkin—her salary in one column, expenses in the other. It didn't look like she and Christopher would be living high on the hog.

Withholding was astronomical, the insurance deduction ridiculous. Elizabeth scratched it out. She would continue Brad's policy, pay his premium, and save a few dollars. She was on a roll: She'd made two major decisions on her own. Elizabeth rewarded herself with a sip of coffee.

Food. Electricity. Mortgage.

How heavy a burden this must have been for Brad— and now it was hers. Damn it, why hadn't he ever told her about all this? She would have helped . . . somehow. She put down the coffee cup and rubbed her eyes again. It was almost three. There was no more time to worry.

Slowly, she pushed herself back, gathered her papers, and picked up her cup, contemplating the changes ahead. No karate, but park basketball was in. No summer vacation, but the pool heater could be fixed. On automatic pilot, Elizabeth scooted around a table. Even McDonald's would be a special treat, and spur-of-the-moment pizza feasts would be out of the question.

" 'Scuse me."

Distracted, Elizabeth moved out of the way just as she turned to toss her cup into the trash can, and her hand hit flesh and bone. Lukewarm coffee doused Elizabeth's hand and the unfortunate man's shirt.

"Oh, I'm so sorry." Elizabeth's breath came out in a gush of words, her problems forgotten. "I didn't see you. Let me help."

She dabbed at his shirt with her napkin. Her napkin! All those figures about to be obliterated. Elizabeth stuffed the wad of paper into her pocket.

"I'll get some club soda. It'll get it right out," she promised. "Trust me." She turned one way only to find it blocked by late-afternoon lunchers. She turned the other way, but couldn't find a path through the tables. The hospital cafeteria was no better than her life; blocked on all sides.

Before she could do anything other than sputter, a strong hand clasped her shoulder, a warm voice laughed. The speaker was so near she could feel his soft breath on her cheek.

"It's not that important." His hand tightened, reassuring her. "Really."

Elizabeth turned around, a smile at the ready. But laughter and gratitude faded and, almost simultaneously, the man's did, too.

Where had they . . . when had they . . . wasn't it . . . he waved a finger her way, a half smile on his face as his mind worked to place her. When he did, he groaned, his smile now a self-deprecating grimace.

"Oh no."

"Oh my God."

Elizabeth paled. She had been distraught when they'd met, not comatose—though that had been the worst day of her life.

"The woman on the road." He held an open palm her way.

"The man in my house," she answered flatly.

"Wow. Small world." He was quiet, almost contemplative, as he looked at her. He was not high on the list of people she would choose to chat with.

"I'm sorry about your shirt." Any semblance of a smile was gone. Her expression was grim, and the man mistook it for anger—which it might have been. "I've got a lot to do, so maybe I could send you a check for the shirt. The coffee won't come out if it soaks in much longer."

"That's not necessary . . ." he began.

"Whatever you like," Elizabeth interrupted. She was mortified. "I *am* sorry." She stepped to the side, but he stepped along with her.

"Hey, wait. I don't give a damn about this shirt, but I do about my conscience. What I did a few days ago has bothered the heck out of me." He touched her arm; gently and respectfully. "Please. Just another minute."

Elizabeth eyed him. He wasn't making fun of her, and she couldn't detect any sarcasm. He stuck out his hand and said, "Max Marino. Embarrassed and apologetic."

Cautiously, she reciprocated.

"Elizabeth MacMillan. The same."

Elizabeth took his hand and it felt good, calluses and all. She looked closer. He was a man who lived in the sun. His skin was tanned, the deep wrinkles around his eyes evidence of days outdoors. A handsome man. A nice man. She inched away, but he moved with her.

"Hey, I mean it," Max insisted, his hand still holding hers. "I am so, so sorry. That was the craziest thing I've ever done in my life. I guess I'm lucky you didn't call the cops and have me arrested."

Elizabeth slipped her hand from his and buried it in the pocket of her jumper. His good humor demanded she be cordial.

"It's not a federal case," Elizabeth said. "I was out of line. You probably were, too. We'll leave it at that. Now, I've really got to get going. If you change your mind about your shirt, you can find me here instead of on the back road. I'll just stay off that."

"I hope not. We're working hard out there. We could use a nice diversion now and again. Just drive slower so we can appreciate you from a distance."

He grinned, coaxing Elizabeth, perhaps flirting with her. But she wouldn't be charmed. She had a man— even if he was missing. Elizabeth managed a polite smile. Max was nice and trying hard to placate her, but he was wasting his time—and hers.

"You're very kind." Elizabeth gave voice to her thoughts. Raising her hand, she displayed the plain gold band she still wore. An adolescent gesture—*see, I'm pinned*—but effective nonetheless. "But I think I'll stick to the normal routes just to make sure."

"Well, that might be best," he said, his smile barely faltering. Elizabeth was impressed. An optimist in the face of obstacles.

Elizabeth nodded. Max did the same.

"Listen," he said finally, "the least I can do is buy you a cup of coffee to replace the one you lost."

"No." Elizabeth responded instantly. "Not a problem. I was finished anyway. I've got to get back to work."

"You're a volunteer. That's important in a place like this. I know the patients appreciate everything you do."

"I've enjoyed it," Elizabeth said as she slipped past him again, not unaware that he smelled a great deal like the outdoors and a little bit like spices. He fell in step beside her.

"You sound like you're quitting," he observed.

"No, just changing directions."

"And you're not happy about it. Which is it—the change or the direction—that bothers you?" Max questioned, overlooking the firm set of Elizabeth's mouth. She clasped her arms in front of her—easily defined body language that he refused to acknowledge.

Elizabeth pulled up fast. In another time, another place, she would probably be going on like a magpie, complimented that one so handsome would want to talk to her. But the time was now, the moment rife with concern, and her life needed a plan, not an adventure. She wanted her husband, not a new friend.

"Look, Mr. Marino, I don't know you. I've got a life that isn't exactly running smooth right now, and although you're very observant, I just don't have the time or the inclination to discuss it. We both probably feel better about clearing the air. Could we just leave it at that?"

"Sure. Sorry. I have a bad habit of butting in where I don't belong. Just thought . . ." Max stepped back to let her pass. He chuckled and ran a hand through the black hair he had meticulously combed away from his broad forehead. "I don't know what I thought. I've always been a pushy kind of guy. Talking all the time. Really nosy. My mother says I've been that way since I was a kid."

"Well, let me satisfy your curiosity, then. I'm transferring to a real job, and I've never had a real job before." To Elizabeth this admission seemed almost more shameful than Brad's desertion. "In this day and age, I'm a woman who's been on a free ride . . ."

"I doubt that . . ."

"What do you know about it?"

"I know that you take care of your house and kids. I know . . ."

"You don't know anything!" Elizabeth snapped and began to walk away. Her step was brisk. He was confusing her. There was no reason on this earth to talk to him, no reason why he should want to talk to her. Dazed, she hurried on, sensory overload shorting out the last of her patience. But he kept pace with her.

"I know you put a lot of love into that house. I know houses. I know how people treat them. People taking a free ride don't treat their homes the way you do. I know about women like you, and believe me you're unique. You're very special in a time when it's hard to find special things. Women like you . . ."

Speechless, Elizabeth stopped and looked him full in the face. His nose was aquiline and his face long and strong. His lips were wide, but not full or pretty. His eyes were dark and heavily lashed, yet there was something behind those eyes that reached out and tried to pull her away from her own concerns. He seemed to want a space in her life when Elizabeth had none to give. But she did have a wide streak of Southern courtesy and a heart that understood when someone was honestly trying to make a connection.

"Thank you for that, Mr. Marino. I love my home. I'm glad it shows."

"It does. You remind me of someone." They fell in step, and Max continued to talk—softer, slower. "I'd like to make up for the trouble I caused. That's really all I want."

He dug into the pocket of his khakis and handed her a card. "I own the construction company that's building the second phase of the Emerald Isle development. I noticed the gutters on the front of your house are looking a little shaky. I could fix them in no time. It's not much, but I would appreciate it if you'd let me ease my conscience by taking a whack at them."

Elizabeth looked at the card, then at him, and knew the gesture was a genuine bid for forgiveness. She also knew it was unnecessary.

"That's very nice of you, but . . ."

Sensing rejection, Max jumped in. "Would you like me to call your husband to discuss this, or can you just give me a start date?"

There it was: The cold water right in the face. A month ago, Elizabeth would have asked Max Marino to call Brad. Man's business. Now, it was her job to make decisions.

"No, I don't. . . . I mean, you can talk to me. I'll have to get back to . . ." Elizabeth stuttered, trying to get hold of the ten thousand thoughts flying through her mind. If she'd been a man, her course of action would have been clear—take the freebie and run.

"Max! Max!"

He turned, forgetting her quickly. Elizabeth looked, too, and beheld, bearing down on them, the roundest woman Elizabeth had ever seen. Oddly, she didn't seem fat, simply circular: back to front, side to side, top to bottom. Her face was apple-cheeked, and soft black curls made her visage moon-like. Her arms were large and her body cinched in the middle by a belt that threatened to cut her in half. Her legs were little barrels, and her feet were stuffed into a pair of impeccably kept low-heeled pumps with polished buckles on the toes.

"Max!" She grabbed his arm. "I've been waiting and waiting. Why didn't you come to the lab to get me? I was so worried something had happened." The woman's voice fluttered, and her breath came in short bursts as if she were fatigued. But the dark eyes that darted Elizabeth's way weren't tired. They ran Elizabeth up and down, then gazed adoringly at Max as the woman pulled his arm protectively closer. Elizabeth couldn't blame her. If she had a man like that in her life, no matter what his role, she would protect him, too. "You should have come back right away like I asked."

"Oh, Mama," Max chided. "What could have happened to me in the middle of a hospital?" The woman huffed and puffed and took great pains to avert her gaze so that Elizabeth was sure she had been snubbed though Max was oblivious to the machinations. "I ran into a friend—literally." Max's large hands covered the pudgy little ones that clung so proprietorially to his muscled arm. "Elizabeth MacMillan, I'd like you to meet Maria . . ."

The older woman leaned toward Elizabeth, but didn't offer her hand. Nor did she allow Max to finish.

"Nice to meet you," she said, and Elizabeth heard the underlying accent. "I'm afraid we don't have time to chat. We've got to get home. It's almost dinner time. Come on now, Max, your friend won't mind that you have to leave. Nice to meet you," she said, once again tugging on Max, who leaned into Elizabeth and whispered, "Call me when you're ready for the gutters."

His smile was gone, and he showed another face to

Elizabeth. Not the first one she'd seen, animated in anger. Not the open, smiling, charming face of a man at ease with himself. But a face void of expression save for some gleam deep in his eyes that insisted this would not be the last time they met. The moon-faced mama was now adamant. They disappeared down another hall, and Max Marino walked out of her life.

Shaking her head and chuckling over the encounter, Elizabeth headed toward the volunteer station. Her mind was still on the basics: a job, food on the table, keeping Christopher safe, finding Brad. The list was short, but formidable. And now she had to add gutters to it.

Shift over, Elizabeth grabbed her purse, stuck Max's card in the side pocket, and went outside. The sun burned low on the horizon, its heat still clinging to everything in sight. These lazy late-summer days had been her favorite until she'd had to spend them alone. Kicking at a rock, she headed across the parking lot. Whom, she wondered, was Brad spending his days with? Did he ever think about the family he'd left behind? With a sigh, she climbed behind the wheel of her car, resting her head against the seat.

"Yes, Mr. Marino, I've got more to worry about than gutters," she muttered.

Three

"Christopher!"

Elizabeth called his name before the car even stopped. Slamming on the brakes, she was out of the car in an instant, running the few yards up the walk to where Christopher sat on the front stoop, his chin cradled in his hands.

"Honey, what's the matter? Why aren't you at Betsy's? Are you all right?" Elizabeth skidded to a halt and collapsed next to her son. Frantic, she brushed back his hair, letting her palm rest against the soft skin of his forehead. No fever. No cuts. No hurts—that she could see.

Christopher shook her hand away and let his own fall between his legs. "Mom, nothing's wrong. I'm okay."

She reached out again, but he jerked back, slashing directly into Elizabeth's heart. She was still feeling her way through the dark passages in his mind.

"Well, if you're not hurt, why aren't you at Betsy's? If I'm going to work, I can't be worried about you every minute while I'm at the office. I made arrangements for you to stay at Betsy's house, and that's where I expect . . ."

"Mom, I went there," Christopher said, his eyes downcast, his full, almost-little-boy lips quivering.

"Then why aren't you still there?" Elizabeth demanded, too tired to play games. Chris remained mute, a reaction that was becoming all too familiar. "Christopher, talk to me. It's been a long day, and I'm in no mood for attitude."

"It's been a long day for me, too, Mom."

Elizabeth paused, angered by his flip remark, but she quickly quelled her fury. In the last few days, she'd frequently found herself cross with her son. But was it Christopher that made her want to scream—or Brad, herself, or this incredible exhaustion that lived inside her now?

Elizabeth's shoulders sagged. It was tiring to fight these feelings, enervating to worry constantly, draining to spend days in an office and nights calling even the remotest places where Brad might be. She contemplated a small stain on her skirt, then she threw back her head, searching the sky for something beautiful to focus on.

Christopher picked up a pebble and tossed it into the flower beds. He clicked his tongue; he tilted his head; he did all the things a child does when he wants attention but would rather die than ask for it. He expected Elizabeth to know what to do. When her mom-magic didn't work, he said, "Mrs. Colby kept asking me about Dad."

Elizabeth took the blow like a pro, extending her body so that the sudden jab in her heart would spread itself thinner. The pain didn't last long; it transformed itself into a real anger directed at the woman next door.

"She wanted to know about you, too." Christopher's eyes darted her way. Elizabeth willed herself to be very still. "She wanted to know where Dad was 'cause she hadn't seen him come for his visits. She even made up some story about needing his work number so she could call him because she wasn't sure if it was okay if she gave me milk products." Christopher's disgust with the thinly veiled treachery of adults was evident. "Then she asked me if you had any *special* friends, and I knew what she meant. I just couldn't stay there, Mom. She was really mean, Mom, the way she said everything, but she wanted me to think she was being nice. I didn't want to talk to her about Dad. I don't want to talk to anyone about him."

Elizabeth's arm went around her son's surprisingly broad shoulders. A big body housed his confused little heart, and it broke Elizabeth's own to realize it. She felt him tense and shiver. She was all he had left, and he didn't want to be with her. Elizabeth had committed the cardinal sin of motherhood: She had left him to fend for himself while she grieved, budgeted, planned, and searched.

She hugged Chris closer, thinking all the while. The tears were hot behind her eyes, the bitterness in her heart all-encompassing. She lay her head against her son's for an instant. They were alone. The women in the neighborhood were nothing to them now except members of the PTA, the moms of Chris' peers—curious people all, but not friends. Who in the hell was Elizabeth MacMillan when she didn't even have one person in the world who worried about her? Where had she lost herself?

When Christopher pulled away, trying to shrug off her caress, Elizabeth held fast until he leaned against her, beaten. She had prided herself on acquiescing in the face of another person's needs. What a fool, to be proud of never stepping fully into anyone's life! She snuggled into him and held on tight until he wrapped

his arms around her. They stayed that way, heads together, for a very long while, legs stretched out in
front of them, his almost as long as hers. Elizabeth
tapped the toes of her shoes together, then held one
up against her son's.

"They're almost the same size," she whispered.

"Mine are bigger," he mumbled. He was right, and
she kissed his head. They watched the sun sink over
the big park. When it was truly dark, when the summer bugs flitted about seeking flesh or light, Elizabeth
kissed Christopher again. With a smile that didn't
quite reach her eyes or convince Christopher that all
was right, she said, "I'm so sorry, honey. I never
wanted you hurt. Not by Daddy or me or the stupid
things people say. Now, what do we say to stupidity?"

Elizabeth popped up, almost turning her ankle, and
faced Betsy's house. She held her thumb to her nose,
wriggling her other fingers and making a noise no
Southern lady would make in public.

"There!" She spun back to Christopher, grinning,
feeling only slightly better, but happy to see her son
fighting a smile. She put out her hands and gestured
for him to stand up. "Come on, you do it."

"Mom," Christopher shook his head, embarrassed
though there was no one to see them.

"Come on," she urged, then whispered, "I have it
on good authority that Betsy wears false teeth and
snores. Some even say she's bald under those flower
hats she wears. Can you imagine what she looks like
when she goes to sleep? She has to take herself apart!"

That did it. An honest-to-goodness chuckle bubbled
up, then Christopher began to laugh. He held his
thumb to his nose and outdid Elizabeth in the noise

game. Encouraged by her approving nod and missing the sadness in her eyes, he snorted and cackled and razzed. When he was finally tired and the close, dark night was no longer welcoming, Elizabeth gathered her things and held out her hand.

"Come on, kiddo. Time for dinner. It's been a long, long day and I'm hungry. Scoot inside and we'll order Chinese. I'll be there in a minute."

"Okay, Mom." He turned in the doorway but saw that she wasn't looking after him, so he disappeared into the dimly lit house.

Outside on the steps, Elizabeth considered her small patch of the world. The grass needed cutting. She hadn't done a very good job the week before. The paint was starting to peel around the dining room window. She wondered if there was touch-up in the garage. And when she looked up, Elizabeth saw that the gutters were, indeed, coming loose from the roof. Wearily, she gave in for an instant to the loneliness, the horrid aloneness, that was now her constant companion.

"Brad, what did we do that was so wrong?"

"So, do I have to go back to Betsy's tomorrow?"

Christopher was washed, brushed, and tucked in, yet Elizabeth sat on the edge of his bed still fussing with the covers, idly wondering if the rest of his teeth would ever be as big as the front two that had come through with such a vengeance.

"I don't think so," Elizabeth said quietly.

"What will I do? I don't want to go to daycare at the camp, Mom. Only the little kids go there."

If Elizabeth hadn't been so empty or felt so drawn,

she would have laughed. A fate worse than death—a ten-year-old made to play with younger children. She could imagine worse things, but she doubted Chris could.

She and Brad had been only children. There wasn't a relative to call on. Other moms had their own children to worry about. There was Donna Burns, who had been as close to a good friend as she had ever had, but even Donna was distancing herself. Elizabeth didn't have time to wonder why. How many married women had given everything to their husband and home to the detriment of their friendships? Her choices were limited, but maybe a choice was what Chris needed to make him feel in control.

"You could call one of your friends from school and see if they wouldn't mind if you went to their house after camp," Elizabeth suggested hopefully.

Christopher shook his head. "I don't think so, Mom. I mean, it would be the same as, you know . . ."

Elizabeth nodded. The MacMillan family was the talk of the town. Another month or two, and nobody would care if Brad ever showed up again. Yet, today, he was probably a hero to half the men in the neighborhood, while the women were trying to decide if Elizabeth were a shrew, frigid, or a spendthrift. With a great motherly leap of faith, she said matter-of-factly, "Ten is pretty old, don't you think?"

Christopher nodded.

"And you do know about nine-one-one," Elizabeth mused.

"I've known that since I was a baby," Christopher reminded her, offended.

"True. You were an exceptionally intelligent baby,"

Elizabeth teased. "And I suppose there are chores you could be doing around the house now that it's just you and me."

"Mom," he objected.

"I mean it," she warned. "Hanging out is not allowed. Chores, homework, television, then I'll be home. Now that I think about it, you'll only be here alone for a few hours." Elizabeth gave one last tuck to the bright yellow sheets on Christopher's bed. "Okay, I think you can do it. I *know* you can. Trial basis, though. You'll come home after camp. Forget Betsy unless it's an emergency."

Elizabeth leaned forward. Had she made the right choice? Yes. The last thing Christopher needed was her chipping away at his delicate confidence. With a kiss, Elizabeth went to the door of the bedroom, looked back, and saw him watching her. She whispered one last good night and was about to leave the darkened room when he called her back.

"Mom?"

"Yes?"

"You'll be home every night, right?"

"Absolutely. On the dot," Elizabeth promised. "Every night. Same time. Same place. Oh, listen. The bell. Someone's downstairs."

Alone, Christopher lay staring at the ceiling, his ears reaching for any sound that might indicate it was his dad at the door, home at last. But he didn't hear his mother squeal with delight or his dad's deep, soft, almost kid-like voice calling up the stairs to him. When he was sure that hope was wasted, Christopher MacMillan slipped out of bed and padded to his closet. Carefully, he rolled back the door and, without turning on the light, felt through the robots and swords, the play guns and Legos, until he found just what he wanted.

Back in bed, he pulled the sheets up close around his neck. In the morning, he promised himself, he would put this old toy back before his mom saw it.

Closing his eyes, he hugged his treasure close, arms wound tight around the worn teddy bear as he tried to shut out the fear and hold back the tears. And, when there was a sob just at the top of his throat, he buried his face in the stuffed head and carefully cried into its fuzzy little ear so his mom wouldn't hear. So his mom wouldn't worry. Even though he wished with all his might that she'd hear him just a little bit.

The doorbell rang again. Elizabeth stood paralyzed at the top of the stairs. When Brad had been home, the sound of the doorbell had been welcoming—a neighbor coming to borrow the hedge clippers, a child asking if Christopher could play, a school mom dropping off a cake for a bake sale. Now the triple dong rang hollow, its deep tones ominous. Irrationally, Elizabeth expected to fling open the door and find Brad. But it wasn't the prospect of seeing him that frightened her; it was how she would feel if she did that was so scary.

The sound of the bell jarred her again. Elizabeth hurried down the steps—one more ring and Christopher would be up. Her hand on the knob, she trembled, then slowly pulled the door open. A woman, half turned away from her door, stood partially bathed in the glow of the porch light.

Elizabeth blinked and actually shook her head, clinging to the door, unnerved by the disappointment. Curiosity and relief fell in on her all at once. She stayed back, as if she could keep her bewilderment hidden.

"Oh, hi. I didn't think you were home." The woman, who turned full face, was blond and familiar but unrecognizable. She seemed to sense rather than see Elizabeth's befuddlement and smiled more broadly.

"Leslie. Leslie Gibson. Around the corner, the yellow house on Dorchestire." She tipped her head and her coiffed hair fell to one side, baring a shoulder. Elizabeth smiled. The woman knew how to wear a tank top. Leslie's grin faded and she looked flustered.

"I shouldn't have come without calling." Leslie backed away self-consciously. "We're usually at the stoplight the same time every morning. I don't know why I got it into my head that you actually knew who I was." She moved slowly away, but kept on talking. "I'll come back this weekend. No, no, I'll call and we can talk on the phone. Or, better yet, you call me." She was almost out of earshot before Elizabeth realized she was losing her. "I just wanted to . . ."

"Wait!" Elizabeth instinctively opened the door wider to the divorcee on Dorchestire. Elizabeth had added her two cents to a zillion discussions about this woman. Every time a group of moms gathered at the ball field, collected clothes for the poor, or laid out a pot luck, Leslie Gibson's name came up.

Wouldn't want to be her for the world.

Poor woman.

All alone.

Well, she must have done something to make him leave. I'd hate to have to work to make ends meet.

She must color her hair.

Bet she sleeps around.

From poor woman to slut, Leslie Gibson had worn every label her neighbors could devise.

"I'm sorry. Forgive me." Elizabeth stepped into the gleam of the porch light, batting at a moth and noticing that the June bugs were gone from the walk. She studied the blonde. Leslie Gibson had a surprisingly gentle smile, incongruous with the expert make-up and the exquisitely done hair. "You surprised me. I wasn't expecting anyone. My mind was on other things."

"Sure. I understand." Leslie's blue eyes softened. All those mornings at the stoplight Elizabeth had imagined the eyes behind the fancy sunglasses would be hard, black, and worn. It was nice to see they weren't.

The two women stared at each other until Leslie's eyes wandered off and her hand reached for the plant that climbed up the side of Elizabeth's house.

"You have such a beautiful house. I've always envied your green thumb."

"Thanks, but it's not mine. My husband did the gardening." Elizabeth was equally quiet, strangely calm. The past tense hung obviously between them.

"Yeah, well, that's why I came." She laughed to cover her discomfiture. "I don't know what possessed me. Pushy, aren't I? But now that I'm here, I'll jump in with both feet. Then you can kick my rear out of here if you want." She broke a stem off the Star Jasmine and raised it to her nose, breathing in the perfume and discarded it an instant later. "Look, I may not be in the mainstream around here, but I did hear that your husband took off. So now that makes two of us bobbing around loose in this sea of happily married types."

"I'm not divorced." A semantic defense. Leslie raised a brow. It was darker than her hair, but it looked good.

Elizabeth laughed. "I guess that was a pretty stupid thing to say. Like there are degrees of being left."

"Maybe there are. My husband left me years before he walked out the door. I used to watch him at night staring at the television. God knows what he was thinking, but he sure wasn't seeing what was in front of him. Then one day he left; a few months later he filed for divorce. Now he lives in a trailer by the beach. Sometimes, I wonder if he's happy; then I wonder what I ever saw in him. And then I wonder . . ." Leslie shook her head. "Listen to me, will you? I came over to offer a little moral support, and here I am telling you my worn-out story."

"To tell you the truth, you're a godsend," Elizabeth assured her, relaxing as the minutes ticked by.

"Yeah, well, I just came to say that if you need to talk, I'm probably the most sympathetic ear you'll get around here. Emerald Isle's a tough place when you're single again. Believe me. The women are afraid you'll take their men—as if we would want them. The men are afraid to blink at you for fear they'll catch hell at home." Leslie grimaced. "Separation, divorce, abandonment, death." She shook her head. "The ultimate social shake-out, and the women always end up at the bottom of the heap. I should have moved years ago."

"Why didn't you?" Elizabeth asked, honestly curious. It hadn't occurred to her that this place might not be home forever.

Leslie shrugged. "Time goes by. Once I got over the grief and the terror and found myself a job, I'd been here so long I didn't know where else to go. Divorcees like to have real homes. I even decorate at Christmas! Garlands, cookies, the whole bit."

"Do tell." Elizabeth laughed.

"Yeah." Leslie giggled. "Aren't I just Martha Stewart?" She took a deep breath and grinned, the shyness returning. "Well, it's late. I know you have a little boy. I'll let you go. Here."

Leslie pressed a brown paper bag into Elizabeth's hands. With a wave goodbye, she disappeared into the safe, dark, family neighborhood of Emerald Isle. When she was nothing more than a shadow, Elizabeth went inside.

Elizabeth secured the locks and went upstairs, bag still in hand. She checked on Christopher, poking her head in far enough to hear his breathing, then went to her room. Sitting cross-legged on the bed, Elizabeth opened her gift. Inside was Leslie Gibson's card. Real estate. Figured. The picture didn't do her justice.

Elizabeth dug in again. This time she came up with two Snickers, a Butterfinger, and a bag of Hershey's kisses. Finally, Leslie had tossed in well-worn copies of two self-help books, a steamy romance, and the new Marigail Mathias fashion catalogue. The latter had a note attached.

A first-aid kit. Enjoy. Talk to you soon. LG

Chuckling, Elizabeth lay back on the quilt she had lovingly stitched. Clutching the books to her chest, looking at the ceiling of the room she had shared with her husband for twelve years, Elizabeth blessed Leslie Gibson. The woman was living proof that life went on and affection could be found in the most unusual places.

Four

"We hardly get to see you now that you're a working woman!"

"Must be fun, Elizabeth."

Elizabeth balanced herself, hands behind her, elbows locked, legs outstretched. Above her loomed the faces of three neighbors, school moms dying for a chance to talk to her since IT happened. At this angle all three looked like the pre-Alka Seltzer segment of a commercial. Better yet, three witches checking to see what the caldron of scandal was cooking up. An Emerald Isle woman, alone, abandoned by her husband, sitting at a Little League game acting like she was enjoying herself was a sight to behold. A curiosity, indeed.

"Everything's fine, Jeanne. Thanks." Elizabeth smiled her most endearing smile. *Cats*. A bit of fun was definitely in order. Her grin broadened as she enthused, "Work is wonderful. I didn't realize how limited I've been these last few years. Living in a planned community like this, you can almost forget there's another world out there. You meet such interesting people when you work, and it's marvelous to get dressed up again. I was so tired of sneakers and sweats." Elizabeth shifted, curling her long legs beneath her, cocking her head to one shoulder. "Oh, I'm sorry. Where are my manners? Do you all know Leslie Gibson? She lives over on Dorchestire."

Leslie raised a hand and grinned wryly, enjoying the game as much as Elizabeth. "Divorcee on Dorchestire. That's me."

There were hellos, but the three women who had been so curious a moment before moved away, their heads together. Elizabeth didn't have to be a lip reader to know what they were saying. One of their own had switched sororities, and the implications would add fodder to the rumor mill for months.

"Can you believe it?" Elizabeth chuckled, watching them walk away.

"Give me a break," Leslie answered lazily, lolling in the beach chair, trying to soak up the last rays of sun. "Do you expect me to believe you were never that bitchy?"

"I wasn't." Elizabeth plucked at the grass, still eyeing the retreating figures. "Really!" She slid her eyes toward Leslie and smirked wickedly. "Well, maybe just a pinch, but no more than that."

"Oh you Southern babes. That voice of yours might make me believe anything if I didn't know the ropes. My name probably passed your lips more than once at one of those mom things."

"Okay, I admit it. I was shallow and stupid, and being on this end of things has opened my eyes."

"Speaking of shallow and stupid . . ." Leslie drawled.

Elizabeth was suddenly on her feet, her mother's eye sharp as she ignored Leslie.

"Christopher! Hit it hard! Make it sail!" Bending her long legs, she was curled up on the blanket a minute later, lying on her stomach, cradling her chin in her hands as she squinted behind her dark glasses. One, two, three times her son swung at the ball. Three times the crowd moaned. Christopher struck out, and it was the last game of the season. Elizabeth sat up again, cross-legged this time, waving as Christopher headed back to the dugout. It was only a game. Chris knew that. But still, after the good season he'd had, it must be tough to perform so poorly. Elizabeth waved again and pulled an exaggerated sad face before smiling sympathetically. She was sure he saw her, yet he walked to the bench without as much as a blink of recognition. Elizabeth had done her duty. She relaxed again.

"What were you saying, Leslie?"

The blonde adjusted her sunglasses. Behind them, she fixed Elizabeth in her sights and said flatly, "I was speaking of shallow and stupid things."

"Yes?" Elizabeth eyed her, knowing what that tone of voice meant. It was as if they'd known each other a hundred years, the way Elizabeth could read Leslie.

Three weeks ago, Leslie Gibson had showed up on Elizabeth's doorstep. Two weeks and five days ago, they had become friends. The phone was hardly put down before one was knocking. Dinner dishes were barely finished before the phone was picked up again. Leslie's kindness had unleashed a torrent of neediness in Elizabeth; her casualness had broken down the barriers Elizabeth had so carefully constructed. They were women bound together by a need no married woman could ever understand. And, when Elizabeth took the time to wonder about this odd and instant relationship, she came to only one conclusion: Leslie was, indeed, her friend.

"Shallow and stupid things is the topic, huh?" Elizabeth's head swung around, her ponytail flipping from one shoulder to the other. "Am I to understand that you may wish to comment on something immediate?"

"Maybe."

"Are you going to make me guess? Come on. We've talked about everything under the sun five times. I can't imagine there's a subject we haven't hit on. Brad. You're mad that I'm not doing more to find Brad."

"You know how I feel; but for the record, I still think you ought to bite the bullet and find him."

Elizabeth threw up her hands. "And I've told you there isn't a bank in the world that's going to let me do it. I couldn't even get a home equity loan because I don't make enough."

"Have you thought about Christopher?" Leslie asked, determined not to let this go.

"I don't think he could get loan approval, either," Elizabeth panned before giving Leslie a playful whack on the shoulder. "Joke, Leslie. Come on, it's a joke. You're supposed to tell me how great I'm doing, making jokes and everything. Wow, I thought that would get a rise out of you."

Leslie closed the distance. She pushed away from her chair and sat cross-legged, too. Her head was down as if someone might hear what she was about to say, even in this huge park. Elizabeth leaned closer.

"I *am* proud of you, Elizabeth. A couple of weeks ago, you would have just as soon burst into tears as make a joke, and that's neat. You're a heck of a lot better than I was; but you're acting like that's meaningful, and it isn't. You're still hurting so bad you can't see your nose in front of your face."

Elizabeth put her hand on her friend's knee. She

meant to be reassuring, although she didn't know who it was supposed to comfort.

"That's crazy, Leslie. Everything's going great. I'm paying the bills and keeping up on insurance; work is a piece of cake, and I'm keeping a happy face for Christopher. What more do you want?"

"I want you to admit that you're still scared to death and that there are a ton of details to work out. Look at Christopher. Look at you!"

"Okay." Elizabeth pulled away and wrinkled her brow. "I'm looking, and I like what I see. We've done mighty well if you ask me. Remember, Brad hasn't been living in our house for more than a year. That was a major adjustment right there. The fact that he's disappeared is . . ."

"Is worse than any separation could be." Leslie threw up her hands in friendly disgust, amazed that Elizabeth couldn't see this most basic truth.

"No, it's not," Elizabeth insisted. "It's just a different part of separation."

"Elizabeth, don't be naive." Leslie sat up straight, frustrated by Elizabeth's blinders. "My God, you've got to deal with the basics: The house is in Brad's name; the car is owned jointly; the savings account is still in both your names and he could tap into it any time. Then there's the emotional baggage, and don't you dare tell me you're not carrying it around every day. I know you're still asking yourself why he didn't tell you where he was going and why he left."

Leslie scooted closer and took Elizabeth by the shoulders, forcing her friend to look her in the eye.

"Chris is lucky. He doesn't have to worry about all the legal stuff, but he does have to deal with Brad's disappearance. Can you imagine what he thinks when he looks at you? He probably worries that you're going to do the same thing one of these days, too. Plus, he's got to worry about the kids at school and answer questions about where his dad is and why you can't volunteer at school anymore . . ."

"My, my, my," Elizabeth interrupted coolly, shrugging off Leslie's hold, her eyes narrowing. She spoke in low and calculating tones. A new voice for Elizabeth, but one Leslie had expected to hear at some point. She'd used it, too: *Don't tell me. I know everything about hurt already.* Human beings were so self-righteous when they were scared. A few things going right made the big wrong things disappear. Elizabeth would be humbled when disaster struck again, but now she needed to be superior just to make the glue of normalcy stick.

"Okay," Leslie sighed. "Let's get it over with. Our first fight."

"I'm not fighting." That drawl was back, and Leslie wanted to smile. Great defense, that accent. Made Elizabeth sound so all-knowing. "I was just curious to learn when you had a dozen kids so that you could know all about how they worked."

"Okay. I'll give you that one." Leslie scooted back to her canvas chair but kept her eyes on Elizabeth. "I don't have any kids. But it doesn't take a rocket scientist to know that if my divorce was as painful and messy as it was without them, then having one must make the whole thing a horror. And what Christopher's going through must be doubly awful. I mean the kid doesn't know where his father is," Leslie said in staccato. Elizabeth talked back before her friend was finished.

"And I've done everything I can short of hiring a private eye to find him. I can't do anything more."

"You can talk about what you have done. Have you even tried to do that with Chris?"

Elizabeth threw away a handful of grass and plucked another. "No, I haven't, because there isn't anything to say. What am I supposed to do, show him the list of phone numbers? The scribbles I make in the dead of night while I rack my brain trying to figure out places he might be? What would you suggest, Leslie?"

"Boy, when you get defensive you are a misery!" Leslie cried, and then she chuckled. "Hey, I'm sorry. I told you when we first met there were lines that shouldn't be crossed. Guess I just put a big fat foot over one. But, honey, all I know is what I see; and I see a kid who can't concentrate, who hasn't smiled since I met him, and who hardly strings two words together. I think that's sad, and somehow you've got to figure out a way to make his hurt come first."

"I am, Leslie," Elizabeth admitted, defeated because the woman closest to her couldn't see how hard she was trying. She hated to blow her own horn, but if all her hard work wasn't evident, then she'd have to raise her voice. If nothing else, it would keep her on track. "I'm bending over backwards to keep our schedule as normal as it can be. I take him out for dinner. We rent tapes. He plays Nintendo and gets the latest *Goosebumps*. I don't make him listen to me cry. I don't constantly talk about Brad. If we find him, then I'll tell Chris. If he comes home, then Chris and I will talk about what that will mean. Meanwhile, I want his life to be normal."

"Yeah," Leslie sighed. "You can shoot for it, but it ain't gonna happen."

"I say it will. And I'll tell you something else," Elizabeth countered, her voice softening as she went on.

"Yes?"

"I think we've just found a subject that's off limits."

"Fair enough. But if you ever do want to talk about . . . anything . . . I'll . . . be . . ." Leslie let her train of thought grind to a stop. Elizabeth was on her knees clapping as Christopher ambled toward them, hat in his hand, his bat dragging on the ground. Elizabeth smiled. The punctuation mark was pretty clear. Her kid. Her decisions. Leslie smiled, too, but refrained from the hoopla.

"Hooray, Christopher! Good game!" Elizabeth reached for him, but Christopher steered clear of her embrace and fell onto the blanket, his eyes flickering to Leslie. She flinched under the honesty of that one look.

"Nice try, kiddo," she offered.

"Yeah." Chris lay his head on his outstretched arm and closed his eyes, a posture of exhaustion his play didn't warrant. Elizabeth was blind to his cry for attention, and it broke Leslie's heart.

"Christopher." Elizabeth's mother-voice was in full bloom. "I think you can properly say hello to Mrs. Gibson."

"Hello." It was a sullen greeting that meant less than nothing. He pushed himself up, banishing Leslie to the netherworld where unnecessary adults dwelled. "Got anything to eat?"

"All your favorites. Put your mitt here and grab a drink. Do you want to see if Joey wants to join us?"

"Nope."

"Okay. Just thought you might. Leslie, what about you? Ham or egg salad? We'll celebrate the end of the season."

Elizabeth was so efficient: expertly unpacking the picnic basket, chattering, fooling herself all at the same time. A good trick.

"Hope you've packed enough for a guest," Leslie said. Elizabeth looked up. Joey was nowhere in sight, and Leslie was staring over Elizabeth's right shoulder.

Elizabeth swiveled. Instantly, her head snapped back. It had taken all of two seconds for her cheeks to fill with the flush of amazement. She dropped the pickles. Her soft drink was the next to go, making a cheery fizzing sound as it soaked the blanket. Instead of helping, Christopher chose that moment to take an interest in what was happening.

"Well," Leslie breathed, forgetting Chris, the picnic, and Elizabeth. "I haven't seen anything like that around Emerald Isle in fifteen years."

"Leslie! Chris . . ." Elizabeth jerked her head toward her son, but Leslie was completely unaware. She was transfixed, hardly breathing, a come-hither smile playing on the edge of her scarlet lips. The smile broadened. She leaned toward Elizabeth. "He's waving!" The smile faltered, then failed completely. "He's waving—at you."

Reluctantly, Elizabeth looked over her shoulder. There was no ignoring the situation. She waved and half smiled as Max Marino made a beeline for their blanket.

"You do know him! Elizabeth! No wonder you're not trying too hard to find . . ."

Elizabeth scampered up, her foot purposely catching

Leslie's thigh. With an "ow" Leslie shut up, her eyes skittering toward Christopher. Maybe she was the last person who should be giving advice about kids after all. Luckily he wasn't paying attention any longer.

"Hello, there!"

Max was upon them; and Leslie was like a jack-in-the-box, popping right up, sticking out one hand while she adjusted her tank top with the other.

"Any friend of Elizabeth's, as they say." Leslie smiled. Elizabeth looked askance at her friend. She had actually giggled. Leslie was all straight, white teeth and a cherry-red mouth, flashing a beautiful smile, as she shook hands with this Adonis-of-the-Park. "Leslie Gibson."

"Max Marino. Nice to meet you." He took her hand. Much to her dismay, he gave it a firm shake.

Elizabeth was smiling, a pickle still in one hand, her other pushing back strands of hair that had escaped her barrette.

"Hi," she said, fully aware that Christopher had let his head clunk onto the hard ground and was panto-miming an excessive hunger in the hopes of catching his mother's attention. When that didn't work he bounded up, too, but not to greet Max. Without a look or a word, he walked away.

"Excuse me," Elizabeth muttered. "Christopher?" she called, embarrassed by this snub. He turned back, attitude etched all over his face. "Where are you go-ing? I want you to meet Mr. Marino." Christopher spread his legs and planted them. He looked his mother straight in the eye. Elizabeth stepped forward, her voice tighter. Leslie tensed. "Chris? Come here. Please?"

One more paralyzing instant, one more cutting edge glare, and Christopher ambled back, stooping to pick a flower. Slowly, he drew up in front of his mother, looked her in the eye for what seemed like an eternity, and crumbled the dandelion.

Elizabeth stared, the mother-child psychic communication in full force. Christopher knew the question she was asking and he ignored it, just as she overlooked the crumpled mass of petals at her feet. Deliberately, she put her arm around Christopher's shoulder and turned him toward Max. A small sacrifice—or shield—she held Christopher forward.

"Christopher, this is Mr. Marino. He's building the new houses on the land behind us."

"Nice to meet you, too, Christopher." Max held out his hand. There was that child-driven instant again, that hesitation of a small hand before it reached for the larger one, the fluttering of the lashes so that they hid those clear ten-year-old eyes that would have said so much if they could have been seen. Christopher did not welcome Max Marino. Then the instant was over and Elizabeth, if not happy, was relieved.

"How was the game?" Max asked, nodding toward Christopher's mitt.

"Lousy." If it were possible for a voice to puff out its cheeks and pout, Christopher's did.

"Sorry to hear that." Max didn't push it.

"It wasn't that bad." Elizabeth took over, wishing that those damn butterflies would stop banging against her innards and making her voice sound so syrupy.

"He's had a really hard couple of weeks." Leslie threw in her two cents, only to clamp her lips shut when Elizabeth's green-eyed gaze impaled her. "I mean, he really did try hard, but it's been a long summer." She was doing more harm than good, not to mention that she felt like a fifth wheel. So, she put out her hand one last time. "Listen, I've got to run."

Leslie moved like lightning, folding up her chair, grabbing the magazines she'd brought along.

"Leslie, don't go," Elizabeth said through her fast-fading grin. Frantically, her eyes bounced back and forth between her friend and the tall man in jeans, but Leslie turned on her heel and waved herself across the park. "Call me," she said to Elizabeth. "Hope to see you again," she threw at Max. "Bye, Chris," she offered gently, hopefully. Christopher didn't respond.

"She's got a lot of energy," Max commented, watching the sway of Leslie's hips as she walked away.

"Her batteries never run down," Elizabeth said just as Christopher squirmed away from her. "Oh, Chris, you must be starved. Have a seat, and I'll get you dished up." Elizabeth knelt by the picnic basket and looked up at Max. "If you have time, join us. There's plenty."

"Mom!" Chris objected.

"Well, honey, there is," Elizabeth asserted. And why shouldn't she? It had been wonderful discovering Leslie's friendship, why not Max's—if that's what could come of these odd meetings?

"Yeah," Chris muttered, off the blanket again. "Plenty. There's plenty for everyone. Have a good lunch. I'm going to Tommy's."

"Christopher," Elizabeth said curtly, peevishly. "You can wait until you've finished eating."

"Tommy wanted me to come right away." Christopher backed off, turned, took a hop, and was gone, running, leaving the lie to hover over them. Elizabeth almost called him back. Instead, she yelled, "Be home by six!"

The sun and the sight of Christopher running away from her made her forget that Max stood nearby. Chris had been alone in the house for weeks by necessity, but choosing to be away from her was another matter. He had left without permission, without Elizabeth knowing exactly where he was headed. She worried, now more than ever. It was unlike him. Then again, he was ten and this was Emerald Isle. What could hurt him?

And that was the last thought of Christopher she had because Max moved closer, his eyes following hers, the heat of his body radiating toward her. Elizabeth's heart twisted. It should have been Brad there watching their son. Her heart thumped. Heaven help her, she was glad it wasn't. Max was exotic, his arrivals in her life unpredictable, perhaps fated.

"He's a big boy for ten," Max said.

Elizabeth lowered the hands she had laced over her sunglasses.

"Yes, he is. Sometimes I wonder how I'm going to keep feeding him. I don't exactly make a fortune."

"Nobody does." Max chuckled. "But we all keep reaching for the pot of gold. That's what life's about."

"Is it?" Elizabeth asked bluntly, annoyed that he should reduce life to such an uncomplicated equation.

"I figure forward movement, no matter what, is victory," Max said quietly. "And, believe me, there's been a lot of *what* these days."

Elizabeth cocked her head. She didn't miss the cloud on his brow or his suddenly contemplative attitude. She forgave him his simplicity of outlook.

"Well," Elizabeth said, "I suppose I shouldn't judge a book by its cover."

"What?" Max shook himself out of his melancholy, startled by her comment.

"Nothing. Just that you seem perfectly happy today, the same way you did at the hospital. I find it odd to hear you talk of troubles. But I suppose everybody's got their share. I hope yours aren't too bad." Elizabeth relaxed, now that she found herself alone with him, the butterflies had lighted. She was able to ask with genuine hope, "So, how about a picnic to keep your spirits intact? I promise, there's no coffee in here, and my car is parked in the garage."

"Wow. Safe at last." Max laughed but made no move to sit down.

"I insist," Elizabeth said, surprised to find that she wanted him to stay. This was here and now. This was living. Waiting for Brad, worrying about the whys and wherefores of his leaving, that was just life. Maybe it was time for another step. Maybe it was time to remember she was a woman. This realization would be worth at least a late-night call to Leslie. But for now, Leslie was gone, Max was here, and Elizabeth was ready to move on.

"I won't take no for an answer," she said brightly, riding the wave of her glorious epiphany.

Spontaneously, she took his hand and led him to the blanket and they both knew this was right. He accepted graciously, ate as if he adored everything, lounged across from her as if they'd known each other for years. But they hadn't, and Elizabeth's nerves reacted with each burst of his rich laughter. Her chatter was as uninhibited as if she were a young girl on a first date.

Stronger now, Elizabeth pushed away what was and let herself enjoy what was right in front of her. The dance had begun, and wonderful experiences lay ahead if only she'd open her heart and let the joy in.

Christopher sat silently on the tree limb, his lips clamped shut, his eyes narrowed, his entire face a mask of resentment and mistrust, anger and hurt. His mom was so dumb, thinking he'd gone off to find his friends. What friends? He didn't have friends anymore. The other boys gave him weird looks. Their dads put their arms around him, and their moms asked questions he didn't like. The kids even made up stories—like that Christopher's dad was a spy or a bank robber. Dumb stuff. Christopher set them straight. His dad had just gotten tired of being a dad. No problem. What was a lie here and there? His mom lied to him every day.

All that crying he heard in her room. That was a lie. Like those times he caught her looking out the window as if she were expecting someone and she said it had nothing to do with his father. That was a lie. All that talk about the two of them making it until his dad came home. That was the biggest lie of all. She didn't even want his dad to come home. She'd been watching for that guy—Max what's-his-name. She'd been waiting for someone to come take care of her, and Christopher didn't like it one bit.

It was disgusting. They were almost lying on the blanket. He couldn't believe it. His mom should have been sitting far away from that guy or, better yet, sending him back wherever he came from. They shouldn't be sitting close together that way. They . . .

"Ow!"

Christopher grabbed his leg and rubbed furiously. Balancing, he held onto the limb above his head and lifted his hand. His calf was bleeding.

"Damn!" Christopher called into the tree. "Damn. Crap!" He thought for a minute, but couldn't come up with any other words he wasn't supposed to say. Tears sprang to his eyes. More tears than the hurt required, but he couldn't help it. He had cut his leg, and it was bleeding bad. Quickly he took off his team shirt and dabbed at the blood. Stupid shirt wasn't any good anyway; nobody on the team had said anything nice to him for the longest time. The coach hadn't played him very much either. Quickly he spit on his fingertips and rubbed the cut.

Furiously he rubbed only to find what he thought was a gash was just a scratch. That was darn disappointing.

Chris heard his mother laugh. Her laugh sounded so pretty as it filtered through the leaves that he looked up, tipping his head as if he could actually breathe in that sound.

Jeez that cut hurt. So bad he really might cry. Then he heard that faraway sound of her laughter again. Now he was sure he was going to cry, except then it happened again.

Christopher slapped his leg and whipped around so hard he almost fell out of the tree. Hanging on, suspended over the hard-packed earth beneath the tree, Christopher called out.

"Who is it?"

He screamed.

"You're a bully."

He hollered.

He started to call again, but his voice caught and the last thing he wanted was for a bully to see him cry. So he shut up. He looked toward the bushes that ran along the fence. The fence was supposed to keep the kids out of the storm drain, but it didn't always. He was sure that's where his antagonist was.

"Come on . . ." He twirled his body off the big limb and landed on his feet. At least he'd done something right. Quickly he shimmied into his shirt, glanced at his leg, and saw he had two cuts now. Christopher scanned the shrubbery. Got him! Christopher stomped toward the bushes.

"Why don't you come out, you bully?"

Ten-year-old words of challenge. To whom? Christopher was so angry with the pain in his leg and in his heart he didn't care if a werewolf sat in those bushes. He hit the leaves closest to him, an awesome feat of bravery. It worked. Out of the greenery crawled a boy with hair as long as a girl's and a wicked-looking sling.

"Good shot, huh?" The kid was shorter than Christopher, but somehow seemed bigger, smarter, even though he hadn't said anything important yet.

"Why did you do that?"

"Felt like it." The kid loaded another sticker ball in the sling, but Christopher was too fast for him. He was on the kid in an instant, arms flailing, fists flying. He'd never fought before, so he had no idea if he were doing it right. He landed a punch to the boy's shoulder and another to his back and managed to wrestle the slingshot away. Breathing hard, swiping at his eyes where the tears had actually spilled out, Christopher danced away. He loaded the homemade weapon and aimed it at the kid.

The long-haired boy winced, but the spiny pod missed him. Christopher loaded again and again and again, tears streaming down his face, nonsense words spilling out of his mouth. But the boy had stopped flinching and leaned back, balancing himself on his palms while Christopher's missiles pinged around him. Finally, frustrated and furious, Christopher flung the slingshot away and turned his back on the kid. Christopher took a step away from the bushes, then remembered his mother and that man. He looked up, hoping to see his mother gathering up her things, the man gone. But all he saw was his mom and that guy walking slowly out of the park. They were going home. To his house. Where his dad used to be.

Christopher sobbed, just once. It was pretty quiet, but he didn't care if that kid heard anyway. Without a backward glance, Christopher started across the park in the opposite direction.

"Hey! Hey! Wait." The kid was behind him, dogging his steps. Christopher's head hung closer to his chest. He wiped his eyes.

The long-haired boy reached up and put an arm around Christopher's shoulder. Christopher shrugged it off, but the arm came around again and this time a grimy hand clamped on and held tight. Chris wiggled and he sniffled, but he kept on walking with the kid.

"Stuff isn't usually as bad as you think," the guy said with the air of someone who knows. That ticked Chris off bad. This kid didn't know spit. He'd tell him. Instead, he said, "Yeah, sure." Chris had his tears under control, but not his voice. He couldn't trust it with more than a word or two, so he'd save the lecture for later.

"Hey, I've been there." The kid stopped and let Christopher go. Chris took a step on his own then realized it felt better to be with this someone, even this new guy in the baggy clothes and the hair that looked like it hadn't been washed in a week.

"You haven't been where I've been," Chris challenged. "You don't know the bad things that are happening in my house." Christopher's lips still trembled, but the kid had the good sense not to call him on it. Instead, he stuffed his hands in his pockets and set his long, thin face in a careworn expression.

"Your house, my house, half the houses around here. It's all the same. Parents causing the problems, and kids taking it on the chin. That about the size of it?"

Christopher nodded.

"Think it's better to sit in a tree?"

Chris' head waggled back and forth.

"Right." The boy grinned, terribly pleased that Chris got all the answers right. "Come on, I'll show you the sights. You gotta get a life if *they*'re not gonna give you one."

His hand was on Chris' shoulder again, and this time it didn't feel heavy or threatening. This time, Christopher reached up and touched it. It felt real and good, and it was the only hand around, so he figured he'd hold onto it. For a little while, anyway. At least until his mom figured things out. Things like he needed her to be with *him*—not with some guy. Not that. Anything but that.

Five

"Screwdriver."

Elizabeth rummaged through the box at her feet, pulled out two, and asked, "Phillips head or regular?"

"Regular."

Elizabeth slapped it into Max's large hand and leaned forward to look carefully at what he was doing. It was tough keeping her mind on the work at hand when she was so distracted by the worker. He was, in a nutshell, perfect.

"See, here? The springs won't work right if you don't keep this tightened up properly. Believe me." He gave a final twist to the screw, then pushed himself upright, towering above her while he considered the garage door mechanism. "I've seen these things snap. If a body's in the way, that person's history. I'd hate to see that happen to Christopher." He handed back the screwdriver, his eyes lingering on her. "Or you, for that matter."

"It's not high on my list of must-have experiences, either." Elizabeth slipped the screwdriver back into the battered red metal box that Brad had paid less and less attention to in the last few years. She flipped the latches, stood up, and lifted the box to its place on the shelves that Brad had put together over one long Labor

Day weekend. She was happy to have the box out of the way, Brad's memory up on the shelf with it. When she turned, she found Max looking at her, a curious mix of interest and pleasure etched on his face.

"What?" Elizabeth laughed self-consciously, wiping her hands on her shorts. She looked away. She was actually blushing.

"What, what?" Max asked.

"What are you looking at?"

"Your smile. You've got the greatest smile when it just pops out instead of when you think about it."

"I didn't know I'd been doing that," she said softly.

"When we met in the hospital, even there in the park, I got the feeling you didn't have a lot of opportunity to use your smile. It seemed hard for you." Max wiped his hands together, then hooked his thumbs in his belt. He was curiously at ease with himself and his body. That was nice. That was something she wasn't used to. Brad, while giving the impression of serenity, was always fussing with something. His sweater would be unbuttoned one moment, yet when she looked again it would be fastened. Funny, she'd never realized that before.

"Has anybody ever told you you're kind of a spooky guy? You should have been a psychic instead of a contractor." Elizabeth dipped her head, ran her hand down the spring he'd just finished tinkering with, then ducked out of the garage, looking over her shoulder long enough to invite him inside. "Come on, you've been working since we got here. You look awfully hot. I'll get you some ice water and show you where you can wash up."

Without waiting for an answer, Elizabeth went up

the walk and opened the front door. He followed and Elizabeth felt a bounce in her step. But when Max closed the door behind them, she felt his presence so keenly that the pain of Brad's leaving wasn't even a memory. Here was a man who smiled and laughed, who talked to her. That feeling was as glorious as his presence was unsettling, showing her the details of her life, of this space she called her own.

The sun no longer lit the house brightly. She and Max stood bathed in shades of twilight: grays and blues and the last pale vestiges of the golden sun. Elizabeth felt these colors on her and knew that they made her face softer, defined by nature not distress. She knew, too, that in this light her shorts and t-shirt caught the shadows and diffused light, making the fabric appear lovingly sculpted into folds instead of rumpled from a long day in the park. And, Elizabeth knew, the light, the silence, the emptiness of the house would make Max excessively attractive if she turned and faced him.

"Through here?"

Elizabeth jumped. He was beside her. Had he read her mind? She was aware only that he was gesturing and aware that she couldn't bring herself to look up and into his eyes.

"The bathroom?" he asked, and there was a wondrous underlying tone in his voice that took Elizabeth a moment to recognize. When she did, it made him all the more attractive. His voice had a casual tone. This was not a man in a hurry. He wanted to stay. He wanted to be with her. Talking. Laughing. With her.

"Yes," she whispered. Then louder, "To the right in the hall."

"Thanks."

Elizabeth watched those first few steps. He looked so comfortable in her house that Elizabeth felt afire with a desire that this be her real life, not an illusion. Confusion had been her home for over a year, yet that tumultuous feeling had only been a prelude to what she was experiencing now. Her flesh prickled with a desire to go after this man she hardly knew; her heart ached with fear that she wouldn't. What if he went down the hall and disappeared? There would be no one to talk with again, no one to look at her as if she, and she alone, were interesting and vital. There would be no one to remind her that she could laugh, joke, converse. But that feeling in the very depths of her body, that desire that had lain so long dormant, was now radiating toward that man. Yes, she felt sexual, sensual, and wonderful. He had opened a door she'd thought would remain closed until Brad came home again.

Perhaps, though, she hadn't been waiting for Brad's return. It wasn't his body she craved through the long, dark nights. It wasn't lovemaking she desired. Answers were what Elizabeth wanted from her husband. She wanted to know the why of it all, the when of it. Elizabeth MacMillan wanted details. Brad had fired missiles that had met their mark, leaving her devastated by self-doubt. He had dropped bombs into her mind until there was nothing left but a black hole, all confidence destroyed, all joy annihilated. Only the blueprint of living remained: wash, eat, cook, care for her child. These were the things Elizabeth did because all life's surety and, with it, the pleasure had been vanquished. She watched Max walk the floors of her home where Brad had so often tread and remembered that she wore a wedding ring. She had taken vows. She was still married.

"Max?"

He turned. His hand was already reaching for the hall light; so when he stopped at the sound of her voice, he appeared poised, as if inviting her to join him. Now she had to tell him a lie and push him from her life because she'd remembered who, and what, she was. She would talk about a forgotten appointment. He couldn't stay. They couldn't be alone together because she was married. Because she had made promises.

Yet, when he looked at her and smiled, Elizabeth could not tell him to go.

"Would you like a glass of wine?" she asked instead.

"I'd love it," he said, the words velvety as they traveled through the twilight. "If it's no trouble."

His eyes sparkled, his smile broadened. He seemed happy to be with her. When Elizabeth turned toward the kitchen, she was grinning. As she walked, her steps became spirited and her hands came together. Without another thought, Elizabeth MacMillan twisted her gold wedding band until it slipped off her finger. She laid the ring on the first surface she passed.

She hadn't broken her vows. Brad had. Whatever happened now would be a part of her new life. It would be a life guided by attention to not only what was said but what was meant. Her life would be counseled by her heart, not by appearances. Elizabeth would not run to the first arms that were held out, but she would not

run from them either. Those were her new vows, given
to herself.

"I mean, I understand how lucky I was to get this
contract in the first place. I'm only thirty-five. I didn't
go to college, but I have a good head on my shoulders.
This company started because I was a talented carpenter. Now, I'm building the next phase of this development—an entire neighborhood! I've got to build
it on time and with the quality I promised. That's
scary. The price of lumber is so volatile . . . I'm never
sure who's going to show up to work . . . and the
weather! It's fine now, but when we get into winter,
who's to say? Those storms we had a few years ago
could shut down the whole project."

Max leaned over and took the bottle of wine in his
hand, considering it carefully. It was obvious he wasn't
interested in the label. He was simply thinking. An interesting man, he considered everything he said then
knew exactly the words he wanted to use when he began to speak. He must make very fine houses if he was
so meticulous about a casual chat. Max held the bottle
her way. When Elizabeth shook her head, he poured
himself half a glass.

"Does anyone ever call you Beth?"

He sat back and crossed his legs, his expression
unchanging.

"I thought we were talking about houses." Elizabeth
was caught off guard, as she had been through so
much of the evening.

"We were, but I thought it might be getting boring.
Sometimes women don't like to hear about a guy's

work. I don't know why. I guess they think it belittles what they do."

Elizabeth shook her head. "I think it's nice. My husband didn't . . ." She looked up. It was so dark. Hadn't she turned on the lights? "Christopher isn't home yet. I've been having such a nice time, I actually forgot about him. What kind of mother does that make me?"

She jumped out of her chair, but the front door opened before she could lift the telephone. Christopher, dirty and disheveled, head down, walked into the house, turned and closed the door, then looked at the two pairs of eyes trained on him. The first person he saw was Max, and his gray-green eyes narrowed with suspicion. Next, he looked into his mother's and his own opened wider, his lips drawing tight in silent accusation and anger. But Elizabeth was oblivious to his disapproval, simply relieved that he was home and that he had interrupted the conversation with Max when he did.

"There you are! I was just about to call Tommy's house. Chris, what were you thinking of—staying out so late? It's almost eight-thirty."

Chris' eyes darted to Max. Without a word, he swung himself onto the first step of the stairs and headed to the second floor. Elizabeth was right behind him, looking up but going no farther than that first step.

"Chris?"

"What?"

She was still talking to his back, half aware that he was dirtier than he should be if all he had done was play at Tommy's. "Did you eat? Did Tommy's mom give you dinner?"

"I'm not hungry." Each answer was precise. He

glanced over his shoulder, his eyes blazing with anger. He turned again, and once more she called him back. The air between them had swelled with tension; it sizzled with unspoken insinuations.

"Maybe you'd like to come in and have something to drink with us. Mr. Marino fixed the garage door and took a look at your bike. He thinks he knows what's wrong with that, too."

Chris' young shoulders broadened as if he had just been handed a great weight to carry upon them. He looked straight up the stairs and, as he began to move, grumbled, "Then let him fix it."

For a split second, Elizabeth was too dumbfounded to speak and Christopher bounded up the stairs and closed the door to his bedroom so loudly it might as well have slammed in her face. She moved, her foot on the next step, her hand sliding up the banister, her head cocked so she could look at the landing above. She didn't see Max standing in the doorway, wineglass abandoned, watching.

"It's okay, Elizabeth," he said kindly. "Really. He's just a kid. I don't know what's what here, but it's important that a kid is comfortable in his own house. I probably shouldn't be here at all. It's my fault."

Her head snapped his way. She showed him her angry face, cold and cut into defined planes of determination and embarrassment. He was right. Ten-year-old boys did do obnoxious things when they were unhappy and confused. But Christopher's behavior went beyond thoughtlessness. His reaction had been downright rude.

She'd been bending over backwards to make his life easy, to make sure as little changed in his routine as possible. She'd been working her fingers to the bone so Christopher wouldn't have to give up sports and video games—pizza on Friday nights. This was her thanks? The one day she had actually found some peace of mind, had some fun, forgotten that her entire existence had been invalidated by Brad's desertion, Christopher ruined it. She wouldn't stand for it. She would hold on to this small triumph if it killed her.

"His father left. It happens to a lot of families. That doesn't excuse him. Please," her voice softened and she could see he understood that this was important to her. "Please stay. I'd love to finish our conversation. I won't be long. Please stay."

She was up the stairs, afraid that if she looked down she would see him walking out the door. Eyes forward, she headed to Christopher's room and rapped twice, but she went in without waiting for an answer.

Chris sat on his bed, his knees bent, a scowl on his face. Elizabeth closed the door and kept her back against it, hands behind her.

"Do you want to explain what just happened?"

Silence.

"Christopher? I asked you a question."

Silence. Cold, miserable silence. Christopher's anger warred with his love and respect and fear. Anger was winning.

"Nothing," he mumbled. "I just said he could fix it. If he's so interested in my bike, then let him fix it. Let him take it. I don't care."

"What is wrong with you?"

Elizabeth's tone was low, so controlled it was evident she didn't expect an answer. Christopher threw his legs over the side of the bed and hunched his shoulders. He picked up a plastic soldier from the floor and adjusted its arms and legs. He might as well have whipped out a trowel and started building a brick wall. Elizabeth skirted the barrier and planted herself in front of him.

"Look, Chris, you may not care what anyone thinks about you. You may not want to hold your head up and smile and act like you're grateful for what you do have instead of crying after what you don't have, but I won't live that way. We don't have enough friends to slap a new one in the face with such rude behavior."

"I wasn't rude," Christopher insisted, looking up, his eyes filled with tears, pleading with her to understand.

"You were, and you have been to other people, and I'm getting tired of it. I'm working so hard, trying to take care of everything, Chris, and all I asked of you was a polite hello. Is that so much to ask? Is it? I want you to go downstairs this minute and apologize. I want . . ."

Suddenly Elizabeth stopped telling Christopher what she wanted because it dawned on her what he needed. Looking at him through the haze of her embarrassment and anger, she finally understood what she should have known all along. Christopher was in pain. His young shoulders shook, and tears fell without a sound.

Instantly, Elizabeth was by his side, gathering him to her, trying to find places for her arms now that he had grown so much. Christopher threw himself away from her and onto the bed as he began to cry in earnest. His sobs were gut-wrenching, tearing through Elizabeth like a jagged knife.

She grappled with him, finding a place on the bed that allowed her to hold him only to have him push her away. She wasn't his comfort; she had become his tormentor, and Elizabeth needed to change it back.

"Chris. Honey. I'm sorry. Oh, baby, I'm so sorry."

"No . . . you're not." A sob. A sniffle that wasn't delicate. Elizabeth sat up and swiped at her own eyes. Her hands hovered over him then found a place to rest on his back, vibrating with the tears he shed, the sobs he tried to suppress. Elizabeth didn't talk. She just waited, sniffing and trying not to let go. He needed her to be courageous and smart. He needed her to listen. "You're not sorry. You're not sorry for Daddy." God, when was the last time Chris had called Brad "Daddy"? He was losing ground, and Elizabeth hadn't seen him slipping. "You keep trying to make everything the same—" A wail. "—then you make it all different—" A sob. "—Then . . . then . . ."

Then there were no words. She understood completely. He didn't want a hair out of place. Christopher's world had to remain the same so that Brad could walk back in and take his place whenever it suited him.

"But things do change, sweetheart," Elizabeth said, letting one hand move from his back to his hair. "Things have to change for us. Daddy may never come back. You don't want us to wait until we're old, do you? You don't want to miss out on growing up because you're waiting for something that might not happen, do you?"

"No?" The half question, half statement was almost lost in his tears. He meant *yes*. Elizabeth knew he did, but she pressed the advantage.

"Of course you don't. And you don't want us to sit and wait for Daddy when we could be learning how to be good people living without him." Elizabeth's voice softened. She continued quickly, speaking gently, stroking her son's hair. "Wouldn't it be nice if he came home, Christopher? But he hasn't. He hasn't even called or written us a letter. I don't think he's coming back for us, honey. He just isn't."

Chris cried harder, filling the room with the sound of his voice. This would probably be the last time he cried. After tonight, something would die in him and maybe never come back, so Elizabeth didn't try to stop him. She simply soothed him as best she could.

"You don't have to accept that right now, honey, but you do have to start acting like it's true—even if you don't believe it. You have to pretend, so you can smile again and make friends. It's time to decide how you want to live your life. That's what I'm going to do. I've got Leslie . . ."

"Why can't you have the friends you had before?"

Chris rolled on his back. His face was red and puffy from grief's extended stay. His skin was mottled, his hair matted to the side of his head where the tears had made it wet. She brushed away that damp hair and took his face in her hands.

"Because friends have things in common, honey. When Daddy was here, I was a mom and a wife. I cooked and cleaned. I took care of you and Daddy, and the women I knew took care of their families in the same way. Now, I have to work. There is no dad here. We're different from the rest of the families. Sometimes people are uncomfortable with that. Not just me, but the other moms, too. Do you understand?"

She took Christopher's silence as a sign that he was trying hard to understand and pressed her advantage, reassuring him that her plight was not his.

"That doesn't mean you can't be friends with the kids. Some kids will think it's weird that your dad just

went away. Others won't care. Those are the ones
you've got to find and hold on to. Those are the kids,
and the moms and dads, who will be our friends now.
And if other people want to be friends, we'll be happy
for that. But we're not going to be sad if they don't.
We'll just go on trying different things and finding
out which ones work. We'll make a good life, Chris.
I promise. If people don't like us for what we don't
have, for a dad who isn't here, then they weren't meant
to be our friends. Okay?"

Chris nodded and Elizabeth smiled. Her tears were
gone, and it felt good to explain what was possible
instead of speculating on what wasn't. She touched
his cheek, and he almost smiled back.

"Good, sweetie. Good. It won't be easy. You won't
wake up tomorrow and feel happy. But if you decide
to start fresh, then you'll find the hurt will go away
that much sooner. Does that make sense?"

"Sort of." Chris sniffled. "I need a Kleenex."

He reached for the box on his bedside table. Elizabeth got there first and handed him a few. He blew
his nose. She wished he were young enough for her
to help. Though he still kept his eyes averted, it was
because of his mortification, not his anger. She continued to touch him lightly, unsure of her child. Was
he a young man? A little boy? Someone who needed
her to hold him or just to be with him or to leave him
alone? How much better it would have been if Brad
had done his disappearing act when Chris was a baby.

Taking a chance, Elizabeth put her arm around
Chris' shoulder. He turned on his side, the Kleenex
wadded into his fist. She scooted further up on the
bed and lay down. He made room for her, trying to

make it seem a reluctant action. She reached back, switched off the bedside lamp, and put her head on his pillow. Quietly they lay side by side, Elizabeth not ready to have him push her away. Minutes ticked by, and Elizabeth could hear each second reverberating in her mind. The next move was Chris'. When he made it, Elizabeth was so touched she thought now was the time she should cry. Without looking, Christopher reached behind him, found her hand, and pulled her arm around him until she lay cupped behind his body.

When Elizabeth heard the deep breathing of sleep, when the hand holding hers relaxed in slumber, she lay with him still. Eyes closed, she thought how wonderful the warmth of his body was against hers. She had carried him for nine months, loved him more than life itself; had he pushed her away once more, she would have been destroyed. Before she slipped off the bed, careful not to wake her sleeping child, Elizabeth thought of God and weighed the question of his fairness. Perhaps He was vindictive because He had made Brad go away. Perhaps Elizabeth had done something to bring this upon herself. More than likely, though, God was a benevolent spirit, because He had given her this wonderful gift, a life to protect with her own. Perhaps He had more good things in store for her. Wouldn't that be wonderful?

Saying a small prayer of thanks for her son, Elizabeth left him to his dreams, hoping they would be good. She hoped he would dream about the future and put the past in its place. Downstairs, Max waited, the black-haired man she barely knew. She went to meet him, ready to take a chance. If she insisted Christopher walk boldly into the future, then she must do the same.

He stood when she walked into the room. Elizabeth raised a hand and lowered it, waving him down. She imagined the air through the open doors in the dining room had a chill in it. Fall was almost upon them, but Elizabeth made no move to shut it out. Seasons changed; so had she. Crossing her arms, rubbing them as if that would warm her on this August night, Elizabeth began to talk quietly.

"My husband left me . . ."

Max remained silent, and Elizabeth watched him. He sat very still, settled in his chair. He had all the time in the world for her. That in itself was amazing.

"It happens," he said simply.

Elizabeth hesitated. To open herself up and lay herself bare was a dangerous thing. To choose to do it with a man she barely knew could be devastating. He could make light of her situation. He could blame her—as she had blamed herself. Worse, he could care less. But Elizabeth had learned a bit about courage in the last many months.

"It doesn't happen often. Not this way." Elizabeth wasn't sure what to do. Look at him defiantly so he would know this situation wasn't really her fault? Look away from him and show how hurt she was? Smile bravely, cheerleader once more in front of an audience of one? Before she could decide which face to put on, he was beside her, his strong arms wrapped around her slight body. He didn't pull her close; he just held her so that it seemed the most natural thing in the world to lay her head against his broad chest and stand in the night with him.

"Brad abandoned us," Elizabeth whispered. "We

don't know where he is. He didn't say goodbye. He took our money. I'm alone."

In the heartbeat of silence that came after her admission, Elizabeth shuddered. Max's arms tightened. He sighed. She wondered what he was thinking and then didn't care when he said, "No, you aren't. Not anymore."

Elizabeth pulled away, looked warily at Max. Slowly, she disengaged herself, gazing curiously up at him, then took a seat across from him. To tell this story she couldn't be so close to him. His arms had felt too right. A small distance was better, safer.

A second later she began to talk. When she had finished her story, when she was sure he would thank her for an unusual evening and be on his way, Max Marino did the unthinkable. He smiled and asked gently, "Would you like to have dinner sometime?"

Six

"I took him to the park, but he didn't want to play; so I took him for pizza and he liked that. Now, I've put money in the envelope on the bulletin board in the kitchen if you want to go to a movie and . . ."

"Elizabeth," Leslie drawled, "I can pop for a movie, and Christopher isn't a five-year-old you have to wear out so I can put him down early."

"I know, I know." Elizabeth fluttered, then paused, her hands to the right of her face as if she couldn't decide whether or not to clip on her earring.

"You know, you're supposed to be looking forward to tonight, not worrying if Chris and I have enough to munch on," Leslie reminded her.

"I am looking forward to tonight. I'm excited. Oh, Leslie, I am," Elizabeth sighed, sounding quite miserable. She snapped the earring in place and collapsed on her bed. She smoothed her skirt and retucked her blouse then couldn't find a proper place for her hands. "Do you think I look all right? I don't know where we're going. He said casual, but I've only got work clothes and my jeans. How casual is casual?"

Leslie grinned and crossed her legs atop the spread. "You look wonderful, kiddo. No man alive could resist you."

"Don't make fun," Elizabeth tsked.

Indignant, Leslie sat up straighter. "I'm not. You look fabulous, and you've only had an hour to pull yourself together. I should have such luck."

Elizabeth laughed. "Don't be ridiculous. You always look wonderful, and you know it. And you're always cool, calm, and collected. I feel like I've got a herd of elephants in my stomach." Elizabeth made a face in the mirror and took a brush to her hair.

"I'd have a herd of elephants in my stomach, too, if I were headed out on the town with Max. Lord above, but he's a honey. What is this, the third time you've gone out?"

"Four counting the park." Elizabeth twisted her long hair into a knot then let it fall, not satisfied with anything about herself. She stepped into her shoes and cinched her belt tighter. "He took me to dinner at that little Italian place. That's where I learned that he loves to cook—and eat! Do you know he can make tortillas from scratch?" Elizabeth chattered, happy to fill Leslie in. "He took Christopher and me out for breakfast. That was when he offered to take Christopher to the next Dodger game. Unfortunately, he made the mistake of putting his arm around me when he asked. They'd been getting along fine, but the minute that happened, all we got from Chris was the cold shoulder. I really thought that was the last we'd see of Max."

"Guess you were wrong."

Elizabeth shot her a hundred-watt smile.

"Guess so. He came back, and he's the most wonderful man I've ever known. Considerate. He keeps his distance just enough so that I know he respects my situation. But he comes close enough so that I know he'd be happy if the situation changed." Elizabeth chuckled, feeling about twelve years old and in the throes of her first crush. "He's bright. He makes me laugh. I've never known anyone like him. I've . . ."

"Doorbell!" Christopher yelled from his room.

"Doorbell," Leslie said, her legs already swinging off the bed as if she should be rushing to answer it.

"Doorbell," Elizabeth reiterated like a mantra as she headed down the stairs, throwing admonitions right and left. "Leslie, make sure he's in bed by nine. Christopher? Nine! And I put some popsicles in the freezer. And I promise I won't be late. Well, I don't promise. I know you're not a sitter, but . . ." Abruptly, she turned on the stairs. Leslie pulled up short. "Do I look all right, really?"

"Except for the green tinge around the gills, you look terrific. Have a good time. My coach isn't going to turn into a pumpkin if you don't make it in by midnight. I'll just sack out on the couch. I know where the blankets are."

"It is all right, isn't it? I'm not doing anything wrong, am I? I don't want to hurt anyone, not even Brad, but Max is so very special."

"Then go for it. Go for it," Leslie whispered. Grinning, Elizabeth ran down the last five steps and opened the door.

Max beamed the moment he saw her. He said hello to Leslie and reached for Elizabeth. He shot a wink Christopher's way and looked so hopeful for his approval that Leslie's heart melted at the sweetness of it. Then they were gone, the door was closed, and Leslie's back was to it. Staring down at her from the top of the stairs was a surly-looking Christopher.

"You want to start with dessert and work our way into dinner?" she asked.

He rolled his eyes, groaned, and turned on his heel. Leslie followed him, up the stairs and past his door. Chris was back at his video game, so Leslie went back downstairs and started flipping through the television channels. But all she could think of was Elizabeth and the way that gorgeous hunk of man looked at her. That was the stuff of which movies were made, and it couldn't have happened to anyone nicer, or more in need of love, than Elizabeth MacMillan.

"Where are we going?" Elizabeth forced herself to look away from the ever-changing, ever-more-beautiful scenery and gave some attention to the mysterious, close-mouthed Max Marino.

The disc jockey on the radio had kept her apprised of the passage of time as they sped toward their secret destination. The high desert had been left behind in the first hour; the second found them winding through the west side of Los Angeles only to slide down the 10 Freeway to Pacific Coast Highway. When they hit a formidable stretch of beach-side road, they were in the middle of Santa Monica.

"We're off to a special place," he promised, and Elizabeth wished she could see his eyes behind his dark glasses. "I haven't been here since I was a kid, but you made me think of it."

"The beach?"

Elizabeth looked past him. The beach was beautiful, blue water and white-capped waves. Sunset hung offshore, keeping company with the horizon. It would be hours yet before dark came.

"Sort of the beach," Max said offhandedly, slowing for the traffic that slithered down the highway on this hot summer evening. Leaning over the steering wheel, he peered at the buildings as they passed. Million-dollar homes were wedged between surf shops, exclusive beach clubs, and bicycle rentals. Families straggled down the shoulder of the road looking for cars they had left hours before when their energy was unflagging and a mile-walk seemed like nothing. Young girls sauntered about, their beautiful young bodies bared save for a strip of fabric that passed for a swimsuit top and cut-offs that hung low on their hips. Young boys followed in their wake, zipped by on skateboards, or lounged as they waited for night at the beach. The show on Pacific Coast Highway was wondrous and colorful and a far cry from the white-hot, relentless heat of the high desert.

Here people were carefree, not careworn the way she had been for so long. Max had chosen well. He seemed to know exactly what she needed, and that alone made her feel giddy at such flattery.

"Come on, let me in on the secret," Elizabeth insisted. He glanced her way, obviously delighted with his surprise.

"For someone with the patience of a saint when it comes to handling difficult situations, you are the most anxious woman when it comes to surprises."

"It's just that I've learned to hate them over the last year," Elizabeth said, regretting the bitter words the moment they were out of her mouth.

"You just haven't learned to figure out a good surprise from a bad surprise yet." Max turned her words around and played with them, as if to show her all was well now.

"And I suppose you can do that?"

"Of course." Max gave a sigh that even he found amusing. He leaned back, throwing his arm over the seat while they waited for the traffic to move. Touching the fall of her hair, he rearranged a wave over her shoulder. He spoke as if he were half asleep, still dreaming while he reached out for her. "If you're very good, I'll tell you how to survive surprises."

"I am very good. I promise," she answered.

"I'm sure you are," he murmured, then shook himself out of his reverie. "And that's why I'm sharing this incredible bit of knowledge with you."

Max leaned close and slipped his glasses onto the tip of his nose. Now she could see his dark eyes, and they were filled to bursting with the sparkle of life. Elizabeth had never seen that look in a man's eyes—not in Brad's, not in her father's. She had missed so much, and settled for so little.

"I'm waiting," she murmured, matching him in movement until her eyes looked over the rim of her glasses. They were so close the world melted away. All Elizabeth saw was Max; all she wanted to see was Max. Her eyes flickered to his lips. Good strong lips, wide, not too full. They moved ever-so-slightly as he whispered to her, telling her the secrets he'd learned in his charmed life.

"The trick is, when it's a good surprise, enjoy it. But when it's a bad surprise, take a deep breath and pretend you expected it all along. That way, all your surprises are good. And sometimes, if you're very, very lucky—" He touched the tip of his finger to her lips. "—and you say your prayers every night—" He trailed that finger across her bottom lip. "—you'll find one or two surprises that are so spectacular you'll want to pinch yourself to make sure that you haven't dreamed the whole thing."

"That's silly," Elizabeth breathed, the words almost impossible to say since her lips trembled under his touch.

"It's the truth," he said quietly, and she believed him.

"Tell me about a surprise like that," Elizabeth murmured as he cupped his hand under her chin.

"You're that kind of surprise, Elizabeth MacMillan. As long as I live, I will remember the surprise of you."

"Surprises can fool you," Elizabeth teased, her voice low and sultry in the close cab of the truck. "Sometimes good surprises become bad realities. Then where are you?"

Max moved away slightly, and his gaze lost some of its sparkle. He pushed his dark glasses into place as if he had just closed the doorway to his soul. Elizabeth felt a sadness envelop him.

"Then you're nowhere, Elizabeth. When that happens, when the happiness becomes misery, then there's nothing you can do at all except your best. Leave it or live with it. Yes, when that happens, you just live with it."

A cloud seemed to have settled over Max; but before she could make sure he was all right, he was smiling again, the moment forgotten.

"Oh, there we go," he said with a little whoop that

banished any melancholy. "I've been waiting for this opening. Hang on to your hat."

Max flipped the wheel, and his little red truck jumped like a nervous filly. They crossed two lanes of traffic in an instant, hit a bump on the wide driveway, and flew down a ramp into the dusky darkness of an underground garage. Max parked and raced around to the passenger side of the car, his hands out to help her descend. Elizabeth went willingly into his arms. He lifted her as if she were as light as air. Her feet hit the ground, but Max still held her, longer than necessary but never long enough.

"We're here," he said, and she could tell he was happy.

Elizabeth grinned, holding on tight to his arms, relieved that whatever had concerned him was gone.

"Where's here?"

"Santa Monica, California. The pier. Video games, bad food, and lights. Families the size of small cities roaming up and down, roller skaters, hunks, gorgeous babes, and even a fisherman or two. Not to mention the smell of salt water, the sound of the waves, a beach to walk on if we want."

He stepped back. Elizabeth's grin spread to epic proportions. She took the hand he held out, playing Wendy to his Peter Pan. She was ready to fly, into the sky or down the pier, with him. Elizabeth MacMillan was free as she had never been before, and she was with a man who wasn't afraid to laugh, pay her compliments, and look her in the eye.

Taking her hand, he slipped it under the crook of his arm and pulled her close as they began to walk.

"What's your heart's desire?" he asked.

"To be as happy as this forever."

Max slid his eyes her way. Elizabeth looked straight ahead. She'd said it. She'd been bold and brave, and now she would find out if she'd chosen the wrong moment for total honesty—or the wrong man. Aware that Max's eyes were forward again, Elizabeth waited for him to loosen his hold, push her away just a bit. Instead, he squeezed her arm tighter.

"I wouldn't have a problem with that. None at all," he murmured and led her up the stairs into a world of noise and lights and sights that she could hardly believe. It was as if he were leading her directly to the place where laughter and happiness were born.

Children no older than Chris roamed the pier. There were yuppies and old people, roller skaters and reggae, hawkers and homeless. Max laughed at her amazement. She'd jumped from Georgia cheerleader to suburban housewife and missed the rainbow belts of life where the alternate was the norm and fantasies were lived.

They threw themselves into the arcade only to find they both loved to win but lost more often than not. Elizabeth's face flushed with excitement with each toss of a ball or a ring that just missed the bottle-neck. They left without as much as a stuffed animal between them. By the time they sat at a corner table in a restaurant that specialized in fried clams and fresh salads, Elizabeth knew that, though their hands were empty, the prize she had sought all her life was within her grasp. The sun was going down; night was upon them, and when Max ordered her another strawberry shake, Elizabeth took his hand and tried to tell him how lucky she felt. Instead, she closed her mouth and grinned.

"What?" Max coaxed.

But Elizabeth remained mute—happy, yet cautious, too. She felt compelled to speak of love. Thankfully, she was smart and thought twice. This wasn't love. But it could be. It could be. So, his hand in hers, she said simply, "You really know how to treat a girl. Thank you."

Max, pleased that she was happy, changed the order to *to go* and they walked out into the now-dark night. Bells and whistles still sounded. They could hear raised voices somewhere behind them, laughter ahead of them. They walked toward the laughter and the music.

"Come on."

Max grabbed Elizabeth's hand, startling her. She followed him anyway as he rushed through a turnstile just as the merry-go-round started to turn. The horses began their futile race, and the pipe organ sounded its song.

"Max," Elizabeth protested, but he wasn't listening. Effortlessly, he swung her onto the platform and followed behind. He picked her up again and placed her sidesaddle on a pink pony with a golden crown sitting on its sea-green hair.

"That's where you belong. On a fancy horse, riding into a dream."

"You're a poet," she said, leaning close so that he could hear her over the noise.

"I'm an optimist," he countered and reached up to touch her face. But the moment was lost. A huge man, swarthy and impossibly wide, clamped a hand on Max's shoulder.

"You gotta have a ticket," he yelled and pointed to the sign near a small booth.

Max shrugged and reached into his pocket. Deftly he stuffed a bill into the other man's hand. "The lady doesn't need a ticket. She's going to ride as long as she wants."

The man opened his hand, approved of what he saw there, and moved on silently.

"Can you always work magic?" Elizabeth hollered just as the pink horse with the golden crown rose high in the sky. Her head was back, her eyes on the lights above her. She didn't see Max's eyes darken with sadness or hear him mutter, "God, how I wish I could."

When she looked again, he was staring ahead as if to chart a trail for her fantasy horse. Knowing it might be time for them to simply be together, Elizabeth rode up and down in silence, Max's hand at her waist. She would ask for nothing more. Not even a word from him because, at that moment, she had everything she wanted.

"Elizabeth, wake up. Come on."

Max shook her gently, not sure he wanted her to wake up at all. She had fallen asleep on his shoulder somewhere near Valencia, and he loved the bedroom silence that enveloped them as he drove through the night. It had been so long since he'd held a woman while she slept. Too long, and he missed that intimacy almost more than . . .

"Are we here?" Elizabeth was awake, twisting her head to peer through the windshield. "Late," she mumbled and let her head fall back against the seat as she put a hand to her head.

"Very," Max agreed, gently helping her push aside her hair so that he could see the sheen of her cheek. She looked pale, still in the throes of sleep, though she was trying hard to appear alert.

"How late?" she asked, her lips barely moving.

"After one. Do you think Leslie's still awake?"

"No. I doubt anyone in Emerald Isle is awake." Elizabeth chuckled, finally shaking off sleep but not her languor. Laying her head back on the seat, she looked at Max through dreamy eyes. "I had a wonderful time tonight. Thank you."

"My pleasure." Max shifted, easing his knee up on the seat so he could look at her. His fingers still played with her hair; his eyes roamed over her face. "I can't remember when I've had a better time, Elizabeth."

"Then you are either the easiest man in the world to please or it's time you got a life."

"I think I'm the easiest man in the world to please. A plate of clams, a merry-go-round, and thou. What else could I ask for?"

Suddenly serious, Elizabeth looked at him closely. "I don't know, Max. But there must be something more you want. This is just too easy, too good to be true."

"What's too easy?"

"Us."

"I'm glad you think there's an us."

"You know what I mean. When we met, I didn't give you a passing thought after you left my house; now, it seems as if you were meant to be in my life."

"Why should that bother you?"

"Because my relationship with Brad was that simple. One day he was *in* my life; and the next, he *was* my life. I didn't question it; we didn't agonize over what we should mean to one another, and now he's gone. Disappeared out of my life as easily as he came into it. I don't want that to happen again. I don't think I could bear it."

"I'm not Brad, Elizabeth," Max said quietly. "I'm just me. Sometimes I'm tired. Sometimes I get frustrated with life, but I'm not the kind of guy to run away from it or analyze it. I've done that—analyzed something to death and never come up with an answer, so I don't do it anymore. It's a waste of energy."

"Sometimes it's hard not to analyze and question," Elizabeth retorted.

"Sometimes it's near impossible," Max agreed, "but this isn't the time to be talking about philosophy. You're exhausted. I should be heading home. I want to end the night the way we started it."

"Me, too," she said, grinning and feeling his goodness envelop her. How silly to want to talk about misery when contentment was at hand.

"Then, come on. I'll set you on your doorstep and wish you pleasant dreams."

"No need to wish them for me, Max. I lived one tonight." Max chuckled and slid out of the truck. As he helped her down, Elizabeth held his hand and spoke quietly all the way to her door. "I've ridden a pink horse tonight and walked on a pier and smelled the salt air. What better dream could there be?"

"I've got to admit," Max said, pulling her hand up and holding it close to his chest as they reached the door, "I can't think of a better one. Now—" He raised her hands to his lips and kissed her fingertips. "—to bed, Elizabeth, and promise we'll do this again."

"And again and again," Elizabeth whispered back.

"As often as you'd like," Max agreed.

Looking at her a bit longer, moving closer as though to kiss her, Max suddenly changed his mind. He dropped her hand, stepped away, and smiled at her almost shyly. "But tonight, I'm gone. Because, if I don't go, Leslie isn't going to be your only overnight guest."

Elizabeth nodded, grinning from ear to ear. How lovely to be wanted—and even lovelier to be left at the doorstep with a kiss on the fingertips. She watched as he walked away. She watched until he was in the truck, his hand held against the window in a good-night salute. She went in first and closed the door. Leaning against it, she strained her ears to hear him drive away. It seemed like an eternity until Elizabeth heard the roar of his motor. Max was gone, but the last thing she felt was lonely. Never in her whole life had she felt so filled with desire and respect and maybe even a little bit of love. It was amazing some woman hadn't snapped Max up a long time ago. Simply, utterly, fabulously amazing. Just like a dream. Yes, a dream where all things were possible.

Max's step was light when he walked up the drive to his home. It looked tiny and vulnerable in the early-morning hours, but he felt large and wonderful. Elizabeth was under his skin but good. Such small things made her feel like a queen. He'd only known one other woman like that, only loved one other woman who was so undemanding. And, as he thought of her, his step slowed until he was exhausted by his memory as he flipped on the kitchen light.

His eyes adjusting to the glare, Max knew the only cure for what ailed him both in the present and the past was a hot shower and a long sleep. But then he saw the slip of paper. Someone had been in his home; someone had been waiting for him and tired of it. The note on the table was carefully written, the wording chosen to let Max know she was quite displeased that they had missed one another.

Max picked up the paper and was duly informed that since he was so late, dinner had been ruined. What was left of it was in the refrigerator. He could eat it at whatever hour he came in. Which, she was sure, would be ungodly. Which, by the way, wasn't a smart idea when the next day was a work day. Which . . .

Max crumpled the paper and tossed it into the wastebasket, then turned out the lights as he headed for the shower. Standing under the hot water, letting the steam do its work, he thought about the note and the ruined dinner.

"Oh, Mama Maria, am I such a disappointment?" he murmured.

He was sorry he hadn't been there for dinner as he had been almost every night for the last many years. He was sorry he couldn't be what she wanted him to be. But he wasn't perfect. And he'd met Elizabeth MacMillan. Mama would just have to understand—someday—when he could explain it to her . . . after he understood it himself.

Minutes later, his hair still damp and curling across his forehead, Max crawled into bed and knew that he'd rather be sleeping with the memory of Elizabeth on her golden-crowned pony than with the memory of another dinner with Mama Maria.

Seven

"I gotta go, David."

Christopher stood up and pulled on his shirt. It was getting too small, but probably his mom hadn't noticed he'd grown. Probably she'd never take him shopping again because things cost too much. But it wasn't really the money; that was just an excuse. He knew what "cost too much" meant. It meant *he* was a problem; it meant *he* cost too much. He'd just wear these clothes till he died. He'd look like a dork. They'd bury him looking like a dweeb in these clothes.

"I gotta go," he said again.

"No you don't. You worry too much. What're they going to do, leave without you?" David didn't bother to look up, too interested in what he was doing and too sure of his own understanding of adult behavior to bother with Chris' worries.

"Maybe," Chris grumbled. "Ever since that guy started hanging around, my mom forgets everything. She'd probably forget me." He plopped himself down next to his new friend. Ever since that day in the park, they'd been hanging out together. Chris couldn't quite figure out why. David didn't look a thing like Chris' regular friends with his baggy clothes and his hair pulled back in a ponytail. At least the rubber band kept it from hanging down in David's eyes. Chris was always afraid his hair would catch on fire or get caught in something while David played his games.

"Come on. Look at this. Just look." David grinned over his shoulder and, as usual, Christopher scooted in beside him even though he really didn't want to. He wanted to play Nintendo or ride his bike, not play these weird games. David pushed a skinny, dirty finger at the stuff in front of him. "See, I've got this little bit of straw and paper just about ready, then you put the cardboard on. You have to tent it, kind of." Meticulously, David poked again as if he were an artist putting the finishing touches on his masterpiece.

Christopher looked closer. Indeed, the paper and straw were beginning to glow under the magnifying glass David held so steadily with his other hand. With a pop, a small flame leapt from the top of the little trash teepee. Christopher reached out and tried to brush away the cardboard, but David stayed his hand.

"Whaddya doin'?" he demanded.

"It'll catch on fire," Chris said, trying to twist his wrist out of David's grasp.

"That's the whole point, stupid." David pushed Christopher's hand away and sat back on his haunches, disgusted by Chris' lack of appreciation for his fine work. "Sometimes you are such a sissy. I don't know why you don't just go home and sit with your mom if you don't want to have any fun."

"I do want to have fun. But that's on fire, David. That's dangerous. What if it got in the grass?" Christopher objected, watching as the flames gained momentum, consuming the straw, licking at the cardboard.

"Then it gets into the grass." David flipped the

magnifying glass shut and stuffed it into the pocket of his too-big jeans. "Then the fire trucks will come, and it will be so cool. We could watch from the park. Then we'd see people sit up and take notice."

"But what if it got to some houses?"

David laughed. "Then it would get to some houses." He stood up and slapped his hands clean, surveying the little blaze at his feet. Then, to Christopher's utter amazement, David performed a feat that made him seem heroic. Without a blink, David stomped on the fire. One foot. Amazing. The flames leapt around his sneaker, licking at the thick rubber of his soles. His eyes, old for ten years, were trained on Christopher. The more impressed Christopher was, the happier David became.

"Wouldn't you care? What if it were your house?" Chris asked breathily, hardly able to take his eyes off that sneaker plopped right in the middle of the fire. One, two, three, and the fire was out with only a little bit of ash left on the ground and a puff of smoke headed toward the sky.

"You're a wimp. Nobody would let a fire get all the way across the park to a house. It's just for effect, you understand? Some excitement? This place needs it. This place sucks."

Christopher nodded. He didn't like that word, but he wasn't about to tell David. This guy was the only one Chris could really talk to. David didn't live in Emerald Isle, but he knew about the people. He lived across the tree line, past the drainage ditch. In David's neighborhood, yards weren't as nice and some people kept trucks and stuff on what was left of the grass. David lived in a house that was smaller than those in

Emerald Isle, and he lived with his mom, who worked all the time. He even went out at night. If he hung around David, Chris would know all the answers.

"You want someone's attention, whaddya do?" David asked. He gave the ash heap one more hard grind with his sneaker. Moving back, he kept his eyes on the ground then slid them sideways. "You light a fire." He laughed, short and unamused. "Light a fire, and then they notice you're there. I've even done it at home. My mom had to come back from work and everything." David giggled, but it wasn't a really happy sound.

Chris didn't like David staring at him, so he looked around. They were behind a dumpster at a small store just on the edge of the park, just outside the gates of Emerald Isle. He had never ventured out of the complex on his own before. With David, though, he roamed where he pleased after school once he checked in with his mom. Her schedule was always the same, so he knew exactly what time he had to be home. And now, with Max coming around, his mom paid even less attention. Freedom was great. Really great.

"It doesn't matter anyway," Chris said, looking at the heap of charred cardboard and ashes that had once been straw and newspaper. "It's out. Let's go."

"Hey, why don't we call your mom and tell her that you're going home with somebody from school. Then you can come to my house. My mom won't be home till late. I found where she's got a new bottle of booze. Ever tried booze? Come on, it'll be fun."

Christopher shook his head, looking at the ground as he kicked at a pebble and headed toward the main street.

"I gotta go. They're waiting for me," he said before he was too far away.

"Yeah," David answered with the resignation of someone who was used to being left behind.

With that, Chris walked away. The minute he was out of sight, Christopher started to jog, running faster and faster until his breath was coming in hot bursts. He was already late; his mom had told him to be home half an hour ago. He picked up speed. It was getting dark earlier now, and she would worry. Even though he was mad at her an awful lot these days, he really didn't want her to worry.

Finally, he neared his house. The porch light was already on, welcoming him. He slowed. It wouldn't do any good to have her think he was really scared about getting home late. David said you had to let adults know that you had some power, too. But he pushed back his hair and stuck his shirt into his pants. They were going out—all of them. Max and his mom and him. That was going to be strange, but he wanted to try again, just to see what it was like now that he knew Max a little better. He wanted to be a part of whatever was happening with his mom and this guy, just to keep an eye on things in case his dad wanted to know when he came back. Hands stuffed in his pocket, Christopher sauntered up the walk, pushed open the gate, and went into the house the back way.

"Mom. I'm home." The house was silent. Not the silence of another person somewhere else, but the quiet of a totally empty place. "Mom?"

Chris ran his hand across the counter and looked toward the refrigerator. No message on the board. He headed toward the living room. Everything was in its place. The house was spotless. Without his mom there moving things around, dusting and stuff, it was like no one lived in this house.

"Mom?" Chris' voice was tentative, childlike as it quavered up the stairs only to bounce back unanswered. His heart beat faster, and his palms were sweaty. He turned on his heel and sat down, his hands clasped and dangling through his knees. He could call again, but he knew she wasn't here. He could always feel his mom: cooking in the kitchen, paying bills while he fell asleep upstairs, watching him from her blanket in the park while he played ball. He could always feel her, and now he couldn't, so that meant she was gone. He was alone and . . .

The doorbell rang. Christopher jumped and ran to open the door, sure it would be his mom saying she'd just stepped out for a minute. No, she'd say she'd sent Max packing and was coming back to take him for pizza. Just the two of them. No, it was . . .

"Mrs. Gibson."

Chris' voice cracked. He moved back, and she stepped in and closed the door. Christopher's arms fell to his sides. They were so heavy he didn't think he would ever lift them again. His eyes were heavy, too— with tears. How could his eyes do that to him? Stupid body. It always did exactly what he didn't want, like his eyes tearing up or his heart beating fast or his ears listening for noises that never came.

"Hi, kiddo." Leslie was beautiful. Christopher had thought so from the minute he'd laid eyes on her. Tonight was no different. She was dressed all in black and her hair looked like spun gold, but he couldn't bring himself to look at her. He was afraid he'd cry because she wasn't his mother. "How long have you been here?" she asked.

"Not too long," Chris answered quietly, shuffling from one foot to the other. Leslie smiled as if that answer were just what she wanted to hear.

"Good. Your mom had to leave, so she called me to come over. I got stuck in traffic. I hope you weren't scared." Leslie edged into the living room and dropped her purse by the sofa, having a hard time keeping up the cheery chat.

"No, I don't get scared anymore. I'm alone a lot." Christopher followed her, lingering in the doorway.

"I know," she said quietly. "That's tough. But your mom's trying hard."

"Yeah, so hard she can't leave me a note?" He pouted, though he hadn't meant to. He wanted to sound sarcastic like David would have.

"Oh, I can't believe that. I bet you just missed it. I'll take a look."

Leslie scooted into the kitchen and headed right to the telephone. Elizabeth kept a pad of paper there. Quickly she scribbled on it and went back to the living room.

"See." She waved the paper over her head. "She did leave you a note. *Chris . . .*" she read, *"Had to rush out. Sorry we had to cancel dinner. Will be home soon as I can. Love, Mom."*

Leslie grinned and looked Christopher's way, but not into his eyes. She hated lying. She hated what Elizabeth was doing just as much. No matter what the outcome of her errand, this kid was in for another major upheaval. Telling him a little white lie wouldn't make that much difference after Elizabeth got home. "There.

See? It fell beside the fridge, that's why you didn't see it."

Christopher was moving around the furniture, stalking Leslie. She kept grinning, her heart sinking when he wouldn't let it go at that.

"Where did she go so fast?"

Leslie shrugged, turned on her heel, and headed to the kitchen. Quickly, she wadded up the paper and slipped it into the trash, then opened the fridge as she chatted.

"I don't know, sweetie. She just left a message at my office for me to come be with you." She bent and checked out the food situation. Not much there. Still, she could stand in the cold a bit longer, hiding there until Christopher lost interest in her explanations. "So, here I am. What do you feel like eating? We've got some eggs and some—" She moved a couple of cans around then stood up. "—okay, there ain't much, so how about a burger?"

Leslie's grin widened, faltered, and faded. Christopher was holding the paper she had crumpled and thrown away. He had unwrapped it, smoothed it, and was holding it in one hand while he looked at her. He had seen the scribbles. He knew the lie.

"She always leaves notes on the fridge pad."

"Hey," Leslie spoke quietly. "I'm sorry. I really am. I thought it would help. Your mom was in a hurry. She had something to do, and had to do it right away."

"What was it?" Christopher asked flatly, all hope gone from his voice now. Adult betrayal was nothing new to him.

"I think she should tell you that." Leslie placed her hands atop the refrigerator door and did her best to look Christopher right in the eye. It was so hard for Elizabeth; Leslie understood that. Her life was a black comedy, but Christopher was too young to understand the wryness of the situation his mother found herself in. He was honestly interested and honestly hurt.

"Was *he* with her?" Christopher demanded.

"Max?" Leslie needn't have asked. Christopher glared at her with a little boy's outrage, saying nothing. She looked away as she closed the refrigerator door. "Come on, honey, let's go get a burger. I'm a good listener. And if you don't want to talk, I'll get you a bunch of quarters and you can take it all out on that video game you like so much."

Leslie stood a few feet from him and held out her hand. Chris' body shook, and his eyes never left hers. There was more she should say and her mind whirled, desperate for inspiration. All the platitudes she knew were old and tired and meant for people who'd lived most of their life already. But she tried again anyway.

"It's not Max, if that's what you're thinking. He just happened to be here when your mom had to leave. She didn't go somewhere with him and forget about you. If she had, she wouldn't have asked me to come."

"It's okay."

Christopher turned and dropped the scribbled note into the trash as he left the kitchen. Leslie followed, steps behind the pained and angry boy.

"What about that burger?"

"I don't want any."

"Then let me make you something."

Chris shook his head. He walked right to the front door. His hand was on the knob. Leslie watched curiously. It was as if he didn't know what he was doing.

He seemed at odds in his own home, and Leslie almost let him walk outside. Almost. When she came to her senses, she was on him fast, her hands gentle, yet firm, on his shoulders.

"Chris? Where are you going? There's nothing out there, sweetie. It's late."

Chris stopped. He took a deep breath and looked up at Leslie. His face was pinched, and she felt powerless to ease his pain.

"It was important, Chris," she assured him. "Your mom will explain when she gets home. Meanwhile, let's call for a pizza. We'll kick off our shoes and watch something on TV. Wait. I have a better idea." Leslie turned him toward her. "I'll play Nintendo with you. What do you say? Can you teach me?"

Chris shook his head. He smiled because she was trying so hard, but that expression cost him the rest of his energy.

"No thanks, Mrs. Gibson. I'm kind of tired."

Chris slipped out of her grasp and walked past her, through the door and up the stairs.

"I'm scared."

Elizabeth held Max's hand tighter. His touch felt good and so right, yet still the fright deep inside her wouldn't be assuaged. Fear of failure—but even worse, fear of success—ran through her like an electrical current. Max squeezed back, cocking his head so he could speak softly.

"It's pretty miserable for you. Are you sure you want to go through with this?"

"What else is there to do?" she asked, hoping against hope that he would have an alternative.

Max eyed her. Elizabeth was as pale as a ghost, her eyes sparkling with an incredible, brittle brightness. Her hand in his was rigid and cold. He lay his other against her cheek, calming words on the tip of his tongue, words that were never spoken.

"Mrs. MacMillan?"

"Yes?" Elizabeth fairly jumped out of her skin, Max forgotten as she waited for the policeman to reach her.

"I'm Officer Black. Sorry to have kept you waiting." The tall man held out his hand. Elizabeth shook it. Her eyes never locked onto his.

"My husband?" Elizabeth whispered, unable to say Brad's name.

"Well, we're not sure about that. The man fits the general description you left with us, so we gave you a call. I'll be pretty upset if the desk got your hopes up on this one. It's a long shot, you understand."

"Can she see him?" Max moved beside her, his arm around her waist, and Elizabeth leaned into him. She could stand on her own two feet, but his strength fortified her.

" 'Fraid not." He spoke to Elizabeth again. "Sorry to put you through the trouble, Mrs. MacMillan, but they took him to St. Martin's Hospital. He had a breakdown. You'll have to go to the hospital if you want to track him down."

"How long ago did they leave?" she asked.

"About ten minutes, ma'am. They'll take him to Emergency to have him checked out. If they release him, we have no reason to hold him. There's no law against losing your memory. He wasn't arrested, you understand; he just showed up here asking for help."

"Are you sure?"

"Sure there's no law?"

"No," Elizabeth insisted, her voice stronger. "Sure that this man wasn't faking. Do you really think his memory was gone? Amnesia?"

"I'm not a doctor, ma'am." Officer Black shrugged. "But he seemed pretty convincing to me. I'm sorry I can't give you more information. The hospital will be able to help you for sure."

With a nod toward Max, the man in blue turned on his heel and disappeared through the door. Elizabeth watched him, unable to move, thinking only that Brad might be sick and in need, with no memory of her or Christopher. Then she thought of Max.

"Elizabeth?"

Max laid his hand on her shoulder. Elizabeth covered it with her own, then laid her cheek against both. Their time together, friends not lovers, the idea of lovers never far from their minds, had been a healing time. She was living happily again. Leslie was her friend. Her job was wonderful. Christopher had settled down—and now this. This!

"I guess we'd better go," she said quietly. Without another word, she walked to the door, Max by her side, his arm around her shoulders. Elizabeth leaned into him, leaned on him, and Max didn't seem to mind at all. Fifteen minutes later, they were walking through the doors of the Emergency Room at the hospital. This time, Elizabeth hurried. This time, they didn't touch.

"Hi, Elizabeth. What brings you here so late? They haven't got you working the night shift, have they?"

The nurse behind the station was so familiar; but for the life of her, Elizabeth couldn't remember her name. Nor did she notice the woman's eyes sliding toward Max with more than a little interest. Elizabeth leaned over the desk and whispered, unable to meet the woman's eyes.

"I'm not working tonight. I . . ." Her voice caught. She tried again. "The police brought in someone they think has amnesia. Do you know where he is?"

"Sure, the guy's in bad shape. You think you know him, do you? You'd be doing him a real service if you could figure out who he is. He's not a street person, believe me. I've seen enough of 'em down here to know when they've been slumming for a while and when they've just hit a bad patch."

Elizabeth nodded. The nurse chatted, walked out from behind the high desk, and flipped her hand for Elizabeth to follow. Before she did, Elizabeth went back to Max. As naturally as if they'd been doing it for years, they walked into each other's arms and held one another.

"Do you want me to come?" he asked.

Elizabeth looked into the black eyes that had never once condemned or questioned her. She shook her head.

"No." After a moment, she voiced the question in both their minds. "What if this is Brad? What if he's been gone all this time because he was sick?"

Max tightened his hold, not to keep her with him but to give her whatever strength he could.

"Then you'll deal with it. On your own, with me, with Chris and Leslie. You've got friends, Elizabeth. You have people who love you." Max's eyes bore into

hers, and Elizabeth saw the reflection of her own sadness and loss. It touched her so deeply she wanted to
weep. Instead, she slipped out of his arms and headed
down the hall. The nurse still held the door open.
When she passed, it closed behind her with a swish
that sounded more like the clanging of a jail-cell door.

Inside Emergency, she slowed her pace and tried to
adjust to the overwhelming smell of antiseptic. The
fluorescent lights made her feel drawn and pale. She
was a ghost of herself floating on to meet her past.
Someone moaned in a space cordoned off by a curtain.
Elizabeth's head snapped right toward the sound. A
woman. There were murmurs and another moan. Two
people in that cubicle. She went on.

"Elizabeth. Here."

Her guide was standing in front of another drawn
circular curtain. No one was hurt inside; there were
no sounds of distress.

"Somebody you know real well, Elizabeth?" the
nurse asked.

"I think he might be my husband," Elizabeth whispered.

"Oh, my goodness." The nurse stepped back; she
remembered the gossip, of course. "You'll want to be
alone." She made a token effort to offer some privacy,
but did not retreat. She wanted to be the first to con-
dense this latest chapter in Elizabeth MacMillan's life.
Hating the blatant curiosity, Elizabeth accepted her return to the limelight.

She crimped the curtain between her fingers, took
a deep breath, then pushed it back just enough to slip
through. Inside the cocoon of cotton, the light was
dimmer, the air closer, the hospital smell even more

intense. She found no paraphernalia—no IV, pans, or medication—only a man, asleep, his knees pulled tight into his chest, one arm flung out.

He didn't move and neither did Elizabeth. She trembled, gripped by a trepidation so overwhelming she was sure the man would hear her teeth chatter. He might look at her if that happened—with Brad's eyes. But he remained still, so silent she wondered if he were dead. Looking closely, she saw his shoulders rise and fall with his shallow breathing. The shoulders were narrow; the legs, long. He wasn't muscular, but slim. Like Brad. Could this be her husband encrusted in dirty clothes, his memory of his past—his marriage and family—gone? Could it?

Elizabeth moved to the left, her eyes trained on his sandy hair. Straight, like Brad's. She moved slowly, hugging the curtain until she could just see the rise of his cheekbone. Yes, it was high and defined, the skin tone the same. Perhaps the face was a bit gaunter than Brad's, but if he'd been sick . . .

Elizabeth closed her eyes and prayed for guidance. Her heart needed to know how she would, should, feel if this man awoke and recognized her as his wife. How? How? And the answer was celestial silence.

Heart thudding, Elizabeth swallowed hard. Eyes open, she realized she had only two roads she could take: turn and run, or walk ahead with courage.

She took those last few steps, courage propelling her to a better vantage point. She tried to study him, but her vision blurred, pulling back into focus three times before she saw him clearly. Her knees buckled; her hands flew to cover her mouth so that the sound of her relief and certainty would remain private.

This wasn't Brad! This was a stranger. How could she have imagined anything else? This face was longer, those lips fuller; and the eyes, even in sleep, were wider than Brad's. And his hands. Lord, his hands, they were broader, the fingers shorter.

Elizabeth backed into the curtain, forgetting there was no substance to this wall; she clutched at the gray fabric. Half laughing, half sobbing, she cried for Max. She needed a warm hand to hold her steady while she sorted through these lightning-bolt feelings of guilt and joy.

"Elizabeth?"

She turned, wanting to look once more at the sleeping man just to be sure. Then she slipped away only to find Judy waiting for her, speaking to her. Lord, she remembered the woman's name! It was so vivid it might as well have been etched in her mind in neon. Elizabeth smiled. She grinned.

"Judy? Judy."

"Is it . . . your husband?"

"No." Elizabeth shook her head and headed for the door, knees still wobbly, heart still pounding. Judy patted her back as she passed. Elizabeth thought she might be sick if she didn't leave immediately.

"Just as well, honey. It would probably be harder to have him back like this than not at all. Why don't you just stay here and pull yourself together? That must have been tough."

Elizabeth nodded. The woman was right. She needed a minute to assimilate all this information. Elizabeth tried not to think of what might have been. She could never have turned him away if he had been sick. Never.

Standing just inside the swinging door, Elizabeth

took a deep breath. Hand to her head, she looked through the porthole of a window and saw Max waiting for her.

With no reason to stay, Elizabeth pushed open the swinging door. Judy was back at her station. Max was watching for her, his expression a combination of pain, curiosity, and hope. He waited for her to speak, but she couldn't find her voice, so she walked into his arms. Without a word, their lips met. They kissed for the first time—without passion, but with relief and the knowledge that the future, for now, was theirs. Finally, after what seemed an eternity, Elizabeth lay her head against his chest, at peace.

"I'll take you home," he whispered, suddenly aware that they were a curiosity. This time, the arm around Elizabeth's shoulders was strong with the certainty that it belonged there. Elizabeth, nestling inside his embrace, felt no regret that the man in the hospital was not her husband. Life went on for Brad somewhere. It would do the same for Elizabeth.

"Elizabeth, that must have been so scary!"

Marsha slid into the chair reserved for those being admitted to the hospital and leaned over the small desk that separated her from Elizabeth.

"What?" Elizabeth asked without much interest. She straightened a pile of forms, clipped two together, and tried to ignore Marsha, busybody and former fellow volunteer. Obviously it hadn't taken Judy long to whisper last night's drama to an interested party and the dominoes had already fallen into place. Elizabeth did have to give Marsha credit. She had the guts to actually talk to Elizabeth face to face.

"You know what I'm talking about. Come on, Elizabeth, don't be coy."

Elizabeth looked up, her expression noncommittal.

"Come on. The thing last night at the hospital. My God," she breathed, "you must have felt like you were in a 'Movie of the Week.' You know, one of those flicks where the woman's husband comes back to claim her just when happiness is on the horizon with a hunk too good to be true."

"I'm not sure the scenario fits." Elizabeth laughed. What a funny way to describe Max. Sexy, yes, but so much more than that. Generous, gentle, wonderful, kind, perfect—her vocabulary was too limited. Marsha wouldn't have understood anyway, so Elizabeth didn't bother telling her about the long hours in the dark, sitting on the couch, talking about everything she was feeling, kissing, her cheek lying against his chest as she talked and talked and talked.

"Well, of course it fits. Your being a Southern belle and all; it's just too romantic. I mean you go from looking at this guy, thinking he was your husband, right into the arms of Max Marino. I would call that a hunk-in-waiting, wouldn't you? Really nice, Elizabeth. I didn't even know he was available. I would have divorced George if I'd known."

Marsha cackled, delighted with her flight of fancy and completely unaware that Elizabeth's attention was now hers completely.

"You know Max?" Elizabeth asked slowly.

"Everyone on Two East knows Max. There wasn't a lady on the staff, volunteer or salaried, married or not, that didn't lust after that bod. Know what I mean?"

"I'm surprised no one bagged him then," Elizabeth commented, looking down, a dreadful feeling growing in the pit of her stomach. She had had the same feeling sitting in Mr. Sawyer's office just before she'd found out Brad was gone for good. Dread was a feeling Elizabeth had learned to pay attention to.

"Well, we do have our rules, you know. Never go after forbidden fruit if the farmer's hanging around." Marsha giggled, and the sound grated on Elizabeth's nerves. The woman sat back in her chair, ready, willing, and able to tell what she knew. "His wife worked here. Really nice girl, but not nice enough to share her husband. Even the worst of us wouldn't do that. Then she got . . . well, I don't know the real story—and who am I to talk—but let's just say she quit . . ."

"Did she?" Elizabeth's fingers trembled as she fidgeted with a stack of papers. Marsha didn't notice; she was having too much fun.

"One day she was here, the next she wasn't. I thought that was nice—Max's business must have taken off and she could afford to stay home. But then I heard she'd started working from home 'cause they wanted to have a baby. She was back and forth here for a while doing fertility work-ups. You know how expensive that can be. I guess they must have had a baby; but, from what I hear about last night, Max isn't home sitting with the kiddies." Marsha giggled. She was a veritable fountain of information. "Anyway, we haven't seen her in a while, but I see her mom all the time with Max. That woman is a hypochondriac, if you know what I mean. I see her and run the other way. Mama Maria's always cornering one doctor or another. Well, anyway, I want to hear all about it: How you felt when you looked at that guy in Emergency . . . where you met Max . . . how long you've been going out . . . and, especially, what happened to his wife. I want to know everything. Just everything!"

Marsha's eyes were wide, her lashes clumped with cheap mascara. Elizabeth had the most awful desire to punch her out. Heaven help her, even a Southern lady couldn't hold up in front of this witch. Feeling her hands fist in frustration, Elizabeth stood up, summoning up every ounce of self-control.

"Last night was strange, Marsha. That man wasn't Brad. I assume the subject is closed as far as you and everyone else in this hospital is concerned. It's private business. Now, since I'm no longer a volunteer, and don't really have time to chat, I'll have to get to work."

With that, she picked up a stack of papers, turned her back, and walked away. Out of sight, catching her breath in the Xerox room, Elizabeth put her papers down and held onto the side of the huge machine. Twice in a lifetime was once too often to feel this way.

Desperate to control her fury, Elizabeth pulled herself together. She still had the capacity to think logically, damn it. Perhaps he hadn't betrayed her at all. Perhaps she was the one who had done Max a disservice by listening to Marsha. That was it, of course. Marsha was a gossip, and gossip was seldom grounded in fact.

Energized, Elizabeth decided to take action. She would drive out to the construction site and ask Max about his wife. Straight out. She'd handle it like an adult. She'd take her lunch hour and go right out there and ask if he was married. He would tell her that he'd been part of a messy divorce . . . that she was the only woman he'd ever cared about. He'd tell her . . .

But why hadn't he already told her? The opportunity to compare notes on errant spouses had come and gone more than once. Unless, of course, he wasn't divorced. Unless he had a wife at home believing his explanations for his late nights and busy Saturdays.

Acting on instinct, Elizabeth formed a second plan of action: She marched to the pay phones. She had neither the luxury of time, nor the guts, to face Max in the open. His work surrounding him, his body and mind strong from a day in the sun, would give him the advantage. If this made her a coward, then so be it.

Elizabeth flipped the phone book open, her fingers fumbling with the pages. Twice she passed the M's and twice she stopped, chastising herself for overreacting. Leaning against the wall of the alcove, Elizabeth closed her eyes and tried to convince herself that Marsha was an ignorant bag of wind. But the seed of doubt had been planted, and nothing would be right until she knew the truth.

Forcing herself to concentrate, Elizabeth found Max's home number, dug in her pocket for change, and dialed. The cadence of the incessant ring slowed Elizabeth's heartbeat and calmed her mind. Each unanswered ring meant no one was home, which—according to Marsha—was where Max's wife should be. Relief came in waves. She let her forehead fall against the phone. No one was home. No one should be. Max was at work. Elizabeth listened once, twice more, and then . . .

"Hello?"

The lump in Elizabeth's throat was big and dense. She could not speak. Triumph gave way to defeat.

"Hello?"

The voice sounded old. Perhaps she was a cleaning lady hired to do what a wife used to do. Perhaps she was his mother. Yes, his mother. Hope sprang eternal in Elizabeth's Southern heart, along with caution born of less genteel memories.

"Hello," she whispered, her voice weak when she wanted it strong. "I'm sorry. I may have the wrong number. Is Mrs. Marino home? Is there a Mrs. Marino there?"

The silence was deafening. It reverberated in Elizabeth's ears like the roar of an angry, destructive sea and she was left breathless in the face of it. Outraged, confined in this small space, Elizabeth wanted to scream. Instead, she put her hand over the receiver, biting back her hurt and rage. *If you stay very still, Elizabeth, everything will work out fine.* If only Mama could be right this time. Pulling herself up, she took her hand away.

"Are you still there? I need to talk to Mrs. Max Marino." Elizabeth stared at a spot on the wall and waited, suddenly and strangely calm.

"Who is this?" the other woman demanded. This was no cleaning lady.

"I . . ."

Elizabeth hesitated. Who was she after all? A friend of a philandering husband? A friend who was so close to him that desire, perhaps even love, was not out of the question? In truth, she was nothing at all, just a woman wronged. "I'm calling from the hospital. St.

Martin's. Her old records. I wanted to give her some information."

"Mrs. Marino doesn't need any information. She has everything she needs from the hospital. She isn't here right now, and she doesn't need to hear from you." The receiver slammed down, the connection cut.

Elizabeth replaced the phone slowly. The lady was right. Max's wife didn't need the information Elizabeth had to give her. But there was a Mrs. Marino. No matter how Elizabeth cut it, the message was clear. Max belonged to someone else.

Elizabeth was sick to death of the nonsensical turns her life had taken. Brad, who wanted nothing to do with a family; Max, who wanted more than his family.

Elizabeth let go of the receiver and walked back to her desk. Once she tried to work, sitting with her back so straight and taut she looked positively inhuman. Every time she thought about this awful situation, she kept the images at bay with her litany: She would not be hurt . . . She would not be victimized. . . . She would be strong for herself this time.

An hour later, her heart gave out and her resolve tumbled like a house of cards. She stood up quickly, automatically stacking her papers and picking up her purse. Dazed, she made her excuses to Frank. Knowing she wasn't lying, Elizabeth left the hospital sicker than she'd ever been in her life.

She drove to the desert, thinking no thoughts at all, wanting only to lose herself in the bleak terrain. At some point, though, she turned around and returned home. She didn't sit on the couch where Max had held her the night before. She didn't look at the two wineglasses still in the sink, one of which Max had raised to her in a salute to her bravery. At home, Elizabeth simply dropped her purse in the entry, kicked off her shoes, and went out back.

Christopher found her there two hours later. She sat on the side of the pool, dangling her feet in the water despite the chill in the air and the stockings on her feet. He looked at her for a long while and thought about tiptoeing to his room, but instead, Christopher kicked off his shoes. Socks on, he put his feet in the water, too, and sat with her. Together, silently, they watched the sun go down. Things were changing again, and it wasn't just the seasons.

Part Two

Fall

Eight

Elizabeth stood at the corner watching Christopher walk to his first day of school alone. In the last weeks, the weeks of her dreadful loneliness, Christopher seemed to grow in stature while she felt herself shrinking. His body had lost the last of its baby fat, and the back she watched was more that of a young man than of a fifth-grader. Wishing he would turn to look at her, knowing he wouldn't, she watched him disappear around the corner, swallowed up by buildings and children. Seconds later, the bell sounded.

Shivering, Elizabeth turned up her collar and looked into the blue, brittle sky. Fall had whooshed into town. Elizabeth's nostrils flared against a short burst of chilled air. At her feet, a few red-gold leaves tumbled past, separated from trees that should never have been planted in a desert in the first place.

She sighed, fingering the piece of paper in her pocket as she walked to her car. She didn't want to look at it again. But like a magnet, the crude missive repeatedly drew her back. The printing was childlike, yet there was nothing naive about the message. *Stay away from him.* Good old married Max. He not only had a wife, but one who posted notes on front doors in the dead of night. Thank God she got up early to get the paper. If Chris had seen this . . .

But he hadn't, and she was tired of looking at it, too. Mrs. Marino needn't worry any longer. She could stop her midnight marauding. Elizabeth wouldn't be bothering Max anymore. And if he knew what was good for him, he'd stop trying to contact her, too.

Crumpling the paper, Elizabeth crossed the street and tossed the note into a trash can on the side of the road. She had no time for nonsense like this. Work was waiting, but there was a stop she had to make before, once more, she jump-started her life.

Elizabeth knocked on the open door, lingering in the hall until Leslie turned around. Phone cradled between her shoulder and ear, she waved Elizabeth in, motioned to a chair, and gave a thumbs-up without ever missing a beat of her conversation.

"No, I'm not going to let these people sacrifice that beautiful home for under four-fifty. Darn right. Four hundred and fifty thousand dollars. Bill! You're listening to all that public relations nonsense. The market's coming back. You know it, I know it, and your buyer knows it, so don't expect me to sacrifice a place that's been updated throughout and even has an enclosed spa. No way." Leslie swiveled back. "Just give me a call when you come around. We're talking a property with a view and a pool, Bill. So what, if it's not quite over the line in Valencia? What's a zip code one way or the other? Okay. Okay. Get back to me."

The receiver cradled, Leslie now belonged to Elizabeth.

"So, what brings you here?" Leslie asked.

"I thought I'd ask you out for coffee while I dine on a little crow." Elizabeth pulled a ladylike, but mortified, face.

"I wondered when you were finally going to crack. I haven't gotten more than two words out of you for the last few weeks. You're not a very good liar. Don't you know monosyllables are a dead giveaway that all is not right with the world?"

"I know. I know." Elizabeth shrugged, a sheepish smile finding a place on a face that had been mighty long for a good while.

"Well, that's something. A smile must mean you aren't dead yet; and if you're ready to talk, I'm ready to listen."

"Can you go for coffee?" Elizabeth asked.

"Sorry. I'm waiting for a call-back on a counteroffer and my beeper's on the blink," Leslie said. Leaning forward, she took a good look at her friend. "God, don't look like that. I didn't mean I don't have time for you. I've got a fresh pot of coffee in the back, and I might even be able to scrounge up a couple of donuts. And look—" She popped up and stood by the door. "—the door closes. We can indulge in girl talk to our heart's content, or until my call comes through, whichever comes first."

Elizabeth smiled. "You're one in a million."

"Yeah, yeah," she said, waving away the compliment as she ducked out. "Back in a sec."

Elizabeth waited, letting her mind rest while she looked at the pictures in Leslie's office. Houses big and small; some expensive, others modest. Each one reminded her of the day she and Brad had walked into their home in Emerald Isle for the first time. How hopeful she had been. How sure she had been of her place in the world every day after that.

Elizabeth closed her eyes. She must be healing if she could actually remember how happy she'd been. A few months ago she would have been reduced to tears by a memory; now Elizabeth felt only a deep sense of ennui. She harbored a dull ache of longing for what had been, and what would never be again.

"Here we go! Coffee. Now, sympathetic ear or a shoulder to cry on? Which will it be?"

"I don't know. A little of both, I suppose." Elizabeth reached for the coffee.

"Okay, let's start with the sympathetic ear. I'm assuming Max said something, did something, didn't do something, and now you're pouting. So, welcome to the dating game!" Leslie raised her donut in a salute, but her bravado evaporated in the face of Elizabeth's misery. "Boy, it must be worse than I thought. I suppose you would have been on the horn earlier if it were just some normal fight. Okay, so what's kept you hibernating so long?"

"He's married."

Leslie froze, instantly aging under her expertly applied make-up. Slowly she swiveled in her chair, put her coffee on the desk, and leaned forward.

"And?"

"And he's married," Elizabeth reiterated sadly. "What else is there to say? I found out from one of the women at the hospital. She knew Max's wife. Not well, but enough to convince me it was true."

"Did you ask him about it?" Elizabeth shook her head. The color came back to Leslie's cheeks, the fairy tale might have a happy ending after all. "Don't you think that might have been wise?"

"I did the next best thing," Elizabeth said wearily. She sipped her coffee, considered the contents of her cup, and said, "I called his home. An older woman answered and said Mrs. Marino wasn't there." Leslie raised an eyebrow and sat back in her chair. "Don't give me that look. There's nothing more to know. The woman didn't say that Mrs. Marino didn't live there anymore. She didn't say there wasn't a Mrs. Marino. She said Mrs. Marino wasn't in and not to call anymore."

"Okay, that last one is kind of telling," Leslie admitted.

Elizabeth nodded sadly and finished her coffee.

"Aren't I just the lucky one? First time out, and I find myself a man who's got a wife at home. For all I know, they have a bunch of kids, too. Marsha—the woman at the hospital—told me that Max's wife was being treated for fertility problems just before she quit work. Well, the drugs probably worked and Mrs. Max Marino is sitting around with angelic babies on her knee, completely oblivious to the scarlet woman in Emerald Isle who had eyes for her husband."

"Oh, come on. Every woman who laid eyes on that guy lusted after him. Give yourself a break. What kind of scarlet woman are you when you didn't even sleep with him?" Leslie hooted, then blinked and lowered her hands. "You didn't sleep with him, did you?" Elizabeth smiled slyly. "Oh, Elizabeth, you didn't, did you?" Leslie squealed. "You did, and you didn't tell me!"

"No. Don't be silly," Elizabeth confessed, chuckling

despite her misery. "But I was going to. It wouldn't have been long. I really wanted him, Leslie. I'm married, and I wanted him."

Elizabeth shook back her hair and looked heavenward. She wasn't fighting tears, only the lingering desire. She waited for words of comfort that didn't come.

"Oh, puleeese! Your husband separates from you for most of a year; then he disappears off the face of the earth without so much as a by-your-leave, and you think you're not supposed to get any? What do you think Brad's doing? Do you think he's being a monk? Do you honestly think he's really concerned about the faithful part of the wedding vows when he tossed all the rest of them to the wind? He probably ran off with some honey. Come on, girl. A nun you weren't meant to be. Not with that body." Elizabeth blushed, and Leslie softened. "Not to mention that big heart of yours. How could you not think of sharing all the love that's inside you if the chance presented itself?"

Elizabeth studied the floor and whispered, "I thought I was failing in love with him, Leslie. I thought it was mutual."

"And it would have been, sweetie." The reassurance was instantaneous and heartfelt. "Believe me. In your heart, you would have been making love. It would have been the same for him. I know he was head-over-heels for you. Now—" Leslie held up her hand before Elizabeth could object. "—I'm not excusing him. I'm just saying, if you had found yourself in bed with him, it would have been right. *Your* feelings were real. Couldn't his have been, too?"

"And it could have been they weren't," Elizabeth countered.

"There's that to consider," Leslie agreed. "You're probably right, but why not give him the benefit of the doubt? Why not smooth it out a bit?"

"Because it shouldn't be smoothed out. This should never be forgotten. I came so close to ruining my life and Christopher's, even Max's wife's. No one should ever feel what I felt when Brad left. I could never cause another woman that kind of anguish. Oh, Leslie, let's face it, I made a fool of myself."

"Just because you were in major lust? Elizabeth, that's silly!" Leslie objected.

"No, not because I wanted him, but because I was stupid enough to imagine he was going to step in and take over for Brad." Elizabeth stood up, her hands clasped in front of her. She walked across Leslie's small office and turned her back to the wall. "I thought he was going to put my life back together. I imagined us married and that Chris would learn to love Max. I would cook dinner again, and do the wash. Max would be that proverbial man of the house," she dead-panned wryly. "I know it was selfish, but I wanted to be sure of myself again by knowing there was a man in my life. I wanted him to define me. I really believe I equated love with how much I'm willing to do for a man and how well a man takes care of me. Leslie, what is wrong with me?" Elizabeth wailed. "Other women raise ten kids on their own, work four jobs, and never complain. I've got one child and a good job; I'm making ends meet, and I'm still looking for a man to take care of me. I must be defective."

"No, you're not," Leslie disagreed. "You just had a taste of the American dream, and you're royally ticked off that you had to wake up. Just because your eyes are open doesn't mean the dream isn't still appealing."

"I know that. But I'm not eighteen anymore. I can't put that letter sweater on and go back and make things right with a cheer. But I wish I could. I want to have stars in my eyes. I want to swoon when I'm kissed. I want love to be a big fluttery thing in the pit of my stomach. All that happened with Max. All of it." She sighed. "To have had that kind of magic again was incredible."

They stared at each other until Leslie broke the silence.

"Elizabeth, you can't go back," she said. "Not to college. Not to being a young wife. And not to falling in love with Max. If you let this eat at you, you won't go forward either. The trick to being happily single is to like who *you* are. You're beautiful and smart. You have a son—God, how I envy that. You're alone, but it is so different from my alone. You have a reason to succeed. The only reason I had was revenge. My best revenge was living better than I ever did when I was married."

Leslie considered her nails, but the introspection didn't last long. She smiled again.

"I don't think you can ever really count on men. In the whole world, there's probably only a handful of guys that are straight out of the storybook. Brad talked like he was, but couldn't cut it in the long run. Max looked like a Prince Charming, but had that black little spot on his resume—a wife. So, just plan on being on your own."

"Does it have to be that awful?" Elizabeth moaned at the prospect.

"Hey, what do I know? I haven't had a date in two years." Leslie cast her a self-deprecating grin.

Elizabeth laughed sadly, pushed herself away from the wall, and picked her purse up from the floor. She hesitated, thinking how nice it would be to hide in this small office with her friend—and how ludicrous.

"You're busy, and I've got to get to work. I've done enough sniveling; you've done enough helping."

"Hey, there's nothing like a good cry and a little outrage to make you feel better." Leslie stood up.

"Then I guess I'd better pump up my outrage, 'cause I've already done my crying."

"It'll get better, honey." Leslie brushed her cheek against Elizabeth's before holding her at arm's length. "I hate to ask, but you haven't let Christopher see you this way, have you?"

"Sure, we've been discussing Max the last few nights. Our discussions have led us to philosophical dissertations on the difference between lust and love," Elizabeth answered seriously. Then she touched Leslie's cheek and leaned close. "Give me some credit, huh? Of course I haven't. Besides, Chris is hardly home these days. He's found a new friend who, I gather, has a huge collection of video games. Usually he manages to run in just before dinner."

"I guess it's better than staying home alone while you work." Leslie walked Elizabeth to the door.

"I suppose. I still haven't met this boy, though. I suppose it doesn't really matter. School started today, so Chris will be doing his homework instead of running around."

"If you say so." Leslie opened the door and Elizabeth paused for a quick kiss.

"Thanks, Leslie. I'm sorry I've been so distant. I just needed some time alone."

"Hey, I've got a sixth sense. No harm done. Have you talked to Max at all since you found out?" Elizabeth shook her head. Leslie sighed. "Just as well. Life's too short for this kind of nonsense, kiddo. You deserve better."

"Thanks, but life is short and that's why it should be about loving someone."

"It is. You just have to make sure you love yourself in case you don't have someone who'll do it for you. Personally, I think I'm fantastic. And I never, ever, ever cheat on myself. Now scoot. I've got work to do, and I venture there's someone at St. Martin's Hospital wondering where you are."

Elizabeth said her goodbyes quickly. Twenty minutes later, she walked into work. In the next instant, love was the last thing on her mind.

"Elizabeth?" the receptionist called before Elizabeth could duck through the side door. Caught. Well, there were worse crimes than being late.

"Laura!" Elizabeth used her brightest voice. "Who's looking for me? An irate patient or a patient's irate family?"

The joke fell flat. Laura held out a slip of paper. "Your son's school called. They want you to come right away."

"Oh my God, Christopher?" Laura nodded, avoiding Elizabeth's eyes. "Accident?" Elizabeth breathed, horrified.

Laura shook her head harder. "I asked. He's just in trouble for something; but from the way it sounded, you'd better get down there pretty quick."

"I've got to tell Frank."

"I already did. He got Sarah to cover for you. He said you should check in with him after lunch if you can."

"Thanks."

Elizabeth hurried down the hall. Then she was running toward her car, trying not to let her imagination run faster than she could.

"With a penknife, Mrs. MacMillan."

The principal held up a small, rusted knife for her inspection. Elizabeth looked him in the eye instead.

"I've never seen that before, Mr. Boden. I'm sure it's not Chris'," Elizabeth insisted.

"Nonetheless, it was the instrument he was using when Mr. Crawford found him scratching obscene words in the finish of one of the stalls. Now, I don't need to tell you, as a taxpayer, what this means to the school budget. We just had those stalls refinished over the summer. They were beautiful. Clean and sparkling . . ."

"Yes, Mr. Boden. I certainly do understand the importance of this. But I must tell you, I can hardly believe it's Christopher you're talking about. I'd like to see him, if that's all right. I'd like to hear what he has to say."

"I'll be happy to let you talk to him during the lunch break. But, Mrs. MacMillan, Mr. Crawford watched Chris long enough to know what he was doing. Normally, Christopher would have been sent home on suspension, but I didn't want him sent to an empty home. I sense that Chris' summer hasn't been the best."

Elizabeth froze, offended that he should make judgments about how she was raising Chris. Luckily, she thought again. This man was trying to do what was best for Christopher, just as she was. She sat back in her chair while the principal waited. She was tired, and this latest phase of Christopher's rebellion brought her close to exhaustion. But she loved him and she wouldn't let him walk down this road alone. With a great effort, she pulled herself straight.

"You're right, Mr. Boden. This summer has been dreadful. Our family problems have affected Chris greatly. I'm sure this is nothing new to you. Children from broken homes all go through a period of adjustment."

"Yes, they do. Unfortunately, I sense that this is not a simple matter," he said kindly.

"No, it isn't. But it is a matter for my family, and no one else."

"Perhaps counseling . . ."

"Perhaps not," Elizabeth rallied, becoming impatient. "I think I'd like to see Christopher now, if you don't mind."

Mr. Boden sighed. "All right." He picked up the phone, punched in a few numbers, and asked someone on the other end to get Chris. Standing, he gestured toward the door. "You can wait in the small office just off the reception room."

"Thank you." As Elizabeth passed, Mr. Boden put a hand on her arm, forcing her to look at him.

"Mrs. MacMillan? What Christopher doesn't say can be just as enlightening as what he does. Sometimes children never come out of their adjustment period. Sometimes they get stuck in the hurt because no one listened to the silences; problems can seem insurmountable in their young minds."

Elizabeth looked him straight in the eye. He was scaring her, but she also knew he was way off base. "I know my son very well, Mr. Boden. I love him. I'll listen, and I'll do what's right."

With that she was gone.

"Mom?"

Elizabeth turned around. She'd been looking out the window, watching the laughing children poking into their lunch bags, trading their treats. Her son should have been with them. Instead, he loitered in the doorway, accused, but not contrite. Elizabeth kept her distance, sizing up his need. What did a good mother say when her son had been bad?

Her eyes roamed over his face, taking in every nuance of his expression. He looked more miserable, perhaps, than at any time during the last year and a half. Elizabeth offered him a smile and spoke softly. He was, after all, her baby.

"Hi, honey. Do you want to close the door?"

He did, but moved no further into the room. Elizabeth went to him and wrapped her arms around him, holding on even when he didn't return the hug.

"I'm sorry," he mumbled flatly and slipped out of her embrace.

Elizabeth let him go, giving him the space he sought to fight his way out of his misery. He wouldn't win because he was shadow boxing and the shadows were memories of his father and their happy life. What formidable enemies!

"I know you are, sweetie." Elizabeth sat on a chair near a small table. Chris still stood, so Elizabeth began to talk. "Sometimes things happen on the spur of the moment. You try to express all that anger you've been bottling up, but . . ."

"Mom . . ." Chris rolled his eyes, his voice plaintive—and disgusted. It was a sound only a child could make and only a mother could understand. *I hate you; please love me.* But Elizabeth was so intent on what she had to say, she didn't hear what Chris needed.

"No, no. I understand. Both of us have done things we shouldn't. I haven't paid enough attention to what you were feeling. I thought if everything *seemed* normal, it *would be* normal. I'm so sorry . . ."

"Mom, stop it." Chris' voice was powerful enough to shock Elizabeth into silence. In the next minute, he mumbled, "It doesn't have anything to do with Dad or you. I just did it. I'm sorry, and I know it was wrong. Mr. Boden says I have to stay later today for detention, okay." It wasn't a question, but a defiant statement.

"Okay." Elizabeth was cautious now that he'd cut her strategy to ribbons. "I want you to write letters of apology to Mr. Boden—and Mr. Crawford, too. Was there anyone else who was doing this with you?" Chris shook his head, his eyes downcast, his hands stuffed in the pockets of his baggy jeans. "Okay, then you'll sand the words away on your own. I want you to ask Mr. Boden when you can do that. Do you understand?"

"Yes."

"Is it going to happen again?" Chris shook his head, but he hadn't yet looked her in the eye. "Well, then." Elizabeth passed her purse from one hand to another, more concerned now than she had been when she walked in. "I guess there isn't much more to say. I think you do know why you did it, but if you don't want to talk about it today, then we won't. But, Chris, one of these days we're going to have to."

Another perfunctory nod. Short but contrite enough to satisfy her. Elizabeth accepted his remorse, little though it was. Privately she breathed a sigh of relief. After all, it wasn't as if Chris had hurt anyone.

"Well," Elizabeth said quietly, "I guess I'd better get back to work. I expect to see those letters tonight."

"Yes, Mom."

"Good. I'll have to work late to make up for the time I took off to deal with this; so when you get home, start your homework immediately." She hoped she sounded strict yet forgiving. At the door, Elizabeth stopped long enough to run her hand over Christopher's hair. She bent to kiss him lightly on the cheek. He stayed still, speaking the minute her caresses stopped.

"Mom? Could I go over to David's? I mean, I hate being alone and I'd feel a lot better if I could be with someone to do my homework. Please? I hate it when you work late."

The guilt card was played and Elizabeth picked it up, assenting against her better judgment.

"Home by eight-thirty. No later." She placed her hand against his cheek, unable to resist a lingering touch. "Go to lunch now. I'll see you later tonight. We'll talk."

Chris pecked her on the cheek, running out the door before she could tell him she loved him.

Nine

Elizabeth's body ached. Every bone, every fiber, every muscle cried out for the blessed oblivion of a hot bath and a cup of tea. Funny, she hadn't realized it until just now. All afternoon, she had sat staring at her paperwork. For six hours, her eyes had been trained on forms, her ears pricked for the answers sick people were giving to her questions. And, for six hours, her subconscious mind was on everything but the work at hand.

Fighting jumbled thoughts of Chris, Max, Brad, and the world at large had exhausted and depressed her. Healing time was what she needed. Her decision to let Chris go to David's had seemed ill-advised halfway through the afternoon. Something niggled deep in her brain, and it was the thought that Christopher was in trouble. Yet, when he called, he was exactly where he had said he would be. Pulling into the drive, she could relax and be ready for Chris when he finally did come home.

The car door creaked when she opened it, and Elizabeth saw that a garage light had burned out. The house was dark and silent. Lonely looking. Lonely feeling. Amazing, even houses got tired.

Chuckling at her foolishness, Elizabeth dragged herself out of the car, put her hands on the small of her back, and stretched. Bending through the open door, she retrieved her purse. A gust of wind blew down the street, lifting her skirts before skittering on. She smiled at the little whirlwind of leaves in the street then headed to the back of the house.

Lost in thought, Elizabeth didn't see the movement near the gate until it was too late. Two, perhaps three seconds passed before the shape registered. Shadowy. A tall man. A big man. A man where he shouldn't be. He was reaching for her before she could turn, touching her before she could scream, pulling her stiffened body closer even as she tried to resist.

"I've been waiting for you," he said softly. Terror crackled through her brain, electrifying every nerve in her body before bursting into an explosion of anger and sick relief. She knew this voice. She despised this voice.

"Get away from me. I don't want you here." Elizabeth twisted sharply to the right, sliding along the side of the house, ripping away from Max's touch. Equally intent, he followed her, hands held out as if he might corral her.

"Elizabeth, what's happening? Come on." There was the high pitch of puzzlement in his voice that Elizabeth found laughable. But she couldn't laugh any more than she could cry again. Max was following her, speaking as if he were hurt. "I've been calling and calling. You can't be that busy. What's wrong?" He stepped in front of her, arms out to his sides. Elizabeth veered right, then left. "Elizabeth. Hey! What's happening? Talk to me. Is it Brad?"

"Hah!" Her laugh was a cry of anguish and disbelief—and enough to repel Max for the instant she needed to escape. She dashed around him, clutching her purse, and almost made it past him.

"Elizabeth. Stop." He caught her arm roughly, his fingers clawing at her as he tried to get a solid hold. Elizabeth tumbled out of his grasp, but his fingers caught on her purse and tangled there, jerking her back. That was Max's moment. Off balance, Elizabeth was at a disadvantage. He moved in, both hands on her shoulders. Bigger, stronger than Elizabeth remembered, Max pressed his edge. He pulled her close, pinning her to him in a vise-like hold. Trying to free herself, Elizabeth almost sobbed in frustration, but Max wouldn't let her go.

"Don't touch me. *Don't touch me!*" She finally snapped, pushing futilely against him until, exhausted, she gave in to his embrace.

"Elizabeth! Elizabeth!" Max shouted. "Stop. Stop it! What's wrong with you?"

"Me? Me?" Elizabeth pulled back, trying one last time to break his hold. She bent over, straining against a grip that couldn't be broken. Finally, giving up, she leaned away and looked him in the eye. "What's wrong with *me?*"

Astonished at her ferocity, Max relaxed his grip. Elizabeth fell back, then scurried away to a dark corner of the house. Fumbling with the strap of her purse, pulling at her jacket, she was half hysterical with fear and defeat and, God yes, desire.

"How dare you come here. How dare you!" Her voice rose with rage and shook with righteousness.

"Elizabeth," Max pleaded, his breath coming in

short bursts, too. "Please. Keep your voice down. The neighbors will call the police."

"Don't you dare tell me . . ." Elizabeth began, only to catch herself.

She was screeching, insane with the shock of finding him here. She lowered her voice, but it still shook with the madness that engulfed her. Until this moment, she hadn't realized how deep and palatable her anger was, such a different fury from the sad, ineffectual resentment she had directed toward Brad. Max Marino's betrayal burned a path of loathing straight through her gut and into her heart so that she not only hated Max, but herself as well. She had allowed need to cloud her vision; she had chosen those rose-colored glasses again. She hated her own stupidity as much as Max's treachery.

"Don't you dare tell me what to do. You have no right to even be standing here, much less to touch me or ask for an explanation."

"I have every right. I thought we were friends. I thought we might be more . . ."

"That is so rich!" Elizabeth crowed harshly. "Of course you thought we might be more. You were probably planning this from the beginning, and I was just needy enough to fall for it. How dare you! Do you think I lost all self-respect when Brad left me? Did you think I'd lost my mind? Well, I didn't. I may have closed my eyes for a minute, but they're wide open now and I see that you're the last person I need in my life."

"Okay. Okay, Elizabeth." Max circled slowly, his hands out in an expression of reconciliation. Even in the dim light Elizabeth could see his face. Damn, he was good. He almost mastered hurt the same way he had perfected bafflement. Elizabeth would have given him a round of applause if she had had the time, but all her energy was directed toward watching him, waiting for the moment he would lose his concentration, allowing her to dash for the safety of the house. Since Max was still talking, Elizabeth eyed him warily. "I don't know what this is about," he cajoled, "but believe me, whatever I did, I'm sure I can fix it. I'm sure I can explain if I've hurt you in any way. Just give me a chance."

Elizabeth drew herself to her full height, unwilling to appear weak though her knees and her heart were feeble.

"Then explain your wife."

Max stopped moving, his expression frozen, so handsome in his statuesque pose. His hands were still held out, a mendicant waiting for absolution from the sins he swore he hadn't committed. They stood in the darkened driveway, face to face, silent now, with only the last word reverberating between them. They moved at the same moment: she away and he forward. This was no longer a gentle stalking.

Max lunged. Elizabeth, catching sight of his shadowy figure out of the corner of her eye, sidestepped. But her maneuver was awkward and she half fell upon him. Surprised, he struggled nonetheless, righting them both. Energy radiated from him; anger added force and substance to his every movement.

"Don't you dare turn your back on me! Not after you've talked about my wife," he cried, struggling with her until he had her back against the rough stucco of the wall.

"There," Elizabeth cried, facing him fully, no longer afraid—not of her emotions or her heartsickness or him. Max meant nothing to her anymore, and that knowledge made Elizabeth strong and cold. She taunted him. "Happy now, Max? I'm looking right at you, Max. Now tell me how outraged you are that I found out about your wife. Tell me how you and she don't get along. Tell me about how you haven't slept together in years."

Max's hands tightened on her shoulders. He trembled, this huge and powerful man. He hurt her, yet Elizabeth was strangely immune to the pain, enthralled—instead—by what was happening to Max. He was shot through with something—anger . . . hatred . . . who knew?—but it coursed through his body and into hers until Elizabeth was on fire with a wild energy.

"Don't talk about my wife." Max's voice was ugly because of its control. No more than a whisper, it made Elizabeth freeze. Speechless and fearful, Elizabeth found the rawness of his hold unbearable. His fingers dug into muscle and bone until she had no doubt her arms would shatter. His eyes blazed, his breath hot on the cheek she now turned to him. She flinched. That Max could snap at the mere mention of his wife was frightening. Yet, though his anger was formidable, Elizabeth's bitterness was even stronger, taking on a life of its own.

"I'll talk about your wife all I please. I'll tell everyone." Elizabeth leaned back in his grasp and raised her head to the sky, her thick hair falling down her back. "Max Marino is married. Max Marino has a wife."

"Stop. Stop it now!"

He shook her and Elizabeth's head snapped forward, her blond hair streaming over her face. But she glared through that silken curtain and her voice matched his in intensity.

"A wife, Max. When were you going to tell me? Or were you just going to let the two of us run into each other at the hospital?" Elizabeth took courage in his stricken silence. Even in the autumn dark she could see his eyes wide with disbelief, a pallor creeping down his neck. She had hurt him and she was glad and wanted more. "See? See how much I know about your wife . . ."

Elizabeth's words were knocked out of her along with her breath. Max pulled her forward until they collided, chest against chest. Two tall, beautiful people in a battle of wills, and Max was winning. He silenced her with the flash in his eye and the menace in his voice.

"You know nothing about my wife," he growled. "But you're going to."

Pulling her after him, stopping only long enough to confirm that Christopher wouldn't be home any time soon, Max dragged Elizabeth over the asphalt, opened the door to the cab of his truck, and all but threw her in. He was beside her in an instant, jabbing the key into the ignition until it finally fit. The motor roared to life. Max leaned over Elizabeth without looking her in the eye and yanked the seat belt forward.

"Secure it," he muttered.

Elizabeth did as she was told, hearing the squeal of tires in unison with the click of the belt. Thrown against the door, she sat ramrod straight in the cab of the truck, not moving, barely breathing, her skirt tucked high on her thighs. She wanted to cover herself but feared moving, dreading Max's angry attention. He was a man possessed, and he was taking her to see his wife.

They drove for an eternity, careening out of Emerald Isle and onto surface streets that gave way to highway, then through a part of town Elizabeth didn't know. Block after block disappeared behind them, peppered with an odd conglomeration of small homes and businesses. Street lights illuminated Max's face, shining on his dark hair, shadowing his deep-set, wolfish eyes. The lights shone on Elizabeth, yellow and red, as the signals changed, her face a prism of color that drained her of all life, waxing her in mannequin-hues. Once she said his name, knowing he understood she was begging him to turn around, but he ignored her. Elizabeth didn't try again. Finally, the journey ended at a long, awkwardly built pink structure. Nondescript, single-storied, it sat on a patch of scruffy, unkempt grass, illuminated by two lanterns at the entrance. Max flipped the wheel, parked on a patch of asphalt, and hopped from the cab.

"Get out," he snapped. Elizabeth looked at him through the darkness. His expression had changed, but she couldn't figure out what lay behind it. She held his gaze. His eyes slipped first. His shoulders hunched as if he had been defeated by her righteousness—or wearied by it. Yet there was more to it than a change of heart. He turned and walked away, cloaked in a mystery that compelled Elizabeth to follow.

Walking behind him, watching him carefully, Elizabeth stole glimpses of her surroundings. This was not an apartment complex, duplex or home. It was not a place for families. Something else loomed behind the door of this structure, and Elizabeth didn't want to go in anymore. Sensing her wariness, Max looked over his shoulder and opened the front door.

Elizabeth pulled her jacket closer. Max stood, stiff and unbending, bathed in warm, golden light. His outstretched arm held back the heavy glass with no more effort than if he were holding back air. He stared straight ahead, as if disinterested in her. It was cold and very dark and Elizabeth wanted to stay where she was, but Max was stalwart in his silence. Head high, heart pounding, Elizabeth passed him, breathing in his scent and despairing of her loss. They would never again be close, not after tonight.

"This way," he muttered grimly and led the way.

Elizabeth stumbled as she tried to take in everything. The high desk. The low lights. The silence, too quiet for an early evening anywhere except . . .

Her eyes flicked to the first room they passed. Two women, as old as the universe, lay on beds from which they would never get up. This was a nursing home. Max's wife hadn't quit working, as Marsha thought; she had simply gone elsewhere. A woman in pink slacks and a matching tunic backed out of the door ahead. She turned, recognized Max, and greeted him brightly with a feathery whisper though nothing on earth could disturb these patients on the threshold of heaven.

Elizabeth's eyes snapped toward Max. He reached out a hand and touched the nurse's arm, nodding in acknowledgment, before walking on. This was not his wife. Curious, Elizabeth hurried after him.

He took a sudden right, and Elizabeth adjusted her course. A night nurse updated medication forms at her station. Somewhere a moan rose and fell, its echo slithering eerily down the hall. Elizabeth shivered, wanting to be gone, away from the disconcerting sounds, the horrid smells, the incredible stillness.

The nurse looked up and nodded. Too old to be Max's wife, too dour. Max loved to laugh. Max loved to make her laugh. But that was in another life. He stopped two doors down, his expression strangely fluid in the shadowy hall as if it might change shape and intent if she blinked. He held out his hand, not for support, but as a challenge.

Elizabeth paused, ready to run, but Max whispered, "Come, meet my wife, Elizabeth."

She went to him, mesmerized.

"This is Anna. My wife."

Grasping her by the shoulder, he stared hard into her eyes before turning her around. He propelled her into the room, holding her tight against him. Elizabeth resisted, burying her head against his strong shoulder. His shirt smelled of starch; his arm felt hard with muscle, and Elizabeth felt weak in the confines of this unintentional embrace. She tried to turn her face into his chest, but he put his other hand gently on her chin, his hold on her no longer tight and foreboding only sadly instructive. Having come so far, Elizabeth acquiesced. The lesson would soon be finished. She allowed Max to direct her vision, and in that instant, her heart shattered.

Alone in the room, on the hospital bed, lay a woman ageless in her suffering. Her hair was thin, nothing but gray wisps on a skull. Her skin, blue-veined and translucent, seemed to glow. Thin, plastic tubing conducted oxygen to her nose. An ugly thick hose forced down her throat supplied her with food. She couldn't breathe on her own, couldn't eat, but she lived. She was still Max's wife, but was she still a woman? Was she still a human being? The sight of Anna Marino would remain indelibly etched on Elizabeth's soul, no matter how much she might try to keep it at bay.

Leaving Max's side, she glided, as if in a dream, to Anna's bed, drawn by the pitiful drama of a vibrant life cut short too soon. She took in the claw-like hands, the shallow breathing, the lips caked and dry for lack of moisture. Death was never more inevitable, yet somehow Elizabeth knew that the end would not come quickly or mercifully.

At last, Elizabeth's eyes traveled away from the woman, her attention caught by the personal fabric of the room. An afghan crafted in many shades of blue by loving hands lay neatly folded at the foot of the bed. African violets were arranged atop a television that probably hadn't been watched in months, if not years. There was a footstool by a big chair in the corner, Max's no doubt. Magazines were neatly stacked beside it, waiting for someone to flip through them. Her personal effects lay on the table between the bed and the chair. Balm for lips that could not speak, water to soothe a throat that couldn't swallow, tissues for a hand that couldn't raise them to wipe away tears. And there were pictures.

Elizabeth reached for one, picked it up, breathed deep, and closed her eyes. When she opened them again, nothing had changed. The picture was as tragic as it had been at first sight.

The Max in the photograph was the same: virile and happy and ready to tackle life. The woman beside him, frozen in time, smiled. Her lips were small and bowed, her smile gentle and shy—as if she would have preferred all her time with Max to be private. Her forehead was broad and her chin a bit narrower, heart-shaped, perfect for someone so small and slight. Everything about her was delicate, almost fragile, except the light in her eyes. That matched Max's twinkle for twinkle. Her head was held high, her face turned toward the wind so her long, magnificent black hair streamed out behind her. She was a beautiful woman, looking confidently toward a perfect future. Now she was gone as the world had known her, as Max had loved her.

Reverently, Elizabeth put the picture back on the small table, careful to arrange it just so. She laid her fingertips on the jar of lip balm, letting them trail along the side of the table. She listened to the sounds of the place where sleep was simply a dress rehearsal for death. Elizabeth breathed in the smells that were so offensive and so much a part of Max's life. No wonder he loved working in the outdoors with the scent of dirt and cut wood and fresh air. No wonder Max was so at ease in the twilight of the day, content just to sit in Elizabeth's home and talk, listen, watch the everyday goings-on of life as if they were the most interesting things in the world.

Knowing she couldn't put it off any longer, Elizabeth turned away from the table, her back to the bed. She couldn't bear to look at this woman again; her courage failed in the face of her suffering. What she had found here made her own predicament seem petty. Elizabeth only hoped she would find the right words to apologize to Max.

But he was gone, replaced by a nurse who checked the tubes, making small talk for the dying.

"Such a shame, isn't it?"

"Yes," Elizabeth replied, surprised her voice worked. "How long . . ."

"Has she been here?" The nurse cocked an eyebrow. "Anna's an old-timer. Four years. This bad for more than a year now, but she's been sick for a long time. Multiple sclerosis is pretty sneaky. It takes a long, long time to get this bad." They watched Anna Marino in silence, and then the nurse said, "I'll leave you alone now. Stay as long as you like."

She was halfway out the door when Elizabeth called to her.

"Can she hear me?"

The lady in pink raised a hand. "Who knows? I believe she can, but then I believe in a lot of things. Even miracles sometimes. Not this time, you understand, but sometimes."

Elizabeth nodded and the nurse left her alone with Anna in her darkened room. The two women to whom Max meant the world were together at last. One unable to open her eyes and let her love shine through, the other perfectly capable of walking up to Max and letting him know how much she cared and how sorry she was.

Quickly, Elizabeth reached out. She touched the woman's curled hand. Her skin was dry and papery, skin that hadn't been caressed in so long. Elizabeth leaned down. They were two women with one purpose. She whispered, "I'll find him. I'll take care of him."

With that, Elizabeth was gone, walking quickly down the corridor, ignoring a nurse and an aide and the sounds of the sick in the night. She walked back through the community room. A lone light shone over a bar that served only milk and juice. On she went, past a fireplace meant to warm bones, not hearts. Books lined the adjacent walls, but the stories that mattered were buried in the minds of those who subsisted in the labyrinth of rooms.

Finally, Elizabeth returned to the front door. There was nowhere for Max to have gone but out. And, if he had run, if he had taken the truck and sped away, Elizabeth wouldn't blame him in the least. She would walk home; and on the long trudge back to Emerald Isle, she would commit to memory the lessons in patience and honor and faith she had been taught that night.

But Max hadn't left her in his despair. The red truck was still there, and he was standing beside it. His arms were crossed atop the cab, and his head buried in the cradle they made. He stood so quietly Elizabeth was reluctant to disturb him, thinking it was privacy he needed, not her. She saw his shoulders shake and a tremor run across his muscled back. She heard a sound and knew this was not the first time Max had cried, alone on this darkened street, in front of this horrid place that had been a part of his life for so long.

Tentatively, Elizabeth walked up to him. She slid her hands over his shoulders, and the touch was so intimate she felt guilty. She lay her cheek against his back and wrapped her arms around his waist.

"It's cold," she whispered. She suspected he couldn't hear her, but she talked anyway. Her voice would resonate, and the quiet tone might soothe him.

God, how could she ever hope to understand this? Her loss had been painless compared to this torture.

Max shuddered, then remained still. He raised his head, tipping it back to look at the autumn sky colored in shades of gray. Elizabeth could tell that he blinked back tears and wondered if he were trying to think of something to say. She held him tighter. Words weren't necessary. Releasing Max, she reached into his pocket and pulled out the keys, coaxing him, tugging on his arm. He remained still, frozen in his sorrowful stupor. She tugged again, tenderly but insistent, until Max gave in, too tired to do anything else. Elizabeth led him to the passenger side of the truck and helped him in. His long body slumped against the seat; his head fell back, and his eyes closed. Elizabeth let her eyes linger briefly on his beautiful profile, then she closed the door, her hands resting against it the way a mother might lay her hands on the blanket covering her precious child.

Elizabeth got in the driver's side and started the engine, threw the truck into reverse, and then, with the utmost care, drove Max home. Her eyes trained on the road, her mind back at the nursing home, Elizabeth's heart fully opened to Max.

"Here."

The light over the kitchen table was on; the living room was dark. Outside the French doors, the pool sparkled black and the night wind blew leaves into the undulating water, bending the branches from which they came. Inside, Max sat, chin in hand, looking at that pool, his thoughts still a mystery to Elizabeth. She would wait all night—a lifetime—for him to share his feelings if she had to.

"Here," she said again and took his hand, pressing the glass into it. Without looking, he wrapped his fingers around it and held tight, but he let it rest atop his thigh instead of drinking. Elizabeth settled herself on the ottoman, close enough to reach him, far enough away to give him space. She glanced at the clock on the mantel, marveling at how little time had passed. Fifteen minutes on the freeway, no more than ten in that horrid room, fifteen minutes back. Christopher would be home at eight-thirty. There was time for the two of them now, adults facing adult problems. Max had shown her there was a life to be lived when he found her in the park. Perhaps she could return the favor now.

"I'm sorry," Max said, his voice cracking. He sounded old and looked worn in the half light. He cleared his throat and raised his eyes for the first time since leaving his wife's side. But his gaze was weary; it seemed a struggle for him to focus.

"There's nothing to be sorry for, Max," Elizabeth whispered, resisting the urge to touch and reassure him.

"I don't usually . . . I mean I feel awful that I brought you there . . ." Elizabeth remained silent as he grappled with dreams and reality, desire and truth. His words were jumbled, the feelings in his heart the same. He passed his hand over his eyes, rubbing away the appalling visions that still lay in his mind. "I'm sorry for you." He sighed. "You didn't need to see her. I'm sorry for Anna. I never meant to use her."

Elizabeth was on her knees in front of him, her

hands on either side of the chair, caging him. She burned with a desire to do—something. But what was it he needed? Her sympathy? Her logic? Elizabeth ignored every possibility and opened her heart. She would listen, stay close, and offer comfort.

"Max, you didn't use her. Don't ever think that." Elizabeth reassured him. "You wanted to show me because there was no other way for me to understand. I've been an idiot. I should have talked to you."

"God." His head swiveled, but it was a movement that seemed to take great effort. The eyes he turned on her were tragic and helpless. "I needed you, and I knew I shouldn't. I felt things for you . . . It was so wrong, but I couldn't help myself. You were there, alone. We talked . . ." Max took a long drink and put the glass on the table in front of him. She waited patiently for him to gather his thoughts. "I wanted to tell you how I felt, but Jesus, Elizabeth, I don't know how to explain it. That first day when you almost ran my man over, I was just mad. But when I saw you, and saw how sad you were, you reminded me of Anna. Then, in a weird way, you didn't. I don't know . . . I kept coming back to you because I wanted you to smile. Then you smiled, and I wanted to touch you. But I'm married. I'm married and I'm not. I'm busy all the time, but I'm so lonely. I need . . ."

Max rested his elbows on his knees and covered his face with his hands, drawing them down as if to rub away the cobwebs in his mind. "I don't know what I need or what I want to say. I just know that it felt right to talk to you and see you. I didn't care about your husband. I just wanted to know you smiling, not crying. I'd been watching Anna the way she is for so long, I wanted a woman I admired to smile at me. To touch me. To talk—to care." Max's hands dropped. He had worked hard to put his emotions into words, and now he was tired. "I don't know anything anymore."

There was a heartbeat of silence. Elizabeth stayed her hand, her mind alive with the implications of what he was saying, her emotions electrified by his admissions. She, too, felt whole in his presence although there was no explanation for it. She, too, needed to talk with him and no one else. Now she understood why.

They both needed a port in the storm where questions weren't asked and circumstances were accepted with grace and courage. That had brought them together; that would keep them together. If only she hadn't been so self-absorbed. If only she had cared enough to draw him out instead of filling him up with her own sorrows.

Max, lost in thought, suddenly moved. He rubbed his legs and pushed himself off his chair. For a long while he stood, hands by his side, his head turned to look out the windows as he considered the matters of his heart.

"I . . . should have told you. I'm . . ."

The sound of his words dissipated until they heard nothing more than the sighing of the wind. He inhaled, and the whisper of his breath followed his words into nothingness. Without another sound, Max stepped between the chair and the ottoman, heading toward the door. But Elizabeth couldn't let him go. It was just Max and her in this darkened house. There were things that needed to be done, gestures that needed to be offered, and words that had to be said. Not everything would happen that night, but something could, and must, take place.

As he passed her, Elizabeth reached up, her fingertips grazing his. It was barely a touch, but more than enough to make Max pause. He still stood in profile, looking toward the door, the way out of Elizabeth's life. Elizabeth still sat on the ottoman, her eyes boring through the opposite wall. She dared not look, fearing he would see what she desired and how uncertain she was of those feelings.

Elizabeth reached once again. This time their fingertips met and the touch lingered. She inched her hand upward, slipping it into Max's. His hand closed over hers, hesitated, then held tight. It was enough. Elizabeth's eyes fluttered shut. This was so right. Brad was gone from her life; in that instant he was gone from her heart and her mind. Max was whom she cared for; Max was whom she would take care of.

While he held her, one hand connecting two hearts, Elizabeth stood, her skirt rustling, her heart beating. Her free hand slid across his middle, stopping when it cupped his hip. Max breathed deep. Elizabeth kept her eyes averted.

For the longest time, an eternity in Elizabeth's mind, they stood that way. Holding hands, her arm wrapped protectively around him. She thought they might not move until morning light streamed through the French doors, but Max wouldn't let the night go so easily. He stirred, moving one step so that they faced each other, urging Elizabeth's hand to his back.

He looked down at her. She raised her eyes. What he thought when he looked at her, Elizabeth would never know. Soon they weren't looking at one another at all. They moved together, neither knowing who was the first. Max held her, his arm coming around her waist, their entwined hands falling to the side as they swayed slowly, dancing to music that didn't play, hearing a beat of their own making. Max turned her, Elizabeth melting easily into him. Slowly, slowly, slowly, they made their way around the room, the heat of their bodies rising with each passing moment, the memory of Anna sealed away in private places.

It was Elizabeth who touched first. Her fingers trailed to the top of his jeans, lingering on the worn leather of his belt. Max drew her closer. This had been so long in coming, this love he had longed for. Elizabeth let her fingers roam further, over his hips and down the side of his leg. Her head was laid against his broad chest, her eyes closed. It had been so long since she had touched a man, been close this way to another human being. In the center of whatever it was that made her Elizabeth, there was an opening, a brightness that radiated from it.

It was her soul, Elizabeth was sure, breaking free of pain and hurt, flying toward Max. She wanted him in all the ways a woman could want a man. She wanted to feel his flesh, hear his voice, drink in every word he chose to say to her. Elizabeth wanted so much more than she had ever asked from Brad, and it terrified her that Max might not be able to give it. Those things had been given to Anna. Perhaps they had been used up.

In the next instant, the fear was gone. Max stopped dancing. They stood still in the dark, listening to their matched breathing. Their anticipation was perceptible.

Their desire stood with them, only to be banished by word and deed. Words came first. Half sentences, mumbled syllables. Both of them whispering as if they might wake a passion that couldn't be controlled if they spoke louder. They moved. Max's hands roamed over her back, cupped her chin, pulled her face up toward him until hungry, needy lips met hers. And those lips were everything Elizabeth knew they would be: full and warm, giving and taking all at the same time. They came down on her roughly at first, as if he might lose her if the first strike weren't swift and sure. And, as his arms tightened, sure of her now, his kiss gentled.

Elizabeth, electrified, could do nothing but lie in his arms and experience the intensity of that moment. The strength she had gained in the last lonely months flowed from her like water from a crumbling dam. Max had reached through her barriers with his kindness then destroyed the wall with this one kiss. This was Elizabeth's nature: to belong, to love, to share of herself. Rejoicing, she gave to him without thought for any consequence to her heart. He was a good man; she a good woman. This was right, and no one could say it wasn't.

"Elizabeth," Max whispered, pulling away from her just long enough to touch her face, push back her hair, convince himself that she was real and had no regrets.

Elizabeth gazed at him, her eyes bright with need and want and love. Yes, it was love. Max had been satisfied with the little she'd given him until now. He had asked nothing of her; Elizabeth had cherished that kindness. He had listened; Elizabeth had been grateful.

He made her laugh; she adored him for that. What else could this be but love?

"Elizabeth," he said again, and the sound of his voice fanned the flames inside her.

"Shhh. No words," she answered breathlessly. "Shhh."

And as she shushed him, as her eyes held his, their hands began their work. She touched his throat where his shirt opened, revealing fine swirls of dark hair. She felt his hand on the back of her neck, warm and sure, his fingers slipping over her shoulders. The buttons of his shirt opened, Elizabeth pushed the fabric aside, her quick hand running over his naked body. Max ran his own over her shoulders, feeling the outline of her body through her clothes, pulling up on the full skirt of her dress so that the cool air nipped at her thighs through her stockings.

On and on they went, a button here, a snap undone there, baring flesh by inches. Their lips met the exquisite tracts, sometimes with reverence, other times with desperation. But when Max's lips trailed down Elizabeth's neck, she called a halt with her touch. Her fingers tipped his chin. Without a word between them, they knew that this was the time, but not the place.

Elizabeth's eyes flitted to the clock. She laced her arm around Max's waist, laying her cheek against his bare chest, her arm covered by the shirt that now fell loosely about his beautiful body. Together they walked slowly up the stairs, so close as to be one. Elizabeth turned at the landing, and Max went with her as if he had walked this way every night of his life.

Neither bothered with the lights; they stood only inches from one another when they parted. Eyes roaming, hungry to record each gesture, they undressed. He dropped his shirt. She peeled away her dress until she stood tall and strong and nearly nude. Max slipped out of his jeans, kicking them away, naked underneath. He went to Elizabeth, and at that moment, she thought twice then discarded any thought of Brad or Anna with the rest of her clothes. Max's lips kissed the crook of her neck as his hands found the snap of her bra. He kissed the side of her cheek and let his tongue roam over her ear as she stepped out of her panties.

Elizabeth moved into him, pressing her body against his, matching his height but feeling delicate and fragile against the breadth of his chest. Her pulse quickened, and his hardness became insistent. Slowly, he lifted her. Holding her even closer, if that were possible, he took her to the bed. There would be no waiting now. Their long vigils alone were at an end. And when Max rolled atop her, when Elizabeth's arms opened to hold him and her legs to receive him, she prayed that these feelings between them would never end.

On and on they went, loving and touching, stroking and pleasing. Time slipped away and neither of them noticed. When Elizabeth heard the door open, when her mother's ear pricked to the sound of her son, she stole away from a sleeping Max and into her robe. By the time she got downstairs, Christopher had turned on the lights and had his head buried in the refrigerator.

"Hi," Elizabeth said, her voice sounding far too sultry, her cheeks burning far too bright.

"Hi." Christopher stood up, his head above the

fridge door, concentrating on the fare inside instead of her.

"Did you have fun?"

"Sure. Always, Mom."

"Good." Elizabeth moved toward the stove. "Did you have dinner at David's? Can I fix you something? Did you get your homework done?"

"Sure, Mom, everything's cool. Don't worry. I got it all done. I finished detention. I didn't get into any more trouble."

"Christopher," Elizabeth admonished softly, the flush in her cheeks diminishing from a stain of pleasure to one of embarrassment. "I didn't expect you to. Here." She walked into the kitchen and took the milk. Her back to him, she poured a glass and talked, wishing she had taken time to put on her jeans, run a brush through her long, love-tousled hair. She handed him the full glass, then sat at the kitchen table. "Come, sit with me."

Christopher was already turned away, but he thought better of leaving. Maybe he even wanted to do as she asked. He sat down.

"Chris," Elizabeth began, concentrating on her entwined fingers, "Max is here."

Christopher nodded. "His car's out front." He took a long drink of milk, a child's equivalent of drowning his sorrows. Elizabeth took a deep breath and tried again.

"He's upstairs, Chris."

"Mom," he objected, looking at her with an exasperated expression. "I know that. I've got friends whose parents do that. I mean, with other people. I know."

"Well, I just thought maybe we should talk about it. I don't want you to think this is—" Elizabeth searched for a word that would sound convincing to a ten-year-old. There wasn't a good one. "I don't want you to think this is casual. I've known Max for a while. He's been so good to us. He has his problems like we do . . ."

Christopher popped up. He pushed the glass away and picked up the backpack he'd dropped in the doorway.

"Mom. It's okay. It's none of my business."

Elizabeth followed suit, catching him before he left the room, putting her hand on his arm.

"Of course, it's your business. You and I are the family here. Someday we may find someone we want to be a part of us. It's not just about me; it's about you, too."

Christopher eyed her, and it was obvious he wasn't oblivious to the changes that had come over her that night. He saw her brighter smile and the softening in her eyes, heard the difference in her voice.

"Yeah, Mom, it's about me, too. All this has always been about me, too. First you, then me."

"Christopher, it is," Elizabeth insisted, her voice harder now. The least he could do was try to understand.

"Is it about Dad, too?" he demanded, his young eyes defiant, daring her to answer that question honestly.

"It can't be," she answered truthfully. "Daddy isn't here. He hasn't tried to come back to us. I've tried to find him, but he seems to have dropped off the face of the earth. So now, we move forward. I'm lucky to have Max as my friend."

Christopher rolled his eyes and Elizabeth's anger flared. How dare he diminish the joy she had just experienced? If he wanted to be so grown up, then she'd treat him that way. "And my lover, Christopher. That's what adults call it. Love happens in many different ways. It happens when two people need each other. Max and I need one another. It happens when people respect and like each other. If you want to roll your eyes and act like you know everything, then I want you to have the right information."

Elizabeth straightened, suddenly aware she had leaned into Christopher. How menacing she must seem, how defensive, and all she wanted him to do was understand, accept, and maybe even be happy for her and try to like Max.

"I'm sorry, honey," she said. "I found out some things about Max tonight that are very sad. He's hurting as much, maybe more, than we are. He's married—I think you should know that—but tonight I saw his wife. She's very sick. She doesn't speak or walk or move. She just lies in a bed waiting to die." Elizabeth saw an unexpected parallel in their lives.

"For a long while after your father left this house," she continued, "that's what I wanted to do, too. But I'm not sick. I was only hurt. Max helped me get over the hurt. I want to help him back. Do you understand that? Can you understand?"

Christopher looked at his mother. He saw how beautiful she was. No wonder men wanted to be around her. But she was his mom, and he wanted her with his dad even though he knew that wasn't going to happen.

But he nodded, and his reward was to see her smile.

Not a big smile. He knew she was afraid he would change his mind, so her smile was small; but it was just for him. He tried really hard to be a good kid. When his mom reached out and touched the back of his neck, pulling him to her so she could kiss the top of his head, he racked his brain for something that he could say to make her like him more and make the always-angry feelings inside him go away. But it wasn't until they started climbing the stairs, until he was almost at the top, that he had a brainstorm.

"I like Max, Mom."

Elizabeth stopped mid-stride, stifling the grin that was desperate to plant itself on her face.

"I'm glad, honey. That means a lot to me."

Christopher nodded. That was as much diplomacy as he could muster. He turned one way toward his room, she toward hers. Max was in his father's bed, where Chris had slept between his parents when he was little. He wouldn't be going into that room for a while. Not for a long, long while.

Looking back over his shoulder, he saw Elizabeth watching him, a strange expression on her face, as if she expected him to do something. But there wasn't anything he could think to do, so he walked into his room and shut the door.

Ten

"I told you, I can't go today. My mom wants me to stop by the store and pick up some stuff on my way home."

"So, go after," David whined, and Christopher rolled his eyes. David was starting to sound like a girl. Always complaining when things didn't go his way. Christopher was getting tired of David's hounding him. It wasn't like all there was to do was baby-sit him. David tugged at Christopher's sweatshirt, danced around him, punched his shoulder. Christopher pulled away and hitched his backpack higher. "Come on, meet me after school."

"Naw, I'm just going to get the stuff and go home. I got homework anyway. Mrs. Ferguson piles it on just before Thanksgiving. She says it gives us something to be thankful for during the holidays when we don't have any."

"Yeah, she's a jerk," David agreed.

"How would you know? You don't even bother to go to school half the time."

David shrugged and stuck his hands in his pockets. Christopher noticed the hole in David's sneaker, but didn't say anything. David was funny about stuff like that. He didn't like to talk about his mom, either, and he didn't like to go home since she had found that new guy who rode the motorcycle. So David hung out at the park a lot again. But now Chris had stuff to do and . . .

"Christopher. Chris, come on, honey. We have to go!"

David looked over his shoulder and grinned. Sort of. He waved. Sort of. David didn't like parents. From the look on Elizabeth's face, Chris could tell that the feeling wasn't exactly mutual, but it was close.

"I gotta go," Chris said, shuffling a bit, not wanting David to think he jumped every time his mom called—even though he was doing it a lot. Still, he felt better lately.

"Yeah." Resigned, David pushed his long hair out of the way. He squinted toward Chris' house. He jerked his thumb. "That guy's still around? Jeez, this a serious thing."

It was Chris' turn to shrug now. The two of them had shoulders that went up and down more often than horses on a merry-go-round.

"He's okay."

"Yeah, but watch out. They change when they get married. If he's going to be your new dad, it'll be weird. I've had two fake dads and my real one. I know about stuff like this."

"I know. You told me." Chris hitched his backpack higher. He didn't want to hear about the weird guys David's mother had had around. His mom wasn't like David's mom. His mom was a good mom and real careful about serious stuff. "Max is okay."

There, he'd said it. And he'd meant it. Max was pretty cool. He'd helped Chris with his math the other day. That was something. Max wasn't just a dumb construction worker. He'd even taken Chris for pizza when Elizabeth had had to work late.

"Aw, I always thought that at first, too. But just wait. They always do something. Always something. Then they make you feel like a real jerk, like you don't even belong in your own house." David considered Max. He watched as the tall, dark-haired man talked to Chris' mom. He watched Max touch her face, lean to kiss her. He saw Max smile. David looked back at Chris. "They always do something. Don't let him fool you, Chris."

"Don't worry about me. I'll see you this weekend, maybe. Unless you're going away for Thanksgiving."

David laughed. "Right. We're going to Aunt Jane's and have a big turkey with all the cousins. Then we're going to sit around the fire and eat pumpkin pie." David laughed so hard it made Christopher sad. Finally finished, David threw a fake punch. "Naw. I'll be here. You might be the one sitting around doing the family thing."

"Maybe. I'll still see you anyway. Maybe you could come here for turkey."

"Maybe. Ask your mom if you want. I could probably come." David tossed his head back. He tried to make it look like he didn't care, but Christopher knew him pretty well by now. He'd come if he were asked.

"Okay. I'll ask. Want a ride to school?"

David shook his head, "Gotta pick up my stuff at home."

"Okay, I'll see ya."

"Yeah, see ya."

David turned one way, Christopher the other. David

was halfway down the block, but Chris was still standing in the same place, looking at his mom, wondering what she was saying to Max while she tried hard not to grin.

"Why don't you just drop Chris off and come back home? My guys are framing today. They could do that in their sleep. All I need to do is check in."

Max smiled at her and Elizabeth almost—almost—gave more than passing consideration to his proposition.

"And if I said *yes,* you'd change your story in an instant. We'd end up in bed and then you'd start worrying if the nails were going in straight," Elizabeth teased him, feeling alive and wonderful and wanted.

"And you'd be having double guilt feelings about skipping out on work." Max sighed. "We're hopeless."

"No way. We're hopelessly romantic and incredibly responsible. That's pretty marvelous if you ask me." Elizabeth tiptoed and kissed his cheek. Not satisfied, she tiptoed up again and kissed him on the lips. Max's arms encircled her. He pulled her against him, adoring the feel of her smile against his lips.

"You're pretty marvelous," he whispered just as Betsy came out from her house next door and, with a great deal of fussing and noise, hurried her children to her car. Elizabeth looked over her shoulder, still cradled in Max's arms. The two women eyed one another. Betsy was not happy. Any display of affection in the driveway of the house next door was definitely unseemly. Elizabeth slipped out of Max's arms, understanding Betsy's feelings completely. She would have hated to have seen so much love and affection with nothing that could compare to it in her own home.

"You look like you're thinking evil thoughts, Elizabeth."

Max ran his hand down her back. She smirked.

"No, not evil at all. I'm just thinking how jealous everyone must be when they see you kissing me this way."

"Maybe they're thinking you're a fallen woman. Not yet divorced, shacking up with a married man."

"They don't know you're married. Besides, you're a man who has suffered alone for a very long time," Elizabeth reminded him with a touch of her finger to his lips. "And I'm a woman who can't be considered married because there is no way she can love, honor, and obey a husband who no longer exists."

"But . . ." Max began.

"No buts," Elizabeth shushed. "Remember? We promised not to do that. We've been so happy together. I'm not going to lose it or beat it into the ground wondering if our poor souls are going to be damned to hell for having this happiness when the rest of our world has fallen down around our ears."

"Well, somebody is trying to watch out for your soul. How many of those notes do you have now?" Max asked seriously.

"Six," she said dryly. "Six lovely reminders that you and I are living in sin, committing adultery, etc., etc., etc."

Elizabeth's brow clouded. As much as she denied it, these odd messages—left on her doorstep, attached to her car, buried in her morning paper—hurt. They did make her wonder if she were being selfish or if she were truly simply moving on with her life. But one look from Max, one touch, and she realized they couldn't possibly be doing anything wrong. Whoever was writing these notes was sick. Whoever was writing these notes had no idea what being alone felt like.

"Hey, sorry." Max tipped her chin up, forcing her to look at his glorious smile. "I shouldn't have brought it up. It's just that it's been on my mind."

"Mine, too. But I talked to the police and they said there's nothing they can do short of posting an officer outside the door and waiting to see who leaves them. Needless to say," Elizabeth laughed, "that doesn't seem to be a serious option."

"Now, why doesn't that surprise me?" Max laughed, too, loving her. "Have I told you today that I adore you?"

Elizabeth shook her head, grinning, her lips tilted up and her eyes closed, dying for one last kiss. Max obliged.

"I do love you, you know," he said quietly.

"And I love you," she whispered back, oblivious to everything around her.

"Mom!"

Christopher was at the door of the car, and Elizabeth laughed. She hadn't even seen him walk by. Courting was a tad different when you had a huge bunch of a boy watching your every move. She smiled, so grateful that peace had been made between Chris and Max.

"All right. Sorry. I didn't see you there." And to Max, she added, "I'm afraid the day must begin."

"I won't see you tonight, remember?"

"Of course," she assured him. "It's Anna's night. Are you going to pick up Maria?" Elizabeth referred easily to Max's mother-in-law, and he nodded. "Did you ask her to join us for Thanksgiving dinner tomorrow? I'd really love to have a chance to get to know her. She's alone too much."

"I asked her," Max replied, but Maria Lopez would not come to Elizabeth's house. "She hasn't been in the mood for Thanksgiving celebrations for years. Not that I can blame her. It has to be hard watching a daughter die."

"As hard as watching a wife," Elizabeth said quietly as she passed him. Then more brightly, refusing to let a black mood start the day, she said, "But when you see her, tell her she is truly welcome."

"I will, but I don't think it will do any good. I've got to go. See you later." One more kiss. One more touch. They went their separate ways. Elizabeth backed out of the driveway first, waved, and headed toward Christopher's school, her mind now on her son and the conversation she had been avoiding.

"Got everything?" she asked. "That extra spelling work you did?"

"Yep."

"Your lunch?"

"Uh-huh."

"The permission slip for the field trip?"

"Mom, give me some credit."

Elizabeth cocked her head and fell silent. It was time.

"Okay, you're right. You deserve a lot of credit, and you deserve to know exactly what's going on in my life because it affects yours." A heavy silence hung between them. "Christopher, I've contacted a lawyer.

I'm going to file for divorce, because it's time I was free of your father."

Christopher, mute with surprise, didn't look at his mother. He didn't breathe. He had never thought it would come to this. Never, ever, ever.

Damn Max.

"It's Thanksgiving. Who would do this on Thanksgiving Day? I thought today would be so wonderful," Elizabeth moaned.

"It still can be. Come on, honey, let's forget about it and just settle down for a nice afternoon. Christopher and his friend won't be here for another twenty minutes. We'll have a drink; we'll put this one with the others and deal with it tomorrow. I'll go to the police station with you."

Max tried to slip the sheet of paper out of Elizabeth's hands, but she yanked it back, out of his reach.

"No, I want to look at it. I want to hold it. I want to see if I can feel the kind of idiot who would do something like this. Look! Look! A dagger through a heart. Not even a very good drawing at that. This is such nonsense, Max. I don't know anyone well enough to have them hate me this much."

Max laughed ruefully. "Don't look at me. The last enemy I made was Billy Horton in sixth grade. He slashed my bike tires because I beat him in the handball championship. He was such a sore loser."

"Max, come on!" Elizabeth wailed. "This is serious. I can't go on like this, wondering if every morning when I pick up the newspaper I'm going to find another one of these notes tacked somewhere. And on Thanksgiving Day, no less. That's really rotten."

"Okay, I'm sorry." He slid next to her on the sofa and took the paper away. This time she let him have it. Watching dejectedly, Elizabeth was about to rail again when they were interrupted.

"Knock! Knock!" Before Max could say another word, Leslie's cheery voice rang out from the entry. "Hope you two are decent," she sang, laughing until she saw Max and Elizabeth sitting side by side looking like they'd lost their best friend.

"This really looks like a fun party. Maybe I should have just stayed home. What's with you two?"

Max waved the paper. There was no need to say more. Leslie walked across the living room, sat next to Max, and took the note, studying it for a minute before reading aloud.

" 'You are married. You are a bad woman.' " Leslie gave her companions a wry look. "Well now, there's a bit of creative writing for you. Come on, Elizabeth, push that vest aside. Let me see your scarlet A."

"Leslie, this isn't funny anymore," Elizabeth complained and pushed herself off the sofa, irritated by the stream of harassing notes. "Did you bring that JELL-O salad you were going to make?"

"It's in the white bag. Watch out, though; there's a bottle of wine in there, too, so it's heavy," Leslie warned absentmindedly.

"I think I'll pop the wine and forget the JELL-O," Elizabeth groused as she picked up Leslie's contribution to Thanksgiving dinner. It would hardly be as jovial as she had expected.

"I'll have a glass, too," Leslie called as Elizabeth

disappeared into the kitchen. When she was gone, Leslie asked Max, "So, what do you think?"

Max shook his head. "I don't know what to think. It's pretty weird, but I doubt there's anything to worry about. These notes aren't actually threatening, and I just don't get the feeling that whoever's writing them is a real bad guy. What do you think?"

"It doesn't matter one bit what I think. The only thing that matters is that Elizabeth is scared. She wasn't at first, but now we can't have a conversation without the subject coming up." Leslie called out Elizabeth's name. Her head poked out of the kitchen door, her expression no more uplifting than it had been when she'd left the room. "Are you scared of whoever is doing this?"

Elizabeth came out of the kitchen, thoughtful, a towel in her hand, her brow furrowed. She shook her head.

"No. I honestly don't think I am. I'm annoyed, peeved, ticked off, miserable; but I'm not afraid. No, I'm not afraid," she decided. "There's something about the way they're written that makes me think of . . ."

"A kid," Max finished for her with a snap of his fingers, delighted with his assessment. "That's it. These things look like they were written by a kid. The spelling isn't all that great, and the printing could use some help. Maybe what we've got here is just a kid's prank. You know how the neighbors are. They're nosy and self-righteous. Maybe someone's kid overheard something. Or—" He paused, reluctantly. "—it could be closer to home."

"Oh, Max," Elizabeth breathed, joining the other two in the living room again. She sat down on the edge of the chair as Leslie reclaimed her seat next to Max. "Leslie, you don't think . . ."

Leslie threw up her hands and leaned back, effectively taking herself out of the discussion.

"No," Elizabeth said adamantly. "No. I won't believe Christopher has anything to do with this. Absolutely not."

"He wasn't really happy when I started coming around," Max reminded her.

"And that was months ago," she shot back. "He's really improved where you're concerned. When you asked him to go with you to check out the foundations and the framing at the new development, he could have burst with pride. I know Christopher. He wouldn't have gone with you unless he really wanted to." Elizabeth looked from one noncommittal face to another, amazed they were even having this conversation. "And what about the two of you sitting up and watching that horrid movie the other night—the one with the robot cop? What about that?" Elizabeth shook her head and stood up. "You're wrong to even think what you're thinking. Totally wrong."

"He may have been coming around, but that was before you filed for a divorce. Even you've noticed how he's cooled off since then," Max reminded her. "He could have something to do with this."

"Do with what?"

Three adult heads snapped toward the sound. Christopher stood in the small hall between the kitchen and the living room. Behind him, lounging against the wall, his shorts and t-shirt hardly the costume for Thanksgiving dinner, was David. David, the bane of Elizabeth's motherly existence, a friend she would rather see Christopher do without. Unfortunately, he was a fact of life; and his surly young face made her wonder, if only for a fleeting moment, whether or not Leslie and Max might be on to something.

"Nothing," Elizabeth said tightly.

"We wondered if you knew who might have something to do with this." Max stood up, the paper in his hand. He glanced at Elizabeth. She half turned from him, unable to fully endorse his actions, but unable to stop his questioning either.

Christopher walked into the room, almost sauntering. He wasn't stupid. He knew what it meant when a bunch of adults sat around with long faces, looking like everything in the world was bad. It meant trouble for a kid, and he was the only kid who lived in this house. Slowly, he took the sheet of paper, held it between his hands, and read while he moved his lips. He read it again. This time, David moved up, hands stuffed deep in his pockets, and looked over Christopher's shoulder.

"You think I did this?"

Surprisingly, Christopher's eyes were on Max, not his mother. His hurt and indignation were real and cut the two women to the core to watch. First, Brad had thrown his son away; now, the man who had stepped in to take his father's place, who had treated him as a friend, was asking—no, accusing—him of this bit of nastiness.

"I didn't say I thought you did it, Chris," Max said, his voice even, his eyes steady. "We're trying to figure out why your mom's been getting these notes."

"I didn't know she was getting stuff like this. I didn't even know it."

Chris looked at Elizabeth. She looked back but didn't go to him. His body language said it all. She had screwed up—again. Just when everything was going so well—Christopher accepting Max, getting back into the swing of things with school—this had to happen.

"I've gotten seven of them counting this one, honey. I didn't want to tell you because I didn't want to worry you. And Max isn't saying you did it." She smiled at Max weakly, an unspoken question in that expression, but she turned back to Christopher without waiting to see if she were lying to her son. "Max and Leslie and I were just trying to figure out who might be responsible or who might know something. We thought it looked like a child had written this, so naturally we thought we'd ask you."

Christopher's eyes darted from one adult to the other. He looked back at David, who didn't flinch. But something passed between them. Elizabeth noted it in a narrowing of their eyes, a drawing together that was so subtle only a mother could be aware of it.

"I never saw it, and David never saw it. We didn't write this stuff. I wouldn't, Mom," Christopher said flatly.

A tremor ran down Elizabeth's spine. It had more to do with foreboding than relief. All their hard work coming to grips with Brad's desertion, Elizabeth's efforts and Max's appearance, seemed to have been nullified in these last few minutes. There was such resentment in Christopher's eyes that Elizabeth could hardly bear to look at him.

"Well, that's that." It was Leslie who decided to lighten the mood and break the thread of tension that was stitching them all together so uncomfortably. She left the couch and headed toward the kitchen, lacing her arms around the boys' shoulders as she went. "Come on, you two. Let's see if we can't hurry that turkey along. It smells great, doesn't it?"

She turned them around and was gone before Elizabeth could move. When she finally did, she went into Max's arms.

"I'm sorry, sweetheart," he whispered, wrapping her as tight as he could. "I didn't see him standing there."

Elizabeth shook her head against his chest. "It's not your fault, just bad timing. But I can't blame him for feeling the way he does. We weren't very subtle, were we?"

Max held her away, brushing at her hair, not because it was out of place, but because he loved the feel of it.

"Do you think I did any lasting damage? I mean, I don't have any kids. I might have scarred him for life."

Elizabeth smiled, but remained unamused. "I don't think you could have damaged that poor little heart any more than Brad and I have. He'll get over this. He'll remember, but he'll get over it. Tonight, I'll explain it again. We were just speculating, that's all."

"That's all it really was," Max said quietly as he pulled her close again, trying to reassure her as much as himself. "I have so much to be thankful for here. You and Chris and the warmth of this home. I wouldn't do anything to hurt either of you. You've got to know that."

"Oh, I do. I do, Max," Elizabeth said and found herself kissing him before she had even thought to do so.

"Excuse me, you two." Leslie cleared her throat and

gave them a wry look when they parted. "The chick has flown the coop."

"What?" Elizabeth asked.

"Christopher. He took off. He said not to wait dinner for him. I thought you should know."

Elizabeth blinked then turned back to Max. She let her forehead fall against his chest. His arms encircled her loosely, and his chin rested atop her head. Raising his eyes, he looked at Leslie.

"I think we should open the wine now."

"I think that's a fine idea," Leslie agreed.

Eleven

"Christopher! Now!"

Elizabeth rushed around the kitchen. Dishes from the night before still sat in the sink. Dog-tired when she'd gotten home from work, Elizabeth had had to deal with Christopher's report card the evening before. It hadn't been a happy discussion, but it was no excuse for not doing the dishes. One of these days, she was going to post a list of acceptable excuses for not keeping one's life in line on the refrigerator door for reference. Topping the list would be Max. He was most definitely an acceptable excuse for forgetting almost anything. But Elizabeth didn't even have that to fall back on.

Max hadn't been around the last few days, needing to concentrate on his work as much as she had to repair the damage done to Chris on Thanksgiving Day. She hoped he was making more progress than she. As much as Elizabeth aspired to mom-perfection, there wasn't time for insightful conversation when morning meant school and work and a sullen son who needed hours, not minutes, of conversation.

"Chris! Ugh!" Elizabeth turned, two dishes in her hand, her mouth open to call one more time, when she bumped right into him. She stopped, looked at him, then smiled. There was time for that. "I swear you grow overnight. We're going to have to get you some new clothes soon." Elizabeth eyed his shoes, his shirt. Both were worn and too small.

"I don't need anything," Chris mumbled, moving out of her way as if she had the plague.

"Well, I say you do," she said brightly, determined to make up for what he considered a condemnation, her lack of faith, her choice of Max over him. She flipped open the dishwasher and kept her tone light. "Not today, though. I've got to run. Grab your back-pack and hop in the car. Maybe we can make a date tonight. What do you say? We can hit the mall and have dinner at the food court."

"It's okay. You don't even have to drive me to school. I told David I'd go with him. I'm going to meet him over by the park. We'll walk to school." Christopher opened the refrigerator, grabbed a carton of milk, and drank from it. When he closed the door, he looked directly at Elizabeth.

She remained silent while another check-list went through her mind. This one listed the new habits Eliza-beth wished Christopher would get rid of: eating food from the cartons, slouching, long hair, baggy clothing, unfinished homework, and hanging around with David to the exclusion of her and their home. She almost mentioned one or two of these particular items, then realized that all the discussions they'd had since Thanksgiving had gotten her nowhere. Better she sim-ply weather the storm, and keep her mouth shut. Un-less Chris was in danger, she would let him make his own mistakes.

"Are you sure you can make it by the first bell?"

Her voice wasn't as polished as before, but Elizabeth was satisfied she sounded normal. Christopher nodded, picked up an apple, slung his backpack over his shoulder, and started to leave the kitchen. "Hey, aren't you forgetting something?"

Elizabeth grinned while her heart cracked into a zillion pieces. *Kiss me,* she wanted to remind him. *Right here on this cheek the way you've done every day since you learned what a kiss was.* But he looked at her blankly, almost sadly.

"Nope. I've got everything," he said flatly, and went out the door. Elizabeth smiled sadly, preferring to believe his polite petulance had more to do with the fact that he was on a downhill slide toward eleven.

Putting the last of the plates in the dishwasher, Elizabeth checked her watch, realized she was really late now, and left without bothering to eat. The phone rang the minute the front door closed behind her. Fumbling with her car keys, Elizabeth listened to it ring once, then twice. She opened the car door. The phone rang a third time. She had a leg inside when the fourth ring sounded. By the fifth, she felt a chill and trembled as it ran straight up her spine.

Abandoning the car, heedless of the time and driven by the insistent ringing of the phone, Elizabeth rushed back to the house. Her premonition extended no further than a sense of impending doom. There was no clear vision of what was to come, but it was Elizabeth who was being called by the harbinger of disaster.

Flinging open the door, she caught her heel on the rise and stumbled, managing to reach the phone before the caller hung up.

"Hello? Hello! Wait . . ."

The answering machine clicked on at the last second, and she had to listen to the interminable sound of her own cheery voice announcing that she wasn't there. Elizabeth listened for the beep, then spoke more calmly.

"Hello, I'm sorry to have kept you waiting."

"That's perfectly all right," came a voice Elizabeth didn't know. Cool and civilized, that voice kept Elizabeth's chill of apprehension on ice. "May I speak to Mr. Marino, please?"

Elizabeth caught her breath. Nothing more than work, and she had almost killed herself to answer the call.

"He's not here. Can I take a message?" Elizabeth asked, worried now about the hour.

"I'm sorry. I understood this was a number where he could be reached at any time." Now the voice wasn't quite as controlled, and the black hole in Elizabeth was yawning once more.

"You usually can. He just isn't here at the moment. I'm sorry to rush you, but I'm late for work. Could I take a message?"

A moment later Elizabeth was sorry she had insisted on hearing what the woman had to say.

"Max! Max!" Elizabeth was hollering before the door was open, almost falling out of the car in her hurry to reach him, almost breaking her neck running over the uneven earth.

"Max!" she screamed once more, and he looked up, squinting as he scanned the construction area, his ears attuned to the sound of her voice. He stood still, plans in hand, hard hat in place. The American-dream man: confident and strong, smart and happy. Elizabeth wished she could simply turn around and leave him that way. But wishes didn't come true on days like this. She couldn't turn away. Max's strength was about to be tested, his contentment shattered.

Catching sight of her, Max raised his hand to wave, his brow furrowing when she didn't stop to return the greeting or smile just at the sight of him. And, when she stumbled, twisting her ankle, Max was over the field and by her side in an instant, plans abandoned, work forgotten.

"Elizabeth, what's wrong?" He took her by the elbow and guided her toward the construction trailer. "You're going to do some major ankle damage if you don't take it easy. Don't tell me I'm so irresistible you couldn't just walk over here."

His laugh was deep and his glorious smile was hers alone, but it brought no warmth or joy to Elizabeth. Neither did the feel of him as she put a hand against his chest, stopping him. She used the other to wipe her brow. Though the day was cool, Elizabeth felt hot and put upon by the overcast sky.

"Max, don't . . ." She took a deep breath, more to stave off the inevitable than to get her wind. ". . . don't joke."

"Hey, hey. What's going on? I'm sorry." Max was immediately contrite and concerned. "Is it Christopher?"

Elizabeth shook her head vehemently, looking first at the ground then toward the burgeoning city that was the product of Max's vision and handiwork. How proud he must be of what he had built. How happy he was in the midst of it. And now she must do this to him. Closing her eyes, she clutched tight to his shirt, then opened them and looked right at Max, hoping he would see in her strength and hope and life.

"It's Anna, Max. I think you'd better come."

His understanding and anguish were instantaneous. Max withered in the blink of an eye, aging while Elizabeth watched. The character lines around his eyes became ruts cut deep by a flash flood of pain. His jaw slackened; his eyes were suddenly shadowed and his energy drained. Unaware that Elizabeth still touched him, Max wandered away without a word. His steps were unsure, his destination unclear. Elizabeth went after him, moving slowly, coaxing him back to her.

"Come on, Max," she said quietly, her fingers plucking at his sleeve. "You've got to go with me now. They said to come now."

"I know. I know," he muttered. Stopping suddenly, he whipped around, engulfing Elizabeth in his arms and holding her close. He buried his face in the crook of her neck. The wind blew her hair over him, a veil to keep him from seeing what was to come. When Max raised his head, he had taken from her what he could, but nothing close to what he needed. He had anticipated this day for years, yet Elizabeth knew nothing could prepare him for it.

Everything would change now.

They would change.

The only question was *how.*

The long pink building looked different in the morning. Cheerier somehow, less threatening. People moved quickly and efficiently, signs of life in this dreary place. Young men in white rolled huge metal carts filled with breakfast trays down the corridors. Nurses chatted at the desks, trading gossip as they fielded phone calls and handled paperwork. They ran in and out of rooms, dispensing medicine and hurried words of comfort.

Elizabeth walked beside Max, aware of the sidelong looks from the people they passed. Sad though they might be for Max, that sorrow didn't touch the part of their heart that actually bled. Dying was dying; young or old, it was all the same.

They turned the corners and traversed corridors that Elizabeth had seen only once before, but she knew the place well. She had seen it in her dreams night after night. Beside her, Max was ghostlike with his pale skin and dark hair. His black eyes were flat, as if he had put up a shield to guard himself from the hurt he expected. Elizabeth started to take his hand, but didn't. If he needed her, he would reach out.

They stopped at Anna's room. Max covered his face and stood very still. Unable to resist, Elizabeth lay just the tips of her fingers against his back. Without uttering a word or looking in her direction, Max let her know her presence was appreciated. The signs were there in the almost imperceptible way he leaned into her touch and lingered with her in the hall. Finally, he was ready; he went to his wife. Alone, Elizabeth leaned against the wall and slid down to the floor. Three hours later, she joined Max.

The woman on the bed breathed desperately, her spent body straining as if she could capture the last part of life by throwing herself at it. Elizabeth averted her eyes and draped her arms over Max's shoulders. He sighed and gathered her hands in his. Together, they kept a silent watch, listening, praying, hoping for Anna's release as the morning turned to afternoon and Elizabeth longed for the night. *Dying,* she thought, *should come tenderly with the twilight.* Outside, the near-winter wind had kicked up, cold and strong. Anna Marino's soul would be swept easily to heaven when the time came.

When Max finally released Elizabeth's hands, when he slipped out of his chair to sit beside his wife on her bed, she knew it was time for her to go. Without a word, she slipped to the door. The last thing she heard was Max's whispery nighttime voice speaking words of love to a woman who had left his life long ago. It was the memory he loved and the memory he grieved for, but it was a shell of that woman that he comforted. In leaving him, Elizabeth took the weight of his sorrow and made it her own. Her tears fell freely, and her sobs were deep sighs of sadness. Whatever else her life might bring, Elizabeth MacMillan promised herself, she would never, ever forget how short life was and how important it was to live while on this earth.

Elizabeth checked her watch as the garage door closed behind her. Five o'clock straight up. Hopefully, Christopher was inside hard at his homework. If he weren't, she didn't have the strength to fight with him. Never had she been through such a wrenching day. Even Brad's desertion hadn't sapped her energy and resolve as Anna's battle for life had. Her father's death had been quick and easy, a heart attack on the golf course. Her mother's passing had been equally tranquil; she'd died in her own bed in her sleep. What she had seen tonight had been too real, too immediate. Elizabeth shuddered. Max hadn't called her at work, so she assumed he still watched and waited. How torturous; how pitiful.

Wearily, she planned her evening as she got out of the car: a quick dinner, a bath. She would rejuvenate herself in case Max needed her. There would be homework for Chris while she waited for a call.

Going through the side door to the backyard, Elizabeth stooped to pick up one of Christopher's roller blades and to re-coil the hose that had been left unwound. Taking some comfort in these routine physical chores, Elizabeth lifted her face to the crisp breeze that blew away some of her melancholy. She closed her eyes, the length of hose slipping through her fingers as it wound around and around itself until the job was done. She picked at a weed, tweaked off a fading impatiens, and, out of the corner of her eye, caught sight of a figure in her driveway, someone leaving her home in an awful hurry.

Elizabeth was alert. Without thinking, she sprinted down the side yard. This, she knew instinctively, was the person who had been tormenting her. The righteous leaver of notes. Elizabeth was going to find out who it was if it were the last thing she did.

"Hey!" Elizabeth yelled. Pausing at the gate she squinted through the darkness. "Hey! Stop right this minute!" She pushed off in hot pursuit of this woman who seemed oddly familiar.

"Damn you," Elizabeth muttered, cursing the entire

world more than the fleeing woman. A leap and Elizabeth's hand made contact with one plump arm. Her fingers twined into the thick cable of a sweater. She pulled back and the woman stumbled, a squeal of terror and opposition cutting through the night. The woman ducked, and Elizabeth thought she might strike out. Instead, her free arm came up and covered her head.

"Oh no you don't," Elizabeth growled, holding on for dear life. The woman struggled to get away but did not retaliate. "You just stand right here. Stand still!"

Elizabeth yanked hard with both hands, but the woman was tenacious. It wasn't until something fell onto the sidewalk between them that the tussle stopped. Still holding on, Elizabeth bent down and swiped it up. She glanced at the tape dispenser just before a huge red blast of indignation exploded behind her eyes. With an enraged cry, Elizabeth twirled the woman toward her and looked without really seeing. She talked, but could only hear half of the words that sputtered out of her mouth. She pulled, dragging the woman toward the illumination of the street light.

"I'm going . . . find out why . . . the police . . . you'll be lucky if you don't go to jail . . ." Elizabeth panted with the exertion of the chase and capture, provoked beyond reason. Finally, she whipped her around, tore off the dark scarf, and looked at the person who had penned the horrid notes.

In silence, they stared at one another, the tall, blond woman and the round-as-a-ball, black-haired lady. Stunned, Elizabeth let her eyes travel down to the chubby little feet pushed into impeccably kept low-heeled pumps that sported shiny buckles. She focused on the buckles. The last time she'd seen them was at the hospital many months ago.

Her grip relaxed; her arms fell to her side, the tape still in hand. Mute in front of the weeping woman, Elizabeth's anger disappeared, leaving a jumbled feeling of bewilderment. Carefully, she touched the woman's shoulder, coaxing her to say or do something, to explain why. But Maria Lopez, Max's mother-in-law, didn't speak.

"Oh, my God," Elizabeth breathed. "Oh, Lord. Why?"

A car rounded the curve of the street, catching them in the harsh glare of headlights. Elizabeth reached for the older woman, but Maria backed away defensively. The car slowed, turned the corner, then drove down the street. The wind buffeted them. Elizabeth looked back. Maria was staring at her purse, dropped in the struggle. Scooping up lipstick, a comb, and a handful of tissues, Elizabeth put them back and snapped the clasp shut. She gestured for Maria to follow her.

"Come on. You can't stand out here like this, and you can't drive. It's cold. It might rain. You've got to come inside."

Elizabeth walked on a few steps, but Maria stood weeping like a child lost on forbidding and unfamiliar ground. Retracing her steps, Elizabeth took the older woman's arm. At Elizabeth's front door Maria covered her face, shoulders sagging, as she saw her handiwork. The last note, the worst yet, still hung on the door. Elizabeth crumpled it without as much as a glance.

"Come on," Elizabeth muttered. She held out her hand, but Maria, dry-eyed, glared at her.

Her round face was swollen, her dark eyes blank,

but hatred illuminated her expression. Elizabeth almost reached for her once more, but a split-second later, everything became clear. Maria wasn't mortified by the things she had done; it was Elizabeth herself that the woman abhorred.

"You should be her," Maria Lopez whispered. "You should be the one in that room. Not my Anna."

Stricken, Elizabeth fell back, her hand at her breast as if the words had been a hex instead of the heartbreaking, futile wish of an anguished mother.

"Why? Why would you want that?" Elizabeth demanded. The strength of her voice surprised the both of them, startling the round-faced woman. She blinked in bewilderment.

"What?" Maria stepped forward, holding on to the side of the house for support. She looked weak and confused.

"Why would you want me to die?" Elizabeth asked, incredulous and appalled.

"I don't," Maria breathed. "I just want my Anna alive. The way she used to be." Those dark eyes filled again with tears; but, exhausted, she couldn't weep. "So beautiful, my daughter. Beautiful and so in love, and not even a baby to leave behind. She had Max, and they were a family. They were a *family*." Her dark head shook, and her black curls bounced. Her eyes lowered. She looked so sad. "You don't understand. You can't understand."

Elizabeth collapsed against the door, her heart breaking. Maria's pain was so compelling, Elizabeth almost wished she could lie down in Anna's bed. Instead, she crumpled to the ground, sitting listlessly in the entry of her home. How on earth had her life come to this?

Max had given her respect, warmth, understanding, and love. In this one moment, this woman had shown her the other side of the coin. Max hadn't given her those things. She, Elizabeth, had taken the love, usurped the warmth, pilfered the understanding that rightfully belonged to Anna. Elizabeth had made the dying woman share, and Anna's mother had tried to make Max's new playmate go away. It was as simple as that.

"I don't want my daughter to die," whispered Maria.

"Nobody wants her to die." Elizabeth raised her hands in quiet frustration. "But Anna is going to die, Maria. You should be with her, because it's going to happen and no one can stop it."

"Max is with her," she snapped. "Max is where he should be. I had to fight you to get him there."

Elizabeth shook her head adamantly, tears swelling behind her own eyes. "No. No, we never had to fight. I didn't try to take him. He came to me. He needed a woman who was alive. Maybe that's not fair, but that's what he needed."

"He needed Anna," the woman insisted, leaning back against the stucco. Her hard fists banged against the wall in short bursts as if she were trying to pound some sense into Elizabeth. "You don't know how it was. How could you? You use Max because you have no man in this house. You use my Max because he is kind and good-hearted, and because he is a man who needs certain things."

"You're wrong." Elizabeth's voice was stronger, and she lifted her chin defiantly. "Because Max is kind and good-hearted, he didn't abandon your daughter. He cared for her; and loved her, and now that she's dying, he's where he should be. But I am here if he needs someone who is strong and concerned about him. Do you understand?"

"No! No!" she screamed, then lowered her voice. "He had me. I was there for him all these years until you. I cooked for him. I took care of his house. I mended his clothes. I kept her alive in his mind and in his home so he wouldn't miss the other parts so much. He didn't need you."

"He did," Elizabeth insisted. "Max couldn't tell you all he was feeling because he worried about you, too. How could he tell you he was despairing when all you wanted to talk about was hope? And how could he begin to mourn when you refused to join him? How could he rejoice in what he and Anna had once when you kept looking to a future and pretending they would have more? You weren't there for him," Elizabeth accused. "You were in their house for your sake. You wanted to be around the things Anna loved so you wouldn't feel frightened, and those things included Max. When you mended and cooked and cleaned for him, you could pretend that Anna had just gone out for a minute. Admit it! You thought she might walk through the door at any time because nothing else had changed."

Maria turned her head, her hands now spread against the wall as if for support. Elizabeth pressed her advantage.

"Max was changing, though, wasn't he? Max wouldn't leave you; he wouldn't move anything in the house or throw away anything that belonged to Anna, but he was healing. You saw it; you understood it; you just didn't want to accept it. He was beginning to live again, and you want him to wallow in the half life you'd made for him."

Elizabeth scrambled to her feet, energized by her words, anxious for this woman to understand that what she and Max had was natural and necessary. Elizabeth would not allow her to make their relationship anything less, no matter how deep her pain.

"Deny it. Deny that you want Max all for yourself. Deny that you don't want him to live a normal life because it will mean your daughter can't."

Maria shook her head hard. She sniffled and wiped her eyes with the back of her hand.

"No. That's not it," she said. "I want him to live the way we used to. Then there will be a place for Anna to come back to. If he has you, there won't be a place for my Anna. No place for her, but her mother's arms. It's Max she wants to live for. Ever since they were small, it was always Max. So I keep him safe for her. You see? I keep Max safe for my baby, Anna." The words were whimpers now, and the old woman crumbled before Elizabeth's eyes. She was fragile and fearful, and Elizabeth was ashamed. "My Anna. My baby. You go away. Not her. I just wanted you to go away."

"Shhh." Wearily, Elizabeth wrapped her arms around the woman. She laid her hand against the dark curls and held the round body to her as she rocked back and forth again and again while Maria cried for her poor, wasted daughter, her once-beautiful child.

"Shhh," Elizabeth whispered. "I know it's unfair. I know. All of it's so unfair." She repeated the litany over and over. Maria spoke, too, sometimes overriding Elizabeth's words, sometimes melting into them. Finally, Elizabeth held her away; and though they faced one another, their eyes were averted. Elizabeth dropped her arms. Neither of them had received the comfort they needed, but both wanted it desperately. Exhausted, the two women walked inside, and Elizabeth flipped on the lights.

"Sit here," Elizabeth said, settling her in a chair by the fireplace. "I'll make some tea."

Her body was heavy as she climbed the stairs, stopping long enough to knock on Christopher's door. When he didn't answer, she opened it and stuck her head in. Christopher lay on his bed, earphones plugged in tight, his fingers working the key pads of his portable video game. A sandwich was on the desk. Elizabeth retreated. She looked like hell and felt the same. There was no need for Christopher to see her like this. Quickly, she went to her bedroom, pausing long enough to look at the novel on the bedside table. Max's book. It was a lifetime ago since they had lain in bed reading side by side. It would be a long while before they were so comfortable again.

Taking a deep breath, Elizabeth splashed her face with water and hung up her jacket. Towels in hand, she went back to Maria Lopez and insisted she freshen up. When she returned, the tea was ready, and it was time for them to talk.

Twelve

Elizabeth tossed and turned. She scooted across the big bed to check the clock. Ten. Only ten o'clock. God bless. She should have stayed up later, but she'd been so tired after taking Maria back to the nursing home that she'd fallen right into bed. Now all she could think about was that sad trip.

They had walked in together, Elizabeth waiting only long enough to see Max embrace his mother-in-law and both of them sit beside Anna's bed. It was their special time to see through together, and Elizabeth feared it would be long and torturous for them both. She didn't speak to Max, or even make her presence known, as much for his sake as for her own. The sum of their personal equation didn't add up in that place. One plus one always came out to be three: Anna, Max, and Maria. Elizabeth didn't count. She left thinking herself stoic and sophisticated, able to bide her time. Alone, Elizabeth proved to be fretful and needy. The memory of the nursing home haunted her. She would have given anything if Max, who had no comfort to give, could have comforted her.

"Mom?"

Elizabeth sat up, alert in the darkness, her heart beating faster, expecting the worst on this long night.

"Yes, sweetheart, what is it? Are you all right?"

Christopher slipped into her room, a silhouette, an adult-like shadow. Elizabeth flipped on the light, blinked, and focused on him. He had taken to wearing plaid boxer shorts and a sleeveless t-shirt to bed, an affectation that didn't quite look manly yet.

"I'm okay. I just couldn't sleep. The more I think about sleeping, the more I can't."

Elizabeth chuckled sadly. "Funny, I seem to be having the same problem." She pulled back the covers. "Too old to have a cuddle with your mom?"

She expected some hesitation or an expertly delivered sound of indignation. What she didn't expect was a shy smile and her son's crawling into the bed without a second thought. Elizabeth arranged the quilt the way she had when Brad was away on business and Chris was very small.

"You want the light off?" he asked.

"Only if you do," she replied, trying to keep her joy to herself. Miracle of miracles, had she been forgiven her transgressions?

Chris leaned over and switched it off. In the dark, Elizabeth smiled, realizing how lucky she was to have this boy. As much as she had thought only Max could help her through the night, it was Christopher who proved comforting. Not wanting to ruin this perfect moment, Elizabeth lay quietly, her head cradled by the down pillow. She could feel him thinking, formulating whatever worried him into ten-and-a-half-year-old thoughts.

"Mom?" he whispered. "I felt really bad about that lady tonight."

Elizabeth waited silently, her eyes closed, and

thanked God for small favors. Christopher, talking, seeking her out, was a miracle in the midst of the turmoil that had been their lives. The tough boy was an act, a chrysalis protecting the ever-sweeter child inside. Elizabeth found his hand and laced her fingers through his as he talked. "She was really upset to do that stuff, to put up those notes and sneak around our house."

"She was very upset. People can do desperate things when they feel there isn't any hope. I'm afraid she's going to be sad for a long, long time. It's hard to watch someone die, especially when it's someone you love."

Elizabeth's voice caught. The mere thought of someone she loved ending up like Anna Marino was almost too much to bear. She squeezed Chris' hand tighter.

"Would you feel that bad if I were sick?"

"Oh, honey," Elizabeth rolled onto her side. In the dark, he couldn't see her face, but he met her halfway, turning so his bright eyes could peer at hers. A little human lie detector. "I don't know what I would do if you ever got that sick. I'm not sure I could go on without you. If anything bad happened to you, the hole in my heart would be so big I could never fill it up again."

Chris whispered, "What if it were Dad? Would you have a hole in your heart, too?" Elizabeth froze. Speechless, her fingers went slack in her son's hand. She turned her head ever so slightly, feeling the coolness of the pillowcase against her cheek, the softness of the down beneath her head. Why was it always about Brad? "Mom? Would you?"

"Yes, Christopher, I would," Elizabeth answered quietly, praying his questions would stop there.

"Would you know if Dad were sick? Do you think you would know somehow if Dad were sick or dying or something?"

How he wanted to validate a family that no longer existed! When would this roller coaster stop? Chris ready to go on, Chris angry that they weren't staying still, Chris anxious to please, Chris ready to disobey. She couldn't take much more—at least not alone.

"I don't know. I suppose I might have a sense if something were really wrong with Daddy," she said, hoping this would satisfy him.

"Then, since you don't feel anything weird, does that mean Dad's okay?"

"Chris, honey, please," Elizabeth pleaded. The day had been too long for her to think about this. Quiet and sleep was what she longed for; yet at every turn, she found questions and hurts and misunderstandings.

"Mom, I want to know." Christopher's plea was equally urgent. Elizabeth reached out and touched Christopher's hair. It was thick and straight, so different than when he was small, still so wonderful to feel. If only he could understand that his hope was futile.

"Chris, I'll try to tell you in the best way I can what's . . ." The doorbell rang, the chimes calling her away from hard questions that had no true answers. Elizabeth patted his hand. "Hold that thought." She flung her legs out of bed and pulled on her robe.

"Mom?" Christopher called, but Elizabeth didn't stop to listen. Intuitively, she knew who stood on the other side of the door and what had happened to bring him here. Hurriedly, she rushed back to the bed, realizing the quiet time with Chris was at an end for now.

"Honey," she said softly, throwing back the quilt, "I've got to see who's at the door. Why don't you hop back into your bed? We'll talk tomorrow, okay?" The bell rang again and once more after that. Elizabeth looked toward the sound, then back to Chris. "Okay, honey?"

Christopher sighed. "Sure, Mom."

But Elizabeth was gone. Christopher's confusion would work itself out and settle itself down as the circumstances of their lives did. But this . . . this call for help downstairs was urgent and vital.

Flying down the last few steps, her robe wrapped tight around her, Elizabeth opened the door and stepped into the circle of light thrown off by the porch fixture. Her hands touched Max's shoulder before moving to his face and cupping his chin.

"She's gone." His voice was tight and hoarse.

Elizabeth drew him inside, holding his arm carefully as she guided him to the living room and settled him on the couch. Without another word, she sat beside him, pulling his head toward her breast, encircling him with her arms and protecting him with her love. She would sit that way with him until he didn't want her any longer. She would sit in silence with him until he felt like talking. And when he started to cry, Elizabeth would cry, too, but for different reasons. In some ways, for Max, this was a fortunate night. Max's wounds could now heal. As long as Brad remained silent and hidden, there would never be an end to Elizabeth's misery, no matter how deep she buried the memory of him.

* * *

Elizabeth watched Max from across the room, admiring the cut of his blue-black suit, the crisp white shirt, the gray-and-beige striped tie. A new Max. A new personality. One as carefully controlled and pulled together as his ensemble. He looked marvelous and tired. Elizabeth wondered if he had slept for any length of time since Anna's passing.

The last few days had been dreadful, arranging for the funeral and the rosary, dealing with poor Maria's grief, fielding phone calls from cousins and aunts and well-meaning friends. Anna's family was big and giving. Elizabeth's had been a neat little package; Anna's was the large, economy size. Max handled it well. He had a good word for all. Leaning close to the elderly, he spoke slowly; lifting children, he kissed their cheeks, making them happy, smiling to celebrate their young lives even on this sad day. He managed to greet everyone, accepting their condolences with a graciousness Elizabeth knew was heartfelt but wearing.

Pushing herself away from the wall where she'd been leaning, Elizabeth picked up the glasses that littered Max's small home. Anna was everywhere: family pictures hung on the wall in meticulous groupings, framed with care; needlepoint pillows were scattered over the sofa; the eyelet cafe curtains filtered the sun's glare.

As she straightened, Elizabeth found herself glancing at Max, wondering how on earth he could care about her when he'd had a wife like Anna. He caught her gaze, and they looked at one another. A pleasure at any other time, but now Elizabeth was uneasy. Max's stare was curiously vacant, as if he were seeing her for the first time, trying to place this tall woman with blond hair in the midst of so many dark heads. She hoped her expression conveyed everything she wanted it to.

I'm here for you, Max. Take your time, sweetheart. Just go with it. Take as long as you need.

Max turned away without as much as a nod. Perhaps she no longer existed. With Anna gone, was there no need for her compassion?

"Elizabeth." She turned toward the tug on her sleeve. Leslie, dressed impeccably in a black suit, smiled at her mournfully. "I'm sorry, hon, I've got to go."

"That's fine. I didn't expect you to stay all day. I'm sure Max appreciated your coming." Elizabeth smiled as brightly as she could, but couldn't shake the feeling that even she shouldn't be here.

"He's a sweetie. I can't believe how well he's holding up," Leslie said, letting her eyes tag him for a second.

Elizabeth nodded. "I think he's doing really well, too."

Leslie raised her eyebrow. "How disappointed you sound."

"I don't mean to. I just feel so out of place." Elizabeth turned on her heel, politely pushed through a group of people standing in front of the kitchen door, and deposited the glasses she held in the sink. Leslie dogged Elizabeth, stopping her before she could begin to wash them. "No you don't. The dishes can wait. I need a breath of fresh air."

Leslie led the way outside. The backyard was tiny, but well kept. A vegetable garden thrived in one corner, and flowers ringed the perimeter. Anna. Anna everywhere. Color had been her contribution to the life she and Max had lived. He'd built it; she'd made it bright. That was quite a talent. Elizabeth and Leslie sat together on a small bench under an apple tree.

"So, what's bothering you?" Leslie asked.

Elizabeth shrugged. The two women looked at the house, not one another. Elizabeth traced the outline of a sprinkler with the toe of her shoe and clutched the bench seat as if she might fly off without something to ground her.

"I don't know. Max stared right through me a minute ago, and it was as if he didn't even know me. He seemed so grateful, bent over backwards to let me know how much he appreciated my coming to the funeral and getting things ready here. Now, I'm not sure it was a good idea to come."

Leslie's hand covered Elizabeth's. "You did the right thing, but give Max a break. We're single because someone chose to leave. He's on his own because Anna died. That's a big difference. And he's got Maria to deal with. She's devastated, too."

Elizabeth sighed. "I know. It's just that Anna had been sick for so long. I thought he'd be relieved."

"He probably is on one level. On another, he's feeling guilty for still being alive. Aren't there stages you go through after someone close to you dies?"

Elizabeth nodded. "I was a jumble of emotion after my parents died, but I wanted the people I loved around me. With Max, I feel like I should just go home and stay there and wait, but I don't know what I'm waiting for." Elizabeth, trying desperately not to whine, failed miserably. She was so afraid; and every time Max looked through her, his features changed and melted and re-formed until it was Brad looking at her, not seeing her. That was what Elizabeth found terrifying.

"Maybe that's not a bad idea. You've got a lot to do at home. He probably does, too."

Elizabeth narrowed her eyes. She shifted on the little bench, sat back, and draped her arm over the back.

"You're trying to tell me something."

"I'm just saying maybe it's time for you guys to take a breather. Max needs to deal with his baggage and, Elizabeth, I think you'd better start dealing with some of your own." Leslie lowered her eyes; she bit her lower lip. This was damned hard, but she had to do it. "Christopher was at the liquor store with that kid—what's his name?"

"David?"

"Yeah, David. The one with the long hair—and some other guys that were kind of spooky-looking. It was after eleven. At night."

"That's impossible. Christopher is in bed by nine every night."

"And when do you go to bed?"

"Ten, ten-thirty, but I don't see how he could sneak out of the house without my knowing. It's impossible," she said, her voice clipped, Max forgotten. It was starting again with Christopher, and she felt powerless to stop him from self-destructing.

"Well, does he ever spend the night at that kid's house?"

Elizabeth's shoulders sagged. "Sometimes. When I'm out with Max. The last few weeks he's been there a lot. I can't keep an eye on him every minute and still help Max."

"You shouldn't have to watch him every second, Elizabeth. I'm not criticizing you," Leslie said gently. "But Chris needs something. Maybe an after-school program with more supervision or someone older to stay with him when you're out. Maybe there's some guy from the high school. A big brother. God, Elizabeth!" Leslie threw up her hands in defeat. "I feel stupid. I'm sorry to be such a doomsayer about Chris. I'm always bringing you bad news, but I look at that kid he hangs with, I see him out late at night, and I get the shakes." Leslie stood up and adjusted her jacket. "I just thought you should know that I saw him. Now, I'll shut up."

"You're sure?" Elizabeth asked, her voice pleading for Leslie to hedge just a bit. She didn't even hesitate.

"I'm sure. It was Chris," she said adamantly. "They weren't doing anything, just sitting on the curb. But, Elizabeth, the other people hanging around that place weren't too savory, if you know what I mean."

Elizabeth nodded and took a deep breath. "Okay. You're right. But, Leslie," Elizabeth said, "he's a good kid. He always has been."

"Oh, hon, I know that. He's the best, and so are you. So is Max. But Christopher needs some real help to get on the right track." She leaned down, laid her hand on Elizabeth's shoulder, and kissed her lightly on the cheek. "Talk to him tonight. Figure out something. Let Max be. He's got plenty of people to help him."

"But none that love him the way I do," Elizabeth said, surprised to hear that sentiment spoken aloud.

"Then help yourself. Make Christopher happy. Give Max some breathing space. Take things slow, Elizabeth. Love is a mighty fine thing. Yours should be real, not rebound."

"After all this time, do you honestly think either of us is on the rebound?" Elizabeth asked incredulously.

"Especially after all this time. Max is a great guy, but love is something else again. Think really hard about what you'd be willing to do for him, how much he's willing to give you right now. Think hard, Elizabeth. Chris might be Max's Achilles' heel. He may have a lot of room in his heart for you, but a problem child? It's something to think about."

"There's nothing to think about. Max adores Christopher. He's said so," Elizabeth insisted.

"That was before he was carrying around a bucketload of grief himself. I'm just saying get your house in order, find out if Max wants you to make room for him."

With that, she lifted her hand in a small salute and was gone, leaving Elizabeth to watch the house and listen to the sounds of life going on. Max's relatives chattered; some laughed and babies cried. They darted by windows and lingered on the porch, all these people she didn't know. Elizabeth watched and thought about Christopher. His deception was like an arrow through her heart. Christopher frightened and confused her. He needed things she couldn't give him, and asked questions she couldn't answer. But she would take more care with him. She would desperately try to be the mother he needed. She would . . .

Then Max stood alone for a moment looking out the kitchen window toward her. She stood up, Christopher forgotten. Max needed her now. She went to him. Once she was done here, she would fix everything else.

Thirteen

The machine was blinking. Three messages. Elizabeth hit the button. The school was requesting a teacher conference regarding Christopher's math grades. This neither surprised nor dismayed Elizabeth. She was determined Chris would get back on the straight and narrow. If one more conference would do the trick, then she would attend one more conference.

A-1 Carpet Cleaning cheerily offered a full-house special while a wrong number rounded off the medley of messages. Then that familiar feeling of melancholy engulfed her.

Two weeks and Max still hadn't called. Once she'd called him, but the uncomfortable edge of their polite conversation was more than she could bear. Patience, she reminded herself. Patience.

At odds with herself, Elizabeth wandered toward the living room, flipping through the mail as she went. Kicking off her shoes, she collapsed on the sofa, put her head back, and realized that, without Max, things had gone from bad to worse. He had been magic, and now the spell was broken, leaving Elizabeth dazed.

"Mom?" The door slammed; heavy steps sounded in the entryway. "I'm home. Mom?"

The pattern of his footsteps told Elizabeth Chris had

made a detour into the kitchen. She managed to lift her head and push herself up by the time he found her. She smiled.

"Hi."

"Hi." Chris tossed his backpack beside the table and flopped himself onto the stool near the fireplace. He smiled. An actual, real, wonderful, warm smile. "What are you doin'?"

"Nothing and thanks." Elizabeth crossed her arms and grinned back. "That's the nicest smile I've had in ages. What happened today?"

"Nothin'." Chris shook his head and pointed to the basket of apples on the coffee table.

She grabbed the biggest one, broke her own rules, and tossed it his way. He caught it easily, his smile widening to show his two giant front teeth in all their glory.

"Well, something must have happened. I got so used to that hangdog face of yours, I wasn't sure you remembered how to smile," Elizabeth said lightly, hiding her relief and her joy.

"Well, maybe something." He took a dramatic bite of his apple, then talked with his mouth full. "I aced the social studies test today, Mom."

"No kidding?" Elizabeth squealed. She was halfway off the couch, her arms out, when he pulled back. Changing course, she raised her hand. They high-fived. Not quite as satisfying as the hug Elizabeth wanted, but she'd take anything she could get.

"No kidding," Chris said, more excited than he'd been in a long time. "Only Tommy Johnson and I got A's. Him and me. Just two of us out of thirty kids in the whole class."

"Well, that's quite a turnaround. Unfortunately, I

have a call on the machine from your math teacher. She wants me to come talk to her about your grade."

Elizabeth sat on the coffee table, anxious to exploit any time Christopher gave her. There were bridges to mend and work to be done just to get back to square one. If nothing else, Max's silence had forced her to pay close attention to the little one still in her nest.

"Yeah, I know. She told me. But, Mom, I'm trying." His triumphant smile disappeared; he changed before her eyes.

"Is there one thing in particular you don't understand?" she pressed on.

Silence. A bite of the apple. Christopher was expert at communicating without saying a word. Elizabeth's shoulders fell. The message was loud and clear. She'd done it again. Chris' moment of pride and happiness had become an opportunity to point out his failings. Throwing her mothering skills into reverse, she backtracked.

"Okay, so I'll find out when I talk to her. I want to hear more about this social studies test."

Christopher got out of the chair and held up his snack. The apple was almost finished. Studiously, he avoided her eyes.

"I'd better throw this away," he said.

She'd blown it.

"Come on, honey, I really want to hear the details." Elizabeth tried again, would have begged if she'd thought it would have done any good.

"It really wasn't that big a deal, Mom. I gotta go do my homework."

"Okay. But how about if I make your favorite tonight to celebrate? Beef stroganoff! I can have it ready by six-thirty. Will that give you enough time for your homework?"

"Sure." The smile wasn't coming back. Christopher slung his backpack over his shoulder, went to the kitchen, tossed the apple core in the trash, and headed toward his room. He hesitated as he passed through the living room again. "Mom?"

"Um-hmmm?" Elizabeth's face was bright with expectation. *Anything you want, Chris. Give me a chance to be better.*

"How come Max doesn't come here anymore?"

Elizabeth swallowed hard. Her smile faltering, then fading. Here was the big question, the one she'd been asking herself every waking hour and dreaming about half the night. The one that was unanswerable.

"Max is getting business taken care of, honey; but I still see him."

"No, you don't. He hasn't called. He hasn't come by."

Touché.

"I mean I see him when he's working sometimes. He just needs time, Christopher. You know, to get over Anna's death. That was very hard on him."

"But you said she was sick for a really long time, so he should feel better," Chris challenged.

"No matter how prepared you think you are for something bad, it always hurts the same as if it just came out of the blue."

"Like Dad leaving," Chris said solemnly. "I didn't feel like talking a lot after Dad left the first time. Then when he didn't come back, that was pretty terrible."

Elizabeth mused, thinking of poor Max and how long he had watched Anna suffer. Half listening to

Chris, Elizabeth responded quietly, more to herself than to him.

"I'm not sure you can really equate Daddy's leaving with Anna's dying, sweetheart. I mean . . ."

"Why do you always say things like that? Why? Don't you think I have any feelings? Don't you think?"

Christopher's outburst was like a slap in the face. His young voice filled the room with anger so intense the walls seemed to shrink from it. Elizabeth blinked at this Christopher she didn't know. His backpack dangled from one hand, his arms akimbo. His face flushed red, and his eyes flashed. Never, ever, had she seen his fury so blatantly displayed.

"Why do you say stuff that makes me feel stupid, Mom? I'm not stupid. I'm not. I know things, and you can't tell me that I don't feel the things I feel. You shouldn't make me feel like a dork. You're my mom."

"Chris," she breathed, half out of her chair. "I didn't mean to. I was just thinking about Max's wife. She's dead. . . . I mean, Chris, that's different from just walking away . . . that's . . ." God, what was she supposed to say? It *was* different. It was! Even Chris had to understand that. "There's always hope that Daddy will come back. . . . It's not like Anna . . . not like dying . . ."

Suddenly Chris swung his backpack, knocking the basket of apples to the floor. He twirled around and around, screaming at the top of his lungs. He stopped and pummeled a pillow. Elizabeth stood, openmouthed and ineffectual, stilled by the shock of his response.

"It is to me! It's just like dying, only I'm still walking around. It's just like that, Mom. Like dying."

Christopher shot toward the French doors and Elizabeth sprang after him, imagining glass shattering as he threw his backpack through the panes. Visions of glass shards, blood, and hurt were all she saw. She grappled with him, but he pulled away, backing off toward the stairs, his hands held up as if that would keep him from doing something stupid.

"It's just like dying, Mom. You don't get it. You never loved Daddy enough 'cause you didn't die when he left. Just like Max's wife, so don't tell me . . ."

The last words were caught on a cry and a sob and a wail of frustration that ripped through Elizabeth until she was sure that if she pulled her hand away from where it lay over her heart, she would see it stained with blood. Openmouthed, horrified, she watched Christopher's face contort with pain and fear and humiliation. There was nothing she could do to help him.

Paralyzed, Elizabeth fell into a chair and watched Christopher's mouth work. Bits and pieces of sentences spilled out—words that made sense to him; words meant to tell her exactly how he felt; words punctuating the silence of the living room.

"You don't know . . . don't care . . . I told you . . . all alone . . ."

Tears flowed down his soft cheeks without washing away the color of his pain. He sniffled. He swiped at those tears with the back of his hand. His newly long hair fell in his eyes only to be plastered to his cheeks as he wiped the strands away through his tears. Then he was gone in a flurry of banging and hurry. He was gone so fast Elizabeth wasn't quick enough to stop him. The front door slammed shut. The garage door was lifted up and never closed again. Elizabeth heard . . . nothing. She dashed through the house calling and calling Christopher's name as she yanked open the front door.

"Chris, please! Chris! Come back. Chris, don't leave."

But he was gone, halfway down the block, his bike rocking back and forth in his frantic escape from the place where the last person he trusted didn't understand what he felt. He had no jacket and the night was turning cold. He had reflectors on the rear wheels, hardly helpful on these black nights. He had no money and the only place he could go was Leslie's or David's. David. She didn't even know his last name. She had a phone number, thank God, but this was absurd. What kind of mother had she become? She had to go find Chris. That was all there was to it.

She was back inside the house in a flash, phone in hand. Her fingers slipped as she misdialed. Taking a deep breath, she tried to control the shaking of her hands. This time she managed the code, but Leslie's machine answered. Elizabeth talked fast, begging her to keep Christopher if he showed up at her place. The second call was to David.

A woman answered and screamed for David. Elizabeth closed her eyes. These were the people Chris had gone to for comfort? That was the home in which he sought refuge? One where screaming was the norm and curiosity was nonexistent? The woman hadn't even asked who she was. Then again, had Christopher's home been any better? A mother who ignored her child in lieu of her lover and her own problems?

"Hello," David said, his voice sullen.

"This is Elizabeth MacMillan, Christopher's mother." She kept her voice quiet. "Christopher just left our house, and he's really upset. I was wondering if you might know where he would go?"

Elizabeth listened, disheartened, as the boy rattled off possible destinations. Parks, stores, malls, corners. She couldn't believe Christopher even knew about half those places and hoped with all her heart he wouldn't be at most of them.

"Mrs. MacMillan?" The boy's voice sounded so small over the phone, hardly that of the tough guy he appeared in person. "I wouldn't waste any time trying to find him. Chris knows where not to go. Don't worry; he'll be okay. I ride out alone all the time. He'll be okay."

But you're not Chris, she wanted to say. *You're not my son who is sweet and gentle. You have a mother who screams at you. A mother who doesn't care where you go.*

Elizabeth didn't say that. He was someone's son and that someone didn't take care with him. Elizabeth would do better with Chris. She would start by respecting his friends.

"You really think so?" she asked quietly while every horrid, dangerous situation Chris could encounter popped into her mind.

"Sure. Why not?" Elizabeth heard the surprise in this boy's voice. Had she been the only one to ever ask his opinion?

"Well then, thanks. I feel better," she lied. "If you really think he'll be okay. But, if he gets to your house, will you tell him that dinner will be ready at 6:30? Will you tell him I'm going to make the stroganoff? And—" She paused briefly. "—and you come with him. To dinner, I mean. If he shows up at your place."

"Sure, Mrs. MacMillan," he said, astonished. "Thanks."

"Okay, David. If you see him, send him home," she said again, hoping he understood how urgent this was.

Elizabeth hung up, trying to still the beating of her heart. Christopher was gone, riding around on a bike in the dark, hurting like hell. And he was alone.

Slowly, Elizabeth walked to the kitchen and looked out over Emerald Isle. It had rained earlier, but the winter promised to be dry. The year had been so hard on them all—on her and Max and Christopher, perhaps even Brad. Elizabeth wasn't sure she could face a frigid winter. She longed for the warmth of family. If only she could light the kindling that would create the fire of closeness for her and Christopher again, she would never let that flame go out. By the time Max was ready to come to her, the blaze of contentment from the MacMillan household would draw him in and hold him there. Yes, she just needed for Chris to understand how much she loved him. She needed to be a good mom and everything would be fine.

She tied an apron over her dress, moving robot-like about the kitchen, chopping onions, cleaning mushrooms. She sliced and browned the beef, and soon the kitchen was toasty warm, filled with the scents of cooking. With each chop of the knife, each turn of the spoon, Elizabeth planned. They would eat, then push the dishes aside. They would talk. They would go out late for ice cream. Elizabeth would wipe away all of Christopher's pain. She would make everything okay again. It was a good plan, the plan of an understanding mother, a woman who has seen her own failings.

Four hours later, the plan failed.

By the time Christopher opened the door and walked into the house, Elizabeth was crazed with worry.

"Where have you been?" she screamed. Chris headed to the stairs, but Elizabeth took his arm and twirled him toward her. Shocked, Christopher had only a moment to hide his expression of hurt and surprise behind one of fury and hatred. Elizabeth pulled him close. "Answer me, Christopher. Where have you been?"

Elizabeth couldn't believe what was happening. Outside herself, she saw Elizabeth MacMillan shrieking like a banshee. Who was this mother? This woman? She had never raised her voice like this to Chris. But then, she had never been so frightened or so angry or so at a loss for what to do. The very things that made her love Chris were draining away, and all she had was a primal scream of indignation and terror to stop the flow.

"I asked you a question. Where have you been?" Her voice was lower and she spoke through clenched teeth, trying desperately to control herself. She backed away, terrified of what she might do if she stayed too near.

"Don't lie to me, Chris. I've talked to David. You never showed up at his house. Leslie isn't home. I've called there, too. So don't lie to me. Don't add that to what you've already done."

Incredibly, Christopher stood his ground, his face pinched and angry. Finally, without a word, he turned on his heel and put his foot on the stair. But Elizabeth was too quick for him. She was halfway up, her hands out to keep him from passing.

"No you don't. No more silent treatment. You're in big trouble."

"For what, Mom? I'm in trouble because you don't care about what I feel? Is that the bad thing I did?"

She advanced a step. "You know perfectly well what I'm talking about. Leaving this house without telling me where you were going. Leaving angry . . ."

"I've stayed home angry, and it doesn't matter. I'm really mad, Mom, and you don't think it's important. I'm really scared sometimes. Everything's different, and you don't care how I feel."

"That is not true. I care. I care so much. I fixed your favorite dinner and now it's ruined. I . . ."

Elizabeth stopped talking, hearing every ridiculous word she spouted. This wasn't about dinner. It was about her son. Insane, that's what she was. She opened her mouth, but no words of apology came out. Christopher, triumphant, walked past her and climbed the stairs without another word. When he reached the top, he turned. Elizabeth lifted her hand, but the look he cast was withering.

When the door to his room closed, Elizabeth dragged herself toward it without the foggiest idea what to do. Humbly, she raised her fist and knocked gently. There was no answer. She knocked once more. This time, Christopher turned the lock.

"Chris?" she called, her voice small. "Chris?" She laid first her hand, then her cheek against the locked door. "Honey, you don't have to answer me. I'm sorry. I'm so sorry." She listened to the silence. "I didn't mean to yell at you; I was just so worried. It was dark, and I was scared, honey. I've been scared for a long time, and I haven't been a very good mom to you because I was frightened—and selfish. Chris?"

She closed her eyes, pressing them together, stroking the wood of the door as if she might rub right through it and touch her son.

"I'm so sorry," she whispered, meaning it so sincerely. Louder, she said, "Chris, I have to go out. I'll be back in a little while. I need to find out what to do. I don't want us to be angry anymore. I need to go talk to someone so I can figure out how I can be a better mom." Elizabeth placed both hands on the door and stared at it, but there was no magic. It wouldn't open. "I know you're a big guy now and you can stay by yourself. But, Chris? If you need anything, go to Betsy's. Please go next door. Don't go out again. It's dark and it's cold. Winter is coming. Please stay home until I get back."

Elizabeth lay her forehead against that door until it was clear that Christopher wouldn't be coming out. There would be no tearful apologies, no throwing around of arms, no hugging.

Devastated, Elizabeth walked slowly down the stairs and out to the car. She drove through the blackness, through the new development where Max's half-finished houses stood like sentinels to guard the families of Emerald Isle. They had failed, those houses. The peace and contentment the place promised had fallen to the enemy of fear and loneliness—at least in one home. Now Elizabeth was going to battle. She needed the wherewithal to make things better, and there was only one place to find the kind of strength she needed now.

Ten minutes later she was knocking on the door that would lead to sanity and serenity. She waited. The door opened. She didn't smile because she'd come begging.

"Can I come in?"

Fourteen

Max stood away from the door, but not before Elizabeth saw his eyes hood to hide an initial flash of—what? Resentment? Disappointment? Ignoring this, she stepped across the threshold of his home, accepting his silent, if reluctant, invitation. He wasn't prepared for company, that was obvious. The first thing Elizabeth noticed was the bottle in his hand. Less than half full. Bourbon. The sight of it sent a chill through her. The sound of the closing door did nothing to dispel her apprehension.

Elizabeth began to unbutton her coat, but stopped on the last button. The apology she intended died on her lips as she looked around the room.

The lovingly appointed living room looked like a garage sale run amok. Clothes were strewn everywhere: a fluffy pale-blue robe; skirts of various lengths and colors; shoes, most with low heels; running clothes; lingerie . . . a white negligee. Jewelry sparkled on the mantel with the glint of gold plate. There was a fedora and a baseball cap. Four purses. A sewing basket lay open, embroidery thread meticulously unraveled into long strands. Max had laid these side by side before curling them into a rainbow that ended in a pile of scarves. Elizabeth absorbed the disarray before she turned and faced Max, her face unreadable, shock and sadness hidden.

"You've been busy," she said quietly, her fingers working hard at the last button until she was free of her coat. Elizabeth dropped it where she stood, unwilling to disturb Max's carefully contrived chaos.

"Busy as hell." Max's voice was low and hoarse from whiskey and sorrow. He lounged against the closed door and raised the bottle her way. "Drink?"

Elizabeth shook her head. "No thanks, Max. Do you have any coffee?"

"Probably. In the kitchen."

He pushed himself away from the door and sauntered toward her, then stumbled on when their shoulders brushed. She was of no more interest than a lamp or table. Max stopped at the top of the thread trail, raised the bottle, took a drink, and sat in the middle of the colorful rainbow. The bottle landed on the hearth.

Elizabeth had seen enough. She walked purposefully toward the kitchen and stopped only when she grabbed hold of the sink. She leaned over and wondered if she might be sick. Finally, with a deep breath, she lifted her head and stared through the window to the darkness outside.

Christopher. Max. Elizabeth. She laughed cheerlessly. Maybe it was Anna who was the lucky one. How on earth could she have been so stupid, thinking that she could be the healer, the stalwart center of Chris and Max's universe? Her hubris was laughable.

She wasn't strong and pure and good. She was scared and made mistakes at every turn. She said wrong words and opened her arms, not to help others, but to seize comfort for herself.

Now it was time to change. First, the coffee. It was cold. She switched on the machine and tried not to watch the pot. Rummaging through the cupboards, she found two mugs. Coffee in hand, her resolve steeled, Elizabeth went back to the living room.

"I brought you some, too," she said softly.

She put his mug on the hearth, shrewdly moving the bottle aside. Max took no notice. Elizabeth waited. When there were no ramifications, she sat gingerly on the brick facing him, knees pulled together, the hot mug of coffee between her chilled hands. A sob grew in her throat. She swallowed it. When Max spoke, it was with a most hateful voice, hard and droll.

"These belonged to Anna's great-grandmother. Pretty, huh?" A pair of embroidery scissors dangled from his little finger. With his other hand, he flicked them so they swung cheerily back and forth. "Can't even get my fingers in 'em to make 'em work." He blinked; the swinging stopped. "Anna could. Tiny fingers. Little fingers. She had the hardest time keeping her wedding ring on sometimes. She'd lose weight, and that damn thing would fall right off. We didn't know why. She just kept getting skinnier." He considered the scissors a bit longer, then tossed them onto the bed of thread. "Anna laughed when she couldn't make these work anymore. Laughed and laughed, and I got so mad I screamed at her."

He sighed and ran a hand across his eyes.

"I screamed at her when she laughed. I'd never done that before. Never yelled at Anna. But she laughed because she couldn't make the scissors work, because she knew she wouldn't be able to laugh much longer. Kind of sad, to know that you're going to break down like that."

Max looked at her with unhappy eyes that might never see the world right again. Elizabeth wanted to tell Max to be happy that he had yelled. Brad had never cared enough to show her such passionate emotion. She had mistaken his silence for serenity when it had been simply silence and, perhaps, boredom. Max's kind of love, this passionate relationship he spoke of, was to be envied.

"She laughed to keep from crying. Told me she was going to be like one of those dolls someday—those puppets guys use that sit on their knees . . ." Puzzled, the word lost in his hazy mind, he looked to Elizabeth for help.

"A ventriloquist's dummy," Elizabeth said quietly.

"Yeah." Max was whispering now, lost in the memory of a day he couldn't quite place. "I'd be the ventriloquist. She'd be the dummy. MS. They shouldn't use the initials on that disease. It's too simple for something that takes everything away. She couldn't talk . . . couldn't put her fingers through the little scissors and cut the threads. She laughed till she didn't have a voice anymore. Anna said the longer she laughed, the longer I'd remember what it sounded like. But I think I've forgotten now. It's been so long since I heard that sound. I think I've forgotten . . ."

Max sighed. The sigh rolled into a sob, and then sobs racked his body. He was devastated by the sight of scissors and a pale-blue robe and the shoes that his beloved had walked in. Elizabeth could no more fill those shoes than she could keep her own tears inside.

She cried quietly, weeping on Anna Marino's sewing box as she slid off the hearth and onto her knees in front of Max.

He reached first, throwing his arms around her and hanging on, hoping against hope that Elizabeth could hold him up or hold him together. For a moment she thought this impossible. Images of Christopher filled her mind, of his pain and his loneliness, and of all the things she couldn't give him. Yet it was for Christopher she found the strength Max needed. If she could help this man, then she could help her son.

"Come on, Max," Elizabeth whispered, her own tears held at bay, the wails pushed back to make room for comforting words. "Come on. Let me help you, Max. Come on."

She stood up, unsteady under his weight. Tugging harder, she spoke longer, until somehow he understood what he had to do. Crying, his head leaning against hers, their arms entwined so that they were closer than close, Elizabeth managed to get Max to the bathroom. Without turning on the light, she felt for him, her fingers fumbling with the buttons on his shirt until she was able to push it off. She placed her hand against his chest as if that loving pressure might ease the burden of his sorrow.

Together they wept while she did what she could for a man drunk on his anguish and guilt. She stripped him and held him up and turned on the water in the shower without once wishing for light. That would have shown her a Max she couldn't bear to see. His pain would have overwhelmed her. Then there would have been no help for either of them.

"Go in, Max." Elizabeth draped his arm around her

shoulder and nudged him toward the shower. "I want you to stand under the water. It's hot. Come on, Max. Don't fight me. Please don't fight me."

"I won't. I promise. I won't fight anymore. I won't be mad anymore." The slurred protestations made his voice sound almost childish, but Elizabeth knew it was the bourbon speaking. There was nothing childish in his hurt.

"Step up, Max. Step up, now. Just a little one. Just enough to get into the shower."

He did as he was told, and Elizabeth realized their tears had stopped as they'd worked together toward this simple goal. That, in itself, was a victory. With one last great effort, Max stepped under the steaming water. Swaying, he reached out to touch the sides of the stall. He slipped and Elizabeth, still trying to steady him, lost her grip and collapsed against the wall outside the shower. She didn't hear him fall. She didn't hear him cry out. She didn't hear him call for her. She only heard the rushing water. Elizabeth's chest rose and fell as she caught her breath, feeling nothing, thinking nothing, aware only that her clothes were wet and the job had been hard. Closing her eyes, she rested. Her tumultuous emotions settled inside her head, soothed by the sound of the water.

Suddenly the house was silent, and Elizabeth was being touched. Max stood naked beside her, his towel raised as he dabbed at the tears staining her cheeks. Ever so gently, he wiped away the moisture but not the tracks of her sorrow. Elizabeth's gut pulled tight, her fingers open against the wall behind her. She watched him, so intent in his task. When his lips moved to her eyes, she closed them and thanked God for his touch. And, as he kissed her, Max murmured Anna's name, reminding Elizabeth that love slept deeply, but didn't die.

Accepting that, needing his love more than she needed to banish Anna's ghost, she reached for him, touching his face. His cheek pressed so sweetly against hers that she felt immense joy in the very simplicity of their closeness. Was it hours or only minutes they stayed like that, the only movement Max's lips against the rise of her cheek? Time meant nothing; there was no time in heaven. Finally, Max's finger touched the base of her throat. Just a touch before trailing down her sweater until he was touching her no more. Once again, he laid his fingers on her. Two this time. Two cutting a wider path down her body, grazing her breasts until he was no longer touching again. Quietly in the darkness, he laid his hands upon her. Elizabeth covered his with her own, guiding them to her breasts before allowing herself the pleasure of touching him. Her hands spread out across his back. His skin, clean and warm from the shower, was inhumanely inviting. Their caresses became urgent. She felt confined; her clothes became cloying. It was he who began to undress her, she who finished the task. Their lips met, hungrily pressing together, biting, nipping, desperate in the begging, joyful language of love and desire. Elizabeth said his name and pulled him toward her, driving their demons and cares away for a moment, an hour, perhaps a lifetime. They twirled away, across the tiled floor and into the carpeted hallway, and then Elizabeth became aware of Max's anger.

Elizabeth's back hit the wall in the hall outside Max's bedroom. He pressed against her, the heat of his body a delicious contrast to the coolness of the painted plaster. She writhed, pushing back at him. Max clasped her hands. He kissed her. He pulled back to look at her. Suddenly he pulled her arms up, pinning them against the wall. They looked at one another. Max's eyes flashed fury in the dark; his grip tightened. Finally, quite slowly, he lowered his head and laid his cheek against her breast. The moment of rage had passed. The tremble of Elizabeth's breath cut through the silence. She let him lie against her, her hands still pinned at her shoulders, her skin slick with the heat of unfulfilled desire.

"Anna," Max whispered, and for a moment Elizabeth's heart stood on a precipice so deep she thought it would tumble over, lost forever in the face of this rejection. Then she realized that he wasn't calling for his wife, he was confessing his guilt. "Anna was dying and . . . I loved you. I loved you, Elizabeth. I shouldn't have. God help me, I did. I do. I love you."

That was enough. The heart that teetered, ready to fall into that black abyss, drew back and flew high with joy. Gently, she let her hands slide down the wall, pushing back on Max's arms until it was she who held him. Without a word, they moved together, collapsing onto the carpeted floor. There, the confession made and penance done, they tangled themselves together, stroking and kissing away the last tears. Together they cast off the shroud of mourning and lay under a blanket woven of passion and love, most of all love.

Part Three

Winter

Fifteen

"Christopher! Christopher, don't you dare leave this house again without telling me where you're going. Christopher! Please."

Elizabeth moved around the kitchen island, trying to retain some of her self-respect, wondering when they would stop this ritual dance. She wanted to chase him to the door, grab onto his jacket, pull him back into the house, and send him to his room. But how could she? The boy who was walking away from her without a word, such a look of disdain on his face, was no longer a boy. His hair grazed his shoulders, and no amount of coaxing or threatening could get him to cut it. He and David looked like street people. Hardly a normal sight here in Emerald Isle. Hardly what Elizabeth would have imagined her gorgeous, bright little boy would look like at ten and a half.

"Christopher!" She couldn't help herself. Elizabeth sprinted for the hall, but Max was there to stop her.

"No. Don't."

"But . . ." Elizabeth hardly heard him. All she saw was the front door closing. All she heard was the slam. All she knew was that Christopher had turned his back yet again.

"No." He put his arm around her shoulders and

pulled her close. "No," he said again, kissing the top of her head, letting his lips linger there as he soothed her frustration. "You can't do it that way. He's almost a teenager. Come on. Come sit with me."

"But I don't even know . . ."

"Where he's going," he finished for her. "I know, and that's got to be an awful feeling. But he's gone off before. The good news is he always comes home. So, come on. Calm down. Sit down. Want a cup of tea?"

He set her on the couch, weighted her down with his touch until he was sure she would stay, then kissed her squarely on the lips. She smiled reluctantly and kissed him back without seeing the shadow of worry darken his eyes.

"Better?" she asked, tipping her face for him to peruse her expression.

"Not much. I can still see the steam coming out of your ears," he joked.

"Sorry." She clamped her hands over her ears. "Better now?" She laughed, but it was an effort. She lowered her hands. "Thanks."

"No problem." He grinned, then added ruefully, "I'm not good for much else around here. You know it's me that's causing all this."

Elizabeth shook her head. "No way. It's everything, all of us, this whole damned situation. All my little mistakes and my big ones. They're piling up on top of each other. Now I've got a mountain of problems with Chris." Elizabeth cocked her head and looked at him narrowly. "And what are you grinning at?"

"You. Do you know that when you're upset, your accent sounds like you left Dixie a day ago?"

"Well, don't that beat all," she clowned, but the

cloud over her head was too dark. Her good humor didn't last. "Nice try, Max, but you and I both know this is getting worse."

Elizabeth stood abruptly and crossed her arms. She looked toward the kitchen, then out the bank of French doors to the pool. The cover was on, thank goodness. The water wouldn't freeze. Winter had been exceptionally cold but not cold enough for her. She wished there were ice and snow on the ground. She wished it were too treacherous for bike-riding and that Christopher had no choice but to stay home. Maybe then, they could figure out how to like each other again. Walking to those windows, Elizabeth placed her hand against a pane. Damn cold. Not cold enough.

"If Brad had just asked for a divorce we could have gone through our misery, dealt with it. This disappearing act just left Christopher dangling from one major loose end." Silent for a moment, she leaned closer to the window as if she wanted to rest there. Instead, her head swiveled, her long blond hair creasing over her shoulder, her green eyes far from playful. "Do you know that Brad didn't even say goodbye to Chris? He hadn't talked to him for about three weeks before he just disappeared."

"No, I didn't. No wonder the poor kid feels like he's on a roller coaster. His father does that, and then I show up. I'd say he has a few reasons to feel out of place."

"I know. But what do I do about it? I can't afford therapy, and I'm not even convinced that's the answer, either." Elizabeth moved away from the windows, going to the fireplace where the logs burned low already. Wood was so expensive, but a fire was inviting, the sign of a home filled with warmth. Why didn't Christopher want to be here where Max loved her and would love him if he'd give it half a chance? "Max, I've tried to find Brad as best I could. Why can't he just understand that and accept it?"

"Because he's young. Look, sweetheart, your son grew up with a family. His own mom and dad living in the same house, having dinner together, going to his baseball games together. Then he turns ten. His hormones start kicking in. He's trying to figure out where he fits in this big, bad world. The kids at school are all jockeying for position; schoolwork's getting harder. More is expected of him. The one thing he can count on is Mom and Dad. Then Dad goes to live somewhere else. Then Dad disappears. Pretty heavy stuff."

"But it happens to other people," Elizabeth protested miserably.

"Did knowing other women had been deserted make Brad's leaving any easier for you?" He opened his hands, that bit of wisdom given. "Did knowing that make you cry less or want less or be less afraid?"

"No," Elizabeth muttered, her answer almost inaudible. She put her hand on the mantel and fingered the slick wood. Three little hooks protruded beneath it. The hooks their Christmas stockings hung on.

"When the doctors told us how many other people had multiple sclerosis, it didn't make Anna's situation any easier, either." Max wrapped his arms around her waist, pulling her back against him. She laid her hands over his, loving these affectionate moments together as much as their passionate times. Max sighed and leaned his chin atop her head. "So if *you* didn't feel any better, and *I* didn't feel any better, do you think

Christopher does when you tell him this happens to other people?"

Elizabeth chuckled. "It does sound ridiculous, doesn't it?"

"No. You just want him to be happy because we are." He laughed as she moved in his arms, facing him now, her hands lying on his chest. "And he will be, because we're going to work on this together. I promise, everything will be fine."

Max touched her chin, two fingers holding her head up until she looked into his eyes and saw the one thing Brad couldn't give her: Commitment. Lord, this was what made a lifetime of love. Nothing would break them up.

"I believe you," Elizabeth said, cuddling into him, letting him hold her while she worried. "But what do we do now?"

"Leave him alone. Let him be an angry kid. I'll keep a close eye on him so he doesn't hurt himself. Believe me, I did exactly the same thing at his age," he lied gently.

"I didn't."

"Then you're a saint."

"Has a nice ring to it," Elizabeth agreed.

Max shook his head and tightened his hold. "I don't think so."

Elizabeth turned her head, gazing up at this man she loved so dearly.

"Why not? I think I'd look great with a halo."

"Saints are only interested in the soul. I definitely like your preoccupation with all this physical stuff."

"Now that," she sighed, "is a great answer. You're right. I think I'll keep my feet of clay awhile longer."

"Thank goodness," he murmured and kissed her long and hard before holding her away. "But before we do anything about that, I've got some stuff to do."

"Max," she said, stopping him at the door just as he was buttoning his jacket. "You do think he's all right, don't you?"

"No doubt about it, sweetheart. This is Emerald Isle. Bad things don't happen in Emerald Isle, not when I've built half the place. I'll be back as soon as I can."

With a confident smile, Elizabeth let him go, but as soon as the cherry-red truck had pulled out of the drive and disappeared down the street, Elizabeth grabbed her coat, too. Dear Max, how sure he was and how wrong he could be. Bad things did happen in Emerald Isle. Brad had left her in Emerald Isle. Christopher was self-destructing in Emerald Isle.

Bundled up, she let herself out the door. She couldn't stay in that silent house waiting, not knowing where her son was. She had to move. A walk was what she needed. A friendly face. Another opinion.

"Oh my God, you must be freezing. Get in here. It's got to be thirty degrees out there." Leslie pulled Elizabeth inside and shut the door. "Give me that coat and go over by the fire. I've had it going all day—and the heat up, too! I don't know who it was that started this rumor about California having the perfect weather. Whoever it was, I'd like to shoot him."

"It could be worse, Leslie. There could be snow on the ground," Elizabeth said through chattering teeth.

"No, that would be better. At least everyone would have a good excuse to stay inside. When it's just cold, you can still drive and go to the grocery store and work. Miserable, if you ask me. I can't wait for spring."

The coat hung up, Leslie put her arm around Elizabeth and hurried her into the living room.

"Spring would be nice." Elizabeth stopped in front of the blazing fire while Leslie scurried to clear a space off the sofa. Papers were scattered everywhere. "What is all this stuff?"

"New sales tools. The company brought us into the space age."

"Looks kind of confusing to me," Elizabeth admitted, abandoning the fire for the coffee table. Holding up a pie chart, she looked at the colors. There were so many it seemed no one had the biggest piece.

"It's not. Just a different way of looking at information. Our office manager got some new software, and he insists we all incorporate his charts and graphs into our sales kit. We're supposed to do this whole presentation when we try to land a new client."

"Do you do it?"

Leslie shook her head. "Noooo, ma'am! I usually hand it to someone to page through. That whole client thing is just chemistry, pure and simple." Leslie's eyes sparkled. "And speaking of chemistry, why aren't you cuddled up with Max on a day like this? You should be sipping hot chocolate and playing Monopoly with Christopher."

Elizabeth set aside the papers, her expression so instantly grim Leslie didn't need a word of explanation.

"Ooops. Spoke out of turn, did I?" She moved a few more papers and sat down next to Elizabeth. "Okay, who is it? Max? Christopher? Or both?"

"Chris."

"Again? Honey, I'm so sorry."

"I know. And I hate to bother you with more of my troubles, but I'm just about at the end of my rope. He walked out again today. One minute I was asking him to take out the trash, and the next minute he was walking through the door without a word. Just leaving. He didn't even answer me."

"Was Max there?"

Elizabeth nodded. She started to put Leslie's papers in order, just to have something to do. Leslie let her go.

"He says all boys go through this defiance thing." Elizabeth abandoned her chore. "I don't know. My gut tells me there's just something more I could be doing."

"Short of tying him up?" Leslie drawled. "Want something to eat?"

Elizabeth shook her head and pulled a face. Food was the last thing on her mind. "Be serious, Leslie."

"I've always been serious about Christopher and what I think he needs. You, however, have always been serious about kindly telling me to butt out."

"Okay, so I've been a bit self-righteous . . ." Elizabeth began. Leslie raised a brow. "Self-centered? Self-absorbed? Can you blame me?"

"No," Leslie said kindly. "I don't. You had more on your plate than most. But you put on blinders when it comes to Chris. You still don't want to do the one thing you have to do to get Christopher back on track."

"And what is that? What?" Elizabeth sank to the floor, sitting cross-legged, disheartened.

"Just find Brad. Really, really try. Christopher can't move forward until he gets some closure. He's got memories, and unfinished business. There have been misunderstandings between you because of Brad and because of Max. He doesn't know where the man is he can look up to. If he sees his father face to face and gets answers to his questions, then Chris can decide who it is that loves him. He's also got to decide whom he should trust and love."

"We've been through that. It's expensive and . . ."

"Not as expensive as it's going to be to rescue Chris once he's fallen through that crack for good," she warned.

"I can't, Leslie. I can't. I don't want to see Brad. I don't want to hear his voice. I don't . . ."

"This isn't about you. Elizabeth, please." Leslie was on the floor beside her friend. She almost took Elizabeth's hand but decided against it. "This isn't about you anymore. You've walked down your road and found your light. There's no reason for you to be afraid of Brad. But you've left Christopher in the dark. Go back for him. Guide him. Prove you're strong enough to at least make the effort. Max can take it, honey. So can you. Give Chris a chance to come to terms with his father. At least show him you're making one last try. Do this for him."

It was a perfect high-desert winter day. Blindingly bright, the sun tilting at windmills as it warred with bone-chilling temperatures. This was the type of day Max loved. He adored the expectation of warmth only to find his skin prickling, his eyes tearing, his ears tingling with cold. These were collar-up days. Glove days. Days when you just wanted to stay inside with your feet up and the game on. A day where you could work and yell at a crew and see your breath in front of you. A day where you could take your woman to bed and heat up the world without a problem.

But Max wasn't doing any of the things he loved. He was out driving his cherry-red truck through neighborhoods nestled at the base of barren hills. His eyes were peeled, not for a new location for another development, but for the familiar flash of electric blue shot with yellow and violet. The colors of Christopher's jacket. The colors not of a gang, but of a kid alone and getting angrier by the day.

Max sighed, fighting his annoyance. Not for the first time, he wondered what possessed him to seek out Elizabeth MacMillan. If he'd tried, he couldn't have made a worse choice. Just his luck to fall in love with a lady with a ton of baggage, the most cumbersome of which was a boy teetering on the edge of delinquency. He leaned his elbow on the window ledge and rubbed his jaw, admitting, just to himself, that it was silly to even think about the downside of the relationship. The upside outweighed it by a mile.

The first time Max had seen Elizabeth he'd thought she was beautiful. When he'd stood in her dining room watching her cry, he'd thought her tragic. She was both. But she was also brave and giving and kind. What other woman would have stood silently by, her hand on his shoulder, as he watched the love of his life pass away? How many other women would have allowed him to mourn for Anna more than he loved the living lady waiting for him? Was there another woman who would love so gently, give so freely, laugh and work and fight for her life with such single-mindedness? Was there another woman who would admit her mistakes and confusion so readily? Perhaps. But there was no other that affected him the way Elizabeth did. Despite all her wonderful qualities, the thing that made her unique and incredibly desirable was indefinable. It was that "something" that kept him coming back, exploring, curious about her—and her son. Yes, he did want them both, and it was time he told Christopher that, man to man.

Max turned east, and more than one head turned to watch him drive slowly down the street. Any other day, the homage paid to his truck would have brought a smile to his face. Today he didn't even notice such automotive adulation. Every kid on a bike came under scrutiny. Every boy standing in a group was his possible quarry. Every quick movement on a sidewalk made Max attentive. And finally, just as he thought it might be time to give up, Max found Chris.

He pulled to the side of the road and looked across the street. A small strip mall—a liquor store separate and apart. The shopping center parking lot was jammed with Christmas shoppers, but the traffic was light. Max had a clear view of Christopher and his friends. Friends, he thought with disgust. Not the boys he would have chosen if Christopher were his son. Since that just might be the case someday, Max opened the truck door without a second thought and stepped out. He waited for a car to go by, then jogged toward the knot of kids.

Chris saw him coming. His eyes slid Max's way with a hint of panic and then a posturing of indifference. Chris was cool. Chris was tough. But, from what Max could see, Chris was not as tough as his companions. Christopher, sitting on the curb, said something to the three young men standing around him.

They looked over their shoulders and checked out the man. Max almost broke stride. These were no kids. Older than Chris, they appeared scary even to Max . . . the kind of boys who yelled at their parents when they were five, stole their first booty at nine, and ended up in jail for assault and battery by the time they were fifteen. Some of them killed. These were the boys that stood on the edge of society and, Max realized, Christopher couldn't hold his own with them no matter how hard he tried. And he was trying hard.

His hair was long, his expression properly surly, yet behind the facade was the sparkle of a good kid, a kind kid, one who simply needed to be shown that the troubles in his life could work out. It was a hard job, but Max thought he could handle it. So he walked right up to the four of them and talked to the kid who didn't belong.

"Chris." Max was a big man, but the three guys at his back made him feel vulnerable. He squared his shoulders, kept his eyes on Chris. He wanted to whisk the boy away pronto, but their escape had to be casual. "I've been looking for you."

"Here I am." Chris had the lazy eyes and the drawl down pat. Max's jaw tightened.

"So I see." Max wandered toward the group, stopping just short of Chris. "What're you doing?"

"He's just about to find God." Behind him, someone laughed. Max tried to resist the urge to look over his shoulder and failed. He turned his head just enough to see them high-fiving each other, palming a tab of acid. Things hadn't changed much since he was young: Bad kids still did bad things.

"I think he'll be getting his religious experience at

home. We're outta here, Chris." Max acted fast, reaching over and taking Chris' arm. He held tight, but Chris shook him off, planting himself on the curb again. Stupid kid. He didn't have a clue what was going down?

"I'm staying," Chris said, without looking at Max. "These are my friends."

"I'm your friend, Chris, and I say you're going."

This time when he took Christopher's arm, he held tight and yanked the boy up. Much as he hated to do it, swiftness of action was the key to success. Don't give him time to react, he told himself, just pull and drag before he could kick and scream. It worked pretty well. What Max hadn't counted on was Christopher's friends. Obviously, they didn't want to lose a convert. They moved fast, too, one of them wedging himself in between Chris and Max, the other two standing tight, a menacing guard behind. Max looked into each of their faces, even glanced at Chris long enough to see trepidation etched there. This was more than he'd counted on. Max let go, knowing full well this show of force had nothing to do with their affection for Christopher. They smelled sport, so he faced them, drawing his shoulders back to let them know he didn't want to play. But they didn't care what he wanted.

"He said he don't want to go, mister. I think you'd better leave Chris right here with us. He's havin' a good time. Ain't you, Christopher?" The leader drew out the syllables of the boy's name, and even Chris understood things had changed. Out of the corner of his eye, Max saw him move slightly. He edged away from the boys toward Max, standing a bit behind him. When he spoke, though, he was still defiant.

"I'm just hanging out," he muttered. "Nothing wrong with that."

"Nothing wrong with that, mister," the leader said again, this time mimicking Chris and sticking his face into Max's. He was a good-looking punk with a matte finish to his eyes that said he didn't give a shit about much of anything. "You're not his father, are you? Come on, man. You his father, or something?"

"No. I'm not his father," Max said evenly.

"Then beat it."

With that the guy with the black hair and flat eyes threw a punch. Max ducked, blocking it just before the fist would have smashed into the side of his head. The guy was vicious, but his aim was miserable. Max stepped back, his hands up in the universal sign of peace.

"I don't want any trouble here . . ." he began.

"Well, you got it," the leader spat back, humiliated that he hadn't taken Max out first try. Behind him, the other two hoodlums bounced on the balls of their feet, sharks smelling blood. They grinned at Max. Christopher had been forgotten, useless now that he'd provided a reason to beat Max to a pulp.

Max stiffened, knowing the situation was grim. His eyes darted toward the window. Behind the counter in the liquor store, a clerk paged through a magazine, a pair of earphones tight on her head. Even if she saw anything, it would be over before she called the police. The liquor store itself sat far back from the main road. The cars that drove by had purpose and, even if their drivers noticed his predicament, Max doubted any would want to get involved in the fray. Christmas shoppers were rushing back and forth into the shopping center to their left, oblivious to the drama being played out. There seemed a slim chance of help, but when it came, it came from a close and surprising source.

"Hey, he's okay. He's not my dad, but he's okay." Christopher stepped forward, standing beside Max in a bold move. "Come on, leave him alone."

"Naw, man, you don't want to go with him. We'll make him go." The two henchmen made agreeable noises. No kid was going to keep them from their fun. But Chris was talking fast, spinning awkwardly yet effectively, his hand on Max's arm.

"I gotta go anyway. I'll talk to you tomorrow." Chris patted the air, keeping his hands low, trying to keep everyone calm. "Tomorrow. Okay?"

Together, Max and Christopher turned away, Max saying a prayer of thanks under his breath. It was Max who looked back once. The leader still watched them, losing interest when he saw they would soon be out of range. Max breathed a sigh of relief, but Chris veered off, heading away alone toward the back of the store.

"Hey, Chris, come on. Where you going?" Chris trudged on, ignoring Max. The older man was on him instantly. This time he grabbed Chris' shoulder and spun him around. "I've had it, Chris. This isn't a game anymore. I want you to come with me right this minute before one of us gets hurt. Believe me, those guys have had practice at beating faces in. I don't want yours to get cracked, and I sure as hell don't want mine to. So cut the crap, kid, and let's get the hell out of here. Grow up. Work this out. Your mom's worried. We've had enough."

"I gotta get my bike," he sniped.

Max hesitated, thrown off by the logic. Flustered,

embarrassed not to have thought of it, he moved past Chris.

"I'll get it," he mumbled angrily.

"I'll get it, Max. Just leave me alone and I'll go home." Christopher sidestepped Max. "I'll go home," he said, making home sound like a four-letter-word. "Just leave me the fuck alone."

"That's it." Max stormed ahead of Chris toward the side of the store. The guys still hung out, watching the two of them with renewed interest. Max stopped abruptly, no longer nervous, feeling mighty in his frustration. He planted his feet, pointing at the three of them. "Stay the hell away from this kid or I'll have the cops on you so fast your heads will spin."

Behind him, Chris wailed, losing face in front of the older boys he wanted to impress. The three delinquents laughed, flashing gang finger signs and insults, knocking each other on the shoulder as Max stomped toward Christopher's bike. Without a word, he lifted it up and slung it over his shoulder. Storming back, he went right past Christopher and growled.

"Get in the truck. Now."

By the time Max had the bicycle secured in the bed of the truck, Christopher was inside.

"Seat belt," Max commanded, buckling his own. He slammed the key into the ignition, and the truck thundered to life. Max shifted. He checked his mirrors and they were out of there, driving without another word until Max swung into the parking lot of the first coffee shop he saw. Five minutes later, he was sitting across from Christopher. The boy was sprawled over the red Naugahyde, staring out the window, cold fury enveloping him. Max gave a tight-lipped smile to the waitress.

Giving Max a knowing and sympathetic look, she handed him the menu and left them alone. Max opened it and, without looking at Chris, said, "Don't you ever use that kind of language with me again. Don't you ever let me hear you using it with your mother, do you understand?"

"I don't have to listen to you," Christopher mumbled.

Max continued to peruse the menu. He closed the leatherette booklet, placed it on the table, and crossed his arms atop it.

"Fine, then I'll listen to you." Max's expression was noncommittal. He looked directly at Christopher, neither challenging him nor slighting him, and waited for Chris to talk. The boy remained silent. Minutes ticked by and Chris squirmed, uncomfortable now that there was no confrontation. Max cocked his head, his invitation a challenge. "Come on. I'm here, I've got all the time in the world, and I'm ready to listen. Tell me what you have to say."

"I don't have anything to say." Chris' voice rose an uncomfortable octave.

"Then you're a baby," Max said quietly.

Christopher's eyes flashed. The view outside the window lost its allure. Max was insulting him. Everything he'd thought about this guy was right. Max didn't care about him at all. Max didn't even like him.

"You're a baby, and those guys back there would have chewed you up and spit you out." Max let that sink in. There was no indication that Chris heard what he said, but Max knew it had made an impact. He waited a beat longer than necessary, never taking his eyes off Chris. He sighed deeply, a giving-up kind of sound. "I thought you were better than that. I thought you were almost grown up. I thought you had ideas. I thought you were mad because nobody would listen, but you're just plain mad. Here's your chance to talk, and you clam up. And if you don't want to tell me what you think, then I guess you're just angry because you're a kid. So, let's order something to eat. Then I'll take your bike out of the back of the truck and you can go wherever you want."

Max looked around for the waitress. He raised his hand, ready to hail her, but Christopher had leaned forward. He was ready to speak. His voice was low, and his face was blazing with the outrage he felt.

"I'm not a baby," he sneered, his hands on the table, his sights straight on his tormentor. Max had to give him credit for that. It was brave for a kid to stand his ground with someone as angry as Max. "I'm mad because of you. You shouldn't be in our house. You shouldn't be with my mother. You're stupid, and you don't have anything that's good. You're nothing but a dumb construction worker, and I hate you for being in our house. My mother forgets about everything when you're around. You're the one who should go somewhere, not me. Not me. That's *my* house, and *my* mother, and *my* dad is going to come home soon and he's going to hate you, too."

Max, still poised to call for the waitress, closed his eyes. He smiled to himself, careful not to let his expression change. Amazing. There was actually a chance he could pull this off. Max settled into the booth, looked at the boy across from him, saw the swelling of tears behind the flash of superiority, and played the advantage. Max lowered his hand, his attention on Chris.

"Fair enough," he said quietly, forcing himself not to smile with relief.

Christopher started. He had the look of a deer caught in the headlights. Confused, he looked around at the other people in the restaurant. Couples, families, people on their own—all intent on themselves. He was captive in this red-vinyl booth. Max wasn't even going to give him a reason to bolt and run. Hesitant, dubious of the game Max was playing, Chris took a chance and began to talk.

"I'm mad at my mom, too," he said quietly, and suddenly the pent-up anger poured out.

With each expletive, the child in him surfaced. Their drinks came, then the food. Max drank and ate. Christopher touched his plate and poked at his meal, his young brow knitted as he tried to find the right words. And he found them, over and over again in so many different ways, but always the meaning was the same.

"People are supposed to do what they promise. She promised to do lots of stuff when she married my dad. I don't think she should have any respect until she doesn't see you anymore. You're the one who made us seem bad in the neighborhood."

"Who says you're bad?" Max asked quietly.

Chris shrugged, a valiant attempt at seeming impervious to hurts, both real and imagined. "Everybody. The lady next door thinks Mom did something bad to make Dad leave. My friends don't have me to their houses anymore. It's because of you, and because my mom isn't waiting for my dad to come home."

"Come on, Chris. It's not any of those things," Max

began gently. "I didn't even meet your mom until your dad had been gone for a long time. We didn't get together until way after that. And what about your friends? Most people don't stop being friends because of something that happens in a family. Come on, buddy, think hard. Why do people stop being friends?"

"You sound like my stupid teacher. You want me to think about the answer and find it for myself. I know what you're doing, and it's stupid," Christopher groused.

"No, it isn't. You know the answer because you've been thinking about this a long time. If I tell you, it won't make it any more right or wrong. I could sit here all day and tell you that your neighbor is an idiot, but not your whole neighborhood. I could tell you that lots of people have lots of different relationships. Some are well-intentioned and some aren't. The way your mom and I feel about each other is good. I love your mom. I promise, Chris, I'm not going to hurt her and she's not doing anything bad."

"But my dad's going to come home. And when he does, he'll find out about the two of you. He'll know that my mom . . ." For all the worldly airs Christopher had acquired during the last few months, he couldn't bring himself to talk about certain things. His voice cracked, a lump of embarrassment and outrage thick in his throat. "He'll know that you've been in her room. Then it really will be over. My dad won't stay home. My dad won't want my mom anymore, and we'll never be happy again. Ever."

That did it. Christopher's reserves were used up. The facial planes that had been chiseled by his anger now fell into the full cheeks of a desperate, scared child.

In Max's eyes, he became very young indeed, and very dear. The revelation was strange and wonderful, interesting and frightening at the same time: He finally knew what Elizabeth felt like. To be responsible for a child's mind and well-being, to soothe his fears and let him grow at the same time, was an awesome task and a frightening responsibility. How wonderful it must be when the child grows up and becomes an adult to be proud of. How awful to fail that child.

"No, Chris," Max whispered. He reached across the table so that his hands lay close to, but didn't touch the boy's. "You'll never be happy like you were. You won't feel the safety a boy feels when he looks at his mom and dad together or lives in the same house with them. You'll always feel that something wonderful was lost. For as long as you live, you'll remember when things were right with you and you'll wish for that time again. But as you get older, it won't hurt so much. Then one day, you'll realize that just because you can't have one kind of perfect doesn't mean there isn't another kind out there for you."

"There isn't," Christopher said, his words punctuated by staccato breaths. Max's eyes softened. How hard it could be not to cry. Hadn't he tried often enough?

"Yes, there is," he whispered. "I know. Because I found your mom. I was married to a lady I loved very much, and I watched her die. Not like in the movies, Chris. She died in a really bad way. And when that happened, I felt worse than when she was sick and I blamed your mom for that. I almost threw her away. I almost stayed in my house and got mad at the world.

I would have stayed there if your mom hadn't come to get me."

Chris eyed him. Max could see he was trying desperately to keep the anger alive but the conversation was extinguishing the flame. They should have had it long ago. Max talked on, hoping he was hitting some of the right notes. He spoke faster, as if he could coax Christopher into comprehension.

"I was mad at your mom for being so understanding. I wanted her to be angry at me and leave me so that I could prove that I was bad. Then I would know that, somehow, I had caused my wife to die. Maybe you feel that this is your fault, your dad leaving. But your dad left for his own reasons and he didn't bother to tell anyone. Don't you think that was a bad thing? Don't you think your mom was scared and wanted to blame someone, too?"

Chris shrugged. "But she went out and got a job and everything stayed the same. It was like my dad hadn't even been there. Everything just went on."

"No, it didn't, Chris." Max laughed sadly, seeing how destructive strength could be. "Your mom worked hard to make it seem that nothing had changed. She didn't want you to be worried or scared. So, you see, you're mad at her for trying her best to do something good. Don't do this to your mom. If you need someone to blame, blame me, but give your mom a break. She needs it, Chris. She needs you and she needs me, but for different reasons, and what she really needs is for us to pull together."

Max sat back, exhausted by the speech. Christopher's face was still a play of conflicting emotions. His eyes, so much like Elizabeth's, burned with a fever

Max was powerless to ease. Max looked out the window at the fading afternoon. All his good intentions—and what had he accomplished? Chris still clung to the most real emotion he had—anger.

"Chris," Max said thoughtfully, his eyes still averted, "your home won't be happy unless the people who are there want to be, unless they stay because they want to stay. Your dad doesn't want to be with your mom, or you. Nobody knows why. Let him go now. Wonder about him." Max looked back at the boy. "Think about him. Still love him if you can, but understand that it's his problem—not yours or mine or your mom's. Let him live his life; then let's start living one just for us." Max leaned across the table again, one last spurt of energy coming to the fore. "Come on, man. Your mom needs you to be strong. She needs you to grow up a little more."

That did it. With those few words he destroyed the bridge he'd almost finished building. Christopher's face clouded, black with fury. Max had committed a mortal sin—he had pointed out Christopher's youth, branded him as infantile. Worse yet, Max had told him his father didn't care.

"Go to hell, Max. You don't know anything. You're so stupid." Christopher tried to slide out of the booth gracefully, but his legs were too short to give him the propulsion he needed. Thwarted, he hit the vinyl with an open hand. The sound reverberated throughout the coffee shop. Chris' cry of helplessness following in its wake. The waitress turned. The people in the booths on either side stopped their conversations and stared.

"Chris, come on," Max said, begging the boy to get hold of himself. "I'm sorry. It was the wrong thing to say. I didn't mean it the way it sounded. Think about your mom."

"You think about her. That's all you do anyway. You eat our food, you sleep in our house; you might just as well move in for good. Go ahead, Max. I don't care. I don't care about anything anymore."

He shot out of the booth, working his shoulders into his jacket.

"And you know what?" he demanded angrily. "You can't make me. You can't make me, Max. You can't make me do anything. You're not my father."

Chris stormed down the aisle of the coffee shop shouting his protestations, but Max could have sworn that by the time the boy got to the door he was crying. Helplessly, Max watched him go. Brad MacMillan might not be around, but he was staring right at Max and laughing.

Sixteen

Needlepoint on her lap, Elizabeth looked at Max sleeping on the couch. One arm was thrown over his eyes, the other over the side of the couch. On the flickering television, two football teams battled it out on a snow-covered field while crowds of fans, bundled to the nose, waved banners and gloved hands. Elizabeth wasn't sure if they were cheering or jeering, because Max had turned the game down to "snoozing" volume.

Outside, the weather was frightfully cold, even for the high desert. The morning frost had made Emerald Isle look like a fairyland; but now, well into the afternoon, it still lingered. The lawn would surely die if the cold didn't break soon. But it wasn't the weather that captivated Elizabeth, it was the Christmas tree.

Decorating with loving care, Elizabeth and Max had shared stories late into the night as they'd strung lights and made memories of their own. He had brought some of his own ornaments and hung them on the tree. Chris had grumbled when they'd tried to include him in the decorating, and, as Christmas came closer and closer, he avoided home as much as possible. Elizabeth understood. Christmas conjured up visions of family and togetherness. Chris chose to believe that could still be a reality with Brad. Elizabeth had made another choice.

This season was a time of hope, a celebration of their victories in the face of what had seemed insurmountable odds. This was the season of beginnings. Elizabeth chose to exalt in the joy Max brought to her life. She chose to look forward, promising herself that in the coming year they would find the magic to heal Christopher.

Almost nine months earlier, she had had to beg for work. Now she was supervising the day staff. A year ago, she had questioned her worth; now Max loved her for herself. Months ago, Brad had walked out, and a few weeks ago, she had hired a private detective to find him. Closure was needed and closure was what she would give Chris for Christmas, no matter how long it took.

There was one other thing she wanted to do, and now the time was right. Elizabeth set aside her needlepoint and made a decision. She pushed herself off the love seat, careful not to make any noise. She walked gingerly to the tree behind the sofa on which Max slept, knelt down, and lifted the paper tags on the brightly wrapped packages.

"Looking for something?"

"Oh!" Elizabeth's head shot up right into the branches of the tree. Ornaments tinkled; lights blinked furiously, and Max grinned at her from over the back of the sofa. Sleep-tousled, he never looked more glorious. Caught, she sat back on her heels and put out her hands to keep the branches from swaying. She admitted her sin—sort of. "I was just checking to see if I'd forgotten any of Christopher's gifts."

"And taking a look to see if any had the name Elizabeth on them?" Max cocked a brow.

Elizabeth tilted her head and raised her shoulder. "Maybe."

"And maybe you thought you might just shake one or two of them? Kind of get a feel for how you're supposed to react tomorrow morning when we open them up?"

"Well, what would it hurt? I mean, what can you really tell from a shake?"

"I don't know. Shall we see?" Max climbed over the top of the sofa and settled himself beside her. Running his hands through his hair, he paused, looked her right in the eye, and said, "Now, remember, you can't tell a thing from shaking a box, right?"

"Right," Elizabeth agreed, properly sobered by being found out, but thrilled to have the chance to rummage around the beautifully wrapped presents.

"Okay. So, let's take a look. Oh, here's one with your name on it!" Max held up an oblong shape with tines peeking out of the snowman paper. "Hmmm. This is a tough one. What do you think?" He held it up and waved it around. "A scepter for the queen of the house?"

Elizabeth reached out and took it from him, "Oh, you're sweet. A pasta server. Just what I've always wanted!"

"Darn. You've a good eye," Max teased. Considering the assortment of gifts, he put a finger to his cheek, reached under the tree, and pulled out a gold one. No wrapping on this one. Store logo. Very nice store. "Go ahead." He held it out to her. "Shake to your heart's content . . ." Her hands were on the box when the phone rang. Max grinned. "I'll get it. . . . Your eyes are the size of saucers. Go ahead. I dare you to figure this one out while I'm gone."

Elizabeth sat back on her heels, not caring what was in the gold box. Max made her happy—teasing her, trying to please her for no other reason than the joy of it. Lifting her face, letting her hair fall down her back, Elizabeth turned a smile Max's way when he walked back into the family room.

"I don't know why you're so good to me . . ." she began, stopping the minute she saw him.

Max stood halfway between her and the door, his eyes darting frantically back and forth as if he needed to run but couldn't decide which way to go. Elizabeth was up, instantly by his side, holding onto his rigid arms.

"Max, what is it?"

"I've got to go. I've got to go now. There's a fire. . . . My houses are on fire. They're having trouble getting the hydrants to work right. I've got to go." Max spoke quickly, his hands moving in mechanical gestures.

"Oh my God!"

Max dashed through the front door before Elizabeth could say another word. Reacting, she hurried after him, grabbing their coats as she went, forgetting gloves and hats. Max was already backing out of the driveway when she screamed for him to wait, tore open the door, and threw herself into the cab. Max hit the gas. Before the gear kicked in, they looked north. Belching into the winter sky, a column of black smoke rose behind the first phase of Emerald Isle. The truck jumped. Elizabeth grabbed the armrest. They were on the back lot before either could think; once there, neither of them wanted to.

Three fire engines had already arrived. Two battled blazes that, if left unattended, would have been devastating, but were now well under control. Max ran to the third engine but was pushed back, away from the blaze.

"That's mine!" he screamed, clawing at the firemen who detained him. Max struggled, a strong man held by those who were stronger and in their right minds. Still, Max bellowed. "That's my trailer. My houses! Damn you, let me through!"

Elizabeth rushed up, grabbing his arm, trying to pull him back.

"Max! Don't! Max, let them work!" she cried, her fingers cold, her face hot from the blaze.

He shook her off. Wild-eyed, he fought Elizabeth and the men, half listening to what they were hollering at him until the tallest of the firefighters did the only thing he could: He hit Max square in the jaw, sending him sprawling in the cold, hard dirt. The man was on him before the stars left Max's eyes. His knee on Max's chest, he shouted over the roar of the fire and the rush of the water.

"Listen, buddy, I don't care who you are. The only thing you could do if you got past me would be to get yourself killed. It's cold, so the water isn't working so good. The wood is dry 'cause there hasn't been any rain, and your whole project's going to go up in smoke if you screw around with us. Is that what you want?"

The man didn't wait for an answer. An explosion popped in the heart of the fire, and he ran off, calling to his men and jerking his thumb at Elizabeth. She knew what she had to do. Instantly, she was on her knees in the dirt beside Max, helping him to sit, then stand. Elizabeth held tight, pulling him back when it seemed he might rush forward again. But he simply stumbled against her, like an animal caged, before standing immobilized on a spot that wasn't quite safe but at least wasn't in the heart of the inferno. From there Max watched the blaze like a man possessed, the towers of flame reflecting in his eyes, cinders falling around his head. Black feathers of charred wood floated in air that was as hot as the devil's breath. Ash colored the air like a dismal snow. Behind them, Elizabeth was not unaware that people had gathered to watch the destruction of Max's dream. She ignored them. She ignored everything but Max.

"Max! Max!" Elizabeth screamed, her hands wrapped around his arms as she tried to hold tight when he moved too far forward. Her voice seemed to egg him on. He pushed against her. Tears of frustration and heat streamed down Elizabeth's face. She sobbed, afraid for him, for them. "Come on, Max, move back."

A wind funnel fanned the building site, and the flames billowed into a huge balloon of golden-red fire that towered above them, a hideous genie that no one, it seemed, could stuff back into the bottle. Max pulled himself up to his full height, arms out, his hands fisted as if he could damn the thing away. His mouth was open but no words, not even those of fury, came from him.

Elizabeth was exhausted, powerless to keep him from moving, so she skittered in front of him. Her back searing as Max's forward movement pushed her closer to the blaze, Elizabeth realized she was nothing more than a minor hindrance. His eyes were wide open and staring, oblivious to everything but the flames. He didn't see the danger. He saw only his life being burned to the ground.

"Max." She breathed hard, pushing with all her might against his chest, slipping on the frost-slick dirt. Her head was against his chest, her arms wrapped around him. She couldn't scream anymore; her voice was raw from the heat and cold, so she talked and held and hoped he would understand. "Max, listen to me. You can't help. Max." She sobbed, wrapping her hands in the fabric of his jacket, losing the battle. "You can't help. Listen to me, dammit. Someone else has to do this. Someone else, do you hear me?"

But he didn't hear or listen. He pushed past her, going around her, moving sideways, his hands now fallen to his side.

"Max," she cried, tears falling without shame. She sniffled, wiping her nose with her sleeve. Hands out, Elizabeth begged, "Max, please. Please come back. I love you."

When he finally stopped, standing as still as a statue, illuminated gold-and-red by the fire, Elizabeth fell on him, sobbing, her hands running up and down his lean, muscled arms, stroking and caressing and begging him to turn away from the horrible sight. At last, as if waking from a dream, Max pulled himself up and put his hands over his eyes. He rubbed, but when he looked again the inferno still blazed and the men in yellow coats still tried to tame it with huge hoses that gushed a never-ending stream of water.

"Elizabeth" was all Max said.

Still crying, she wrapped her arms around his waist

as he pulled her close. Together, they stood—she crying, he stoic. They watched until the last lick of flame had been defeated. They watched until nothing but gray, ghostlike columns of smoke wafted over what remained of the second division of Emerald Isle.

It was only three in the afternoon, but it might as well have been midnight. The sky was dark with clouds that threatened rain. If only they had made good on their threat hours ago . . . if only God had opened up the heavens and poured down every ounce of angel-tears onto Max's beautiful work . . . but God had blinked and left it to the firemen to do what they could. Now, the air was clearing and they wandered through the mess in shock. Stepping lightly where they could—as if their care could save a beam that hadn't been completely consumed, nails that hadn't been melted. They went in silence. Max stooped now and again to pick up something important to him. These he piled in a pitiful heap.

Elizabeth couldn't watch; nor could she cry anymore. Her eyes were swollen, her hands cold, her feet aching. She was aware of all this, yet she felt numb and empty. Hands stuffed deep in the pockets of her jacket, she wandered away from Max but resolutely returned to his side again. On and on they went in small circles and squares until Max called a halt to their journey. He stood on a small rise, surveying the scene. "Forty still standing—sort of."

Elizabeth nodded and pulled her chin deeper into her collar. She tried hard to focus on those that were untouched, but found herself looking at the charred remains instead.

"The trailer is gone," he said flatly. "My files."

"Do you have copies?"

Max nodded. "Plans. They're filed. I can get them from the city. Correspondence, no; but I remember enough. I've got some copies at home. It'll take awhile to pull things together."

"I can help. On the weekends. At night," Elizabeth offered wearily.

Max sniffled and tried to smile. He reached out, touched her cheek, but put his hands back in his own pockets almost immediately. He needed to stand alone with this, look at it, and take it all in.

"I've got insurance."

Elizabeth nodded.

"Time. I don't know about that." Max kicked at a piece of wood that lay at his feet. It looked perfectly fine, normal in every way. But as Max's foot nudged it, the exterior crumbled, destroyed from the inside out. Max gave a sad laugh and stepped over the mess, shaking his head. Elizabeth trailed behind, head down, stepping where he stepped. "There's a clause in the contract. I get docked for every day I'm over the deadline. I cut the bid tight. I can't afford to lose that money."

"Is there any chance you can still make it?"

Max raised his head. He looked at the damage now with the discerning eye of a professional, not the eye of a man whose heart and soul had been put into every beam raised.

He nodded tersely. "I could. I can . . . if I can get the suppliers to float me until the insurance pays off. If they have the right lumber available, I could do it. But it's not just me. It's . . ."

"Mr. Marino!" Max turned. Elizabeth looked over her shoulder and moved to Max's side. The fire chief, weary and dirty, halted two feet from Max. "We're going to be taking off now."

"Is everything all right?" Max asked. "It won't start again? A wind? Something?"

Elizabeth looked askance at Max. She heard the anguish in his voice though he tried to hide it. Christmas was over before it had begun. The new year was looming. No joy for Max. Not here. The fireman shook his head, his eyes downcast. His eyelids were black with soot, his forehead white where his helmet protected him.

"Naw. I've checked it myself. You're fine for now, but don't get a crew in here for a while."

"How long?"

"I don't know. Tomorrow's Christmas. I'll try to get the inspector out here today, but not much is going to happen. Lab's closed. Christmas and all, you know."

Max nodded. Elizabeth stepped forward, slipping her hand into Max's, her attention riveted on the other man. She heard something in his voice that frightened her.

"What kind of inspector? Why does an inspector have to come here?" she asked warily.

"Arson inspector, ma'am," he said flatly.

"You don't think someone did this on purpose, do you?" Elizabeth breathed, horrified at the thought.

"People do this kind of thing all the time on purpose," he said matter-of-factly.

"But why?"

"They want to see the fire. They want to see if they can get away with it. They want to hurt someone else." The man looked knowingly at Max, his eyes narrowing. "Anyone like that been around here lately? Someone you fired maybe?"

Max shook his head adamantly. "Not a chance. Everyone's solid on my crew," Max answered, his voice flat and defeated.

"Okay. Well, guess that's about it then. I'll be heading out."

Max and Elizabeth stood looking after him. There was nothing to say, not much to do. Max wandered around what used to be the job trailer. Finally, gathering his salvage, Max, with Elizabeth close behind, went to his truck. Elizabeth sat quietly inside while he slowly piled his treasures into the bed. When he eventually joined her, he sat with his eyes forward. Finally, he started the engine, looked over his shoulder, and hit the gas. The truck flew back, kicking up a cloud of ash before Max slammed the gear into first and sped away from the ruins without another backward glance.

"I'll make coffee."

Elizabeth got out of the truck and headed up the walk without looking at Max. He called after her, his voice lifeless.

"Hit the garage door opener. I want to try to clean some of the tools and see what's salvageable."

Elizabeth paused, then turned and went back to him. He was reaching for some blackened remnants when she lay her hand on his arm.

"Don't, honey," she begged. "Don't do this now."

"I have to," he said, his jaw set, eyes like flint as he surveyed the mess in the bed of the truck. "I have to do something. If I sit in the house without working off what's inside me, I'll bust, Elizabeth. This isn't something we can talk about. I need to do some work or, I swear, I'll explode. Okay? Just leave me alone now. It will be all right, but you've got to give me this, Elizabeth. Okay?"

He shook off her arm and never looked at her. Elizabeth moved away, knowing he was right. This had nothing to do with her. Not now, anyway. She watched as he plucked things out of that truck he loved, watched a moment longer just to make sure he didn't stop and look around for her. When Elizabeth was sure he was wound tight into his protective cocoon of hard labor, she turned her back.

"There'll be coffee when you want it."

Inside the house, Elizabeth made sure to reach around through the garage door and push the button. It was a small thing, but at least she felt connected to the man outside.

It was incredible how dirty Max felt. He was tired and empty yet energized by rage and filled up with despair. There was so much inside him, he could neither go forward nor back. Luckily his sanity was intact. This was not the time to make decisions or seek answers. Methodically, he unloaded the tools in the back of his truck and lay them side by side in the garage: little corpses he hoped to bring back to life; bounty rescued from the inferno—a pickax, a metal box, two saws their teeth askew, a hammer. Some wood. Not much. Nothing really. All of them dirty. Cleaning would make them right.

He grabbed the hose at the side of the garage and pulled it to the front of the house, then went back to turn on the faucet. But the rush of water caused him such pain he turned it off, twisting the faucet until he was sure it would never be turned on again. He had solvents and acids, stuff he could use to clean his precious treasures without water. He made a beeline for the cabinet on the other side of the garage.

Elizabeth's car was parked close to the wall, but he sucked in his gut, slid across the doors of the car, twisted left, and reached for the cabinet door, thinking how much easier this would have been if he'd just asked Elizabeth for the keys and moved the damn thing. As he stretched, he realized he wasn't alone. From the corner of his eye, Max caught a glimmer of movement, as if the air were shivering. Probing the shadows, Max focused and saw what had caught his attention. There on the garage floor, knees pulled up to his chin, sat Christopher MacMillan.

They stared at one another before Max slowly, carefully, and silently edged his way across the car and back to the empty side of the garage. He glanced toward the door, then back at the boy. There was something about Christopher—the way he looked, the expression in his eye—that Max wanted to see again.

This time he rounded the back of the car and peered down the little corridor between the garage wall and Elizabeth's car. Once again Christopher and Max locked eyes. Max stepped back.

"Come out here," he said quietly.

Christopher pulled his legs closer, locking his arms firmly around them. He shook his head.

"Get out here now, Christopher." Max's voice rose in timbre and lowered in tone. Christopher scuttled further into his hiding place, pushing back against storage boxes until he could push no further without their tumbling down. The boy was quick, but not quick enough. Max was on him in a second, his huge hands wrapping around Christopher's shoulders, pulling him up like a rag doll and setting him on his feet. There was no place for Christopher to go, barred from moving on one side by the car, on the other by the wall; boxes behind, with Max in front, the most formidable obstruction of all.

The boy's eyes widened. His lips trembled. He quaked with fear as Max loomed above him, more frightening because of the coldness of his appraisal. Finally, slowly, Max backed out of the garage pulling Christopher with him. Still silent, still looking the boy up and down, he back-stepped until the two of them were in the driveway.

Christopher's knees gave out, but Max set him upright. He whimpered, his hands covering Max's, working at his fingers. Max held tighter and looked closer. Christopher was a very little boy; a very frightened little boy. Christopher was also a very, very dirty little boy.

Max touched Chris' cheek, still holding him tight with his other hand. He let his fingers linger against the soft skin, then slowly wiped away the dirt. Instead of rubbing the mess on his jeans, Max raised his fingers to his nose and breathed in. His eyes lost focus. His jaw tightened. Max backed away, his retreat more terrifying to Christopher than the closeness had been.

"You were there?" Max asked. Christopher was mute, his eyes widening. Max said again, "You were there before the rest of us, weren't you?" Max stepped closer and Christopher stepped back, raising his hands over his heart. "How long? How long, Christopher? From the beginning? Were you there when this started? Did you start this fire? You did, didn't you!"

This time Max bellowed, and the imperceptible nod of Christopher's head was enough to unleash an incredible wrath. With lightning speed, Max bent to the garage floor, his tall lean body arcing to sweep up the first things he touched. A hammer, a saw. The first he flung with such force the head buried itself in the wallboard. The second he flung behind him with a roar— part word, part curse, part cry of anguish. Moving closer to the boy, he raised his hands before storming away, afraid of what he might do if he came too close.

Chris backed up, paralyzed with fear. Max ranted and the boy cowered. Suddenly Elizabeth was there, her voice joining with Max's. His curses were deep and warlike, her questions shrill and shocked.

"Oh my God! Christopher, move back!" she screamed. "Max! Chris! What is it?"

She held out her hands, curving her body as if she could take the force of any blow—verbal or physical—and keep it from Chris.

"You did it! Oh my God. You did it, didn't you?" Max raved, rampaging down the drive. He turned and pointed a finger. "You did it, Christopher. You set that fire, and you burned down my work. You burned down my life, you stupid little asshole."

"Max!" Elizabeth pulled Christopher close, protecting him with her hands over his ears. "Have you gone crazy? What are you saying? What are you doing?"

"What are *you* doing?" he spat back, eyes flashing black and vicious, lightning bolts of hatred flashed toward them. Elizabeth pulled Christopher's face into her, deflecting Max's wrath. "What are you doing, Elizabeth? What are you doing with this kid? You've protected him while he dumped all over you. When he couldn't get your attention at home, he ran away and worried you sick. When that didn't work, he turned on me. You're trying to protect an arsonist—an arsonist, for God's sake! He played his stupid little games and burned down what was mine!"

"No! No! Shut up, Max. Shut up!" Elizabeth screamed, begging and crying at the same time. She shook her head as though she might keep the words from penetrating her mind. But Max wouldn't let up.

"Don't tell me to shut up." He was on them, ripping Elizabeth away from her son. He held her tight, his fingers firm on her chin so she couldn't look away. "Look at him. Smell him. Smell the fire and smoke that's clinging to him. Look, Elizabeth, and open your eyes. I should have months ago. I was wrong about him just being mixed up. I was wrong, by God." Max shook so hard and long, she thought he might fly apart. He strode, he stopped, he bellowed, and he dragged Elizabeth with him all the while. "I've got his number now. If you don't look and admit what he is, then I'm out of here. I'm gone, because he'll destroy everything around him. If you don't look and open your eyes, he'll destroy you, too."

"Chris?" Elizabeth swooned, and Max let her go. He didn't have the strength to hold her up. He could hardly keep himself upright. "Chris? Chris?" She reached out for him, his denial so necessary; but he pulled back, moving into the darker recesses of the garage.

Scared, eyes flashing, tears shimmering, Chris cowered, and his chest heaved up and down. He opened his mouth but was mute. Elizabeth stirred and once again Max held her tight till Chris cried out.

"I didn't mean to. I didn't. It just happened."

"Oh my God!" Elizabeth's knees buckled; her hands went to her mouth.

"Mom," Christopher begged, but she could do nothing to help him. "It was just a little fire. I found some matches. I didn't mean . . ." Suddenly Chris was quiet. In a split second, he changed his tune and his attitude. "I didn't mean it, but I'm glad it happened. Now you'll go away." Christopher glared at Max and even dared a step forward. When nothing happened and Max didn't retaliate, Christopher became bold in his anguish. "I hate having you here. No one looks at me anymore. No one wants me. No one does anything, but go to work and . . . and . . . I don't want you here, Max. Go away. My dad's coming home, and you've got better things to do now. Go fix your houses. It was an accident, but it's better this way. Better because my dad is coming back to this one."

"Forget your father," Max raged, appalled at what he was hearing. Christopher's determined logic escaped him and hurt him and burned his heart as surely as Christopher's negligence had reduced his work to cinders. He let Elizabeth go roughly and zeroed in on Chris. "Christ, forget him. Burning down my houses won't bring him back. Destroying something good is not the way to make something else better. An accident? No, this was arson, and that makes you a criminal. You're the bad guy, kid, not me." Max cried out in torment, and this time it was the end of everything.

"Goddamn you and your father," Max hissed. Elizabeth backed away, horrified by Max's pain and Christopher's. "I'm the one that's here. I'm here, and you've never even tried to understand that. Never once did you cut me some slack, and now you do this. My God, you did this? To me? And I've been here, for you." Max looked at Christopher and there was such disbelief and pain in his voice that even the boy seemed to melt under the sadness of it. "Christopher, I've been right here in this house with you the whole time. I've been holding out my hand to you. I've tried to love you . . ."

"Max, it was an accident. You have to believe that . . ." Elizabeth finally whispered.

"Elizabeth." Max pleaded for her understanding. "Look at him. Look at his hands. Smell his clothes. Look at him. Please, Elizabeth. Please look and see that he isn't sorry no matter how it started."

Elizabeth's eyes never left Max. Instinctively, protecting what had been hers longer, she moved toward Christopher, her arms out to pull him in. Max watched quietly, vanquished by this final blow. She had chosen wrongly, and there was nothing he could do about it. Yet there was still life in Max. He made one more valiant effort to save her.

"Elizabeth, please. I love you. I've loved you since the minute I saw you. Look at what's real. Christopher isn't real anymore. He's not the child you think he is. He won't just suddenly come back. Look, Elizabeth. See."

Her gaze faltered. She couldn't refuse Max's request. Her eyes fluttered; her head twisted as if it were an awesome burden. But she did as Max asked and, when her green eyes, her mother's eyes, rested on her son, Elizabeth saw exactly what Max did. Not a dirty boy tired from a day at play, not a kid confused by adult treachery and failings, but a young man who knew that what he had done was wrong, that his play had been potentially deadly. And he had run from it rather than try to make it better or help.

"Chris?" She backed off, dropping her arms, standing between the two of them, neither protecting nor supporting either one.

"Mom, it was an accident," he implored, his voice trembling at the very brink of the childish scale. "And you were going to give up on Dad. You were."

Suddenly childish fear became near-adult rage. Chris ran from the garage, screaming as he went, hollering senseless words. He struck Max's truck, grunts of futility and dire need the only sounds he could utter. Christopher kicked and yelped with frenzy until he lashed out at Max, who, protecting himself, reached out and caught Christopher's arm.

The boy stumbled, grasping for the hood of the truck, and fell to his belly, half crawling to escape. But Max was upon him, grappling with the squirming boy. They breathed in tight, sharp puffs, wrestling on the cold, hard concrete. Rolling to his knees, Max held on as Christopher continued to struggle.

"Stop, Christopher. Stop now." Max's breath was labored, exhausted by the emotions of the day. He clawed at the squirming boy, trying to get a better hold. Though his fight was valiant, Chris was no match for the big man. Chris' strength gave out; his energy flagged. Max leaned close, straddling him until his face was against Christopher's cheek.

"Stop now, Chris. Just stop. I'll take care of it." Chris wiggled; he moved; he sobbed, and then, when he was very still, Max reared up. Instead of punishment, he pulled Christopher into his lap and cradled him.

Elizabeth stood back, her fingers tented over her

mouth, paralyzed. She listened, and she prayed, her eyes closed. She was as still as an angel hovering over those she found herself powerless to guard. She waited in the cold and stillness of Emerald Isle, aware that eyes watched them from behind curtains. The next sound she heard was the answer to her prayers. It was the sound of forgiveness.

Opening her eyes, she saw that Christopher still lay strapped tight in Max's arms as Max stared toward the horizon. It was Christopher who cried and Christopher who spoke.

"I'm sorry. I'm so sorry. Max . . ." His apologies tumbled over one another, the word Max getting mixed up with Mom.

And Max, having lost everything, having every right to simply leave Christopher where he was and walk away from the MacMillan house, began to rock the boy. Slowly, gratefully, Elizabeth went toward them.

She reached for Max, her arms winding around him. Her hands fluttered to Christopher's face. She bent and kissed him, kissed the skin so sweet and soft underneath the soot. Then she kissed Max, her fingers brushing back his dark, dark hair. Everything would be all right now. Everything.

Part Four

Spring

Seventeen

"I couldn't believe it. He actually had a twang. A twang, and he's lived in California for about twenty years! I swear, this is the last time I will ever go out with anyone in my entire life. And I certainly will never, ever, go out on a blind date again."

Leslie jabbered, her mouth moving faster than her hands as she passed Elizabeth a shovel and pots and fertilizer. She brushed dirt from her gauzy floral skirt. It was an exceptionally warm spring day, and Leslie was taking advantage of it to the fullest, tank top and all.

"I need the azalea," Elizabeth muttered, too intent on the hole she was digging to look Leslie's way. Leslie pushed herself off the grass, retrieved the plant, then plopped it and herself beside Elizabeth. "Thanks." Elizabeth reached for it and gave it a sharp whack on the bottom, expertly freeing it from the pot.

"Have you been listening?" Leslie asked.

Elizabeth shot her friend a grin. "How could I not? A twang after twenty years. Pushes peas onto his fork with his fingers, and his socks didn't match his suit. Yuck. Sounds awful. Did you at least go somewhere nice?"

Leslie sat cross-legged and settled in for a good long afternoon of watching Elizabeth work.

"Actually, yes. It was very nice. The steak house over on Cedar."

"Oh, that is nice," Elizabeth said absently.

"I suppose. No, it wasn't." Leslie changed her mind. "I guess I'm just jealous. I don't want to be at a steak house with a twanger. I want to be home with a real man. I keep thinking, if you can find a guy like Max, then I should be able to, too."

"Well, thanks a lot!"

"Oh, come on." Leslie laughed. "I didn't mean it that way. I mean, if there's one out there, maybe there're more."

"I don't know about that. I think they're few and far between," Elizabeth said mischievously. "Don't be too jealous, though. It's not like he just fell into my lap and we lived happily ever after. Our yellow-brick road had a few patches of mortar missing."

"Isn't that the truth! I've never seen two people . . ."

"Three." Elizabeth pointed her shovel to underscore her point.

"Sorry," Leslie said. "Three. I've never seen three people go through so much. Actually, it kind of renews my faith in humanity that you're still together, know what I mean?"

"Sure, we're so tough we walked through hell and came out the other side with only singed eyebrows and a blackened heart—literally," Elizabeth said wryly, filling the hole and tamping down the fresh dirt.

"Don't be ridiculous. I mean it renews my faith because none of you ran away. I think that's pretty neat.

In fact, I think that's downright incredible. How come Oprah never has people like you on her show? How come everyone you ever hear about is ready to pack it up and give in?"

Elizabeth smiled and moved over to the next section of the garden, ready to start another planting. Leslie accommodated her and moved a foot, too.

"I don't think anyone would be interested in a happy ending. Besides, people like us don't go on national television and bare all." Elizabeth laughed, so pleased with the day and her life. "It is kind of amazing, isn't it? I can't believe my life has changed so much. I don't think I've ever been happier."

"Anything new with Christopher?" Leslie asked, lowering her voice, ready for a serious talk.

"Only good stuff. We've been working with the school counselor, but you know what? I don't think he needs the counselor. I think what he needed all along was just to be sure of things."

"Do you think he is now? He doesn't worry about you or Max leaving . . ."

"Better than that. He *knows* neither of us is going to leave." Elizabeth slid her eyes toward her friend, shooting her a sly grin. "We're going to be a real family. Max and I are getting married."

"Oh my God! I'm so happy for you! But how can you do this? I thought you were still working on the divorce."

"I am. Another month and it's final. Three months after that, I will be Mrs. Max Marino. He's at the bank right now, but he's due home any minute. You can ask him if you don't believe me."

"Not believe you! Of course, I believe you. And I'd

better be the maid of honor or I'll never speak to you again. I'm so happy for you. It couldn't have happened to anyone nicer. And have I got the dress for you! I saw it just the other day. A really simple column of cream-colored silk. We'll do some kind of wide band in your hair, maybe a cameo—kind of twenties-looking. You'll be gorgeous. Max will look fabulous. He'll be a great husband and . . ."

"And a stunning father. That's so important. Christopher needs that so much," Elizabeth sighed, content because she'd already seen the fruits of Max's selfless labor where Chris was concerned.

"And a great provider!" Leslie said.

"Not to mention a fabulous handyman!" Elizabeth countered, getting into the spirit of the game.

Leslie lowered her voice. "Can we add great lover to that list?"

Elizabeth howled with delight. She was still smiling when she sensed they weren't alone. Elizabeth was grinning from ear to ear when she looked over her shoulder, just as a shadow covered them both.

"Max, I don't know what else to tell you. I've been to the loan committee, and we've reviewed all the paperwork you've given us. We just don't see how we can extend the life of this loan. We're going to have to insist that you satisfy the full note when it comes due and payable."

Max sat back, looking more the international businessman than a contractor anxious about his livelihood. His shirt was starched and white; his tie, old school. His suit, navy with only a hint of a white pinstripe, was perfectly tailored. He held his fingers to his chin and considered the man who was destroying his future.

"I appreciate what you're saying, Mr. Harrigan, but you've also got to appreciate that what you see on paper isn't the whole story."

"I'm afraid it is, Mr. Marino. From what we can see, you won't be able to make the deadline on the project at Emerald Isle. You only need to slip by six days and you'll not only have an unprofitable situation on your hands, you'll be personally unprofitable. Slip another two, and you won't have a chance of meeting the loan."

"That's exactly why I'm asking you to give me an extension—so I can set things right, make a profit, and pay off this note." Max threw up his hands, unable to contain his frustration.

"Listen, my insurance company promised to have a check in my hand by the end of the month. If that happens the way it should, then I'll be able to hire more men. We'll meet the deadline and earn the bonus dollars. You'll be paid back; I'll be profitable, and everything will be fine. I'm not asking for the world, only thirty days."

"That's a lot of *ifs,* Mr. Marino," the banker said smugly.

"Of course, it is," he said, exasperated. "Nothing is ever certain, Mr. Harrigan. Not my job. Not yours." Max let that sink in, then went on. "The reason I came to this bank was because everything you print, every advertisement you run, every line of bull that comes out of your mouth says that this bank is kind and caring and worried about the small-businessman. Well, now's the time to prove it, Mr. Harrigan. I'm sitting here with all the good faith in the world. My wife and I—my late wife—we built this business from nothing. We didn't do it with your help. We just worked damn hard. I came to you when I was ready for the next step, and you welcomed me with open arms. Now, just when I need you, you're telling me that you can't offer a helping hand. Well, Mr. Harrigan, that's called false advertising. That's also called unethical and immoral. And if you really want to stretch it, I'd say we're bordering on criminal."

Max gave the man a minute to think about his words before he continued.

"But since you're the bank and I'm just a working guy, I guess there isn't a whole lot I can do about any of this." Max stood up, shot his cuffs, and picked up the satchel he used for a briefcase. Mr. Harrigan stood also and put out his hand, but Max ignored it. "You'll have your money, Mr. Harrigan. Don't you worry. Then I'll have the pleasure of taking my business out of this bank."

"If I can think of anything else, I'll call you," Mr. Harrigan said with an appropriately concerned expression.

"Right."

Max walked out of the bank knowing hell would freeze over before he ever heard a creative banking idea from Mr. Harrigan. Tossing his satchel into the front of the truck, he rounded it and hopped in, taking his tie off. He tossed it aside before he shrugged out of his suit jacket and unbuttoned the top two buttons of his dress shirt. Loosening his cuffs, Max rolled them up and sped off.

Twenty minutes later, he was at the work site, sitting in the newly purchased, badly used trailer that would be his headquarters until this project was done or the bank reclaimed it. He had stopped for a burger on the way, but now it sat cold in its bag. Instead of eating or working, Max looked at a photograph of Anna.

"Oh, babe, how did it come to this? I feel like I'm letting you down."

He looked away from the photo, then put it carefully back in the drawer. Now he could look at her picture, say her name, and remember the good times and so little of the pain. He had Elizabeth to thank for that, too, not just time. But it was nice to sit and remember Anna without feeling his heart breaking.

What, he wondered, would she say to all this? Max smothered a laugh. She would get up, thump him on the back, and tell him to make his deadline. And before he'd be able to answer her, she'd be out there hammering nails herself. Max stood up and leaned in the doorway of the trailer, surveying the work.

It was May already. Where had the time gone? Eighty percent of the houses were finished except for detail. Plasterboard was up, roofs on, concrete driveways poured. The other twenty percent, the victims of Christopher's handiwork, were back to where they were before match met lighter fluid. But that wasn't the kind of progress Max needed. He needed the lagging twenty percent to catch up with everything else. Unfortunately, he didn't have the money to pay the extra labor to make that miracle happen. If he didn't have to spend his time begging banks, making appointments with insurance adjusters, bargaining for new lumber and labor, things would be different. But corporate wheels turned slower than Max's.

Smiling sadly, Max accepted that there was nothing more he could do. The skeleton crew who opted to stay worked double time. They would give it a good run, he and his men. Maybe they could make it. But not today. Today no one worked because he hadn't been able to afford the lumber he needed. There was nothing for him to do, so he packed up; it was time to go home. It was time to let Elizabeth know exactly how bad things were. She deserved the truth, and he needed to hear that it didn't matter. God, he needed to hear that most of all.

Christopher pedaled harder, trying to jump over the rise in the street, succeeding only in making his knees pop as he stood straight on the pedals. That felt weird. As weird as his head felt. His mom had made him cut his hair, and his ears still weren't used to being naked. Not that he'd really liked all that hair around his face, but David looked so cool with it that Chris had thought he would, too. He hadn't. He had known that every time he looked in the mirror, but he hadn't been about to admit it to his mom, not when he knew it made her mad that he had it.

Chris pedaled slower now, thinking of all the really stupid things he'd done. The hair, skipping school, bad grades. The fire. He still shivered to think of the fire. Boy, he'd been scared. Scared of the fire, of someone finding out, but mostly scared of himself. He hadn't known that could happen, but when he'd been hiding behind his mom's car he'd been afraid to move. He'd been so sure that if he moved he was going to hurt someone—not just something. That had been the scariest thing of all, because he'd known he wasn't bad. Not really. He was just . . .

He swerved, his mind on the huge trash can that sat in the middle of the street. Chris laughed. Boy, his bike felt good. He was really flying today. Then he remembered he'd been thinking really deep thoughts about all the stuff that had happened in the past year, so he went back to thinking—just to make sure he never forgot.

But it was a beautiful spring day. He was older, eleven now, and wiser; but he was still a kid. It was too nice out just to go home. School was almost over, so homework had lightened up. Max usually wasn't home till after six. They wouldn't be shooting hoops before then, and maybe not at all, 'cause Max seemed kind of down. Since it was Friday, he didn't have to go help with the houses. It was hard work but not a bad punishment considering Max hadn't pressed charges. In fact, Chris felt he was really starting to be a good carpenter. Maybe tomorrow Max would let him work the big saw.

But today was today, so he veered off and headed toward David's house. David was still the only person Chris felt really comfortable with. That would change soon because, in a year, Chris was going to junior high. David would probably still be cutting classes. And his mom still wasn't home with him very often, so he was really on his own, and Chris had rules again. But for now, Chris and David still needed one another, and Chris pedaled on harder and harder, skirting Emerald Isle, the park where he used to play when he was a little kid. Bigger stuff was waiting for him now. This summer, he'd play Little League. It was amazing how things changed, day to day, week to week, season to season. It was just amazing all the junk that had happened to him and his mom. He sure was glad it was over now. He was tired of crying and tired of wondering what was going to happen. Now, Chris knew exactly what his life would be like. His mom would keep working; she would marry Max, and they would all live happily ever after. It was a good ending to their story.

Flying free, Christopher stood higher on the pedals of his bicycle, let go of the handles, and threw his arms out against the wind of his own creation. It was great being eleven, especially when things went just right.

Max picked up the shovel on the grass and carried it into the garage with a glance at the flower beds, surprised Elizabeth hadn't cleaned up. It was getting late, and Chris would be home soon. She was really punctual about getting dinner on the table for both of them, so he'd probably find her in the kitchen. He smiled, thinking about how hard she was trying to be perfect. Elizabeth had no idea that the mere fact that she was there, waiting for him with open arms, meant more than dinner at six. But if it made Elizabeth happy, who was he to complain? Besides, she was a hell of a good cook.

Hanging the shovel on the tool board, Max hitched his jacket on his shoulder and walked into the house, still rehearsing his speech, trying to find the best words to describe a bleak situation. He would, of course, offer to postpone their wedding. She'd had enough uncertainty, so if she wanted to wait until he was back on his feet, he would understand. He would put it to her that way. He would . . .

Max's ears pricked. Taking a few more steps, he hesitated. Elizabeth wasn't alone. She was speaking, and the vibration of her voice was low and urgent. This wasn't the kind of voice she used with Leslie. He hoped Chris weren't in trouble again and listened more intently. Then he remembered Chris' bike wasn't in the garage. Chris wasn't even home. Whatever was going on, it didn't sound good.

Elizabeth had stopped speaking. Perhaps she was on the phone, but Max didn't think so. There was something in the air that wasn't right. Without calling out, he walked the few steps into the living room—and saw her.

Elizabeth, dirty from her gardening, her hair still pulled back and tucked under the baseball cap she wore, sat on the sofa. She twisted and turned the dirt encrusted gloves in her hand, sending a shower of soil onto the carpet. Her shoes had been muddy when she came in, for he saw the clear outline of her footprints. She had walked directly to the sofa and sat down. Max's first thought was that Elizabeth was sick.

Memories of Anna fell in upon him until his breath was almost choked off. Anna had sat the same way when she'd learned her diagnosis—so still, as if death were sitting right beside her and she were afraid to look him in the face. That's how Elizabeth sat. So still. In that moment, Max remembered what Elizabeth had told him one night as they'd lain in bed. It was the advice her mother had given her. Advice Max had thought rather silly. *If you sit quite still, Elizabeth, bad things will go away.*

Bad things.

Bad things.

How still she sat. Bad things again.

Max shook his head, denial almost stronger than curiosity. But when Elizabeth dropped her gloves and bent to retrieve them, she caught sight of him. She raised her hands and reached out to him. Max stepped right into her plea. But someone else moved in the room, too, and Max was forgotten. Elizabeth's big green eyes were on the man who was looking out the French doors in the dining room. Her eyes followed him as he moved into the full light. His bearded face was tired and drawn, his eyes dark and soft, his mouth held tight under his mustache.

Elizabeth's head whipped back toward Max. Her tortured eyes caught the gaze of his inquisitive ones. Her hands fell back into her lap, her head lowered. She made her introduction, made her confession.

"Max, this is Brad. My husband."

Eighteen

"Please, just let me handle this, okay?"

Elizabeth danced around Max, who kept turning back toward the house as if his mind were as changeable as the seasons. But Elizabeth had her arms out; she touched him, she cajoled, she was terrified.

"I can't, Elizabeth. Who the hell does that guy think he is, waltzing back in here? You told him, didn't you? You told him about us?" Max's eyes blazed. He spoke through clenched teeth.

"Max, please," Elizabeth begged. "I haven't had a chance to tell him anything. We've just been sitting there. I don't know how long. Leslie was here. She stuck around for a bit just to make sure everything was okay. Max, I can't think straight. I haven't really found out anything, and that's why I need to be here alone with him to find out what he wants and why he's here. Max, please understand that I don't know what to do or what I'm supposed to say and feel."

"What do you mean you don't know what to feel? How can you even say that? You should feel angry and you should feel intolerant and you should feel damned put upon that guy who caused all your problems just showed up and is sitting in your living room. That's how you should feel. And you should be asking *him* to leave, not me. I belong there. I've been there when you and Chris needed me."

Elizabeth talked over him. "And I've been there when you've needed me. Max, this isn't a contest and this isn't a test of the love I feel for you. It's just something that's happening, and it's got to be dealt with somehow. I'm just not sure what that *somehow* is, and I've got to figure it out before Christopher gets home. I've got to think of him, too."

Max took Elizabeth by the shoulders. "You're not going to tell him, are you?"

"Of course. Don't be absurd," Elizabeth said, aghast. "Max, you're hurting me. Let go." Elizabeth pried his fingers from her shoulders. "I'm going to tell Brad about us and I'm going to tell Chris about him."

"Elizabeth, I'm sorry. I just . . ." Max let her go, turning in circles, pushing his hands through his hair. "This is just ridiculous. Elizabeth, can't you see how absurd this is? And telling Chris! That's not the way to handle things. You're just setting him up for another fall. Kick the bum out. He's the one that caused all this. He didn't care enough to say goodbye to Chris; why should you care now?"

"I don't know!" Elizabeth screamed, then lowered her voice. "I don't know why he's come back. The only thing I am sure of is that Christopher deserves to know. Can you imagine how he would feel if he found out a year from now? Ten years from now? Ten minutes from now!" Elizabeth's drawl was pronounced, and it made her arguments seem almost sarcastic. But her actions belied scorn. She went to him, stroked his arm, softened her voice. There were tears hiding inside her, but her fear and uncertainty kept them at bay. "Max, you've got to understand. What Brad did, and how I handled what he did, turned Christopher into an angry, destructive boy. If I expect Chris to want to be a part of the family we're going to make, then we have to be honest. We have to let him be involved in what's going on now. I'll choose the degree of involvement, but I won't choose to keep him out of this completely. I love him. I don't want to hurt or disappoint him anymore. If *I* want answers, imagine how he must feel. If I send Brad away without giving Chris a chance to ask his questions, then I'm no better than Brad—I'm choosing my feelings and my fears over the needs of my son."

Max covered Elizabeth's hand with his own then pulled her into him. Swiftly, he embraced her, holding tight and burying his face in the crook of her neck. She smelled like spring sun and dark earth and new flowers. She felt light in his arms, though he knew how heavy her heart must be. The last thing he wanted to do was leave her with that man, which was exactly why he had to leave her.

"Elizabeth, what's he going to do to us?"

But Elizabeth remained silent. She had no answer—yet. She wanted to assure him that Brad MacMillan was powerless to hurt them; but even as she stood in the arms of the man she loved, Elizabeth felt cold tight fingers close around her heart. She couldn't whisper the assurances he—and she—sought. Selfishly, she took from him his comfort and handed back nothing. But she would. Eventually, he would have all of her. She would commit to their life together, offer him her heart and soul—as soon as she had some answers.

"I have to go, Max. I have to go back in and find

out—so many things." Elizabeth slipped away from him. "Go see Maria. You haven't visited her in weeks. I'll call you."

"When?" Max insisted, but Elizabeth shook her head.

"I don't know. I can't tell. Chris will be home soon." Although she was being unfair, Elizabeth didn't want to talk anymore. It was too difficult to look at Max's crestfallen face, too easy to want to leave with him, and too hard to stay. "I'll call as soon as I can . . . tonight." She held her fingertips to her lips, throwing him a kiss as she turned back toward the house.

"Elizabeth," Max called. She looked back at him. "Will he stay the night?"

Confused, Elizabeth paused, trying to understand what he was asking. When she did, she ducked back through the front door, leaving Max without an answer. He watched. He listened. There wasn't a sound and there was nothing more for him to do, so he left and drove back to the house he'd shared with Anna.

Through the long night, Max sat in the house he hardly stayed in anymore. He sat and he thought. He didn't call Maria, who had seen enough of his heartache to last a lifetime.

If Max had anything to say about it, Brad McMillan would be strolling out of Elizabeth's life.

He wasn't going to lose Elizabeth and he wasn't going to lose Christopher.

He wouldn't!

* * *

"I'm tired, Brad. I'm tired of talking. I want you to leave."

Elizabeth's long blond hair lay in a tangled rope down her back. The only nod to civility were her hands, scrubbed clean after she had left Max in the driveway. But she picked at her nails and wished that she could wash her hands again and again and somehow scrub away Brad.

"That's pretty cut and dried." Brad sat in the chair that had always been his, pinning her to the sofa with his eyes. Those eyes hadn't changed. They were still probing, still softly imperious, yet strangely needy. "Not even an ounce of feeling left for me?"

"Brad, don't. Don't try to just walk back in here and pretend that you didn't leave us. You have no idea what the last year has been like. It's been hell. Pure hell."

"I can see that." Brad's brows tipped. "Mephistopheles is awfully good-looking, Elizabeth. How long has this been going on? How long has he been lord of the manor?"

"Don't you dare use that intellectual nonsense with me, and don't you dare talk about Max. He's the only thing that kept me sane while I tried to hold what was left of this family together."

Elizabeth shot off the couch. A year ago she would have wilted under his scrutiny. But she'd listened to the mental tapes of their marital conversation until she'd thought she'd go mad. At some point she'd realized Brad had never talked to her—he'd lectured her on everything from keeping house to solving world problems. He had reminded her that he was a professor, her better, in so many subtle ways. Now wiser, Elizabeth knew his knowledge was nothing more than opinions spouted to young kids who were easily impressed—the way she had been. She wouldn't fall for it again.

But then she felt his soft dark eyes on her. She admired the litheness of his body, the way his skin was now tan. Always attractive to her, he was even more so now. She couldn't deny that any more than she could deny her anger or her fear that Christopher might walk in before either of them was ready. Elizabeth flinched. Brad was still talking.

"You did a beautiful job holding things together. I honestly didn't think you could do it."

"Stop it," she snapped, running a hand across her brow, trying to calm herself. "Just say you thought I was stupid and leave it at that. But I'm not as stupid as you thought. I finally realized I'm not your cheerleader anymore. I'm not anything to you."

"You're my wife."

"On paper," Elizabeth shot back. Rearing the hurt in her own voice, she lowered it. "On paper, Brad, and not for much longer."

"I know. You've filed for divorce. Your private investigator told everyone within a mile of my apartment. I'll be honest. It scared me, Elizabeth. I think we should try to work things out."

"Hah!" Elizabeth paced, first in front of her husband, then behind him. "I'd bet my last dollar that sentiment had nothing to do with your decision, Brad. And believe me, I don't have a whole lot of dollars to bet. There's something else going on here, and I want to know what it is."

"We've been over that. I realized how much I had to lose, how much we had together. It's as simple as that." Brad swiveled in his seat, his eyes following

Elizabeth's every move. She waited for him to continue, but his mind was on other things. "You look wonderful, you know. I'd forgotten how beautiful you are."

Elizabeth stumbled. She didn't want to hear that. His protestations of love would be her downfall. They had slept together for twelve years; they had made a home and a child. The pull of that connection was strong and scary.

"Don't talk like that."

"Why not? It's the truth." That gentle ripple of his voice again. Elizabeth shuddered and faced her nightmare.

"Brad, I doubt you'd know the truth if it bit you." She turned on him. There were no rule books for something like this, so she lashed out blindly. "Try telling me the truth from the beginning. Let's start with when you decided you didn't want to live in this house anymore. What was that all about?"

"Elizabeth, that's history. Why rehash it? I needed space; I needed time to myself. I've had it now."

"I won't accept that," she said, standing tough. "Do you have any idea what's gone on here, Brad, just because you wanted time to yourself?"

Brad pushed himself up and faced her. He waved a hand as if he were weary of conversation that was beneath him.

"There you go. You're trying to make me out to be the devil incarnate when I did the only thing I could do to make your life easier. I walked away from here before I went crazy." He left the living room and went into the kitchen as if it were still his. Speechless, Elizabeth waited as he sauntered back with a glass of water, still talking. "You have no idea, Elizabeth, what my life was about. I agonized over the decision to quit the university. All I ever wanted was to teach. To be denied tenure, to have my entire life negated by a committee of intellectually stagnant men and women, was almost too much for me to bear. How can you possibly know what it is to have your entire existence nullified by the people you felt were your peers?"

"You're right, Brad," Elizabeth drawled. "I don't know what it feels like to be left hanging without any explanation as to why my performance wasn't up to snuff." Elizabeth walked up to her husband. She stood away from him, and still that was too close. "Listen to yourself. How self-centered. How selfish. I don't know what it's like to have my existence nullified?" Brad flinched at her sarcasm and Elizabeth was empowered. "What do you think you did to me? I was a wife, for God's sake, then I was nothing. Not a divorcee. Not a widow. Just a woman who'd been left. Little money, Brad. No security. A child to care for. But that never crossed your mind, did it? It never occurred to you that you hadn't just left me, you'd also left Christopher. I could go on and on about myself, but let's talk about Christopher."

"There's nothing to say. I couldn't tell him I was a failure, Elizabeth." Brad set aside his glass and hung his head.

Elizabeth threw up her hands. "God, Brad! What are you saying? You were an executive in a fine firm. You had everything."

"Except my self-respect. I was meant to be in academia. I was meant to teach young people . . ."

"How could you teach anything when you couldn't

even teach yourself some restraint?" Elizabeth questioned. "How could you communicate anything when you couldn't find the courage to tell me you weren't happy? You couldn't do me the courtesy, Brad, the kindness, to share your problems the way a husband should share with a wife. My job was to help you, and you didn't give me the tools. God, that's so basic—talking to each other—and you're worried about trying to teach poetic philosophy to a bunch of kids. Whatever gave you the right to think you could teach anything when you hadn't even learned the basics of living?"

Elizabeth found it difficult to look at him. There, behind the beard, were the eyes she had loved, the lips she had kissed, the person she had adored. She didn't know him anymore. Disgusted, she turned her back and looked out the window, calmer now.

"I've had a lot of time to think, Brad. I've gone over every conversation, every look, every moment of lovemaking and silence in our marriage." She looked over her shoulder and smiled wryly. "There wasn't much else to do when I'd run out of tears, when this house was as quiet as a tomb." She looked away again, not necessarily seeing anything but preferring the flowers to the sight of her husband. "I realized that you weren't at all what I had thought you were. Not that you had changed in twelve years, but that I had grown up. I was able to look at you in a different light. You see, I used to think that your silences were necessary so that you could think deep and intellectual thoughts.

"That was so stupid, but I adored you, Brad. Can you imagine what it felt like to be a student and have an associate professor not only show interest in you, but profess to love you? It was heaven, and I walked through those gates you opened with stars in my eyes. It could have gone on like that forever, Brad. To have a husband and child was all I ever cared about. You had given me everything I ever wanted. You could have been adored and cared for because of that, but you walked away from it."

Brad moved beside her. He didn't touch her. He looked past her with that deep-in-thought look Elizabeth had seen so often. She was no longer moved. He had probably been looking for a hole in the fence that he could squeeze through all those years they were together. He'd only wanted to run from her.

"That was exactly the problem," he began quietly. "You were so content. You had me and Christopher, this house, your life. You wanted so little, asked for so little. There was always a smile. How could I have shared these deep, disturbing feelings with you?"

"How could you not?" Elizabeth responded coldly. Sitting on the couch she pinned Brad with her eyes. "I don't want to have this conversation now. We should have had it two years ago, three years ago. Maybe we should have talked to each other *about* each other before we got married. You're obviously not the person I thought you were, and I'm not the person you left. If you care, I'm better than the person you left." Elizabeth looped her thumbs in her jeans' pockets. "Listen up, Brad. The new Elizabeth is going to speak to you. I don't have any more time to waste, because I have a son to care for, a house to pay for, and a future to live for." She paused. "Where have you been, Brad? I want to know now."

"Colorado," he replied. Hardly the dramatic answer she'd expected.

Elizabeth laughed harshly.

"Nice. Aspen?"

"Don't be ridiculous," Brad said in that gently contemptuous tone that let her know she was barely worth the effort of his attention. "I wasn't on vacation."

"What were you doing?"

"Finding myself. Searching my soul. Working at odd jobs."

"You went all the way to Colorado to live the life of a college student?"

"What's wrong with personal exploration?" he demanded, sounding hurt.

"Nothing if you're single and rich and have nothing better to do with your life, or you're old and lonely. But you were a husband and a father and a man with a job. You had responsibilities, people who loved you. You threw it away because you wanted to play. That's the bottom line."

"I needed to get in touch with myself and my goals again. I was lost. Depressed."

"You were selfish," she spat back, eyes hard and dark now. "I hope you had a fine time, because while you were gone looking for yourself, I have been keeping body and soul together working as an admission's officer at the hospital. We have a son who has gone straight downhill from a sweet and kind little boy to an arsonist."

"What?" Brad was coming straight at her, but she held out her hand.

"Forget it. I've taken care of Christopher with Max's help. Max was here for both of us when we needed him. A man who didn't ask for anything in return—not money, not affection, not space and time when things got too hot for him."

"I don't give a damn who this man is. You obviously needed support from someone, but I'm galled that you're blaming me for Christopher."

"Brad!" Elizabeth laughed harshly. "Of course I'm blaming you for Christopher. I'm blaming you for everything: all the misery, all the tears, all the heartache. Whom else am I going to blame? *I* didn't go anywhere." Elizabeth had thought her question rhetorical, but when it looked as if Brad were about to speak, she gave him a warning. "Don't you dare try to turn this around and make it my fault or the university's fault or anyone else's. You did this, Brad, when you didn't have the guts to at least write us a note and say you were going."

"I thought about it. But one day led to the next, Elizabeth. I thought I'd only be gone for a day or two. Then I took my vacation. Then the days just sort of melted into one another. It was very strange, to be so free." Brad's eyes took on a faraway look as if, given half the chance, he'd do it over again.

"Calling in to quit work was possible, but leaving a message on the answering machine wasn't?" Elizabeth demanded, her Southern drawl coming to the fore.

"No, it wasn't possible," Brad said all too patiently. "I could call work because I knew how I felt about that. I couldn't call you, I couldn't talk to you, because I didn't know how I felt about you."

"And you do now?" Elizabeth asked wryly.

"I do," Brad answered solemnly.

"Really? Well, now that you've found your voice—and your guts—just spit it out and let's get on with this. How do you feel about me now, Brad? Make it quick, because I don't want to sit here and listen to what a shrew I've been and how I've ruined your life."

"On the contrary, Elizabeth, you *are* my life. I know that now," Brad said quietly, his eyes boring into hers. "I love you, and I want to come home."

Stunned, Elizabeth had no voice. She couldn't move; she couldn't think. Love. Home. How could he use those words? And how could he not? This was his home and she was his wife.

Wearily, Elizabeth pulled her fingers through her long blond hair. She wiped her hand over her eyes, blinked, and still Brad stood there waiting for her to react. There was no more time, though. They weren't alone.

"Dad?"

Christopher stood watching them, holding himself up against the wall, his face alight with happiness. A moment later, Christopher threw himself into his father's arms and Elizabeth's world began to crumble.

Nineteen

"I hope it's okay that I came down, Elizabeth." Leslie looked over her shoulder, nervous ever since Brad's reappearance.

"Relax," Elizabeth assured her, "Brad's not going to pop out of a closet. The way I've been acting the last few weeks, I'm surprised I even have a job left to come to."

"That bad, huh?"

"Worse. My whole life is upside down. I can't concentrate. Brad walks around the house as if he never left. Christopher is walking on air, he's so happy his father is home, and I'm . . ."

"You're not sleeping with him, are you?" Elizabeth's withering gaze stopped that line of questioning. "Just asking. I mean he has been living there with you, and he has a certain charm."

"So has Max, the man I was going to marry before Brad showed up again." Elizabeth set aside the papers she'd been shuffling, knowing she wouldn't accomplish anything before noon. "Max is coming to take me to lunch. Leslie, I don't know what to tell him. This is such a hard decision."

"I don't know why, honey. You should have sent

Brad packing the minute he showed up. Max is a god, and you should be planning your wedding."

"I was going to do that the day he showed up, but Chris walked in just as I was getting ready to toss him out. Leslie, you've never seen anything like that boy's face. And now it's like Brad never left. If Chris weren't so darn big, he'd sit in the same chair with his father and never let him out of his sight. Then he tells me how great it is that we're together again. He thinks because Brad is physically in the house that makes us a family. How can I send Brad away? It would break Christopher's heart."

Leslie scoffed. Her bravado was exemplary because Elizabeth saw real concern behind her eyes. "Don't be ridiculous. If you don't get rid of Brad now, you're going to be stuck with him for the next twenty years."

"Lord, Leslie, I know that," Elizabeth wailed, giving up that thread of courage she'd been hanging on to every day. Her shoulders slumped. "You know, Max and Christopher were finally starting to connect. It was wonderful. But what I'd overlooked was that Max was second best. The fact is, Brad is Christopher's dad."

Leslie sighed, tired just listening to Elizabeth. "Honey, if Christopher gets Brad, you get nothing. You're not a wife; you're not the breadwinner, and you can't go back to being a homemaker. You're giving up Max, and for what?"

"I didn't say I was going to give up Max," Elizabeth said quietly.

"Do you think he'll wait around forever?"

"No, of course I don't expect him to wait," she insisted. "But I expect . . ." Elizabeth lowered her eyes in defeat. "I don't know what I expect. There's so much to worry about: finances, Chris, legalities."

"No, you have to worry about just one thing: Yourself."

"Kind of selfish since there is a child involved," Elizabeth said sorrowfully.

"No, it's not. Your best interest is Christopher's, too. *You* didn't run away, and yet you're punishing yourself. If you rely on Brad and Christopher, everything will get screwed up. Christopher is a kid, and Brad hasn't exactly shown himself to be a responsible adult. He shouldn't be given any consideration . . ."

"Stop it." Elizabeth spoke quietly. "Please, Leslie. Stop."

"You still love him," Leslie whispered.

Elizabeth shook her head. "No, but I remember. It's like being at the beach all day and then lying down to sleep and suddenly remembering the heat of the sun as if it were still shining on you. You remember how good it felt to be that warm and lazy and comfortable. That's what it was for me and Brad. Twelve comfortable years."

"For you, Elizabeth. Brad ran away."

"Now he's back, and I can remember how it felt to be in that sunshine. I can remember how it feels to be warm."

"But that's familiarity, Elizabeth, not love." Leslie talked fast, hoping to convince Elizabeth, but her friend wasn't listening. "Elizabeth," she went on gently, "you know about real love, the kind that stays put through thick and thin."

"I do," she said, half defeated, half frustrated. "Max never gave up on us. But then there's the beach and the sun, and I start drifting off. Chris is happy, and

Brad doesn't want anything. He just wants to stay. That's not so much to ask."

"Is Max asking for anything?" Leslie asked, squeezing Elizabeth's hand tight.

"Yes," Elizabeth said dully.

"That's good. He's fighting for you. Brad's just offering to pick up where you left off—and that wasn't such a great place."

"But it was predictable and good for Christopher. I could be a mom and bake cookies and volunteer at school. Now, I run to a job and . . ." Elizabeth flinched, startled by the ringing of the phone. "Sorry," she breathed and answered. "Hello? Yes. Okay. I'll be right out." She hung up a second later. "Max is here."

"Mohammed coming to the mountain?"

"I guess. I haven't quite known what to say to him or where to say it. I thought neutral territory might be the best. We made a date."

"That's exactly what you need, but it should be overnight. You should lie in his arms, and you should . . ."

"Leslie, please! I thought you were my friend." Elizabeth dug into the desk drawer, found her purse, and tucked it under her arm. Leslie reached over the desk and stopped her.

"I'm not kidding, Elizabeth. Do it. Before Brad came back, you were ready to marry Max. This great, incredible man chose *you* to love. I'm telling you, go home with him, let Brad baby-sit. Let Max hold you all night. Let him make love to you; close your eyes and feel what he means to you. If you don't, you're going to lie down on that beach again. You'll fall asleep and wake up burned when you're too old to do anything about it. Think, Elizabeth. You can be completely alone with someone else in the house, and that's how it's going to be if you stay with Brad." Elizabeth remained silent, and Leslie was disgusted. "Sometimes you make me so mad, Elizabeth." She stood up. "Call me if you need me, but don't expect me to come sit at the dinner table with you and your 'family.' I just couldn't bear it."

In the next moment, it wasn't a cream-colored suit Elizabeth was looking at but a tall, black-haired man in jeans. She almost looked away from Max, needing a second to herself. Thankfully, she didn't, because he smiled. It was a gentle, patient, and most wonderful expression. It made her feel weak with sorrow.

"Ready?" he asked.

Elizabeth hesitated, selfishly allowing herself to look at him for one long, loving minute.

"You're not eating."

Elizabeth surveyed the hero sandwich still in its wrapper on the park bench. The soft drink was now swimming in water, ice long melted. The chips hadn't been touched. Max, squinting against the sun, looked askance at his food, then at Elizabeth's lap.

"You haven't exactly made a dent in your lunch, either," he said quietly, a small laugh managing to bubble to the surface before losing steam.

Elizabeth set aside her sandwich. "It was such a lovely idea . . . a picnic." She sighed and studied their surroundings. The park was beautiful. Not as big or as pretty as Emerald Isle, but lovely nonetheless. Spring was like that in their neck of the woods.

"I always loved spring," Max said, as if reading her mind. "Anna did, too. She called it a 'possible' season."

Elizabeth laughed gently. "A what?"

Max shifted, lowering the arms he'd thrown over the back of the green bench. He leaned forward and put his elbows on his knees as if he could get closer to the memory.

"A possible season," he repeated. "She said that every year when spring came around, she felt that everything was possible. Even getting better."

"I always felt like that at Christmas time," Elizabeth said, her eyes roaming over the park, her ears pricking at the sound of the traffic on the street behind them. "That's when I would make promises to myself, resolutions."

"That's different. A possible season isn't about promises; it's about rejuvenation and hope, not about any one special thing. And it's not about changing anything, either. It's just—possible."

Max held out his hands. How could he explain this deep and marvelous philosophy? "I've been thinking a lot about that lately. About Anna's season of the possible."

Max got up and linked his thumbs in the pocket of his jeans. He paced in front of Elizabeth, tall and handsome and so willing to do whatever it took to make things right. He didn't look at her and, eventually, Elizabeth averted her eyes, too. He spoke again. "A few weeks ago, life was good. After all the heartache, the questions, the destruction, it looked like we were headed right into one of those great sunsets you see in the movies. I thought this was our possible season."

He stopped pacing. Elizabeth was looking at the

toes of his work boots and found that particular take endearing. She looked up at him and smiled.

"I thought it was, too, Max," she whispered. "I didn't know that's what it was called, but I thought it was going to be our springtime."

Max sighed. Never, even at the worst with Christopher, had she seen such a look of despair. It pained her to the depths of her soul. He started to speak; his voice caught, and he swallowed the words before starting again.

"I suppose that means you're staying with Brad, then. If you're using the past tense, that's what it must mean."

Elizabeth shook her head and abandoned their uneaten picnic to walk beside him. The park was small and intimate; a canopy of trees lined the labyrinth of concrete paths that wound round in random pattern. She didn't take Max's arm as she would have liked; he didn't reach for her hand the way he would have weeks ago. Elizabeth tipped her head and looked at the sun. It was bright with promise, but there was no warmth in it. It was only spring sun.

"I don't know, Max. I don't think that's what I'm saying."

"Then say you'll tell Brad that he has to leave the house. Say we're still going to be married," he intoned.

Elizabeth dropped her head and looked at the ground. The concrete was cracked and well worn. She felt that way. Just like the concrete.

"I can't say that, Max. I can't."

"Then you have to say it's over."

Elizabeth stopped, a sudden, horrid fear stabbing into her heart. Max had walked on. Slowly, he turned around, clasping his hands behind his back as if that would keep him from reaching for her.

"You have to tell me that, Elizabeth, because by not choosing me, you choose him." Max tipped his head and the light caught on the tears in his eyes. "I can't do this anymore. I watched one woman leave this world bit by bit. I won't watch you leave me the same way. I'm not that strong."

"Max, don't," she cried and threw herself into his arms. She held him tight and buried her face against his chest. It had been so long since she'd touched him, kissed him, since she had felt whole. Brad couldn't make her feel this way. She didn't want to be close to him, or love him. She didn't. *She didn't!* Every time that thought crossed her mind, her arms tightened and she moved ever closer to Max. And when his arms came around her, she thought for an instant that all would be right. But that second of pure bliss was destroyed in the next moment. Max wasn't holding her the way a desperate lover should; Max was saying goodbye.

"Max . . ." Her head fell back, her hair escaping the pins, her green eyes deep with despair. "You can't mean this. Max, please. You know I love you. This has nothing to do with how I feel about you."

"It has everything to do with that." Max let go of her and laid his palms against the sides of her head, his eyes drinking in every nuance.

"No, no. It has to do with Christopher. Just with him. He believes in miracles. He believes his prayers have been answered. How can I shatter his world again by rejecting his father out of hand? How can I, Max?"

"You wouldn't be rejecting him. You'd be putting

him in the proper perspective. Elizabeth, do you want Christopher to grow up thinking that someone's presence means they love you? Or do you want him to know that love is full of heartache and work and happiness and that it never ends but you never give up, either? Don't you want him to know all those things?"

"I do. But I also want him to know security, Max." He moved away from her. She followed him. They were headed down that endless concrete path again, all circles and curves that ended up right back where they started. "At his age, security is important. You should see him. You should see how happy he is."

"I'd like to. Don't you understand that?" Max said, stuffing his hands into his pockets. "I'd like to shoot some hoops. I'd like to help you make dinner. I'd like to make love to you and plan our future."

"I can't plan it until I know what Brad is going to do."

"And when will he tell you what he's going to do?" Max stopped briefly, then continued when she didn't have an answer. "Brad might decide to leave tomorrow. He might decide to hang around for another twelve years. He might decide that you're making life awfully easy and that he'll just sit back and watch all the rest of it go by."

"I know that," Elizabeth said, angry now that he should dare voice the worries she'd been engulfed in day and night. "I know the dangers, but what's the harm in letting Christopher enjoy this time?"

"The harm is that it's not real—and that this time may never end. It isn't real, Elizabeth," Max said more quietly, more forcefully. "Even if you decide to cut me loose, even if you decide to stay with Brad, you won't have a family. Not unless," he added, "you really do love Brad. Maybe that's what this is all about."

"No," Elizabeth answered honestly. "That's not what this is about. It's about being a mother. I don't know any other way to explain that to you."

"You would sacrifice your happiness for Christopher's?"

Elizabeth nodded.

"I see."

Max watched her a minute more, then took the two steps needed to close the space between them. He stood beside her, shoulder to shoulder, looking down on the woman he loved. Ever so gently, he lifted his hand and placed it against her cheek. He bent and kissed her temple, letting his lips linger as if he could somehow wordlessly make her understand what she was giving up.

Elizabeth's eyes closed. She felt his heat, and wanted more. She longed for him to convince her that there was another way, but that was something Max was unable to do. All the pain she had caused her child, all the mistakes she had made with him because of her love for Max, came back now to haunt her. The one thing he wanted was his father. That was the one thing she could give him.

Max pulled away first. Reluctantly but firmly, he left her standing straight and tall in the little park, and her heart began to crumble. Bereft, she followed Max, and they rode in silence back to the hospital, their fingers laced, holding hands for the last time. Elizabeth had made her decision. Since they had used up all their words, Elizabeth got out in the hospital parking lot and watched until the cherry-red truck disappeared.

"He didn't mean it," she whispered to herself. When he didn't return, Elizabeth repeated the words to herself and walked into the hospital, knowing, but not admitting, that she was lying.

Max had been headed to the only place in the world that felt right—work. Deadlines were closing in, and still he had so much to do before the last houses could be finished. Missing the bonus deadline was a certainty he had come to accept, but he sure as hell had a chance at making break-even. Yet he found himself off course, driving through the front entrance of Emerald Isle instead of around to the back, parking in Elizabeth's drive, knowing there would be only one person in the house at this time of day: Brad MacMillan.

Max got out of the truck, sensitive to every sound he made: the slight squeak of the door, the thudding of his heavy boots on the concrete, what seemed a resounding crash of metal against metal as he slammed the door shut. He hadn't meant to do that. It seemed such an angry gesture and he was sorry for it. Walking toward the front door, he saw things he had come to think of as his and Elizabeth's: the flowers, the new gutters, the little mat she had placed outside the door for him to wipe his muddy boots. This was his home, and someone who didn't belong anymore was trying to take it away. Max couldn't let him do that. Without another thought, he rang the bell.

Brad was wearing glasses when he opened the door. He took them off, swinging them by one end as he looked Max up and down, a wry look of satisfaction mixed with one of weariness on his face.

"I suppose it had to come to this," he said dryly. He opened the door wider. Max stepped through. Brad skirted around him, waving toward the living room. "You know the way. Unless of course you'd be more comfortable . . . elsewhere?" Brad's eyes flitted toward the stairwell and the bedroom above. "I meant the kitchen, or the backyard, of course," he explained.

Max walked past him into the living room, refusing to be angered by innuendo or action. Until this moment Max hadn't been sure why he had come. Now, looking into Brad MacMillan's smug expression, he knew what he had to do to save Elizabeth and Christopher from a man who cared less about them than his own comfort.

"You have to leave this house and never come back."

"Blunt." Brad chuckled. "I suppose that's to be expected from a man like you. It surprises me that Elizabeth found you attractive. She could have had her pick of the jocks when we met, but intellect won out."

Max glared, ignoring his remarks. "I want to know what you intend to do."

"I intend to stay here." Brad's supercilious attitude disappeared. He was on his guard now. "This is my home; Elizabeth is my wife, and Christopher is my son. If Elizabeth doesn't ask me to leave, then I have no intention of doing so."

Brad moved around the room slowly, cautious of Max, who stood so still, only his eyes following.

"Do you love her?" Max asked, his voice quiet and deep. "Do you want to be here?"

"I need to be here," Brad snapped, controlling himself with equal alacrity. "I don't believe that you could quite understand the concept; but in its simplest form, without Elizabeth and Christopher, I'm nothing—neither father nor husband, just a man on his own like so many others. I wouldn't have anything to show for my life."

"You are an obnoxious bore," Max said, disgusted by Brad.

Unfortunately, he could also understand Elizabeth's attraction. Brad MacMillan's sense of other-worldness, or intelligence, perhaps serenity, would appeal to a young girl. It would be like a man marrying a centerfold only to wake up one morning and realize the beauty had all been manufactured. Max's fury bubbled, but he beat it back, determined not to give Brad MacMillan the satisfaction of feeling a superiority he didn't deserve.

"It doesn't matter what you think, does it?" Brad baited him. "You have no place here. Elizabeth understands that I've been confused and that I had to contemplate my past and future before we could continue as a family. I'm not stupid enough to think she'll drop dead from happiness. I'm not without fault, and there are pieces to be picked up. I will do my best to regain Elizabeth's trust. With Christopher, I'd say I'm halfway home."

Brad circled the coffee table and sat on the couch. He put his glasses back on, blinking at Max as if surprised to see him still there. He gazed without further comment, as though trying to decide how best to make Max understand his unique position. At last, he went on.

"You can't possibly have any idea of what I've gone through in the past years. To be left by the wayside in your chosen profession is something I wouldn't wish on anyone. To know that you had something valuable to give, only to have it rejected, is painful. To look at your wife and realize she loves you for what she thinks you are—when you're nothing of the sort—is humbling. To live the same day every twenty-four hours is horrible. Nothing ever changed. Not Elizabeth's optimism, not her joy with living a life that had become routine. That joy was a slap in the face every day. Or so I thought.

"When I left, I thought I would find a life that fit me better. I thought I would find answers, other people searching the way I was. But most people seem happy with their lot in life, so I had to conclude that what I wanted simply wasn't out there. When I realized I would never find my heart's desire, I came back."

"Bull," Max said quietly, delighted to see Brad sit up and take notice. "You came back because Elizabeth was going to divorce you and take away your fall-back position."

Brad chuckled, recovering his composure. "There is that. Money was running low, and I hadn't found anyone interesting to help me through my dilemma. So, in the grand scheme of things, I realized that I needed to come back and make amends. What I had here wasn't perfect . . ."

"Says you," Max growled, and that seemed to give Brad pleasure.

"It's better than being alone. The moments when I feel the closeness of this family are wonderful. They may not happen as often as I'd like . . ."

"God, you make me sick. Why don't you just say what you mean? It doesn't have to do with this nonsense you're spouting. You don't want to be part of a family, you want to feel like a god. You're looking for adoration."

"The thought crossed my mind," Brad admitted, smiling secretively, as if sorry to be found out. "I'm surprised it crossed yours. But then, I suppose that's why I married someone so much younger than I. Elizabeth always accepted whatever I said or did. I was surprised to find any consequence on this end when I came back. Elizabeth has changed, but she'll change back. Christopher is still the same—bigger of course—but still loyal. He makes me realize that there is still someone I can make an impact on. There's still someone who believes just in me."

"And what are you giving back?"

Brad started, surprised by the question. "Stability, of course. The sense of belonging. Education. I can teach him things schools can't."

"No wonder they didn't give you tenure," Max muttered, turning away. Pompous ass. The thought of Elizabeth married to this fool was almost more than he could bear. But Elizabeth had made it clear: Christopher was her priority. He was almost ready to admit defeat when Brad MacMillan made a dreadful mistake. He opened his mouth again.

"You have no place here, Marino. I think the best thing for everyone would be for you to turn around and leave this house. You're nothing here," Brad sneered, fully enjoying himself. "Nothing except the man who screwed my wife. A gigolo. A man who uses his body to please women, and Elizabeth is a fool . . ."

Brad never had a chance. Max was on him like lightning, his hands wrapping around the other man's neck without a second thought. A roar of anguish ripped through the quiet living room like a sonic boom as Max pushed Brad into the soft cushions of the couch. From his throat came a guttural wail of shock and surprise. Max didn't care.

"You ass. You goddamn creep. You don't have any right . . ." Max, aware that he could break the man's neck with a twist of his hands, tried desperately to control himself, but the sight of him lying there, unable and unwilling to defend himself, enraged Max. With a cry, he slapped his hands on Brad's shoulders and yanked him to his feet. "She's your wife. Your wife and you are . . ."

"Stop!"

Max released Brad suddenly and stumbled backward. The other man fell back, gasping for breath, his hands going round his own neck as if to make sure it was all in one piece. Max grunted, whirling to see who had attacked him, who it was that had thrown the kidney punch. He twirled and looked into Christopher MacMillan's flushed face and saw those boyish fists heading toward any part of Max's body they could connect with.

"Stop!" he cried again. "Don't hurt my dad. Don't hurt him. Go away, Max."

Christopher's arms flailed, and it took Max a minute to rein them in. When he finally did, he held them both in one huge hand and put the other on Chris' shoulder, bending to try to soothe him, to explain what it was that had happened.

"I'm sorry. Chris, I'm sorry. But he was saying . . ."

"I don't care what he was saying. I don't care," Chris cried, his sobs sounding more and more infantile by the moment. It wasn't right to leave Chris and Elizabeth with a man who held them in such low esteem, but Christopher was doing his best to change Max's mind. "Max, let me go. Let me go. If you don't, he'll leave again. Daddy! Daddy! Make him let me go."

Stunned, Max did as Christopher asked. *Daddy.* That cry meant so much more than just the person on the couch. It meant safety and normalcy and happiness to Christopher MacMillan. With that one word, Christopher convinced Max that he was wrong. They stopped struggling and looked at each other for a long, long time. Christopher looked through Max with his child's eyes, and then Max raised Christopher's fists and laid his lips against them. With that kiss, he lowered his hands, stood up, and left Elizabeth's house.

Behind him, Christopher watched until Max disappeared. On the couch, Brad MacMillan slowly righted himself and adjusted his glasses. He pulled at his shirt, trying to find a comfortable spot on the sofa. All the while, his angry eyes remained on the spot where he had last seen Max Marino.

"What a cretin. What a stupid display of macho strength." Brad pushed himself off the sofa. He stood by his son without touching him. "Your mother was so stupid to be taken in by someone like that."

Blinking, Christopher swiveled his head and looked at his father, who looked right back.

"She's an idiot," Brad said.

Christopher blinked again.

Twenty

"Brad! Brad!" Elizabeth flew through the door and rushed into the living room. "God, there you are."

Brad stopped pacing and looked at her. "Catch your breath," he commanded.

"I will, if you just tell me . . ." The words caught in her throat. Her hand went to her chest as if she could hold her heart in. She tried again. "Just tell me what happened. Where has he gone?"

"How would I know where he is?" Brad snapped. "He yelled at me, and then he ran out. You're his mother. You're the one who should know where he is."

"But why did he run away? He's been so happy," Elizabeth wailed. She threw her jacket on a chair. "I can't believe this is happening all over again. What, Brad? What happened?"

"Your friend, that's what happened," Brad answered sarcastically.

"Leslie?" Elizabeth asked, thoroughly confused.

"Don't be ridiculous. It was that he-man you've been seeing. He came in here and tried to strangle me. I suppose that upset Christopher. It's the only thing I can think of." Brad turned away, hiding the face of truth. Elizabeth followed him back to the couch.

"I can't believe Max would do something like that." She confronted him softly but insistently.

"Believe it. If Christopher hadn't come in when he did, that guy would have killed me."

"You're exaggerating, but whatever happened between you and Max, I'm sorry Chris had to see it. It hasn't been easy for him. He and Max had a special relationship."

"And it's ended as far as I'm concerned."

"I'm not sure you have anything to say about it," Elizabeth answered coolly, peeved he should assume what she already knew was inevitable. "Right now, the important thing is to find Chris. Don't you agree?"

"Of course, I do. Whatever you think best. I'll call the police if you think that's the thing to do now."

Brad sat down again and Elizabeth saw him as he really was. Gone was the tan that had made him seem so vital, gone was the litheness of body that she had admired so. He slumped on the sofa, unwilling or unable to make a decision about his own son, waiting petulantly, instead, like a child needing directions.

Elizabeth sat down beside him, looking closely, trying to find the man she had once admired so much. He was gone. The man in her living room was a pitiful person, without direction or passion. Elizabeth breathed deeply as if coming out of a long, dark sleep.

"Brad, why did you come back?" For the first time since his return, Elizabeth realized Brad had made no attempt to touch her. Not a kiss, a hand to hold, a hug of relief and welcome. Nothing. Curiously, she asked again, "Why, Brad?"

"Because this is where I belong," he answered, his voice a whisper.

"But *why* do you belong here?" Elizabeth insisted. "Please, no more lies, Brad. No more made-up stories, excuses, or fabrications. No more silences. Just the truth, if you know how to tell it."

He hesitated, a look of panic in his eyes. The inevitable had happened.

"I belong because there's nowhere else for me. Out there, I wasn't anyone, Elizabeth. Not a professor, not a manager, not a husband or a father. I really had nowhere else to go. I ran away, and there was nothing to run to, so I came back."

"And you know you can't stay, don't you?" she asked quietly.

Brad nodded. He looked out the paned doors toward the pool and the garden. "But it would be so nice, Elizabeth. So easy to stay here and be what we were before."

"We can never be what we were before, exactly for that reason. You found you didn't want to fight the world; I found out that I could. I'm strong Brad, and I want to live with someone who admires that. I want a man who isn't afraid to stand by my side and fight when it's necessary. I want to live with someone who treats me as if I matter, not as if I'm a pleasant diversion. I want to know that Chris and I are in his thoughts. I don't want to settle anymore." Slowly, Elizabeth stood up. She felt strangely calm and inordinately free. "You have to go, Brad."

"Where?" he asked.

"I don't know, but you can't stay here. Max belongs here. That man stood by us through thick and thin. He gave us more in a year than you gave us in twelve. You don't know how to give, and you never have. I'm sorry I didn't realize that before we took our vows. We would have both been better off if we'd been truthful from the beginning."

Elizabeth didn't bother to kiss him. His place was in her past, not her future. Turning on her heel, she slung her purse over her shoulder.

"Don't be here when I get back, Brad."

"You can't do this to me, Elizabeth," he said weakly. She looked at him once more, and he pressed his opening. "Think about this before you do anything rash. Think about what this means."

"I've thought about it, Brad. It's over. All this while I imagined this was about my surviving, but it's not. This is about Christopher and what kind of man I want him to become. This is about me and what kind of woman I have already become. You don't have a place in our lives anymore. It's spring, Brad. It's the possible season. Start fresh, but start somewhere else."

And she was gone, out the door and into her car, stopping only when she reached Max's impeccably kept house. With a sure step, Elizabeth walked up the path and knocked on the door, and she had to wait only a minute before he opened it.

"Christopher is gone. Run away," she said, without giving him a chance to speak. "I know I have no right to be here after what I told you this afternoon. I know I have no right to ask for your help. But I've come to take back everything I said, to apologize for all the time we've lost over the past few weeks. I want us to be a family, Max. No matter what happens, I can't face the future unless you're with me. I think Chris will feel the same once we find him. I think he'll

understand that it could never work for Brad and me.
I . . . I . . ."

Her breath had run out. There were no more words,
only the wanting. She would beg him if she had to; she
would throw herself at his feet and promise the world,
if only he would give her one more chance. Elizabeth
had almost let him go and she was shamed that her
faith in their love had been so minimal, that her strength
to fight for it had waned so badly. Now she was ready
to do battle if that were what he wanted. She would do
anything he wanted, if he would just give her a sign.

Before Elizabeth could utter another word, or debate
him on the finer points of her stupidity, Max pulled
her close and buried his face in the warm crook of
her neck. Surprised, Elizabeth hesitated only a second
before wrapping her arms around him. She closed her
eyes and breathed in his scent, the smell of outdoors
and hard work, the scent of life.

"Thank God," she whispered, the words caught in
the tremble of her voice.

Holding her away, brushing back her long hair as
if there weren't an inch of her that didn't enthrall him,
he kissed her forehead, kissed her eyes.

"Will you help me? Will you help with Chris?"

"I don't think I have to," he said. "I think Christopher knows exactly what he's doing."

Gently Max drew her into the house, turning her and
moving away so that she could see. There on the couch,
surrounded by Anna's needlework pillows, sat Christopher.

Epilogue

"Elizabeth, come away. He'll see you."

"I don't care." Elizabeth laughed, but Leslie scurried about, herding her back into the room. "This is my house now, you know."

"How could I forget? I spent the last week moving everything but the kitchen sink from your old one."

"It's nice, isn't it?" Elizabeth sighed.

"Yes," Leslie agreed, matching her sigh for sigh. "It's nice. But now isn't the time to do a walkthrough." Elizabeth shot her a petulant glance. "Okay, it's better than nice. I still can't believe Max managed to come in on time with these places and get you one at such a low interest rate to boot."

"I'm so proud of him. He did a beautiful job. I'm only sorry he lost his bonus. A few more days, and he could have had his dream."

"I think most of his dreams came true, so don't you worry about the money."

"I'm not, really," Elizabeth said, sitting down at her dressing table in front of the mirror. She tried to look at herself, but all she saw was the reflection of Max's handiwork. The clipped ceilings, the fireplace in the bedroom with the beautiful mantel. Amazing that this could have risen out of the ashes of Christopher's discontent. Max the miracle worker. It was good to be in this house, good to put the past behind her.

"Elizabeth! Elizabeth!"

"What?" Startled, Elizabeth finally focused on Leslie in the mirror.

"It's almost time. Come on, we've got to go."

"I know. Christopher is waiting."

Elizabeth rose and Leslie put her hands on her friend's shoulder before they turned away from the mirror. "We look pretty damned good for two ladies who've seen our share of troubles."

"That we do," Elizabeth whispered, taking a good look. Leslie wore ice blue; Elizabeth wore beige, a silken column that ended just above her knee. High on her shoulder was a brooch cut from alabaster. Her hair was pulled back, wrapped in a chignon at the base of her neck. On her feet were shoes of satin, the heels high and the toes pointed. She seemed to shimmer like a shaft of sunlight suddenly made solid, a dream become reality.

"Now don't do that," Leslie said gently. "Don't you cry and get that make-up all messed up. Not after the dickens of a time I had getting you to wear it. Come on. Max is waiting."

"But Christopher," Elizabeth said, the tears still in her voice, not easily banished.

"We'll find him. Don't you worry. But it's time for you now. Okay?" Elizabeth nodded, and the two women walked through rooms that promised a wonderful new life.

"Christopher?"

Elizabeth called to him when they reached the living room. He was surrounded by Anna Marino's pillows, but now they peppered Elizabeth's sofa. A perfect blending of the old and new. Never had Christopher looked more grown up. Elizabeth's eyes lowered as he stood, feeling oddly shy as if he alone could pass judgment on her this day. When she looked up, it was just in time to see him smile at her.

"You look really beautiful, Mom," he said, coming toward her, equally shy. He held out his arm and Elizabeth laced her hand through the crook of it. Together they stood, side by side facing the door to the garden. He had come to her! Never again would she watch him running away. From this day forward, they would stand together against the world and walk together to the future, just as they were doing now.

"There's the music," Leslie whispered and handed Elizabeth her flowers. With a smile, Leslie turned away from them and, head up, walked through the door.

Christopher and Elizabeth were next. Together, they stepped into the late-spring sunshine and paused while the people gathered amidst the blooming flowers turned to smile at them. But neither Elizabeth nor her son looked back. They stared instead at Max, who waited only steps ahead with Maria by his side. The woman grinned, ready to give her blessing to this union, this blending of families. For that, Elizabeth would always be grateful.

Chin up, her eyes locked with Max's, she walked on. His smile embraced them, his hand reached out to them. And when Christopher took his mother's hand to give to Max, Max took both of theirs, instead. Together, the three stood before God and made their vows, and Elizabeth let her tears fall, slipping gently down her cheeks until she closed her eyes. In her mind she saw all that was hers from this moment on.

Here, in this house, with this boy and this man, Elizabeth MacMillan began her possible season, the season of her contentment.

Dear Reader:

Sometimes the most exciting and poignant stories are found in everyday places, lived by people like Elizabeth MacMillan and Max Marino. They aren't wealthy, nor are they well known; they don't move in powerful circles or do business with moguls. They are people like you and me, who search for happiness through commitment and love and respect.

There were moments when I was writing this book that Max and Elizabeth's problems seemed insurmountable, but I knew that couldn't be because their hearts were good and their motivations so decent. They didn't worry about making a million, but about the right choices, fairness, and each other. I was delighted that they could rejoice in the happiness they had earned so dearly.

I hope you enjoyed this story, and I wish you the best in this season and all to come.

Rebecca Forster
P.O. Box 1081
Palos Verdes Estates, CA 90274